Other books by Kyell Gold:

Argaea Universe:
Volle
Pendant of Fortune
The Prisoner's Release and Other Stories
Shadow of the Father
*Weasel Presents**

Forester Universe:
Waterways
*Bridges**
*Science Friction**
*Winter Games**
The Mysterious Affair of Giles (February 2014)*

Dev and Lee Series:
Out of Position
Isolation Play
Divisions
(Fourth book, July 2014)

Dangerous Spirits Series:
Green Fairy
Red Devil
Black Angel (2015)

Other Books:
In the Doghouse of Justice
*The Silver Citcle**
X (editor)

Published by FurPlanet Press

Red Devil

by Kyell Gold

RED DEVIL

Copyright 2014 by Kyell Gold

Published by Sofawolf Press
St. Paul, Minnesota
http://www.sofawolf.com

ISBN 978-1-936689-35-4
Printed in the United States of America
First trade paperback edition: January 2014
Third Printing: November 2019

Cover and interior art by Rukis

For the Russian LGBT community

любовь-для мечтателей.
так что мечтай.

Contents

Prologue

The first tsars came from the north, fierce tigers with blood on their claws and death in their eyes. They cut into the soft southern lands as easily as they opened the bellies of their prey, and they named the land after their home: Siberia.

For centuries, the wild tigers of the north ruled the empty reaches of the eastern deserts, the western mountains and fertile river valleys, and all the land between. All around them, the savage horses of the steppes, the cunning malaya-pandas of the river valleys to the east, the bloodthirsty wolves of the west, all of these rose to power and shouted challenges or hissed threats. Still the Siberian tigers dug in their claws and held fast to the land while their rivals and neighbors faded and died.

Throughout the world, Siberia's legend grew; her death-eyed rulers were spoken of in whispers, her soldiers used as bedtime stories to frighten children. Wars flared, revolutions blazed, but Siberia stayed straight and true, the will of the tigers guiding the nation to prosperity. Where people questioned that will or threatened rebellion, the tigers moved quickly and brutally to crush dissent so that none would doubt the divine right that led the tsars to their noble position. For years, that right remained the surest proof of God in a Siberian's life.

But the softness of the southern lands dulled the claws of the tigers over time, weakened the fire in their eyes. By the time the world celebrated the dawn of the twentieth century, Tsar Nicholas had only enough strength to whine at the incessant politicking in his life, unable to defend himself against the currents of power that coursed around him rather than through him. As the leader of a proud people, he lost the faith and following of all but his most devoted subjects. For the first time in centuries, Siberians looked to the West with envy, and many left their ancestral lands, a journey that would have been unthinkable but a generation before. Had the old emperors—even Nicholas's own grandfather—survived to see him, they would have gutted him on the spot.

And to think I named my son for him.

Chapter 1

Even in the height of summer in Samorodka, back in his native Siberia, Alexei Tsarev had not panted this hard. He was in better shape than he'd been in years: not underfed like in Samorodka, not gorging on fried chicken and peach and pecan pies like six months ago at his host family's home. But that didn't help on a summer day in Vidalia when the humidity thickened the air, made breathing an effort even when the young fox wasn't running around playing football—no, it was 'soccer' here in the States. On defense, he didn't run as much as the strikers did, but he ran enough that after an hour, he had to rest with his paws on his knees while his muzzle hung open and his tongue dripped onto the grass.

Sol, whose athletic body Alexei envied, panted just as hard. Of course, the black-furred wolf had it worse than the red-furred fox, even with a white shirt and shorts to reflect the sun's heat. Alexei knew how much warmer his own black paws and feet felt compared to, say, his white-tipped red tail. But Sol didn't complain, just said, "Good game," then gulped and panted again. He looked ahead to a thin muskrat in a gold and blue polo shirt, standing with paws in his pockets, watching the game. "I think he'll be impressed."

"Hope so." Alexei appreciated Sol's support, but still, he didn't want to go talk to the muskrat with his tongue hanging out. The muskrat's name was Colin and he played for the Vidalia Peaches, a semi-professional soccer league. If they sponsored Alexei, he could apply for a visa that would allow him to stay in this country indefinitely, so he would wait until he'd recovered his breath and could be bright and friendly.

Mike, the big Dall sheep who played at one of the forward positions, walked up to them with a big smile. "You did great," he said, patting Alexei on the shoulder, and then he, too, turned toward the muskrat. "Think he'll be impressed?"

Where Sol spoke with a southern twang that helped him fit in with everyone else in Vidalia, Mike talked with a broad, slightly nasal Midwestern accent—not as out of place as Alexei's Siberian, but still foreign. Alexei smiled broadly up. "Sol thinks so," he said.

"I'm gonna get a drink." Sol raised a paw to Alexei and hurried off to the open cooler on the sideline without even a look at the sheep.

Mike watched him go, big brown eyes creasing. Alexei bit his lip. "I am sorry about Sol. It is not your fault. I have told him to give you a chance.

His former boyfriend was a sheep."

The sheep's eyes widened, and he nodded slowly. "So that's it. Well, don't force him. I know it's hard." Mike shook his head, great golden horns swinging from side to side, and brought the smile back to his muzzle. "I mean, my ex is a rabbit, and still when I see a rabbit, my first reaction is, like, 'I bet you don't have a real job.'" He laughed shortly. "Then I have to slap myself."

"It is like me seeing another fox," Alexei said. "Only backwards. I always feel more comfortable."

"Oh yeah, they've done studies on that." Mike reached up to scratch the base of his ear, and Alexei got a whiff of his scent, which made it hard to concentrate on the words. "It seems like it's at least partly based in the family. Like, if a fox was adopted by rabbits, he gets that feeling around rabbits as well as other foxes."

"What if you are raised in a terrible family?" As Mike's eyebrows rose, Alexei added quickly, "Like those gay cubs you have told me about."

"Oh." He shook his head. "You mean, like, if a rabbit is raised by abusive parents, does he not trust rabbits? I don't know. That's a good question, though. I'll look it up."

Alexei looked after Sol again. "It was a very bad experience for him." He realized he was on the verge of revealing something private about Sol, and shut his muzzle.

Mike stood awkwardly for a moment, then forced a smile and said, "Hey, if you go play with the Peaches, does that mean you can't play these games anymore?"

"I will always come play with you," Alexei said, though he really had no idea.

"We appreciate it." Mike stared at the sidelines. "I think Zayda would have to play defense if you left, and Kendall would hate that."

Alexei stiffened reflexively and then forced himself to relax. "I would not want to upset Kendall," he said.

Mike either didn't catch his tone or ignored it. "It'd be worth it—I mean, you could stay in the States without having to worry about your student visa. And without going to those bigots in Millenport. I swear it's as bad as—well, not Siberia, I guess."

"No." Alexei breathed in the sweet, humid air, and exhaled slowly. "It is not as bad as being gay in Siberia."

It was still a marvel to him that he could stand out in a public space and say the word 'gay,' and that Mike—everyone on their team, of course—was also gay. It was incredible that Alexei was standing here talking to him and wishing Mike would have left that big hand on his shoulders a little longer, that the brown eyes would stay focused on him just a little more. Warmth spread through his chest. *Ask him now*, he urged himself.

"You could always go to Port City," Mike said, and rubbed his head. "They're pretty good with Siberian immigrants. You'd have to stay there for about six months while they process you, though. We'd miss you back here."

Now! His mind yelled at him in Siberian, but what if Mike didn't want to go out with him? What if he just liked Alexei as a friend? What about all the time he spent with Kendall? All the fox managed to say was, "I would miss you, too." Sometimes English, with its unspecific 'you,' was a curse.

"How's your sister doing? Any word from her?"

Alexei shook his head. "I have written her twice, and sent her my new address here."

Mike nodded. "Maybe she's on her way over?"

The fox smiled thinly. "I would like to dream that. But I think it is more likely that our father does not allow her to write. She graduated a month ago and she always wrote me from school."

"I can't believe he won't let her call." Mike held up a hand. "No matter what they think of you leaving…but I know, parents aren't rational."

"I wish I had your parents," Alexei said, because he did not want to tell Mike about his father breaking the phone and nearly breaking Caterina's arm. "I would never have left."

Mike laughed, and his eyes lit up when he did. "Oh, I don't know. Maybe with your thick fur you'd be okay in Hilltown, but the food there is terrible." His smile retreated slightly. "Is it so bad in Siberia?"

"Siberia, no." Alexei sighed. "Moskva is lovely, the hills are beautiful, and the river and the flowers around my town—"

"Somoroka?"

"Samorodka." He smiled. "There are many kind people. Just…not in my house. I worry about Cat."

"My older brother worries about me, too." Mike's smile was fond, slightly sad, and his eyes focused somewhere far off. "He keeps asking if I'm staying safe."

"He knows about…?" Alexei gestured to the field, the team.

"That I play soccer?" Mike laughed, his attention returning to Alexei. "Just kidding. Yeah, he knows I'm gay. My whole family is pretty supportive."

"I cannot imagine that," Alexei said wistfully.

The sheep paused, but didn't let the silence go on for long. "Oh, my brother—younger brother—sent me some MP3s of his metal band. Did you want to trade for your Siberian death metal? I can't wait to hear it."

"I would like to hear your brother's band, but…you could find Siberian metal on the Internet." Alexei did not particularly want to listen to his Siberian metal anymore, but Stateside metal was different, more comical.

"Yeah, but I don't know what's good. I want to hear the stuff you like."

The warmth of Mike's smile overcame any reluctance he had to revisit his childhood music. "All right," he said with a smile.

"Cool. I'll bring them to Jerry's barbecue Saturday. You guys are coming, right?"

The fox nodded. *Let's listen to them together sometime. Let's get a cup of coffee. Let's have dinner.*

He opened his muzzle, and just then a slender pine marten jogged up and slapped Mike on the rear. "Mikey boy! Come meet Colin."

Alexei's ears flattened. Mike elbowed the marten lightly. "We were waiting for you, Kendall."

Kendall wrapped an arm around Mike's waist and squeezed. "Come on, then." He glanced across Mike at Alexei, both of them half a foot shorter than the sheep. "You too, dear. Don't worry, he won't care about your English, but if you want, I can talk for you."

"I can speak for myself," Alexei said tightly, trying not to look at Kendall's brown paw on Mike's red athletic shorts. "And my name is Alexei."

"Pity he's not trying to recruit you," Kendall said up to Mike. "You're stunning." After a slight pause, he added with a sly grin, "And you played pretty well, too."

Alexei clamped his jaw shut, lagging behind the other two. "You were pretty good yourself," Mike said as they approached the muskrat, who lifted his whiskers and smiled. Kendall's arm slid off Mike's waist.

"Not too bad, K," Colin said. "I thought for a minute you were going to let that raccoon waddle past you with the ball."

Kendall affected a laugh with a pretentious toss of his pointy muzzle. "We were up three-nil, and he was trying so hard. I thought about it."

"Hi," Alexei said, and as soon as his muzzle opened, he was panting again. With an effort, he closed his mouth and smiled. "Thank you for coming."

The muskrat turned away from Kendall. Alexei could see the embroidered logo on his shirt more clearly now: a cartoon peach kicking a football—soccer ball. "Sure. Alex, is it?"

"Alexei," the fox said as Sol came up beside him, holding a Bolt Energy Drink in one paw. "This is Sol."

Colin's eyes flicked back and forth between them, and his whiskers twitched. "Okay. You're the one who needs the visa, though?" Alexei nodded. "Good. Well, we're in the middle of the season and we don't normally do tryouts, but you've got a deadline or something?"

"My student visa is only valid for three months after graduation."

"We graduated the first week of June," Sol put in. "Almost a month ago."

Kendall stretched, showing off his lean, sinuous form with his back to Alexei, his chest and stomach and smile toward Mike. The damp shirt clung to his muscles, which wasn't fair at all. The marten sweated and it made him look good; Alexei's tongue hung out and it made him feel awkward. He focused on Mike, who had muscles he didn't need to show off.

"...be a little more aggressive," Colin said. Alexei's ears snapped forward; the muskrat was talking to him. "I know it was just a community game—"

"Yeah," Kendall said, relaxing out of his stretch and leaning up against Mike. "You guys don't ever have to stop a game when four armadillo kits roll out onto the field, do you?"

The muskrat laughed, and kept talking to Alexei. "But you hang back a lot, waiting for the play to come to you. If you can show some more movement..."

Of course, he would list off all the things Alexei was doing wrong right in front of Mike. Frozen, the fox nodded without opening his muzzle, fighting back the urge to flatten his ears and tighten his tail.

Sol jumped in. "We're playing a college team in two weeks, Vidalia College or something. They're probably better." They all looked at him. "And, uh, Alexei'll do better against them. That's what I mean."

"I might actually get to make a pretty good save or two, too," Kendall said. He might not have his arm on Mike's waist, but he was still standing close, closer than most same-sex friends would normally stand. Sure, most of the people around were in the Vidalia Lesbian and Gay Alliance, but they were still in a public park, Alexei thought.

The muskrat turned back toward Alexei and Sol. "You guys aren't playing next week?"

"Westside Insurance." Kendall laughed and leaned his whole body into Mike. "I bet the big guy here outscores their whole team by himself."

"All right," Colin said to Alexei. "I'll bring Vic to that game in a couple weeks, and we'll see how it goes. You got good footwork, and you could help the team."

Sol clapped the fox on the back and said, "Good footwork!"

"Yeah, I've helped him out a lot." Kendall had his chin out, chest puffed up. "He's got a lot of potential. Say, if you guys need a backup goalie for the playoffs, I'm free…"

Alexei's paws scuffed the dirt. Between his father's house and the dam in Samorodka stretched a long dirt path along which Alexei had spent countless hours kicking an old, grimy football. His feet remembered the feel of a ball, and the years of practicing along the path, away from the eyes of the other cubs, had worn themselves into his reflexes. In the States, he had found arcade dancing games, and he and Sol enjoyed playing them. But the training in Samorodka felt primitive, the dancing game juvenile, so Alexei hoped the muskrat wouldn't ask further about his footwork, even though it would give him the chance to say that Kendall had done nothing to help him, which he itched to do. He forced a smile. "Thank you very much."

Fortunately, Colin didn't follow up. "Glad to help out a friend." The muskrat turned from him to smile at Kendall.

Alexei looked over to see if Mike had noticed the muskrat's praise of him, but the sheep was smiling at Kendall, too. "So, if we bring you on the team," Colin added, "that would be enough to qualify you for a new visa?"

The fox nodded. "Liza says so." He gestured to a bright white ermine standing farther down the sidelines, talking to a rabbit and a red squirrel.

Kendall laughed as they all turned. "Those are the 'L's in our VLGA family."

The muskrat brushed his whiskers back, squinting at the ladies with a hungry look. The ladies were pretty, Liza especially, but Alexei wondered if Colin realized what the 'L' stood for, and how uninterested Liza and Alice would be in him. After that first look, though, the muskrat just twitched his thin tail and returned his attention to Alexei. "Well," he said, "we won't sign you if you're not qualified, you know. But you looked pretty good. You guys go for beer after games?"

"Sure," Kendall said.

"Alexei and I are underage," Sol put in.

The pine marten laughed. "So what? We can go to my local bar. If you're with me, they won't card you."

"I do not drink much anymore," Alexei said.

"Yeah," Colin said. "You don't want beer after a workout anyway. How about a Bolt now, then we can go out? We can go to a place where you guys can get something non-alcoholic."

As they walked down the sidelines, the white ermine detached herself from the conversation to reach down into the orange plastic cooler and toss

Alexei a Bolt Energy bottle. *"Catch,"* she said in Siberian, and then, without looking at the muskrat, *"So does he like you?"*

"I have to work harder," Alexei said, before cracking open the plastic screw-top and gulping down the blessedly cool, sweet drink. Lizabeta, a friend of his from the Internet, had not only introduced him to the VLGA, but had gotten him his job. Since moving to Vidalia, he'd gotten more used to speaking Siberian with her. In the past year, he hadn't spoken his native language with anyone but his sister on their infrequent phone calls. And that reminded him that he hadn't heard from Cat in several weeks.

Liza grinned. *"This is what I always tell you,"* she said. Then, in English, "How is the job? Vlad is treating you well?"

He nodded. "Good. The job is mostly moving boxes, learning postal codes. He says I am doing well."

"No wonder you're in good shape." Mike grabbed a Bolt of his own. "Your job is a workout. I just sit at a computer and file documents all day."

Alexei saw Kendall talking up the muskrat, no doubt pushing him again about the goalie job. He swallowed down the sour taste in his muzzle. "You both did very well in the game," he said, stepping close to Mike to draw Liza over to them. "I enjoy watching you."

"Aw, it's a pleasure to watch you, too." Mike nudged his shoulder with a bump just gentle enough that Alexei didn't quite lose his footing. "You're always in the right place and you make it look so easy."

"You could also try out for this team," Alexei said in a burst of joy at Mike's compliment. Liza was grinning hugely at him and he tried to ignore her.

Mike laughed. "That's sweet, but I'm not that good. Anyway, I'm trying to find a permanent job, and I don't think 'minor league soccer player' pays as well as paralegal work."

"I like that you want to help people," Alexei said. "My sister also wants to help people back in our home country."

"She sounds pretty awesome. I hope I get to meet her." Mike turned his big, beautiful brown eyes full on Alexei.

The fox swallowed. "I do too," he said, and took a moment to figure out how to tell Mike more about Caterina.

In that moment, Kendall grabbed Mike by the wrist and tugged. "Everybody had their Bolts?" he said. "Let's get going."

Sol glanced at Mike and hesitated. A half-second later, he turned to follow, but Alexei had already noticed, and Alexei had had enough of Kendall for one day anyway. So the fox said loudly, "I am tired. I think I will just go home."

"So does he like you?"

"Oh," Sol said. "I'll come with you, then."

Most of the departing group stopped long enough to wave. Mike tried to, but Kendall pulled him along, so the sheep just called over his shoulder, "See you at the barbecue Saturday!"

Alexei tossed his empty Bolt drink bottle into a nearby garbage can and grabbed another out of the cooler, the melted ice chilling his paw as he opened the bottle. Sol, still nursing his original one, walked beside Alexei through the park gates. "Why didn't you want to go?" Sol said when they were well out of earshot of the group, back on the hard, warm sidewalk.

"I am tired." Alexei gulped the cold, sweet, chemical-orange-flavored drink.

Sol's tail swished from side to side. "Uh-huh. Why don't you like Kendall, anyway?"

"Why don't you like Mike?" Sol went quiet, and Alexei lowered his ears and kicked at a stick on the ground. "I am sorry. But Mike is nice, he is not like—" He breathed in. "I do not like the way Kendall talks about me."

"What, the comment about the footwork?" Sol's ears came back up. He waved the paw with the bottle dismissively. "Everyone knows he doesn't do shit to work with you. What's the harm?"

"And the comment about my English last week. And how he explains my not drinking. And always it's in front of Mike." Alexei kicked at a piece of trash on the ground. "I don't want to talk to Mike with him around."

"He's just teasing you. Like a big brother."

Alexei focused his slit-pupilled eyes on Sol. "Did Natty tease you that way? Talking about how you have 'potential to improve'?"

"Sometimes, yeah."

"Did he also help you? Really help?"

Sol scratched behind his ear and took another drink while they waited to cross a street. "I don't get you," he said at last. "You stood up for me against Tanny that time, and you stand up for me against Meg."

"It is—it's different," Alexei said. "Easier to stand up for you than for me. And he is president of this group."

"I don't think that means anything." Sol made a slightly exasperated noise, but didn't let it affect his voice. "Well, I'll tell you what. How about if I stand up for you, then?"

Alexei turned his head. The brotherly concern alone relaxed him. Sol wouldn't abandon him, and as long as they were friends, he had hope. After all, Mike was only the second most important person at the VLGA to him. It was important he remember that. "It's okay. You don't have to."

"No," Sol said. "At the barbecue—we're going, right?—I'll keep Kendall's attention away from Mike. Give you a chance to talk to him a while. Which reminds me, uh…"

"There's our bus." Alexei pointed ahead to where the #45 was pulling up to the stop. They ran for it, which set them both panting again. The bus was full of people and smelled it, but in the refreshingly cool air, it was easy to ignore the various scents around them. Anyway, when they were seated together, Alexei mostly smelled fox and wolf, and that was fine.

"What did I remind you of?" he asked, but Sol shook his head, looking at the mule deer sitting next to them. So they talked about the game, the weather, the Typhoons (the Millenport baseball team), and anything else Alexei thought of as their "public-safe" conversations: things that did not touch on gay relationships. They could use the acronym for the Vidalia Lesbian and Gay Alliance if they needed to, but it was safer to just leave those discussions for home.

The bus let them off at their corner, where even though the sky was brilliant orange and gold with the sunset, the air remained oppressively hot and thick. Here, in the midst of several blocks of run-down apartment buildings, heat assaulted them from the pavement, the bricks, and the exhaust of the bus as it pulled away, a choking cloud of gas fumes that left both canids breathing into their shirt sleeves. Alexei's shirt was damp when he took his muzzle away from it.

Sol was quiet the rest of the half-block to their building, but when the fox put a paw on the door handle, the wolf tugged him back. "Let's not go in right now," he said.

Which meant that he wanted to talk to Alexei without Meg hearing, and that was impossible in the apartment because Meg rarely left her room. They could sit on the front stoop and talk, though, because their apartment faced the rear of the building, and Meg's room, at the back, looked onto what was now a construction site, so she kept her window closed most of the time anyway.

Alexei curled his tail around his hips, sitting on the warm concrete, and Sol did the same beside him. The wolf hunched his shoulders so that he was the same height as Alexei, though the fox was sitting up straight. At first, Alexei thought something was wrong, but then he felt the twitching of the wolf's tail wagging beside him. "I got a date," Sol said softly.

He grinned when Alexei gaped, and then the fox laughed. "Just this morning? That's wonderful," he said. "Who is it? Do I know him?"

Sol shook his head. "He was a customer at the store. He bought 'Up and Out'—that's a movie that came out about ten years ago, with that cougar Devin Murphy? He plays a guy everyone thinks is gay—anyway, I said, 'Nice movie,' 'cause you don't see many people buying gay movies. I mean, I'm surprised we even stocked it. Probably it's been on the shelf since it was released. Anyway, I just felt like I could say that to him. And he said, 'I haven't seen it since it was out and I was in middle school.' So it turns out he's only three years older than me, and he asked if I wanted to have coffee with him Friday." He laughed. "Well, he asked about today, but I told him I had a soccer game. He thought that was cool."

The wolf was so excited that Alexei found it easy to quell the pang of jealousy he felt. "What's his name? What's he like?"

"He's a bear, another predator, so that's good. His name is Mitch, and he's pre-law at the U. That's really all I know. I mean, maybe he just wants to talk about movies, but…but I have a feeling."

"Aw, I'm glad." He was glad, but still. This had just fallen into Sol's lap, without any effort. Why was it so much harder for Alexei, when the sheep he wanted to date was right there in front of him on the football field for hours? And why couldn't Sol accept that Mike was different? As soon as he thought that, he chided himself. Sol was going to help him talk to Mike. The wolf was trying to get over his prejudice, to be a good friend. "You don't want to tell Meg?"

"Not until after." Sol laid his ears back. "You know how she is. She'll be all like, 'I'm not going to call your parents after they find your dismembered corpse,' or something."

"Ha." Alexei smiled at Sol's imitation. "She means well."

"I know," Sol said. "Just sometimes I don't really want to deal with it." He stared down at his paws, fingers rubbing over his right wrist. "I was wondering if, uh…if you'd…come along maybe."

"On your date?" Alexei perked his ears.

They waited, growing quieter as a skunk couple padded up the walk, around them, and into the building. Sol rubbed his paw again. "Not on it," he said. "Just…to the coffee shop. I'd feel better knowing you were there."

Alexei patted Sol's knee fraternally, feeling like an older brother even though he and Sol were pretty much the same age. That wasn't how things normally were, but Sol was all abashed and his ears were half-down and he looked like he needed an older brother, just as Alexei had needed one a half hour before. "He will not do anything bad in public."

"I know." Sol exhaled, and his shoulders sagged further. "It's stupid. But I'd feel better."

"All right. If you would feel better." He didn't have any plans for tomorrow evening anyway, not if Sol was going to be busy elsewhere.

He could stay in and watch a movie with Meg, but the smell of the close apartment grew difficult to bear after a short time, and Meg rarely wanted to go out to movies.

"Thanks." Sol's tail twitched again. "Don't tell Meg, would you? I feel stupid enough about this."

Alexei leaned against the wolf. "You have not—you have no reason to feel stupid. You had a bad experience, and you need to have a good time to forget about it." He put on a smile he didn't completely believe, but knew was necessary. It had been only a few months since that ex-online-boyfriend bastard had tried to rape Sol, and had only been stopped by—Sol claimed, and Alexei believed—a ghost.

"It's just a date," Sol said.

"It's good." Alexei wagged his tail, too. "I thought you would meet someone in the VLGA, but this is also good."

Sol shrugged. "None of them really clicked like this guy. I mean, when you feel that click, you've got to do something about it, right?"

The question followed Alexei into the apartment, which tonight smelled of noodles and soy sauce. Meg, a stocky otter about Alexei's height, sat finishing her meal at the table. She'd dyed most of her head fur black, either to set off the many silver studs and rings in her ears, or just to be a black otter, and even when she wasn't eating, she sometimes lost herself in her own moods and didn't talk much. Alexei had learned that if she didn't respond right away when he said something, he was better off just waiting to ask her later. At least she did cook most of her own meals and was happy to share with the boys when they wanted. Tonight, Alexei was not hungry, though he knew he would be soon. He waved to her, walked past the small kitchen table, and into the room he shared with Sol.

Sol sat down to talk to Meg and tell her more about the game—he hadn't scored, but he'd stolen the ball and passed to Mike, who'd kicked it forward to Liza for a goal. The bedroom door hung ajar, so Alexei could hear every word of their conversation, but he tuned them out.

When you feel that click. He knew he'd felt it with Mike, and yet every time he tried to talk to the sheep alone, he had been headed off by Kendall. Still, Sol was going to block for him at the barbecue, and Mike wanted to get to know Alexei, so perhaps things would start to improve.

If anyone in the VLGA were a potential rapist, Alexei thought darkly, it would be Kendall. Everyone else seemed to like him, so maybe that was just Alexei's own insecurity. He muttered to himself in Siberian, a habit that made him feel better on one level and worse on others.

He breathed in his scent and Sol's, and opened the window. Sol had shown him how to set up the box fan to blow the hot air out, but Alexei still wanted to feel a breeze on his fur, so tonight he set up the fan to blow inward and stood in front of it, closing his eyes.

When the smell of construction dust became too much, he sighed and turned the fan around, and then stood looking at Sol's side of the room. On the wall above the wolf's bed hung a framed picture, a reproduction of a painting of a nude fox just getting up from a park bench in autumn, the kind of autumn Alexei knew from Siberia, where the trees gave up their leaves in a defiant blaze of brief color, like a warning fire: winter is coming! The fox did not seem bothered by a chill in the air, his lovely fur unruffled by any breeze. This might be the artist's license, or it might be because Niki, the fox in the picture, had been Siberian like Alexei (though Alexei had rarely gone out shirtless, even at home).

Niki had been the ghost Sol claimed had rescued him. After drinking absinthe with Meg, the wolf had dreamed he'd met the ghost of that fox, or lived his life, or something, and those dreams had resulted in Sol's eyes turning the bright green of Niki's, in the painting. Alexei had not previously begrudged Sol his dreams and the lasting bond with Niki, but now he could taste the sour tang of jealousy as he looked at the picture. Sol got help from a ghost, Sol had a date tomorrow night, Sol was a citizen and going to school in a month and a half, and where would Alexei be then? "*Why can you not help me with Kendall?*" he asked the painting in Siberian.

He expected no answer, and received none. So he dropped into the chair at the desk he shared with Sol and pulled open the top drawer on his side. His sister Caterina, the only person in Siberia he still loved, was very real, and yet she had been silent for nearly as long as Sol's ghost had. Two pieces of paper covered with her neat, precise writing lay atop his school notebooks. He took out the letter, leaving the envelope in the drawer, and read over the words again.

Chapter 2

May 20

Dear Alexei,

I am sorry I have not called you in so long. Here is what happened: After the last time I called you on the phone, Mama looked into the history and saw your number. She got very angry and told me I could no longer use the phone as I could not be trusted with it, but she did make Papa let go of my arm. So I have no phone now and I must ask my friends to pass messages to me through Mama and Papa, which none of them want to do. Sometimes we make plans at school, but they do not tell me when they change. I went to the square last Friday night, but they had all decided to go to the club in Vdansk instead and I waited for an hour before I went home.

I pleaded with Mama, and with Papa, but they will not relent so far. Papa locks the new phone he had to buy in the case where Grandfather's war medals used to be. I think he meant to teach me a lesson by doing that but it only looks pathetic. It works, however. I cannot open the case as you did because now Papa keeps the key in his pocket all the time.

So I will write you letters at school, like right now when Mister Oblonsky is talking some dull nonsense about maths, and I will practice my English so that someday when I join you I can speak as well as you do. I have already improved in the year since you left! I looked up 'pathetic' and 'relent' in my dictionary. Kisha has agreed to mail my letters for me, and you may send responses to her. It is the same address as where you sent my Christmas presents.

It is already lonely without being able to talk to you. But I have promised myself that I will work hard to study my English and that even if I cannot find the same path that you did, I will come to the States. I approached Miss Vladenka, but she said she thought that you had Papa's approval when she helped process your paperwork and she did not want to help me. I know that she is lying, but what can I do if she will not help? Kisha says I should take the train to Moskva and work my way out from there, but we have heard many stories of the terrible things that can happen to young girls who go to Moskva, especially foxes, and I will not jump from one trap into

17

A second home of sorts

another. Prababushka would not wish it and I think perhaps she might come back to haunt me.

Spring has finally come to us here. After a month of grey skies, we saw sun for three straight days this week! Birds sing outside my window again, and the tree outside your window has flowered, full of white blossoms that fall like snow when there is a wind. The walk to the river is full of color and song: Blue stars and cornflowers, the red somlatha flowers, white daisies with their yellow hearts. I picked a bunch and placed them in an old tin cup in our shed off the path. Half of the roof collapsed from the snow, but the three walls are still standing. I miss you most when I am in the shed, because that was a happy place. When I am home and sniff through the crack in the wall to your room, I also miss you, but I feel happy that you have escaped. Also there is a hive of bees that has come to live in the wall outside your room, and their buzz makes me feel as though you, or someone, are there. Mama tells Papa he must get rid of them, but he does nothing, and she is too afraid. I am glad. They do not hurt anyone, and I like their company.

The shed on the river path had been a second home of sorts to Alexei and Cat, a place where they could sit and not be disturbed. It was the site of his earliest memory of Cat, when he was six years old and she barely five, and she'd sobbed against him for an hour after their father had thrown a bottle at her and struck her on the shoulder. Alexei remembered the smell of her fur as he held her, the light smell of blood where the bottle had broken the skin, her slight frame shaking and her cries echoing across the sluggish water. Most of all, he remembered his surprise that the bottle had not been thrown at him.

Up until then, Alexei remembered feeling that he was a bad fox, that his beatings were all deserved, and that Caterina was the good girl who did not get beaten. She must have been hit before then; he dimly recalled sitting in the waiting room of the hospital once with his parents. But it wasn't until that day that his view of himself changed, and the reason was the sobbing cub he held in his arms. Cat had done nothing wrong, and this, he began to understand, meant that perhaps neither had he.

That Cat was spending time at the shed meant that their parents had been in a bad temper. Probably they had hit her, but she was trying to spare him the details. He felt again the surge of anger he'd felt when he'd first read the letter, and went on.

Yesterday the purple blooms of onion made the air smell sharp on the path up the hill. Kisha and I ran away from school to sit on the hill above the river, because the sun was out and we wanted to spread out our tails and sit back. We watched ravens and jays wheel and scream while little bushy-tailed grounders chased each other around and around. The green was bursting to life all through the hills and songbirds were singing. I did not see how anyone could be unhappy. Kisha, of course, pointed at the garbage strewn on the hill, the holes in the roof of the schoolhouse, the ruins of the dam, and the small cluster of ugly four-story office buildings. She lifted her nose and smelled the rotten fish and stink of vodka, and said she could understand why I was so desperate to get away.

I am not sure she does. I want very much to know what the birds in Midland sound like, and how the trees smell there, and to taste the real pizza you have told me about. I would like to have a computer of my own, yes, and learn the wonderful things and go to the wonderful places, but I mostly want to go to be with you. Escape for its own sake is not an answer. You must always run toward something, not away, because how do you know that you are not running from the monster to the witch? What monster is that horrible that nothing you run to could be worse?

Now I am in history class with Mister Lanin. It is so close to the Last Bell and I feel no sense of joy. It will be a celebration that promises freedom and yet most of us will remain in Samorodka, no more free than we are now. We will simply arrive at a job rather than a school, we will have less homework but longer hours, and there will be a different Last Bell to look forward to, many years off. The school is determined to have a joyful celebration, but I would just as soon remain home and study my English.

Mister Lanin sympathizes, at least. He teaches us history, how the great male and female Siberian leaders believed that freedom lay in structure, that with our lives held in the claws of the state, we would be liberated from concerns of livelihood and welfare, and such is our tradition. When teaching us of the Revolution, he waves his paws and his long, striped tail about, and becomes very excited at the idea that the peasants of Siberia chose to determine their own fate. Then he teaches us of the dictators that followed and his tail loses its life. I suppose when he thinks of all the tigers killed under those dictators, he must be as sad as Prababushka when she thinks of her family lost in the War. But Mister Lanin does not dwell on loss. He tells us that we are part of a new Siberia, that we are in an age where we may decide our own fate, free of the mistakes of our parents.

I hope he is right. I have already decided that if I go to Last Bell, I will read him a short poem. Kisha will laugh at me, but she used to laugh at me when I picked up garbage on our way down the hill, or when I stopped to smell the flowers or laugh at the grounders. She will marry Vaclav sometime next year and they will live in his parents' house and have a family, and that, she says, is enough for her. For me, there must be more beyond this town, and I am eternally grateful to you for showing me the way.

   With love,
   Caterina

Last Bell, the graduation ceremony, should be a joyful party. Alexei had gone last year—owing to differences in the educational systems, he had been advised to take one more year of high school in the States, and therefore had graduated twice. The ceremony in Midland had been muted by comparison to the party in Samorodka: the class assembled in caps and gowns, heard speeches, and then…it was over. No partings of the students and teachers, except small personal ones after the ceremony. No town-wide party, although he had heard that Sol's friend Xavy and some of the athletes had gone down to a local dance club to celebrate.

He and Sol and Meg had taken barbecue fixings to an evening picnic in the park and cooked for their own party; Sol's parents and Alexei's host family had understood that it was something just for them. Some of the others from their class joined them, arranged through phone texts and quick calls, which brought Alexei's attention back to his sister's letter.

Again, she had not included a photograph. Alexei's only picture of her had disappeared during his exit from Siberia, probably during the search of his luggage by the Siberian customs officials to make sure he was not smuggling anything out of the country. He hadn't missed it until arriving in Midland. Then he had remembered her well enough that it hadn't seemed important to ask for a picture, and over the last few months, when he'd asked, she had promised to try, but still he had no image of her. Her face was harder for him to remember, but when he read these words, he could picture her smile as clearly as the crescent of the moon in the sky outside his window.

Since getting this letter, he had written to tell her that she should go to Last Bell, even though he'd gotten the letter on May 25th, the day of the ceremony. Then he had written again to give her his new address in Vidalia, and to ask her the question he hadn't formed until re-reading the letter.

Cat had been seeing a wolf named Miroslav—Slava for short. The last time she'd called, she'd told him that although Slava wasn't as good at English as she was, he was quite clever with his paws and knew enough about electronics that she thought he could find a job easily. He was even willing to explore moving to the States with her. But the letter of May 20 had no mention of Slava, not even when she talked of her friend Kisha's fiancé. And Cat had not answered either of his letters since then.

He dropped the letter into the drawer and went to sit on his bed, feeling his mood darken. He wondered if Mike had gone out with Kendall after the beers, if he had kissed the pine marten yet.

Alexei set the letter aside and rested his forearms on the desk, then turned his head to Sol's side of the room to look at the painting again. Sol got strength from the portrait, and soon enough would be in here to search for guidance from Niki before his date the next day. All Alexei could see in the picture was his own reflection in the glass, the confused, uncertain fox over the confident, assured Niki, his eyes grey and cloudy against the fox's bright green.

He thought he might write to his sister about Mike, and he took out a piece of paper to do so. He got as far as, *"Dear Cat, My life in Vidalia has been good. There is someone,"* before he lifted his pen from the paper and tried to think of how to describe Mike. Each time he thought he had come up with an adequate phrase, the words fell away from him and seemed to lose their meaning. "A sheep I like"—but it was more than just "liking" with this sheep. "A good-looking friend"—but Mike was not just about looks. "You would like his smile and his eyes"—no, none of that was right, none of that spoke of Mike's easy grace and assurance, both on the field and in meetings, the moments he'd taken to speak just to Alexei, that "click" Sol was talking about. Alexei was sure Mike would feel it as strongly as he did, if only that pine marten were not forever interfering.

"Writing your sister?" Sol asked, coming in. Alexei, who had heard the creak of the wood under the carpet, hadn't bothered to hide his letter. After all, he'd barely written anything.

"I am trying. She has still not responded to my earlier letters."

"I'm sure she's okay. The mail is probably just slow." Sol sat on his bed and opened his laptop computer, but stared up at Niki's portrait as he did.

"Yes. Or perhaps her letter has been lost." He scratched out "~~There is someone~~" and wrote, *"I still have not received a letter from you. If Kisha sent it, then it has been lost."*

"When she graduates, will she be able to move out of your parents' house and get her phone back?"

"I suppose so." Alexei stared down at his writing. "She wants to move here."

"Here? To Vidalia?" Sol looked around the bedroom. "Like, here?"

Alexei shook his head. "This country. Perhaps here with me, but she will go anywhere she can learn." He wrote, *"I would love to believe that you are on your way here right now."*

"Oh, okay." Sol relaxed, his tail tip hanging over the side of the bed. "I'm sure she's okay."

Alexei nodded. He forced himself to write a little about the soccer game, remembering to call it "football" for his sister's benefit, and he told her about his little VLGA family and how he was looking forward to introducing her to them. He wrote about his job moving boxes in the shipping warehouse, how his pay came in a small envelope every week, how it felt to be earning money. After a little while, he had a page of writing that told much about what he was doing and very little about his life.

Sol typed away at his computer. Alexei could see that his word processor wasn't open, so he wasn't writing the story he kept saying he was going to work on. Probably he was chatting with some of the other soon-to-be freshmen to the College of Charlton, making plans for the fall. None of the others were gay—that they admitted—but they were impressed that Sol had been a baseball player, and mostly they all talked sports.

Meg, like Alexei, didn't know what she was going to do this fall, but her plans depended on his situation. Alexei thought they could continue to rent this apartment by themselves, if he stayed in the country, but Meg hadn't talked about the fall with him yet.

Sol's typing stopped. Alexei glanced over and saw the black wolf gazing up at the painting. In the silence, the sound of Meg cleaning dishes clattered loudly, so the fox swept the letter and pens into his desk drawer, closed it, and went outside to talk to her.

Above the sink and stove, the two small kitchen cupboards were closed, their white paint chipped enough to show the brown wood below in a pattern like rot, though the wood smelled clean and fresh if Alexei put his nose next to it. If Meg had been cooking, the kitchen overflowed with the smells of oil and butter and (usually) fish, unless she opened one of the small windows; if she had not been cooking, the strongest smell was the grease that accumulated underneath the cupboards over the stove. Now the kitchen smelled of fish and salt and dish soap, and splashing sounds echoed from where Meg stood over the scuffed, dirty sink.

Alexei's claws clicked on the cool tile floor as he walked up to the black-furred otter. "Hey, fox-boy," she said, scrubbing at her plate with a sponge over soapy water. "I have a new drink recipe I want you to try."

The fox stopped and sighed. "I would prefer—"

Meg held up a paw. "I know, I know. But I'm trying to make this drink that's, like, special for you. It's got local flavor and Siberian flavor and I just need someone to tell me if I'm making it right."

"All right." Alexei picked up a dishtowel and the clean, wet saucepan.

"You don't have to dry," Meg said. "That's what a drying rack is for."

"I don't mind," he said, wiping the water carefully away. "How was dinner?"

"Fish cakes and noodles and plenty of soy sauce," she said. "I expect 'Top Chef' to call any day now."

He grinned. "It smells good. Salty. What is 'Top Chef'?"

"The salt is the soy. 'Top Chef' is a reality show…"

"Oh. Like 'Survivor'."

"Kind of. Except they have to cook. I have it on my computer if you want to watch sometime. It's pretty good."

"Sure," he said to be nice, though he hadn't really enjoyed "Survivor" when he'd watched it with his friends in Samorodka. He put the dry saucepan up in the cupboard and picked up the plastic spoon. A grain of rice was stuck in the gap in the handle; he poked at it with a claw.

"My vampire fox friend hasn't seen it either. You can watch it with us when he comes to visit," she said.

He nodded. "When is he coming?"

"In a couple weeks. I told Sol. He'll sleep on my floor, don't worry about it."

Alexei smiled. "We can leave if you would like time alone."

She turned, paws soapy, and scowled at him. "We don't need time alone. He's just coming to see the apartment."

"Uh-huh." Alexei grinned, and Meg splashed water at him. He jumped and wiped his fur with the towel. "Does this mean you are going to be a vampire too?"

She rolled her eyes. "I don't believe in that crap."

He glanced toward Sol's room, and Meg saw the look. "Even him," she said, lowering her voice, because even though Sol had started playing music, he had good canid ears. "I don't know what he thought he dreamed with that painting…"

"His eyes," Alexei said softly.

She shook her head, and then held her fingers an inch apart. "Maybe I believe in it this much. But people just believe what they want to believe. Our minds are more powerful than we give them credit for. You have to remember what's real and what's not, or else you just lose yourself in the shit you want to be real and you can't find your way back to be any use to the shit that actually is real."

"How do we know what is real?" he said. "How can we know that there is not more to be seen? In Siberia, we believe that our ancestors watch over us."

"I thought ancestor-worship was an Eastern thing." She squinted at him.

"'Worship' is like in church?" She nodded, and Alexei shook his head. "It is not like that. Here…" He thought. "My host family, their grandparents had died years ago. They went to where they are buried and put flowers. Kyree—my host mother—she sometimes talked to her mother as if she were alive."

"Not everyone does that." Meg finished washing her plate and shook it, then slid it into the rack. "My grandparents died like ten years ago and I don't even know where they're buried."

He nodded. "Yes. But in Siberia—in Samorodka, I know—it is much more common. We thought there was a house where an ancestor came back as a ghost, but also my sister and myself remember our great-grandmother and we think she would like to try to help us escape. She was born in Baranowicze, which was then Lechia, and she fled into Siberia when the war started."

"Which war?" Meg asked. "They were having them every ten years for a while."

"World War Two," Alexei said. "Nineteen thirty-eight."

"I thought they didn't persecute foxes."

Alexei lowered his ears. "Foxes with proper coloring. Great-grandmother was a cross fox."

"Fucking hell." Meg lifted a paw to her whiskers, the black dye in her fur. "So she went to Siberia?"

"She stopped in Samorodka because she…" He frowned. "She twisted her ankle so that she could not walk. Sprain, is this right?" Meg nodded, and he inclined his head, searching for words. It was harder to tell the story because he could hear Prababushka laughing in her cracked voice, the Siberian words so familiar that he had fight to speak in a language Meg could understand. "My great-grandfather was the son of the doctor. He helped take care of her and they stayed. She said that it was the happiest time she ever sprained an ankle."

"She could have sprained her ankle in any town, though," Meg pointed out. "She might still have met someone, and then someone else would be here telling me this story."

Alexei shook his head, annoyed that he was telling the story badly. Prababushka would scold him, would tell him to start again. "She had a small doll from her grandmother, who had died the year before. When they were traveling through Samorodka, the doll slipped from her paws. She tried to catch it, and…" He mimed twisting his ankle. "So she always said that her grandmother's spirit made her stop to meet Dmitri—my great-grandfather."

Meg smiled. "It's a nice story, but it's still just putting meaning into randomness. What about you? You're running away from a horrible place and you ended up here. What ghost did that?"

"Perhaps I am not meant to stay here," Alexei said. "I have not met a…" The word 'husband' didn't sound right. "Special person."

"Thanks."

"I mean," he said quickly, "someone to build a life with. And anyway," he added before Meg could argue more, "I may still have to return."

"You can't go back. They'll fuck you up. It's just getting worse back there for gay cubs, y'know?"

"Not only the gay ones." Alexei thought of Cat. "But I will say prayers to Prababushka that I may remain. That is what I mean. We do not put our ancestors in churches, but we say prayers for them and thanks to them."

"Whatever works." Meg washed out her glass and one of Sol's and put them in the drying rack. "I guess it's no stranger than praying to a guy who died two thousand years ago and nobody knows what species he was and he wants you to eat part of him."

"Does your vampire fox not want to eat people?" Alexei said, to tease her.

"He drinks fake blood," Meg said. "It's fruit punch."

Alexei laughed. "So everyone believes in something strange. Who can say what is true?"

"I can," Meg said. "It's whatever I can touch, what stays the same from one day to the next. I never saw a ghost, I just saw Sol acting weird and then somehow screwing up his eyes. My vampire fox friend says there are chemicals on the Internet you can get that change your eye color."

Alexei started to shake his head, then said, "Your vampire friend, does he have a name?"

Meg scowled. "I call him Athos, but that's not his real name."

"Are you going to learn his real name before he comes to visit?"

"You sound like Sol's mother," Meg said. "I trust him. I talk to him just about every day."

"I only ask," Alexei said, "because of what happened to Sol. Not the ghost, the real world."

"Sol believes in a lot of things I don't. Ghosts. Nice people. Love. I'll be okay. He won't try anything."

"Okay." Alexei smiled. "You will tell us if you need help?" He picked up the plate she'd put in the rack and wiped it dry.

"Of course," Meg said, "but I won't need help. What about you? Bringing anyone over we should know about?"

"You do not believe in love," Alexei said, teasingly.

"I believe that you believe in it." She shut the water off, but left her paws in the full sink, moving them back and forth, eyes half-closed as she turned to smile at him. "So I'm trying to respect your beliefs. Not be too biased, you know? So?"

Alexei shook his head. "No. I do not think so."

"Oh well." Meg looked in at Sol again. "He's got someone. Did he tell you?"

The fox raised an eyebrow. "He said he didn't want to tell you because you do not believe in love."

"He didn't tell me," Meg said. "He's just all distracted the way he used to be when he was texting that asshole rapist all the time. Did he really say he didn't want to tell me?"

"They have not had a date yet," Alexei said, turning the plate over. "I am sure he will tell you when he is more sure."

"Hm." Meg nodded. "Well, don't tell him I know. But I wouldn't make fun of him for it. I just want to make sure he's okay. He's… Well, even though you believe in ghosts, I think you're more grounded than he is." She peered at him. "You've been through more."

Alexei put the plate down and dried his paws on the towel. "Should I say, 'Thank you'?"

"Nah." She sighed and lifted her paws from the sink. Alexei held the towel out to her as he heard the gurgle of the drain. The water level lowered slowly. "I need to get out to the pool," she said.

"I will go with you if you like."

"Okay." She dabbed at her paws and then dropped the towel on the counter. "Tomorrow?"

Alexei shook his head. "Tomorrow is when Sol has his…" He smiled. "He asked me to be there to watch just to make him feel better."

"Good. So he's not entirely off in dreamland." She looked past Alexei to Sol's bedroom. "Day after tomorrow, then."

Alexei nodded, and picked up the towel to hang it up as Meg went back to her room.

◆

That night, he lay in bed wondering whether he would meet his special person in Vidalia, if there were a reason he'd ended up at high school with Sol and Meg. It could be Mike, but maybe someone else would join the Vidalia Lesbian and Gay Alliance, or maybe someone would notice him at his job, or maybe while he was sitting at the coffee house watching Sol and his date, someone would sit with him. But the more he thought about it, the more that mysterious person always became a white sheep with gold curving horns and wide brown eyes and a smile that made Alexei feel like a small sun was glowing in his chest.

And who liked Kendall, of all people. The pine marten smirked through Alexei's half-dream, with his painted claws and his flouncing manner and his way of speaking that was so quick, so slick. Alexei had known someone like him back in Samorodka—not gay, of course, but that fast-talking manner. At home, he had enjoyed sparring with his classmate, because he was clever enough to match wits even if he wasn't quick enough to match words, and also because there was much less depending on whether he could prove himself superior. He had played pranks on Tomas, and Tomas had played pranks on him, and sometime around their year 9 in school they had grown bored of it and stopped.

But Kendall, Kendall was like a Tomas who was living on the way to Alexei's house, a malicious fairy living in the wood near his home. Alexei fell further into sleep, imagining the pine marten chasing him away from Mike over and over, until a high whine reached his ears and woke him.

He turned over in bed, facing Sol's wall, where a light shone from outside. It fell on the portrait of Niki, on the fox's one visible green eye, as though Niki were peering through a long, dark night directly at Alexei. The room rumbled as though something huge were approaching, though Alexei's bed remained solid and still.

He got up slowly, and the light went out and Niki vanished back into darkness. A moment later, the whining and rumbling died away, and only the soft clanks of machinery and voices, the smell of dirt and oil, came through the warm air to him. He peered out the window. Two wolves and a raccoon at the construction site, doing something at—he checked his phone—midnight. Whatever it was, he didn't know and couldn't hear. He closed the window and lay back on his bed.

He'd never been woken up at night before, never seen a light come through the window so late. "Prababushka?" he whispered. "Niki?"

His ears stayed perked straight up, but only the murmurs of night outside broke the silence.

Chapter 3

In the morning, Alexei was no longer convinced that anything supernatural had happened. The painting looked the same as it had every morning, softly lit by the reflected glow of the sunlight from Alexei's wall when Sol pulled the blinds up at six-thirty. He stared at the fox's eye for a long moment and then, just as Sol looked about to ask him what he was doing, turned away and got dressed.

They ate breakfast bars on the way to the transit center, changed busses, and rode the ten minutes to Alexei's stop together. Sol had to ride another ten minutes to downtown where his store was. "You'll come down after?" he asked as Alexei got up to get off.

"Yes," Alexei said with a smile. "Six o'clock, at the coffee shop at your bus stop."

"Thanks." Sol's tail wagged against the seat.

Alexei's work was dull, but he enjoyed the exercise of lifting boxes, and he felt safe and anonymous as one of a team of fifteen who sweated out the day shift in the warehouse. His supervisor Vlad, a second-generation Siberian tiger who smoked constantly, had told him that in a another month he would be eligible to move to the cooler evening shift, but this did not appeal to Alexei. For one thing, the heat of the day was no worse than the muggy Samorodka summers, and for another, he enjoyed spending his evenings with Sol and Meg, and the VLGA soccer games were also in the evening.

Alexei had not told Vlad about the VLGA, even though he had gotten the job through Vlad's friendship with outspoken lesbian Liza. He did not think Vlad would mind having a gay worker, but there was no call for his relationships to be part of the job, so he talked to the tiger about his hometown when he had a chance, and sometimes about Sol and Meg, and little else.

The others on his shift barely even wanted to talk about that. They had families, most of them, but their conversations consisted of sports and their church activities, or about the nights they'd had at the topless club. Sometimes the same conversation would encompass all three topics, which had confused Alexei at first, but he just nodded and smiled, and over the first two weeks came to realize that though a fellow might be married with a lovely daughter and attend church on Sundays, still he liked to go out with the boys on Saturday and look at half-naked ladies.

They had invited him to the club with them this week, and he'd declined politely, saying he and Sol and Meg had plans—he always included Meg even if she weren't coming, because then it was "three friends" and not "two boys." Alexei, of course, had never had an interest in looking at half-naked ladies, so he had never really thought much of it other than that it was a thing that the boys in his class liked to do on the shared school computer when the teacher was out of the room. He had rather vaguely supposed that the urge would pass once you were married and had a wife to look at, but his co-workers acted as if their fondest dream would be to walk out of the warehouse into a world where it was illegal for female breasts or behinds to be covered.

His co-workers accepted him as a quiet fox, although if he chose to talk about his family, they listened well enough. Pierre, a hutia from an island to the south called Havane, had a younger sister who had remained behind as Cat had, and he constantly told Alexei he was lucky not to have to worry as much about his sister as Pierre worried about his, living under a dictatorial regime. It was worse, he said, because he had defected, and they would be watching her closely. Cat's situation was not so different, Alexei thought, only the dictators were his parents.

This day, as Alexei retrieved boxes from storage and put them onto conveyor belts, or took boxes from conveyor belts to the appropriate storage area, he told his co-workers about the scout from the soccer team and his prospect of getting a visa. Vlad thought it was wonderful, but Pierre, also undocumented, was not so sure. "You know then Vlad has to sign you up regular, right? More paperwork, maybe the job here not so good for you."

Vlad swatted at the hutia when he said that. "Always is job here for hard worker."

"Siberian worker, you mean." Pierre put on an accent. "If I talk like this, I can have more hours, da?"

"You talk like that, you may have claw where sun does not shine." Vlad extended his middle finger and the claw at the end of it, and Pierre and the others laughed.

After work, Alexei took the bus to Sol's stop and found the coffee shop easily. The black wolf must have just come from work; he was still in his red polo shirt, sitting across from a bear. Sol acknowledged him, but only briefly, and so Alexei sat in a corner with a latte and leaned back.

He knew he was supposed to be watching Sol, but his attention kept drifting. It was so strange to be sitting here watching his best friend have a date with a guy. This was why he had left Samorodka, and yet, it was frustrating to watch Sol smiling, engaged with the bear, while Alexei thought about Mike, and Kendall's arm around his waist. At the barbecue, things would be better.

Sol would keep Kendall away, and Alexei would ask Mike out. He *would*. He had not fled Siberia only to remain just as unhappy here.

Not *just* as unhappy; that was unfair. Here, he did not have to be afraid when he opened the door of his house; he knew that someday the life he wanted would be within reach. He just wished it would hurry and arrive.

And Vidalia was interesting in a way that Samorodka never could be, a profusion of people and worlds crammed between hot asphalt lines. Though it had been just a year since he'd left Samorodka, it was hard to remember the neat stone buildings, the decrepit abandoned houses, or anything outside his parents' house or the schoolhouse. Only the path to the dam and the little shelter he'd so often sat in with Cat remained clear in his mind; he could see the flowers she talked about when she listed them, and he could smell the fresh water and the scent of grass crushed under their paws. Even his life in Midland, only a month removed, had receded into the fog of "things he didn't need to think about anymore." He could see the house where he'd lived and the painting on the wall he'd stared at every dinner, and he remembered the smell of the cheap disinfectant Richfield High had used in its corridors, but most of his other memories of Midland, like Samorodka, were of people: the nasty coyote who'd tormented Sol, a squirrel he'd studied with, the wolves on the baseball team.

And his host parents, of course. He had e-mailed them twice to let them know that he had an apartment, and then a job; his host mother had worried about him being paid unofficially, while his host father had congratulated him on doing "real work." But neither of them had written since then to ask him how he was. He'd asked about their daughter, who had just returned from spending a year in Zhangou, and about the mother's job—she had been up for a promotion. There'd been no e-mails since then, and Alexei realized that when he was no longer at their dinner table, his presence was no longer forced into their busy lives.

"Hey."

He looked up into Sol's bright green eyes. How long had he been thinking, off in his own world? He started to apologize, but the wolf was smiling. Alexei saw the bear waiting at the door. "Oh. Is it...?"

"He's nice," Sol said. "I think we're going to get dinner. You'll be okay?"

Alexei nodded. "Oh, yes. Good." He smiled back up. "Have a good dinner."

"Thanks for coming." Sol lowered his voice, and his ears flicked back. "I feel silly."

"No, no, I understand." Alexei wagged his tail. "I am glad to help."

He followed their progress down the sidewalk, watching them talk and gesture to each other. Sol looked completely absorbed in the bear, and

Alexei was glad to see that the bear returned the interest. He didn't know how good he was at telling character from appearances, but the bear looked like a nice fellow. What had Sol said his name was? Mike? No, not Mike, he would have remembered that. Mitch, that was it.

The two of them disappeared around the corner. So he would be on his own for dinner, or else he could go home and eat whatever Meg was cooking. He sighed, and then perked up his ears, looking out the window. The downtown bustled around him, full of buildings and scents, and sparking his spirit of adventure. Maybe he could find a place he hadn't tried before, and tell Meg and Sol about it. If it were really good, he could write to Cat about it, too.

He finished his latte and left the coffee shop, walking down the street amidst all the other people. Even though the crowds were larger than in Samorodka, the mix of scents was similar. He supposed that beyond a certain number of people, scents just mingled into a haze. There was a muskrat in front of him, alone; a jaguar stalking the edge of the sidewalk. He followed the progress of another fox, a little chubby and older, checking his phone as he crossed the street. Any of these people might come up to him and be the right one for him, mightn't they? Only they never would. Even here, where he did not know everyone he met, where there was a group of gay people who met and dated and (in private rooms) held paws, even here, he was walking to dinner alone.

The restaurants that looked interesting to him, the ones whose smells lured him to the door with fried onions and peach pies and roasted chicken, they all had tables where groups of two and three and four sat and laughed together. He wondered if Mike would want to go to any of these places with him. Sol was out with his date, and Alexei ached to share something like that with Mike, a dinner at an interesting restaurant or a movie they were both seeing for the first time.

He did not want to go sit alone by himself at a table, so he ended up at a takeout chicken place, with gleaming white tile and chrome and the smells of oil and ammonia mingling in the air. At least the oil in this place smelled good: chicken rather than burgers. Alexei had heard throughout his childhood the sour-grapes jokes that the delicious-looking burgers in the States included pieces of rats and vermin, and those jokes had worked their way so far into his consciousness that now he found it difficult to eat burgers, at least from fast food places.

This place at least looked clean, and the chicken smelled better when he stepped inside, so he walked up to the counter and ordered his chicken sandwich and Coke. And then he reached into his pocket and found it empty.

"Sorry," he said, checking the other pocket even though he knew his wallet wasn't there. He'd had it at the coffee shop, he'd been sitting next to the window, he'd gotten up…it must still be there.

His sandwich and fried potatoes plunked down on the counter, dropped by a breathless coyote who barely spared him a glance before running back to fill another order. The doe behind the register looked at him dully.

"I don't," he said, ears folding back. He panted as though the air conditioning in the restaurant had failed. If Sol were here, Sol could help him, either give him money or tell him how to react in this situation. Or if he'd been on a date, he could turn and see the sympathy in Mike's eyes, and Mike would take care of things and together they would go look for his wallet. But there was nobody there to help. "I can't find…"

Everyone simply stared at him. He turned and ran from the restaurant.

◆

The kitchen smelled of salmon, butter, and a salty-sharp spice. "You were out late," Meg called.

Alexei didn't say anything, postponing the moment when he would have to say, "I lost my wallet." He walked into his bedroom, directly to his dresser and the drawer where his shirts lay neatly folded. In the moment he reached his paw into the drawer, he half-expected his money to be gone, magically transported to wherever his wallet had disappeared to. But no, it was there, two hundred dollars saved over three weeks of work. Even without the…whatever twenty minus his latte came to, he was still doing rather well, he thought. Honest work.

The thought did nothing to improve his mood. Stupid fox, he thought, can't ask Mike for just a cup of coffee, can't keep track of his wallet, can't speak English properly. How was it so easy, so natural, for Sol to go to coffee with Mitch the bear? He was an idiot to think things could be different even in a relaxed setting like the barbecue.

When Sol was frustrated, he'd told Alexei, he just looked at Niki, whether on the wall or on the background of his phone, and he remembered that Niki had believed in him. Alexei had Sol, but Sol was off with Mitch; he'd had Cat, but he couldn't call her anymore or do anything but send increasingly worried letters out into the darkness.

He turned to the picture of Niki, facing the green-eyed fox behind his reflection in the glass. "*Where is my ghost?*" he said in Siberian. "*Why don't you help me find someone?*"

"What are you going on about?" Meg appeared in the doorway and looked at Alexei, then at where he was staring. "Oh god. Don't tell me you've started dreaming about him too. You know about collective hallucinations, right?"

"Collective?" He knew both the words, but they didn't seem to go together. "No," he went on before she could explain, "I am just…"

"Mind you, at least it would be familiar. Sol could help you handle it. So could I, for that matter." Her grin faded. "You look like someone shaved your tail. Sol's thing not go well?"

He shook his head. "It was fine. They went to dinner. They are still there, I suppose." His muzzle dipped. He stared down at the carpet. "I lost my wallet. I had to walk home."

"Oh, shit. Well, wait, you don't have a driver's license, and you didn't have credit cards." She sucked in a breath. "Your ID."

"I can send for another one. It is not important. Nobody asks to see it. And it was not a lot of money. It was…" He held his paws in front of his muzzle, trying to work out how to convey the feeling of shame and loneliness and anger. "It made me feel stupid."

"Well, asking that painting to find your wallet for you isn't doing you any favors on that count. Maybe you should just get some candles and something that was in your wallet at one time." She laughed. "But I think a drink might be more help. You game? I got the stuff for that one I was telling you about."

"It is vodka?"

She nodded. "Yeah, with just a little schnapps for flavor. Sol always felt better after he took a shot of absinthe, or had a couple beers. Anyway, the vodka should make you feel at home, and it sounds like you need a drink."

Alexei understood the expression, "I need a drink," and how here in the States the word "need" lost some of its urgency when put into this expression. Back in Samorodka, he and his friends had emptied many bottles of vodka, but those had not been the times when he'd *needed* a drink.

No, but he "needed a drink" in the English sense of it. Alcohol could loosen the knot in his stomach, mute the endless replaying in his mind of him walking out of the café without his wallet. The only bruises sustained had been to his pride, and he would be able to sleep eventually—but he did want that dullness, that relaxing of the body that followed the burning of vodka.

As long as he didn't drink too much…his tail twitched. He wondered if Cat still drank, if there were nights when she *needed* to. There was nobody to hold her, to tip the bottle to her muzzle if it were shaking. His paws clenched, and the knots in his stomach twisted, tightened. She never mentioned it in her letters, but then, Cat never would.

A moment later, he followed Meg out to the kitchen. "Do you have a saying in English, something like, 'Trouble never comes alone'?"

She paused, a bottle in one paw. "Misery loves company?"

"Maybe." He sighed. "When you have one bad thought and it attracts all the others to you, things you have maybe not thought about for months."

"Oh." Meg shook her head. "'Misery loves company' is more like, um…if you're miserable, you want to make other people miserable too."

"That is not quite right." Alexei smiled. "I do not want to make you sad."

"Fox-boy," Meg said, starting to pour from the bottle into a glass, "I think that's one thing you don't ever have to worry about. So let me try to cheer you up."

Her manner did ease Alexei's worries, at least a little. Of course Cat was all right. She was just having trouble finding time to write now that school was out. He was being silly—there was no reason she was in trouble just because he'd lost his wallet. He lifted his ears and muzzle and tried to right his mood. "What did you mean when you said I should get candles?"

She laughed. "My vampire fox—Athos—said if Sol wanted to summon his ghost again, there's a ritual, and there's candles and stuff. He's kind of a dork sometimes. And don't tell Sol. Jesus, the last thing I need is for him to get all weird again."

He watched her pour clear vodka into a glass and add peach schnapps and some grenadine syrup. It was a mystery to him and Sol where Meg managed to procure alcohol. It happened during the day while they were gone; they would come back to find two six-packs of beer in the fridge, or Meg would announce margarita night and bring out margarita mix and tequila. Alexei usually declined, and he worried as much about the speed with which the bottles vanished as about their appearance, but Meg didn't show any signs of being worse off for drinking, so he kept his worries to himself. And right now, he'd just told himself to stop worrying about Cat; he wasn't going to start worrying about Meg.

"Do you know the ritual?" he said.

She stopped pouring and set the bottle down. "No," she said, turning to him. "No, I am not going to help you chase after something just because Sol did it."

"It is not for that," he said.

She squinted at him and then turned back to the drinks, adding a shot from a bottle marked *Southern Comfort*. "It's supposed to have a couple other alcohols in it, but all I have is SoCo and vodka." She swirled the drink around, then poured half into a small glass tumbler and held it out to him. "It's regional cause of the peaches."

"Regional?" Alexei sniffed, caught the strong scents of peaches and grenadine, and not much else.

"From around here," Meg clarified. She emptied the rest of the drink into a black coffee mug, wider-mouthed for her wider muzzle.

"You should mix drinks at a bar." He sipped the drink at the same time she lifted her mug to her lips. Though it had the sting of alcohol, the overwhelming taste was peach, but it wasn't peach like the fruit. It was swaggering, smug *peach*, as if—as if someone had mashed an overripe peach into his nose and held it there, as if—

As if Kendall were a peach. It was the fruit taste, but stronger, and the grenadine added sweet cherry flavor, but not enough. "Too much peach," he said.

Meg said, "Needs more grenadine," and took his glass.

The association of Kendall made him not want to drink any more, but when Meg gave him the tumbler back, he took another sip to be polite. The flavor was smoother, not as intensely peach, and the sting of alcohol only brushed the back of his throat. "It's good," he said.

"Right." Meg drank hers and looked pleased. "Not too bad. I wonder what the other alcohols add."

Alexei shook his head. "I have no experience of that." He tipped the cup to the end of his muzzle again and let the sweet-sharp tang roll across his tongue as the peach-cherry filled his nose.

"Hey," Meg said, "don't drink it too fast."

The drink warmed his stomach and chest. Already his shame was receding, drowned in vodka and peach and camaraderie with Meg. "I am Siberian," he said. "This is vodka. I am born to it." He said it without knowing where he pulled the words from, and then remembered that it was something close to what his father'd used to say when his mother said he'd had enough. He set the drink down.

"You don't like it?" The otter tapped her coffee mug. It had a chip on the rim where the white ceramic showed through the black glaze.

Alexei flicked his ears. "You are right. I should not drink it so fast."

"A second ago you were 'born to it.'"

"What do you call it?" he asked, to change the subject.

Meg lowered her broad nose to her mug. "The original recipe is called a Red Devil, but I changed it around a little."

He traced a claw around the rim of the glass. "Red Devil. My sister and I called our blood that, sometimes."

Meg arched an eyebrow. "I get enough fake blood with Athos, okay? Anyway, this looks more orangey."

"It was a story." He stared down into the cup, seeing the orange of the sunset over the river, of Prababushka's fur, her long-remembered scent, her voice in his ears.

"Well?"

Meg was staring at him, tapping one finger on her cup. He blinked, and Samorodka fell away from him. "Well? What?"

"Are you gonna tell me the story?"

"Oh. If you like." He pulled the words from his memory, taking time to translate them. "My great-grandmother told me. Give me a moment to get the words." Fairy tales here started with a different phrase, so he used that one. "Once upon a time…a fox prince lived in a castle near a wood. His father—the king—had lost his oldest son to, er…" He clucked his tongue. "Not wolf, but wild wolf? In Siberian, the word is wolf-monster." Although his great-grandmother had used a different word still. She had grown up in Lechia, one of the Slavic regions to the west that was now part of—Alexei couldn't keep track of which country was which now. But she'd used still a different word for it.

"Animal-wolf," Meg said. "Some people say 'feral-wolf,' too."

"Animal." Alexei nodded. "So the king tells his son, you may not go into woods. Tch—into *the* woods. But the son, he loves the trees and the—the animals. All the peasants, all the servants, all the people can go to the woods to hunt, but he is trapped in the castle. 'As long as my blood runs in your veins,' the king says, 'you will be my heir and stay here.'

"One night he watches the full moon rise over the forest, and his wish calls to it. 'Free me from this red devil in my veins!' he cries.

"A wood-witch hears and comes to him. The prince is suspicious, but the witch cuts her arm and shows him the green sap in it. 'I can put this green sap in your veins,' she says, 'and then you will be able to wander the woods free of danger, free of duty.'"

"I wonder why people in fairy tales are so stupid," Meg said.

Alexei and Cat had sat together in that old ramshackle shed, looking at the river and the scraggly woods beyond, and had cried out the prince's plea. They would have taken the wood-witch's bargain, if she'd come to them. "The prince wanted desperately to escape his life. He could see no other way out."

"He was a prince." Meg shook her head. "Some people don't know how good they got it."

"'Prince,' in Siberia, may be simply head of a tribe. It is not…" He waved his arms. "Gold and money and fancy clothes. Not like that cartoon movie."

"He lived in a castle," Meg pointed out.

Alexei sighed. "The prince said yes." He ignored Meg's eyeroll. "So the witch took his blood and poured it into a wood-golem."

"A what?"

"A golem is a…" He gestured up and down his body with a paw. "Made in the shape of a fox, but of wood, but can move. A statue that can move."

"That holds blood."

"The wood-witch animated the golem with the blood of the prince, and put her green sap in his veins." Meg opened her mouth to comment again, and Alexei hurried on with the story. "So the prince was able to escape the castle, and he ran into the woods he loved so. But away from the fires of the castle, the sap in his veins thickened and slowed. When he returned from the woods, thirty years had passed, and his father was dead, and the wood-golem sat on the throne."

Meg watched him expectantly. When he didn't go on, she said, "Then what?"

He blinked, and picked up the drink again. The orange liquid left traces on the glass where it surged up and fell back. "Er. That is the end of the story."

"Did he get the throne back? Did he get his blood back?"

Alexei breathed in the peach aroma, the cherry flavor, the sting of the vodka. "I do not know. I suppose he was made to live with his decision."

"That sucks." Meg finished the rest of her drink and set the mug in the sink. "I mean, he was the prince, right? Don't those spells always have a way of reversing?"

"I don't know," Alexei said. "You could ask your friend."

Meg looked levelly at him. "I'm not going to ask him how to summon a ghost. I told you, it's stupid."

"I did not mean that." Alexei paused, the idea resurfacing in his mind. "But if you do not believe, what harm is there?"

Her eyes slid to Sol's room, then to his glass. "If you're not going to finish that, I will."

"Please." He handed her the drink.

She lifted it to her lips and then met his eyes again. "Sol went through a lot of crap, and he's still kind of hung up on that dream, in case you haven't noticed. I'm sure he'd tell you to do it, but I feel like it's my fault for pushing the absinthe on him, and I don't wanna encourage you to believe in it too. Last thing I need is both of you moping around after dreams." Before he could mount an answer to that, she drained the glass and set it down with a clack. "So you escaped, right, like that prince in your story? I guess you don't care if you go back. But your sister's still there?"

"Yes."

"Do you miss her?" She didn't face him as she asked, staring instead at her claws on the tabletop.

The vodka's warmth, cushioned by the sweet syrups, did not distance him from the world as much as Siberian vodka had. "Very much. This is one of the things I was miserable about."

Meg turned quickly, her piercings clinking. "Whoops. Sorry. You don't have to—"

"I don't mind. But no, I would not go back." He tapped the table with a claw. "She would not want me to. She wanted me to come to the States because I could be happy here."

"Uh-huh." Meg brought the glasses to the sink. "Is she happy there?"

Alexei saw the shed, the small flowers sitting against the rough, diseased wood. "I promised I would bring her with me, that I would find a way."

"Very noble." Meg's thick tail tapped the table leg while she washed the glasses. "But maybe you should keep yourself here first."

Chapter 4

When Sol came back a little later, Meg had disappeared into her room and closed the door, and didn't come out. Sol talked effusively about his date, how Mitch had been just so much fun and talkative and real (and not like that guy he'd met on the Internet, Alexei heard even though Sol did not say it). He'd asked Sol about the story he was writing, was impressed with his creativity, and wanted to get together again Saturday night. "I figure the barbecue will be over by six, so I told him eight."

"Do you want me to come along again?" Alexei asked.

"No, no." Sol laughed. "Thanks so much, though. I felt a lot better knowing you were there." And he went on, his tail wagging still, so that Alexei didn't feel like spoiling his evening by telling him about the lost wallet.

He told him the next morning on their way to work, and Sol said he would look out for it around the bus stop, but Alexei knew it was gone. He must have dropped it outside on the street, or else someone had found it in the coffee shop and taken it. So he came by Sol's store after his shift ended and bought a new wallet for ten dollars, a cheap bright yellow nylon thing that he hoped would not disappear easily.

And Saturday afternoon, with the sun blazing overhead and the humid air almost thick enough to swim through, they went out to the VLGA picnic in the backyard of Jerry's house. Jerry, a tall, slightly awkward rabbit, alternated between hurrying to ask if any of his twenty or so guests needed food or drink, and standing with his back to a tree, ears down, eyes wide. Alexei, sitting with Sol, asked Liza if the rabbit were okay.

"He is always like this," she said. "He wants company, then is afraid something will go wrong. But he loves to host." She glanced up at the second floor of his house. "His mother never comes down. Maybe she is just up there decaying in a rocking chair."

Alexei wasn't used to this gruesome imagination from Liza, and his flattened ears must have reflected that. She leaned over. "Norman Bates? *Psycho?*"

"Oh," Sol said. "Didn't they remake that a few years ago?"

"The remake is terrible," Liza said. "Go watch the original."

After that, Alexei kept looking up at the second floor windows, looking for a shadow of ears or any sign of movement. Sol didn't seem bothered by the prospect of being watched by an old rabbit who might be dead. But Alexei knew from Samorodka that ghosts would not always be as helpful and friendly as Sol's Niki had been.

Jerry grilled hot dogs for the carnivores and small squash and corn for the herbivores, and the smells mingled pleasantly with the smoke of the coals. The hot dogs were juicy and salty, and Alexei liked the sharp bite of the mustard, the soft sweet bread of the buns. He ate two while chatting amiably with Liza and Sol about movies and some of their friends, and besides the second floor windows, the other thing he watched was Mike.

It seemed to him that Kendall was pursuing Mike, and that the sheep tried to escape from time to time, but he couldn't be sure. Maybe Mike was just being polite and trying to talk to all the people at the picnic. Twice, though, Mike excused himself and turned to someone else only to have Kendall come back to join him and the other person. Not that the sheep looked irritated; in fact, Alexei had never seen Mike upset. Either he was very good at hiding it or he was the kind of wonderful person who didn't get annoyed at other people. Sol, meanwhile, had either forgotten his promise or was waiting until they'd all finished eating, because he didn't even look at the marten. Alexei didn't mind; he was working himself up to talk to Mike, rehearsing what he wanted to say.

Kendall, reminding everyone that he was VLGA president, started organizing games when most of the group had set down their plates. This took him away from Mike; Alexei watched as the sheep walked over to the grill and took an ear of corn and one of the squashes, then spread hummus on a small tortilla and wrapped it around the squash.

An elbow caught Alexei in the side. He turned to see Sol grinning at him. "Go," the wolf hissed.

"He's eating."

"He's alone. Go say hi." Sol practically shoved him off the bench. "I'll go help Kendall with the games so he doesn't interfere. Not that he would."

Alexei laughed nervously, looked up at the second floor windows, and then hurried over to where Mike was just taking the first bite of his squash-hummus wrap. The sheep looked up and smiled as Alexei approached.

"Hi there," he said. "Fun party. Hey, here's the music, before I forget."

He gave Alexei a small USB drive. The fox slipped it into his pocket and held out the CD he'd made. The sheep reached for it, but Alexei held it close. "Is that your Siberian metal?" Mike asked.

Alexei nodded. "I made this for you, but..."

Mike smiled. "You don't have to be ashamed of it. I'm very open-minded."

"It is not that. It is…" He lowered his voice. "When I listened to this, I was…younger. It is not something I listen to very much now."

The sheep smiled and patted Alexei's shoulder. "You know what? I used to listen to boy bands not so long ago. I promise I won't think less of you. Okay?"

Alexei smiled. "Okay." He held out the CD. "But you must also give me some music of boy bands, then."

The disk caught the light as Mike took it, a shimmering rainbow dancing along the silver edge, and the sheep's laugh was just as bright. "All right, I'll see if I can dig some up. Fair's fair." He shoved the disc into his back pocket.

"How's the squash?" Alexei nodded toward the wrap.

"It's good. The hummus is a little bland, but not bad. How were the dogs?"

Alexei smiled, tail wagging. "They were good. The mustard is very nice."

He cursed himself immediately—talking about mustard? But Mike looked toward the condiment table and said, "Really? Maybe I should try that instead of the hummus."

"Or together," Alexei said.

Mike grinned. "Or together. Do you cook?"

"Only a little. I am learning. My roommate cooks."

"Sol?" The sheep turned his large horns to where the black wolf was arguing with Kendall about some rules. Sol's tail wagged and he was grinning, so it was a friendly argument.

"No. We live with Meg, an otter. She is straight—I think—and very practical about the world. She believes in things she can see and touch, like fish. Not in things she cannot. Like—ghosts." He'd almost said, "love."

"Well," Mike said with a laugh, "I can't say I blame her too much."

"Liza says that Jerry's mother might be a ghost." Alexei shook his head and smiled. "We had a house in Samorodka that was haunted."

"Oh, come to think of it, we had a haunted house too!" Mike lit up with the memory. "I didn't really believe, but you know, I went out there once with some friends and there were weird noises and my friend Jas said he heard something talking. None of the rest of us did, and we said he was drunk, but…" He rubbed his muzzle. "He never liked to talk about it after."

Alexei's tail wagged. "I know some ghost stories as well. Meg laughs at them, but Sol says, 'Who are we to say that what others see is not real?'" Stop telling Mike what other people think. He kept his smile on. "I think Sol is right."

"You believe in ghosts?" But Mike didn't say it the way Meg would have, with snark and edge. He said it with a "convince me" expression.

The conversation had headed abruptly into territory that Alexei wasn't sure he wanted to be treading. "Is that strange?"

"Well…" Mike finished his wrap and rubbed his paws together. "Maybe a little. But I haven't seen what you've seen. Maybe ghosts are just rare."

"Maybe." This would be a good place to end the conversation. Mike had turned those brown eyes on him and was still smiling, and his golden horns caught the sun, and oh, the fox thought, if some spirit were conspiring to produce the perfect moment for Alexei to ask him out, its plans had come to fruition now. Alexei struggled with the words, flipping through phrases in his head, but his chest and throat felt tight, and he kept worrying, *what if he says no? What if he is just being polite?*

"Heads up!" came a shout from the other side of the yard, and Alexei half-turned.

A hard blow struck his chest, hard enough to send him staggering back a step, and for a moment he was back in his living room. But there was no dull thud of a bottle to the wood floor; water exploded at his muzzle, into his nose and even into his ears. The world slowed, chill and wet, and his head spun. "Wha—?"

Water trickled down his sides, into his pants, even as he held his shirt away from his fur. The rubber scrap of a balloon fell limply to the ground. Laughter and cheers surrounded him on all sides.

"Kendall!" Mike stifled a giggle and then put on an annoyed voice. "Don't be an ass."

"What? I'm trying to get people to toss water balloons around," came the pine marten's voice. "Just having a little fun."

"Maybe you should wait 'til people expect it." But Mike's annoyance was diminishing.

"I said, 'Heads up,'" Kendall replied, closer now. Alexei looked up to see him next to Mike, shirtless, drops of water beading on the fur of his arms and his broad chest. The oils in his fur kept the water from soaking in, as it was doing to Alexei's thin summer coat. Behind Kendall, Sol stood with flattened ears, one paw rubbing the back of the other. The pine marten, in contrast, just swaggered, grinning, paws on his hips. "You okay?"

"I am wet," Alexei said, hating himself for looking at Kendall's chest and arms. He scowled and stared at the ground.

Kendall laughed. "That's what happens when you get hit with a water balloon. Take your shirt off, come on." He gestured, showing off his chest and stomach to Mike.

The sheep was smiling now, perhaps reassured that Alexei was okay, perhaps just amused by Kendall's prank. Alexei made one more ineffectual brush at his shirt and then stalked back to the picnic tables. "Hey," Kendall called after him, "you can throw one at me if you want."

Alexei plopped down on the bench. Sol sat beside him, tail brushing his, and put a paw on his knee. "Sorry," he said. "I didn't notice until he was about to do it. But he's just playing around."

Alexei crossed his arms on the table and dropped his muzzle atop them. "Because I was talking to Mike, he wanted to make me look stupid."

"He was trying to include you. Come on, don't sulk."

But Alexei, lost in his own thoughts, spiraled downward. He would always be mocked, always be pushed aside by the Kendalls of the world. He had run away from exactly this in Samorodka, where a pudgy fox could not be allowed to play football, where a fox who did not want to play war with his friends would be pushed down and shut out, where a fox who was not interested in vixens would be subject to curses and demeaning insults and threats of being sent away with drug addicts and criminals. And here he had found freedom, he was playing football and had gotten into shape, and none of it mattered, he was still that pudgy, gay fox being laughed at. He felt that even the ghost of Jerry's mother, there on the second floor, was staring down at him. He imagined her with greying fur, drooping ears, grinning ear to ear and cackling.

"I want to go home," he said, worried that he might embarrass himself further.

"I think they're going to do egg races," Sol said. "You don't want to—"

"You can stay." Alexei stood up, even though he did want Sol to come with him. "I don't mind. But I am going home."

Sol did stay, and Alexei walked out quickly, without saying thank you to Jerry or good-bye to Liza or Mike. He thought he heard someone call out after him, but he was already in a black mood in which he wanted no pity from anyone, so he turned the corner of the house and walked down the path to the front gate, and nobody followed him.

The sun beat down on his black ears, but he didn't want to sit on a bus with a water-splattered shirt. After three blocks, he looked around at all the people walking shirtless through the streets and thought about taking his shirt off. Then he remembered Kendall saying, *Go on, take your shirt off,* and he kept it on.

Panting harder, half a mile farther along, his shirt was drying out but his fur was still wet. Kendall was back in Jerry's yard, and would never know. So Alexei stopped on the sidewalk, grasped the bottom of his shirt to lift it over his head...and stopped. What if some of the people around him laughed? What if Sol or Mike decided to come after him in a car? He released the shirt. His fur would dry out eventually. Even if it was a hot day, even if the fox across the street had a bare white-furred gut hanging over his belt, even if the deer jogging by was wearing nothing but a tight bra and shorts…

He arrived home, panting, to find the apartment even more stifling than the outdoors. "Can I open a window?" he asked Meg, closing the door behind him.

"Open yours," she called from her bedroom, and then her head showed through the doorway. "Picnic over already? Where's Sol? He go right to his date?"

"He is still there." Alexei strode to his bedroom, letting the door swing closed behind him, though he didn't shut it all the way. His scent and Sol's hit him in a wave in the oven-like heat of the room. He leaned over the desk, fumbled with the window catch, and then shoved the window up.

The air he'd just walked in from, hot, muggy, and thick with construction dust, felt refreshing compared to the oppressive apartment air. Alexei pushed the fan into the window and breathed in, sitting on the desk with his head against the window screen.

Meg pushed the door open. "Everything okay?"

Here, back in his home, the specters of the past receded. Alexei nodded, curling his tail across the top of the desk and resting one paw on it. "I got tired of the picnic," he said.

Her eyes drifted downward. "Spill something on your shirt?"

"Someone else did."

"Ah." She folded her arms. "And Sol just let you leave on your own?"

"I told him he could." He looked away from her, back out at the construction site. Two bulldozers sat idle amid huge piles of dirt behind the chain-link fence. A rack of lights loomed above, two of them aimed directly at him. "Do they work at night on those sites?"

"When it's really hot, yeah." Meg stepped into the room. "So what happened?"

Alexei shrugged. "It does not matter." He turned his head and stared up at the painting of Niki. "I want to do the ritual."

"What—" She followed his gaze. "Oh. No. No way."

Niki looked back at him with one friendly green eye. He knew what it was like to grow up Siberian, an outsider. He had overcome his childhood. "Why not?"

"Because if you pretend you're talking to Sol's dream boy, he'll be pissed. Or haven't you noticed how he looks at that painting all the time, how it's on his phone and his computer?"

Alexei bit his lip. "If I can talk to him, then Sol can again, too."

"No, he can't. And if—when you try and fail, he'll just be more depressed." She folded her arms.

"*I* will be depressed!" Alexei was trying to keep his voice down, but his shirt clung to his fur and he could still smell the tap water from the balloon and see Mike laughing at him and Kendall's smirk. "Sol has a date and a ghost and I have—I cannot even—"

"Okay, settle down. What's bothering you? Is it because you're all wet? Get that shirt off and let me get you a towel."

"No—" But she was already gone. He inhaled and pulled his shirt off, throwing it in the corner.

Meg returned with a towel and tossed it to him, not commenting on his physique or fur or anything. "So what is it? Your sister?"

He rubbed his fur dry and shook his head. "There is someone I want to ask on a date...but..."

"A date? Fuck, is that all? Why don't you just ask Sol?"

"I did—I mean, he is helping, but—"

"You know there are books, right? 'Dating for Dummies'? I don't know if there's a 'Gay Dating for Dummies,' but probably. Anyway, you're in a gay club! What could be easier?"

He threw the towel at her, his tail curled tightly against his leg. "If you do not wish to help me, then go away. I will find something on the Internet and I will do it myself."

Meg dodged and then picked up the towel. "Fine, then do that. Don't tell me how it goes."

She walked out of the doorway and Alexei fumed, fists clenched, staring at the painting of Niki. The fox had talked to Sol, and now Alexei needed him, and he was right here in the room. There had to be a way to get through to him. He cleared his throat and said in Siberian, "*Niki...please come talk to me...help me...*"

He'd never had to summon a ghost in Samorodka; there, the problem was keeping away from the ghosts. He fixed his eyes on Niki's until they watered, said variations on the same thing in Siberian and English over and over, and then went to his computer to search for ghost summoning rituals. All of them seemed ridiculous, and required incense or bells or chalk or (in one case) a blood sacrifice.

At that last one, Alexei put the computer to sleep and shuddered. It had been easy for Sol. He'd drunk the absinthe from Meg...

The fox stood up. Meg. She would have to get him some absinthe. He would just drink it himself, and then she wouldn't have to be involved. He hurried out to the living room and knocked on her door.

"Go away," she said, muffled.

"I just need some absinthe," he said.

"Go. Away."

"Please." He slumped against her door. "I...don't know what else to do."

The silence lasted for so long that Alexei nearly trudged back to his room. But then Meg rattled the door handle and pulled her door open, and stood there staring at him. "You don't need absinthe," she said. "Anyway, Athos doesn't have any more of it. Sol asked too."

"Then—"

"Jesus." Meg scowled at him. "If I help you do this ritual, will you promise to leave it alone and go pick up a self-help book or get a motivational CD or something and stop going on about ghosts?"

He perked his ears straight up and beamed at her. "Yes! I promise, yes." Because of course the ritual would not fail, and then he would be able to talk to Niki and ask him for help, for confidence in talking to Mike. And if by some chance Niki refused to speak to him, well then, he would have to find something else to do anyway, and he wouldn't involve Meg. But he knew in his heart that the ritual would work.

Meg sighed. "Fine. Let's get it over with, then. Are you eating here tonight?" He nodded. "All right. Want to go with me to get fish at the market?"

His eyes lingered on the painting. "Can we do the ritual now?"

"No." When he gave her a pleading look, she folded her arms. "One, you don't know when Sol's going to get back. Two, we have to do it at night."

"Why?"

"We just do, that's all. Ghosts come out at night."

He thought of the second story of Jerry's house, of the old abandoned house in Samorodka. "Not always."

"Well, we're doing it at night. Anyway, I need to get a list of stuff from Athos. Want to come to the market?"

Because it was better than sitting around the apartment, he went with her, hoping his fur would dry more quickly in the sun. She didn't ask any more about the picnic; instead they talked about Sol and his date, about Alexei's job, and about what movies were coming out. Meg tried to get him to make fun of some of the other shoppers with her, but after the picnic, Alexei didn't feel comfortable mocking people, so she stopped quickly.

Athos texted her a list of ingredients and a ritual, supposedly—she wouldn't show Alexei the message, but made him get some wormwood incense, some candles, and a bell. "Do we need chalk?" he said, and Meg gave him a strange look.

"I have some," she said. "Why did you think that?"

"On the Internet, some of the rituals wanted things drawn with chalk." He grinned at her, glad that he'd figured out part of it.

"Yeah, well." She pointed at the bag she'd made him carry. "We got what we need, except the painting. Let's go home."

"The painting?"

"Yeah." She tapped her phone. "You need something related to the ghost to call it, and unless you want Sol to lie in the circle with his freaky green eyes…"

"I suppose…" Alexei said slowly. "If Sol is away, and we can put the painting back afterwards."

"He'll never know. And it's not going to work anyway, so it doesn't matter." Meg swatted his shoulder, and he flicked his tail back at her with a conspiratorial grin.

Alexei's good spirits lasted until Sol returned. "Kendall feels really bad about the water balloon," was the very first thing the black wolf said. Alexei didn't say anything. Sol waited and then went on. "He wants to make sure you're coming to Game Night on Saturday."

The previous week, Sol had talked Alexei into going to the restaurant/arcade Playtime with the VLGA, and the fox had convinced himself that in a more relaxed setting, he might get to talk to Mike. "We have a soccer game on Wednesday," Alexei said. "I will see him there."

"Yeah, but we don't usually hang out that much at the games. He said he wants to buy you a drink at Game Night."

Alexei shrugged. "We will see."

Sol let it go at that, either because he didn't want to argue any longer or because he was getting ready for his date. He had bought a cologne with a musky scent on the way home, "Because he's a bear and his nose isn't as good," he said, when Alexei wrinkled his muzzle at the thick odor. The bottle was marked "subtle," but Alexei thought it was rather strong, and his nose was relieved when Sol, dressed in a nice shirt and slacks, took his scent out the door.

The sun wasn't quite setting, so he didn't ask Meg about doing the ritual, but grew more excited as he helped her prepare for dinner. When she scolded him for flicking her with his tail, he tried to keep it more demurely tucked away, but it kept flicking around and wagging when he stopped paying attention.

They'd bought a white fish, which Meg fried in butter, but Alexei could not recall afterwards how it tasted, apart from the seared butter. He devoured the fish and bread, all the while looking at the fading light through his bedroom door. Patiently, he helped Meg clean the dishes, and when she had given him the last plate and he had dried it, he looked at her and smiled, and she said, "Oh, all right, let's go."

He went to his room first, but she didn't follow. "Bring the painting," she said. "We'll do it in my room. Otherwise Sherlock Wolfy will wonder why you were burning wormwood in your room."

"I can just tell him I like the smell," Alexei said.

"Yeah, but if he smells it from my room, he won't even ask that much. Besides, if he comes home early…. Easier to move the painting."

Alexei climbed onto Sol's bed. He gripped the edges of the frame with both paws and lifted it away from the wall. For a moment, Niki's eye met his, and he thought he felt the painting quiver in his paws. Then it was still, and Alexei backed gently off the bed, searching for the floor with one foot before putting his weight back on it. He held the frame sideways, maneuvered it through the door, and walked with it to Meg's room.

She was already sprinkling the chalk dust in a circle on her floor. "Put the painting in the center of the circle," she said. "Then put one of the incense holders on the side near the wall and put the incense in it. Don't light it yet. And don't brush away any of my lines with your tail."

He found it difficult to keep his tail still, but he did at least keep it curled up as he followed her instructions. She finished her circle and started drawing small symbols in the dust, pausing frequently to check her monitor. "This is never going to come out of the carpet."

"I will come vacuum it for you." Alexei would have promised her anything. "Where do I sit?"

Meg pointed to a spot at the edge. "Sit there and stay still. I'm just about finished."

While Alexei arranged himself cross-legged beside the painting, Meg sprinkled a lavender-scented oil on the symbols she'd been drawing, then arranged the three candles in a triangle. "You have the bell?" she asked.

"Right here." Alexei held it up, pressing the clapper against the side so it wouldn't make any noise. The lavender oil tickled his nose, but he repressed the urge to sneeze.

"Set it down in front of you. We're going to say this ritual and then at the end you're going to ring the bell. And then you have to ring the bell again to send it back."

"All right." Alexei had so many questions to ask. He had been trying to organize them in his head, but they kept pushing past each other for precedence. *How do I get someone to notice me? How do I deal with someone who takes all the attention for himself? How can I find out if I really love someone?* He would say the questions in Siberian, so as not to embarrass himself in front of Meg. Niki was born in Siberia, so he should speak the language.

He was about to speak to a ghost. Alexei squeezed his paws together. He pulled the end of his tail into his lap to stop it from wagging, and watched Meg check the monitor against the carpet one last time. Then she sat down across the painting from him.

"Rest your paws on the painting."

"Not the glass," Alexei said hurriedly as she moved her paws forward. "Sol will notice."

"Oh, all right." She rested fingertips on the wood frame. "Now focus your mind on the spirit, and listen as I speak the summoning ritual."

"Could I speak it?" Alexei asked.

Meg looked at him for a second before answering. "Athos is funny about his rituals. He said I could do it, but he didn't want me to tell anyone else."

"I will hear it when you say it," Alexei pointed out.

"But you won't have memorized it like I did. Now just close your eyes." Meg stared down at her paws, then lifted her head to the ceiling. "Spirits from the land beyond," she intoned. "Hear the call we send to you. Feel the circle's mystic bond. Niki, come across and through."

Alexei had his eyes squeezed shut, thinking about his questions, so Meg had to hiss at him. Then he remembered, and picked up the bell to ring it.

"With the tolling of the bell," Meg went on, "the gate is opened wide. Whether from heaven or from hell, appear thou spirit at our side."

Alexei felt a chill in his fur. Nothing else happened. He looked at Meg and lifted the bell, but she shook her head. They waited in silence, Alexei with his ears perked for the slightest sound.

But the sound, when it came, was not what he expected. It was not an ethereal wailing, nor a high-pitched eerie background noise like in a movie, nor a comforting Siberian vulpine voice. It was the rattle of the door handle.

"Sol!" He gasped, and Meg looked up.

"Nothing yet?" she hissed. Alexei shook his head. "Do you know any more of his name?"

He shook his head again, eyes wide, and stared at the picture, at the green eye looking back at him. A scrap, a buried memory surfaced. "Konstantinov," he said, running the syllables fluidly together to get the word out faster.

Meg closed her eyes. "Niki Konstantinov, hear us and come forth."

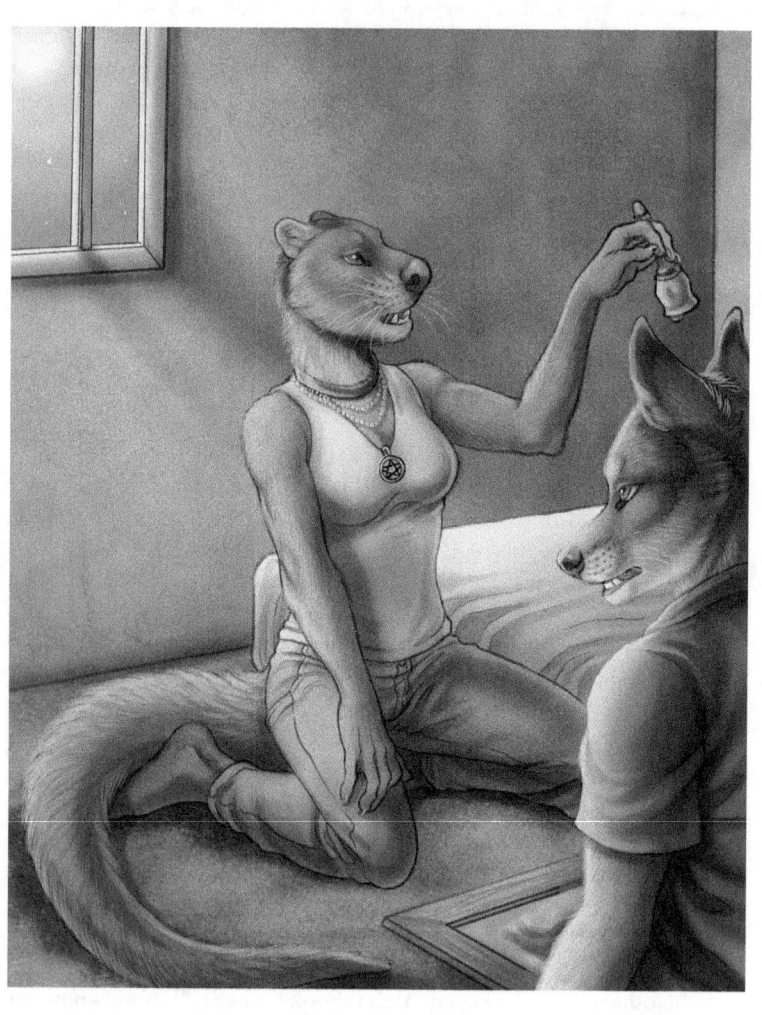

"The gate is opened wide"

Sol's key clicked; the lock threw back. Meg's eyes met Alexei's, and he saw that despite her cynicism, she was invested in the ritual as well, hoping for some revelation. "Nothing?" she whispered to him.

Alexei closed his eyes as the front door opened, straining to feel anything beyond his normal perceptions. Slowly, he shook his head.

"All right," Meg said. "Go, go."

He got up, then stared at the painting in horror. Meg saw where he was looking and sprang to her feet, her thick tail sweeping across several of the symbols. "Ask him how his date was," she hissed. "Keep him talking until he goes to the bathroom."

Alexei darted out the door. Sol, locking the front door behind him, turned just as Alexei reached the table. "Hey. On the computer?"

He hadn't seen Alexei leave Meg's room. Alexei gulped and nodded. "How was your date? You are back early."

"He has a study session Sunday morning. It went pretty good." Sol smiled, tail swinging lazily from side to side. "He kissed me."

"Really?" The painting fled Alexei's mind. "A real kiss?"

"Well, on the side of the muzzle." Sol smoothed his whiskers back. "But it was nice. We had dinner, and talked about food and wine. He knows a lot about wine. And then we talked about movies and his college and where I was going."

He started to walk to the bedroom. Alexei stepped into his path. "Please, tell me about it."

The black wolf stopped, looking bemusedly at Alexei. "All right. Well…let me go to the bathroom first."

"Yes, of course." Alexei couldn't stop the first wag of his tail, but then he curled it around his leg.

Sol disappeared into the bathroom, and Alexei ran to Meg's door, only to nearly bump into her. She made as if to go past him, but he took the painting from her and ran to their room. As he got up on Sol's bed, he heard the toilet flush. Alexei settled the painting against the wall and lowered it, but it didn't stay. He tried again. The wire would not catch on the hooks.

The bathroom door opened. Desperate, Alexei lifted the painting, lowered it—and this time, it stayed against the wall. He hopped down from Sol's bed, landing on the floor with a light jolt. "Hey," Sol said, poking his head in the door of the bedroom. "Want to talk in here? Meg's room smells funny. You know what—"

With a crash, the painting fell from the wall.

Chapter 5

Alexei stood and stared at Sol, and Sol stood and stared at the painting. "What were you doing with Niki?" he asked.

"I…" Keeping Sol unaware had made all the sense in the world when he'd started. But now, the wide eyes and gaping mouth of Alexei's best friend swept all that nonsense aside, and Alexei stared at the confusion on Sol's muzzle with no idea how to explain his actions, even to himself.

Sol strode forward and stood at the edge of his bed, one paw outstretched as though afraid the face-down picture would crumble if he touched it. "I'm sorry," Alexei said, fumbling for the words. "I meant nothing harmful…"

His command of English deserted him. He stayed pressed back against the desk, watching Sol tremble as the black wolf reached out and tenderly lifted the frame from the bed.

Meg appeared at the edge of the door. Alexei waved frantically for her to go away, but she mouthed something at him. He couldn't interpret it, so he waved harder, and finally, with an exasperated look, she left. The smell of wormwood invaded the room, strong enough for Sol to smell, but the wolf's whole attention was focused on the picture he was lifting carefully from the bed.

He gave a low moan, and Alexei, without seeing anything, said, "I didn't mean to hurt him. I promise."

"It's cracked." Sol's voice came low and rough.

"I'm *sorry*!" Alexei said. "Is…is the painting damaged?"

"I can't tell." Sol traced a finger along the glass. Alexei moved to his left and now saw a line running through the glass, through the base of the stone bench and through the leg of the fox. He winced, but could not look away.

"I will pay for the repair." Alexei moved to his dresser and opened the drawer.

"Yeah, you will." Sol turned; his voice was louder. "What were you doing?"

Alexei swallowed. "I was…I was lonely. I thought I could…I thought I could talk to him too."

"So you had to pull the picture off the wall? Couldn't you just stare at it?" Sol's bright green eyes bored into his. "You could've broken the whole thing! I can't just go down to the store and get another one."

"I know," Alexei said.

"I should never have moved in here with you," Sol snapped.

Alexei folded his ears back. He wanted to pull himself inward and disappear, to get away from here; more than that, he wanted to go back in time and not take Sol's picture from the wall, to find something else to use in the ritual or just to ask Sol's permission. How would Cat have felt if he'd betrayed her this fundamentally? He had nothing but useless, inadequate words that sounded worse because they were not in his language. All the things he wanted to tell Sol were trapped in the only words he could think of. "I'm sorry," he said softly, and ran out of the bedroom.

He yanked at the front door, found it locked, and threw the lock back, hoping Sol would tell him to wait. But Sol didn't say a word, and Meg must have been staying in her room. He pulled the door open and slipped out, and ran to the front step.

But he stopped there, breathing in the hot evening air, insects and cars buzzing low in his ears. Up and down the sidewalk, streetlights cast islands of light onto the cement, but the light in front of their stoop was broken, and Alexei stood with the dim light of the windows behind him, murky clouds above him, and the cement walkway stretching through relative darkness ahead of him. He had no idea where he was going to go or what he might do. He didn't really know anyone else in Vidalia except Vlad and Liza, and didn't know if either of them would welcome him showing up at nine-thirty at night needing a place to stay.

He sat down on the stoop, and curled his tail around his hips, then sank his muzzle into his paws. It wasn't as if the ritual had even worked. It had all been for nothing, and worse than nothing, because he had betrayed his best friend.

The sick feeling in his chest grew stronger and stronger, and the urge to get to his feet and leave this place grew with it. He stood, took a step toward the street, and then stopped. A pair of goats walked by, into light, into darkness, and back into light. He watched them walk on, envying them the surety of their destination.

His feet took him to the edge of the sidewalk, to the edge of one of the pools of light below the streetlamps. To the left, their street met a large busy road; that was where the bus picked him up. To the right, it stretched down into block after block of streetlamps and anonymous apartment buildings, broken by the glow of an all-night convenience store and, perhaps half a mile down, the rush of cars along a freeway overpass. There were busses there, too, he knew; they ran to other parts of Vidalia, places he'd never been.

This was not at all like leaving Samorodka and his parents behind. He had been moving forward then, toward a brighter future. Now he was living in that future and he had ruined it, tainted it. Did he have another future to go to? He thought about Cat's words, that one should always run toward something rather than away. What would she do, in his place? He ached to ask her, hated that he could not.

In the tortured moments weighing his decision, the front door opened behind him. He swept his ears back to listen, but didn't turn around.

Sol's voice came through the night. "Hey," the wolf said. "Come back inside. I'm—I'm sorry I yelled at you."

Alexei shook his head slowly, and turned. "You were right. I did a terrible thing."

The black wolf did not contradict him, but he did stare down at the pavement and his tail was as tightly curled as Alexei's was. The mirrored emotion relaxed the fox a little. "I still shouldn't have yelled." Sol took a breath. "Meg said...she said it was all just a mistake."

Alexei nodded, hesitating. "But still, I should have asked."

"Well," Sol said. "Yeah." Undercurrents of anger remained in his voice. "But it's...it's okay. I mean, you said you'd pay for it."

"I will."

"So...come back inside."

It was half a request, half an order. Sol's ears remained flat and he didn't meet the fox's eyes, but Alexei believed the apology was sincere. He looked again to his left and his right, and then stepped toward Sol and back to the apartment.

"Thank god," Meg said as the two of them walked back in. "I can only imagine where you might have ended up, going off on your own. Where *were* you going?"

"I don't know," Alexei said.

Sol leaned against the kitchen table, his back to the bedroom. "Meg said you were really down. I guess I didn't realize that." His words came slowly and begrudgingly, but Alexei found it easier to listen for the sincerity behind them. He was aware that things were not the same with him and Sol, might not be again for a long time, and he chose his words carefully.

"I never meant any disrespect to Niki," he said softly. "I would never do anything like that."

Sol turned away. Meg coughed and said, "Hey, he even remembered your dream-fox's last name. How's that for caring?"

"Last name?" Sol flicked his ears, his eyes narrowing. "He doesn't have a last name."

Meg's expression when she met Alexei's eyes was part apology, part conspirator. "Well, he made one up for him, then," she said.

Alexei knew that Sol didn't want to hear the name, and knew that Meg knew that, and also knew that she was about to make things worse by telling him. So he broke in. "It is not important," he said. "I will take the picture to a shop this weekend." He had no idea where to take a broken picture, but Vlad would tell him. "I will have it fixed."

And that was the end of it for that night—almost. The matter certainly remained in the minds of each of them, Alexei most of all. As he lay in bed trying to sleep that night, one thing kept returning over and over. When he'd said, "Konstantinov," it had had the certain feeling of an uncovered memory, something Sol had mentioned and Alexei had forgotten. But Sol had been immediately certain that Niki didn't have a last name, which meant that he'd never known it.

Then where had that name come from?

Chapter 6

The people of Siberia belong to the land, and the land belongs to the tsars. We are born in the smell of earth and carried on our mothers' and fathers' backs for the plowing, the planting, the harvesting. We know hay from wheat before we can count to ten; we can swing a scythe before we can hold a pencil.

For centuries, this was the order: the tsars ruled the people and the people worked the land. We would no more wish to rule ourselves than the tigers in Petrograd would wish to come to the sowing. We met in villages to decide questions that were not worth their time: which of us would work which field, who would care for the sick family, whether dim Sergei Alexandrovich, who was a good carpenter, was responsible for the roof he'd repaired that had collapsed when a child leapt onto it. Life was not easy, but it was simple.

In the middle of the nineteenth century, Siberians began to look outward, to the nations where merchants were rising in power, to the great nations built on coin and trade rather than on honest work and earth. They saw the possibilities and grew greedy, and the village meetings became centers of revolution, discarding the words of our ancestors like wheat husks left to rot in the fall rains. Out there, they said, those who work reap the rewards, and the monarchs answer to them! Why should we labor for others? As a fungus will spread through a storehouse, these ideas clung and gnawed at the people, and grew potent.

But the emperors—what the tsars called themselves—were not yet weak, then. Alexander II bared his claws and crushed the would-be revolutionaries, raking the land and leaving scarred villages, empty seats at the meetings. The peasants left in their wake had to work still harder, but that is how a country heals.

Our village thought it had been spared, until one cold night two weeks before the end of the year. Under the new moon the tigers came, in the winter when their scent would not carry in the dead air and their feet could not be heard in the new-fallen snow. Silent as ghosts, they surrounded the cottages and houses, and then burst in, taking the villagers unawares. The soldiers pulled us easily from our homes, and we blinked stupidly and stumbled after them. There was no fighting; those who fancied themselves revolutionaries had only ideas and dreams, no real strength.

The tigers tied and gagged us, and threw us into a cart, piled atop each other. My parents and the others who would have fought against the Tsar were taken a mile outside of town, pulled from the cart, and made to kneel. A tiger

I had nobody else in which to place my trust

pulled me down as well, but another stayed him, brought me around to the front of the cart to stand with the steaming, panting horses while the cracks of gunfire rained around us. I am ashamed to admit that I cried, I clung to his leg and breathed in his gunpowder scent as the bodies fell. He whispered down to me in the cold night that my parents were wicked people, and that my life would be different, better, from this moment on.

I had no way of knowing that he was right, but I had nobody else in which to place my trust. I was six years old.

Chapter 7

Alexei stands on a barren rocky field. The wind is familiar and cold, like a family member he left behind in Samorodka. In Samorodka, though, wind comes from one direction, blowing down from the north or the east; now, whichever way he turns, it burrows into his ears and chills his nose. He turns, looking for features on the land, and sees nothing but rocks stretching out to the horizon in every direction.

He wraps his arms and tail around himself. The shirt and light pants he wears around Vidalia have never met a temperature below sixty (or fifteen, as he still thinks of it), and offer no protection from the slicing wind. This cold is as sharp and bitter as the January wind in which he had to stand for an hour as punishment for "dreaming" when he failed to bring enough fish home.

The landscape is the same in all directions, and he has turned more than a full circle when he spots the other figure. Where there had been only rocks there is now a tall fox facing away from him, wearing a blue military coat with a gold belt—not the kind from the heroic pictures on the wall of Alexei's schoolhouse, but the kind that he has seen mostly in old movies and history books, knee-length, drawn tightly around a scrawny body. The coat's red collar bears dark stains, the fabric is torn in patches, and the gold belt is spotted with rust-red. His tail, ragged and so dirty that the white tip appears grey, shows below the edge of the coat, and a sword hangs from the belt.

Hello, *Alexei calls, but the fox's ears do not move and he does not answer. Alexei takes a step toward him and finds himself the same distance away, perhaps ten feet. He takes another step, and another, and still the fox remains ten feet away, immobile as a statue.* Hello? *Alexei raises his voice.* Niki? Nikolai?

At that, the fox's ears swivel back, but still he does not turn. A rough, cracked voice makes its way to Alexei, speaking Siberian: Leave me alone.

But I need your help, *Alexei pleads.* I've nobody left.

The winds swirl, bite his ears, and he feels the emptiness all around him. The fox's ears flick. Why, *he says,* do you come to me, then?

Perhaps, Alexei thinks, this is Nikolai before Sol knew him, before his years in Lutèce. But this fox feels older, and Alexei knows it is not Sol's Niki, not any Niki. He stammers. I...I know you...someone...helped a friend of mine.

Then you have friends. You have family.

That last word rings hollowly, is caught and swirled by the wind and driven into Alexei's ears. He folds them down. My family, *he says,* my family cannot help me. And my best friend...

He sees again Sol's expression, the flat ears and flatter eyes. The wind rips the words from his muzzle to die.

The fox before him stirs. The ragged tail twitches. Go, *he says.*

The wind keens. Alexei struggles forward and reaches out an arm, but the wind sears his eyes, and when he blinks, he is alone again.

Chapter 8

Sol didn't speak much to Alexei in the morning. It wasn't only that Sol was still upset, though he was; it was also that Alexei remained quiet, struggling to figure out what, if anything, his dream meant. It had felt very real, but he had had realistic dreams before and nothing had come of them. And the fox wasn't Niki, that was almost certain.

The dream left him in a bleak mood, whether there was anything to it or not. Though the day was already hot and humid, he still felt chilly inside, especially when Sol said he was going out for a walk.

"I'll chip in to fix the picture," Meg said. "I told him not to be so butt-hurt over it, but you know how he is." When Alexei didn't answer, she went on. "Sorry the thing didn't work. You know, you can't predict what's going to happen."

He wanted to tell her about his dream, but he was worried she would laugh at him and call him crazy like Sol. Sol would believe him, but the black wolf was still upset, even though he'd supposedly forgiven Alexei. How would he react if Alexei told him that he was having vivid dreams about another time? Jealousy? Smug satisfaction that he had connected with his dream fox, while Alexei's had told him to go away? Alexei didn't even know how he himself felt about it, so he had no idea how to expect Sol to react.

Most Sundays, he and Sol would go kick a ball around, and he had little doubt that if he walked over to the park, he'd find the black wolf there. But Alexei stayed seated at his desk, tail curled around his hip, the clean white tip twitching.

The loneliness of the dream and the Siberian fox had sharpened his worry about Cat. He searched online for her friends, but he did not know the last names of many of them, and he guessed that most of them didn't have computers anyway. It had been strange for him, going from a small town where all the cubs fished or hunted and families shared cellular phones to this country, where his host family bought him a phone of his own right away so that they could keep in touch with him. They also gave him their daughter's old computer, which was more advanced than the one computer in the Samorodka schoolhouse that the students shared only for research, not communication. These had been startling gifts to him, but to his host family, they were necessities.

As a last resort, he sent an e-mail to the engineer who had helped him get into the exchange program, telling him he was worried about his sister and asking for any help the fox could provide. Then, guilty because he had not kept in touch, he told the engineer more about his life, how he was happy living in Vidalia, he had found friends here and was hoping to become a citizen.

When he had finished typing the words, he stared at them on the screen. They felt false to him, but what else could he say? The truth would be depressing to a fox who had taken some risk in getting Alexei out of Samorodka, even if he didn't tell him anything about ghosts and rituals. His benefactor deserved to think he was happy.

He would be again, one day, he presumed. After all, he remembered nights in Samorodka when he would lie in bed and believe he would never smell anything but fish again, that his fur would always feel grimy with mud, that he would never be able to tell another boy that he was attractive or ask to hold him. And here he was in Vidalia, smelling of fish only when he helped Meg cook it, with clean fur and friends who thought there was nothing so natural as a boy who loved boys. So surely, the trouble with Sol would pass, and maybe if he worked at it, he could gain the courage to ask Mike out.

It was not precisely when he had that thought, but close to it, that his phone buzzed with a text message. He didn't recognize the number, but the message started with, *It's Mike,* so he called it up.

It's Mike. Hi. Sol gave me your number. I wanted to say sorry if I was laughing at you yesterday. Sol said you were okay but you seemed upset.

Warmth thawed Alexei's mood. Maybe he would be able to talk to Mike after all. He typed: *Thank you. I am fine, it was just a shock.*

He sat and stared at the words, thumb hesitating over the Send button. He could ask Mike out. "Maybe we could have dinner sometime." No, that was stupid. In all the comedies he'd seen here, people were made fun of for saying important things over text messages. He would wait until Wednesday at the game, or maybe Friday at Playtime. But at least he could say something more, tell Mike how much he appreciated the sheep's concern.

Before he could add those words, his phone buzzed again. *Kendall says he's sorry, he thought you were expecting it.*

So Mike was with Kendall now. Out to lunch somewhere. Maybe Kendall had made him text Alexei, or, more likely, Kendall had been reliving the moment. Alexei could see him laughing, could hear the sneer: "Did you see the look on his face when I hit him?" And Mike smiling, feeling a little guilty, making Kendall apologize, and Kendall saying, "Well, yeah, if he can't take a joke then I'm sorry."

Alexei just sent his message as it was. He would try to get Mike alone at Playtime, ask him for a date. Then he would show Kendall who was sorry.

Monday morning, Sol still did not talk to Alexei very much, and when Alexei suggested they practice that evening for Wednesday's game, Sol nodded without a word. On their way to the bus, he responded to Alexei's attempts at conversation with subdued tones, as though preoccupied with some far-off problem. The thick, humid air had them both panting by the time they stepped onto the air-conditioned bus, and the blast of cool air reminded Alexei of his dream again. He sat by the window with his head against the glass, and Sol sat with earphones in, and when the wolf got up, Alexei waved shortly good-bye.

At work, he asked Vlad where he could get a framed picture repaired, and spent the rest of the day quiet. He would have to do something to make things right with Sol, and he had no idea what that would be. Once he'd fixed the painting, he would still need to earn Sol's trust back. He thought up and discarded several schemes, and left work frustrated, hoping the physical exertion of practice would help.

Unfortunately, Kendall also showed up to their practice session in the park, and Alexei had to wave off his apologies twice. Sol remained quiet, and Kendall's presence put Alexei back into a dark mood. He didn't seem to be able to do any of the practice drills properly, especially when Kendall was watching, and he rode home with Sol in silence on the bus.

But at home, a letter from his sister waited on the table.

Chapter 9

June 19

Dear Alexei,

I had to write this letter today so that it would not be one month since the last one. I have received your letters, but without a schoolroom to write in, it takes me longer to get away, and also I hurt my paw after Last Bell and it was painful to write. When I am not being made to do chores, I am given your fishing rod and told to catch supper. Friday nights I am allowed to play with my friends, and that is why I have some exciting news in this letter.

We, Kisha and I and some friends, were in Vdansk, and I happened to be talking about you in a small shop where our friends were buying earrings, when a short corsac fox turned around and said that his son was also in the exchange program. He told me that he is on leave from the civil service, and so he had privileged access to those programs. When I said I wished to join an exchange program as well, he said he would try to get me into one this fall so that I might join you in the States!

Alexei, I cannot express how light my heart was with this news. Things have been difficult since you and Slava left. I have not known what I would write to you even if I did have the time, because I would not want you to worry more. But now I have good news I can tell you! His name is Bogdan and he said that it would be difficult for me to call him as he is traveling around while on leave, but he took down my number and told me he would call me when he had more news about how I could join the program. He is such a nice fox and says that my English is quite good enough to go to the States, that a pretty vixen like me will certainly be accepted into the program. Kisha says all he wants to do is sleep with me, but she says that about every male we encounter.

I spend every moment of Friday night that I can with my friends, because without you, I do not like to be at home. Mama and Papa have changed since you left, and sometimes it is better and sometimes worse. Papa says he wishes you were still here, but only when I bring back one or no fish. More often he does not talk at all, simply sits in his shed and drinks his drink as it comes out. I like those days better. Sometimes when he has drunk a lot of vodka he thinks I am you and once he shut me in your room and shouted for nearly an hour. I worried that the bees would sting me, but they merely went about their business and ignored me.

I wish Mama could do that. She tells me nearly every day what I must do to become a good wife, and I could write out for you from memory the list of available boys to become my husband. You know that there are not many foxes any more in Samorodka, so Mama has written to friends in other towns and tells me of young Shchavlev, the son of the schoolteacher in Kirovka, or young Chistyakov, whose family in Myatlevo regularly travels to Moskva. These are only the two she has been talking about most of the time for the entire year. I will not waste your time reciting the entire list, either of my prospective husbands or of my faults as a vixen of the Tsarev family. Mama likes to remind me that we were once servants of the emperors, even though it has been a hundred years since that meant anything.

Two weeks ago, the engineers returned to repair the dam, but while they were here, a fire burned down Madam Zvereva's boarding-house. None of the engineers was harmed, but they all left the next day without finishing their work. The children say the fire was started by the ghost of Katya Bobrova who drowned in the river, but everyone else knows it was someone in town. Nobody has made any attempt to rebuild the house. Ivana Zvereva took her mother in, and now she complains loudly to anyone who will remain close enough to hear that there is no justice in the town. Wolverines are never happy, I know, but I think in this case she has the right.

I thought of you, of course, but the engineer you befriended did not return this year. So if the burning was done because of your departure, it was for nothing. Although it might also have been done because everyone fears that if the dam is completed, the fishing will be gone and then what will we eat on the days when we have nothing else? We learned in school that the dam would bring power and money to Samorodka, but it is difficult for people to accept the promise of the future against the loss of the present. They no longer trust the government to do the right thing, but try to make decisions for themselves, and the government is not willing to stop them. This is what Mr. Lanin tells us.

The only other thing I think I must tell you about happened last week. I told you about Ksenia Tsyzyreva, the roe deer who left for Moskva in the middle of winter with the military trucks, yes? She returned last Tuesday and is living with her parents again. I have not seen her, but Kisha says both her feet were bleeding, and that she lived on the streets of Moskva and only survived by doing things she will not talk about. We all know what those things are. Kisha and I brought her vodka and bread and a bunch of cornflowers and we sat with her, and we will go over again on Friday. Kisha wants to take her to Udansk when we go, but I think she would prefer to be among friends here in Samorodka, where we know everyone and there are no strangers. She says she missed the peace of the river, and I told her I would bring her fishing. We can sit together with our tails to the town and our noses to the woods and breathe in the clean smell of the water (if we sit upwind of the garbage). I want badly to ask her about Moskva, but I cannot bring myself to make her think of it again. If she chooses to tell me, so be it.

No, there will be no Moskva for me. ~~It will be either joining you,~~ or It will be joining you, however I must make it happen.

With love,

Cat

Alexei folded up the letter, tail twitching as crazily as his thoughts. He was glad to hear from his sister, but the letter had plunged him back into Samorodka and reminded him that if anything, it had gotten worse since he'd been there. He imagined the burned-out shell of the boarding house, smoking in the town's streets; he imagined the half-finished dam slowly rotting away because the engineers returning to Moskva reported that the town was no longer a suitable location for it. He imagined the reek of alcohol in his house getting worse—or perhaps better, if it were drunk even before it was set out in open-mouthed bottles. He could hear the buzz of bees, could smell the rotting wood, could hear the shouts and his sister's cry as something struck her paw. It was no mystery to him how her injury had come about—another thing to hold against his parents.

At least the letter had a hopeful note. If Cat had included the civil servant's last name or rank, Alexei might have been able to find him and send him a note of support or offer some assistance. He had to tell himself several times that Cat would have told him if there were any way he could help.

His first instinct was to tell Sol about the letter, but Sol was working on his computer, the barrier of silence still between them. He unfolded the letter and read it again and then went to Meg's door.

"Sounds like her life sucks," Meg said when she'd finally opened the door and let him tell her about the letter. "Good thing she's getting out."

He did not feel like explaining the whole process by which an under-18 student could get out of small-town Siberia. Sol already knew, and would have been sympathetic, appropriately worried at his sister's prospects. Mike would have been concerned about his family, but Alexei still had the lingering association of Kendall with Mike and he didn't want to text him anyway; it felt too early to take advantage of their newly-formed phone connection. So he settled for telling Meg that he hoped she would get to meet his sister soon, and then sat in the kitchen with his iPod and headphones.

First he called up the songs from Mike's brother's band. They were enjoyable, a little rough but at least as accomplished as any of the metal he'd picked up in the States. But the songs felt shallow, scratching at his malaise without cutting deeply enough to penetrate it.

For most of the year he'd been living in the States, he hadn't listened to the Siberian death-metal music he'd had growing up, because it reminded him of thirteen-year-old boys drinking, and burning the foulest-smelling thing they could find. But he'd transferred it to the iPod his host family had given him for Christmas, because he could not bring himself to throw it out. Even when he had been reluctantly burning the disk for Mike, he hadn't listened to the songs. Now he found the tracks easily—one of the few with a Siberian name—and played one.

The deep throat-scratching bass voice above the cacophony of guitars exhorted the destruction of government, of society, of family. They brought Alexei back to a time when he'd half-believed that burning everything down to start over might be the only way to salvage his world. Then, he and his friends—his schoolmates, rather, for few if any had been friends—escaped their life through the raw visceral destruction in the screams, the words, the tortured guitars. Now he closed his eyes, letting the words flow past him, focusing on the guitar and staccato-like drum. The music filled his head, blocking out everything else, Cat's problems, Mike, Sol.

Unbidden, before his eyes, the image of the fox he'd seen in his dream arose in his mind. The fox's ears were flat, his shoulders hunched as though he could hear Alexei's music. Alexei kept his eyes closed, but his fur prickled. The fox's tail curled upwards, and this did not feel like an ordinary daydream. He had the sense that the fox was trying to say something that he could not hear over the heart-racing, ear-rending music.

He fumbled with his iPod and knocked it off the table. His earphones tugged at his ears and then popped free from them. Plunged into silence, his eyes flew open and he lunged to catch the music player, managing to pinch it between two fingers and then gather it into his paw. Breathing hard, he squeezed the player and closed his eyes again, but the vision was gone.

Chapter 10

Tuesday morning, grumpy from his lack of dreams, he brought the painting with him when he and Sol left to catch the bus, not caring that it made Sol quiet and flat-eared again. It took up so much room on the seat that Sol sat elsewhere, and only raised a paw to Alexei when he left.

At the framing store, they told him that to replace the glass would be a hundred and fifty dollars, and Alexei said yes, because he had to, but that he didn't have the cash on him and could he leave the painting and come back? The clerk told him he could just use a credit card and Alexei said he didn't have one, which led to an awkward silence of five seconds and the clerk just taking the painting and his name.

He had the cash, barely, but he would have very little left after that. He could ask Vlad for an advance on his pay; it would only be for four days, but the thought of imposing on the tiger who had already generously hired him gave him flutters in his stomach. Meg's offer to help pay was kind, but he didn't know where she got her money, and anyway it hadn't been her fault.

So he called Liza on a break and asked her if he could borrow fifty dollars from her until Saturday, when he would see her at the VLGA outing. "Of course," she said, without even asking what he needed it for. "You want me to come over tonight?"

Riverwalk, where Liza and a lot of other gay couples lived, was only a fifteen-minute walk away. But Alexei didn't want the extra conversation that a visit would entail. "I don't need it right now, thank you."

"No worry. I'll bring it tomorrow."

And Wednesday evening at the game, Liza took Alexei aside first thing and passed him two twenties and a ten. "No rush to pay me back," she said.

"I can pay you Saturday. Like I promised." He shoved the money quickly into a pocket.

She patted him on the shoulder. "No rush. Now let's go kick some Westside Insurance tail."

The muskrat from the Peaches, Colin, was there again, though this time he'd brought a folding chair and was just relaxing. He, like most of the team, seemed to think this would be an easy game, but Alexei didn't know anything about the insurance industry and treated each game the same. And it was a good thing, too, because the insurance team came out aggressive and fast, and Alexei, on defense, found himself engaged from the very start.

They gave up a goal quickly, which brought yells from Kendall to tighten up the defense, as though it had been Sol or Alexei who'd let in the score. He started directing the two of them, which didn't seem to bother Sol. It made Alexei grit his teeth, and made him look over at the sidelines to see if Colin was watching. When the muskrat was paying attention, Alexei either ignored or deliberately contradicted Kendall's instructions, even when they were reasonable.

About fifteen minutes from the end of the game, the Westsiders sent a pass down the field to Alexei's side, one striker following it with Mike close behind him. The big sheep wasn't going to catch the Westsider, a quick white-tailed deer, and Sol was too far away to intercept him, but Alexei was back near the box around the goal. He moved forward and then saw Kendall out of the corner of his eye as the pine marten sprinted up, yelling, "I got it!"

But Alexei was slightly closer, and although technically the goalie had the right to come stupidly out of position the way Kendall was doing just to show off for Mike, it was Alexei's play. With Kendall charging, Alexei properly should hang back and defend the goal, just in case something went wrong. He hesitated for a moment.

The field darkened as though a cloud had passed across the sun. Alexei felt a chill and was reminded of the cold wind of his dream. And in that moment he clenched his fists and leapt forward, the grass cold beneath his paws though the sun was out again, wind streaming through his tail. He ignored Kendall's furious shout and reached the ball a second sooner, taking in the Westside deer charging toward him and in an instant smacking the ball to his left, out of the path of the deer, across to Sol.

Kendall plowed into him from behind, knocked him down, and didn't say a word before sprinting back to the goal. Alexei followed the ball as he got up; Sol received his pass and launched it back down the field to one of the VLGA strikers, and the action was back on the other side again. Mike had already turned to follow it, so Alexei didn't see how the sheep had reacted to his save, but Sol gave him a big smile and a thumbs up, and Colin was standing on the sidelines, watching Alexei closely.

The moment stuck in his mind, replayed over and over. He thought it might have been one of those transcendent moments the great players talked about, when the game took you over and you found yourself anticipating, moving before the opposing player made his move, before you could even think about what you were doing. It cheered him to think that those kind of moments were coming to him now, and it cheered him even more that Kendall stopped yelling directions at him, focusing all his advice on Sol. He could not completely forget the chill, the echo of his dream, but that shiver faded in the warmth of the day.

They lost the game 1-0, but the mood afterwards was generally upbeat anyway; few people cared about the score. Kendall, though, stalked up to Alexei and talked in a low, even tone that was at odds with his tense body language and slight snarl. "Listen," he said, "I don't know how you played in Siberia, but 'got it' means 'I'm going to kick the ball.'"

"I know what it means," Alexei said, cutting off Sol's protest. "I was closer." The muskrat was coming their way.

"But I called it," Kendall persisted.

Alexei shrugged. "In Siberia, the goalie stays in the goal box." The words, like his sudden decision to attack the ball, felt oddly both his and not his. Though the day was every bit as hot and humid as the previous Thursday, he felt cooler about the head and chest, and when he panted, it was deliberate, like sticking his tongue out at the marten.

Sol, panting as well, broke in. "Look, he got the ball out and they didn't score, so let's let it go."

"Next time," Kendall said as Colin joined them, "we might not be so lucky."

"So stay in goal." Alexei stared back at the pine marten and let his jaw drop in a tongue-lolling smile. He didn't know if Mike was watching, and found he didn't care.

The muskrat looked between them, picking up on the tension. Though he was Kendall's age and therefore a few years Alexei's senior, he hesitated before saying, "Nice move there. Good aggression on defense."

Alexei flicked his tongue back into his mouth, close enough that drops of his saliva almost sprayed Kendall. "There, you see," he said. "The professional player agrees."

Kendall looked as though he might choke, but obviously didn't want to say anything in front of the muskrat. "Sure," Colin said. "I mean, in one of our games, the goalie would've stayed back, but in this case it's a casual game. I might've let Kendall have the play, but you did a nice job."

"Anyway," Kendall said, "Colin and I were going to get a beer." He glared at Alexei.

Sol tugged at Alexei's arm. "Come on," he said. "Let's get dinner." And as they walked away from Colin and Kendall, Sol said, "What's gotten into you?"

The fox couldn't keep the grin from his muzzle. "He made a bad play."

"I didn't mean that," Sol said, and then waved a paw as Mike came over to them. "Never mind." He started to walk away, but Alexei grabbed his wrist and made him stay.

"Hey," the sheep said. "Nice play."

Alexei's ears flushed, and his grin widened. "You played well, too. They have a good goalie."

Mike stood with one hand in his pocket, the other hovering at his side. "Don't worry about Kendall. He just really wants to win."

"So do I," Alexei said, looking right up at the tall sheep.

They stood for a moment, eyes locked, and then Sol said, "Well, we all do," and the moment was broken. An answering smile blossomed on the sheep's face and he stuck out his hand to Alexei.

Alexei clasped the hand in his paw and impulsively said, "Would you like to join us for dinner?"

Mike opened his mouth to reply, looking surprised and happy. Alexei's heart raced faster. And then Kendall's sharp voice interrupted them. "Hey, Mike! We leaving, or what?"

The smile died. "Oh yeah," Mike said. "I was supposed to…"

The confidence that had filled Alexei on the field deserted him, replaced with a flush of warmth in his flattened ears. If Mike *wanted* to go with Kendall, if he was taken in by that act, then Alexei certainly wasn't going to stand in his way.

"Well, uh," Mike said, half turning and taking a step toward Kendall. "Maybe you guys can come with?"

"No." Alexei walked out across the field because that was the direction that took him away from Mike, away from Kendall. He stalked across the grass, past the goal, into the fading light. He barely saw the brilliant pinks and oranges in front of him.

Sol caught up to him just as he was leaving the field. Alexei didn't slow his pace. "So where do you want to go?" Sol said.

"Don't care," Alexei replied. His mind whirled furiously. What good did it do him to be aggressive on the field if Mike still didn't see the value in him? That moment of certainty, when he'd leapt forward—he'd never experienced anything like it. Now, with Mike walking away from him and Sol barely registering that he cared about it, that moment felt tarnished in Alexei's mind.

He and Sol got fried chicken and talked about very little, except when Sol brought up Meg's friend. "We've got to keep an eye out for her," Sol said. "She's only known him on the Internet."

"He seems nice," Alexei said cautiously. "Meg says they are just friends."

"Have you talked to him?" Sol's voice held a challenging tone, and Alexei shook his head, afraid to bring up the ritual again when they were talking so freely. "You don't know what he wants. Nobody knows. Not even Meg."

"I will help watch out," the fox said. "Although Meg may not talk to us if there is a problem."

Sol chewed another bite of his chicken off a drumstick. "We're all she's got. I don't think she'd tell her parents anything."

And while Alexei felt good about being someone Meg could count on, he felt bad for her because he knew what it was like to have no parents one could rely on. At least hers had been neglectful rather than abusive, from what she said. Sol seemed to think they were nice people, but Meg said he didn't know, and there the exchanges usually stopped. Still, Meg had him and Sol now, and they had her, and the three of them looked after each other. Usually.

When they returned home finally, Alexei let Sol use the desk and the computer. Rather than sit and stare at the blank space on the wall, he took his sister's letter out again and read it at the kitchen table, and then continued his response.

He told her how excited he was that she might be able to join him, wrote about his play in the soccer game and Colin being impressed, and then, almost without consciously making the decision to do it, he told her about his attempt to talk to a ghost. He had already told her about Sol's adventure with Niki, one of the last phone conversations he'd had with her, and he could still remember her laugh and joy at the thought that a ghost might be clever and helpful. *Sadly,* he wrote, *I have not met Sol's ghost. I have only had a strange dream about a fox who would not help me.*

And a moment in a daydream, he remembered. And then the moment on the field, when he'd felt the cold chill. It hadn't occurred to him to connect the moment with his dream until he was staring at the words on the page, the pen hovering in his paw above them. Even then, he didn't feel confident enough to share the thought with his sister. He closed by asking her to tell him quickly if there was anything he could do to help.

When he went into the bedroom to go to sleep, he said good night to Sol, and then lay in bed with his eyes closed, trying to summon the image of the fox again, the blue coat, the yellow belt, the ragged tail. *Was that you?* he asked. *Did you help me? Why?*

He had the sense of staring off far into the distance, toward a distant, empty horizon. Even the sound of Sol's breathing faded away.

Alexei knew he was still lying in bed, but he felt the chill of his dream creeping in on him. If he opened his eyes, he would see the wall he was facing, and he could still smell the sheets and Sol and the pasta Meg had cooked for her dinner.

He opened his eyes. The wall in front of him, painted ivory but deep in shadow, seemed to be receding. His heart raced, and he put a paw out.

His fingers touched smooth paint. The illusion was broken. The wall was just a wall.

Alexei sighed and closed his eyes again. He didn't know if he was scared that something might be happening, or scared that it wasn't.

Chapter 11

Under the protection of the officer Vasily Petrovich, I grew up a loyal cub to the Emperor. I played with tiger cubs and learned the military discipline and structure that made them such effective soldiers. There was a time during which I was teased and beaten by my peers for being the son of foxes who had plotted to kill the Tsar. Gregor, two years older than my eleven years, slashed at my face with a sword, leaving me a scar that brought his father's wrath down on him. My parents' actions were not my fault, we were both told, and I was making amends for them by living a virtuous life. After that, I had no trouble with Gregor; his father's word was law, and protected me as effectively as if Vasily himself stood beside me.

That is not to say that I did not feel Vasily's claws. Indeed, he believed in discipline, administered physically, not only when I transgressed, but also when my progress in studies and training did not meet his strict standards. "A soldier who doesn't dream of becoming a general is a bad one," he told me often. This served to drive me to do better, to earn those rare words of praise. By the time I was twelve, he rarely had cause to state his disappointment; by the time I was sixteen, he cuffed me without claws, more out of habit and affection than for correction. Unlike Gregor, I would never grow as strong and tall as my adopted father. He was a tiger often said to be second only to Emperor Alexander in physical prowess.

Vasily belonged to the Preobrazhensky Guards, the Tsar's elite force of tigers, and he had been the Tsar's presence on many raids of revolutionary towns. The officers of the Guards were the noblest and fiercest Siberia had to offer, and some of my earliest memories of life in Petrograd are of standing beside the training grounds, watching the magnificent tigers in their smart blue coats, golden epaulets and buttons shining in the sun. During presentations of the guards, I stood as proudly at attention as I could manage while the glorious march played, keeping my bushy tail tucked neatly between my legs.

I could not join the Preobrazhensky Guards, but the Semenovsky regiment which trained alongside them was nearly as prestigious. Nothing, I thought, would please Vasily more than to have his adopted son attain the highest honor available to a non-tiger soldier, proving my loyalty, proving that Vasily's noble action had saved me from the accident of my birth. For no aristocrat's son was more devoted to the Tsar than I. I flew into a rage if a word was spoken against him, at least until the age of eighteen. Perhaps I felt in my heart the terror that if I did not defend the Tsar, the dreams that haunted me would become truth, nightmares in which I returned to the cart, to the age of six, and watched Vasily extend a sword rather than a paw to me. I woke always with the terror, not of death, but of disappointing my Papa.

And that is why, when Gregor called me a little traitor's son and kicked me in the ribs, I leapt upon him, scratching and biting, until he drew his sword and slashed blindly at me. I was not punished, not as he was, and I bore the scar proudly as a badge of my loyalty to the Tsar for all the days thereafter. I became known for it among the soldiers I trained with; they called me Notch for the piece cut out of my ear, and I arched my tail when I heard the name, remembering that I had earned that name with my loyalty and passion.

Though proud of my status, I did not hold it above the others, not at any age. Vasily would not stand for it, and I learned quickly that I would be given the same opportunities as anyone else at my station. So I trained with the other soldiers, offered and accepted advice, and did my best to be a soldier like the rest. I wanted to excel, of course—I dreamed of becoming a general—and I did distinguish myself. But I never held myself above my peers; I strove to help them reach their own potential, the better to reflect on the glory of our beloved empire, and the Emperor at its head. In the small, insular world of young soldiers, we were all aimed at that goal. Or so I thought.

Chapter 12

The wind howls past Alexei's ears again like the cries of the dead. He does not stand on a rocky plain now; it is a field, but the ground has been torn by more than plows. His feet stand uneasily on mud frozen into the twisted shapes left behind by horses and boots, tufts of grass lying trampled and broken, and unidentifiable pieces of metal and cloth. Yards away, large boulders lie strewn in the ground, and to the other side of the field, a forest squats, shadowy and more black than green. The sky above him swirls, dark grey on light grey, turbulent and restless.

Alexei smells only the emptiness of winter and impending snow. His whiskers, buffeted by wind, nevertheless register a presence at his side. He turns, and crouched beside him is the old fox in his blue military coat. His arms fold over his knees; his tail spills across the ground. The collar, which Alexei can see over his shoulder, is a deep blood red, trimmed in the same golden yellow that circles the fox's narrow waist.

But it is his face, which Alexei has not seen before, that draws the young fox's attention. The muzzle is broad, like his own father's, but with more grey on it. Above the eye, a clean scar bisects the eyebrow, and in the left ear, a long notch runs almost five centimeters in from the edge. Many of the foxes in Samorodka had similar notches, their longer ears a target for the other children in schoolyard tussles. But none of their notches ran so deep. Their ears were chewed, and healed. This notch has been inflicted by a weapon.

The fox stares out across the field, and his paw reaches down to brush a long piece of metal. It gleams like a knife blade under the black-furred fingers. When they lift, Alexei sees a patch of red on it. Not fresh blood red, but the rust-red of ancient blood, of tiger's fur, of a dying sunset.

I have been watching you, *the fox says.*

How?

You called me.

I called *you*?

The fox turns. A dark eye fixes Alexei. I have decided, *he says,* that you require my help.

Did you do something to me on the field? During the game?

If you are to be a worthy servant of the Tsar, Alexei Tsarev, you will have to learn pride.

Alexei's ribs and stomach feel like ice. His feet shift on the frozen mud, unstable. There has not been a tsar in a hundred years, *he says.*

The fox narrows his eyes, the scar wrinkling as he glares. He places a paw across his chest. The tsar, *he says,* lives in our hearts and spirits. He is the force that guides us and sets our place in the world, the father of us all. Without knowing your place in the world, how can you take pride in it? Without a tsar to serve, how can you know your place? You have been lost, alone. You have no family, no country.

The words strike him like cold needles in his chest. I don't want a country. I want a—I want a companion.

How can you be someone's mate when you do not know where you belong?

But a specific someone, *Alexei says.*

The fox turns to him. A vixen?

He does not know how closely the fox has been watching him, if this is even real. Y-yes, *he says.*

The older fox's muzzle turns, points straight ahead. He speaks in a low voice: When I first set eyes on Mariya Frolova, I was an attendant in the honor guard at the Ostaltsev ball, and she was the youngest sister in the Frolov household. I could not dance with her then; I was on duty and she was a daughter of a noble family. But I caught her eye, and when the night was over, I waited in the crisp spring night air. She accompanied her family out, and turned to look at me.

Ten feet before them, shimmering in the air where the fox's eyes are fixed, the image of a vixen in a long dress appears. Her dress is a deep blue untouched by the dust and dirt of the field, trimmed with pearls and lace, a hundred years old but still elegant and becoming. She is young, perhaps Alexei's age, and though she is turned away from them, her head bends back over her shoulder so the bright blue of her eyes shines back at them. The wind's cries soften and the clouds overhead go still.

After a moment staring at her in silence, the old fox goes on. I could have stayed by my post and waited. I could have let her walk off into that night, to marry one of the many noble foxes she danced with. But she stopped, and she turned, and she looked. There was a moment, a chance, and I knew that if I let that chance go, I would forever be left to wonder what might have happened. My destiny was to have a family of my own, ones who would be loyal and who would put to rest the crimes of my parents.

Your parents? *Alexei looks down at the fox's ear and wonders if the notch came from his father. Many of his friends—his schoolmates—in Samorodka bore the marks of their parents. Some parents left less visible marks.*

The fox ignores him. I left my post, *he says,* and I walked up to her. I told her that I would be deeply honored to receive the pleasure of her company. Loudly enough so that her mother could hear, I told her that I was a junior officer of the Semenovsky Guards, in the event that she was not familiar with the uniform, and I told her that my adopted father was the fourth military officer in line from the Emperor himself.

She could have smiled politely and walked away. She could have laughed. But she turned to her mother with the most beautiful tilt to her ears, and asked for her mother's favor. And when her mother hesitated, she could have lowered her muzzle, met my eyes with a secretive look of longing, and acceded to her mother's will. But she added a heartfelt plea, and I stood smartly at attention, and her mother allowed that I might be permitted to call upon the family.

The image of the vixen vanishes, but the fox keeps staring off into the distance. Alexei looks down at him. What happened?

They respected my uniform, the place I held in society. My rank assured them that I would be a worthy husband to her.

He waits for more, but the fox does not speak, only reaches down to the knife blade again and strokes it. When his paw rises this time, it reveals the patch of rust not on silvery steel but on a dirty white bone. Alexei looks up quickly. Why are we in this place?

The fox lowers his eyes. The wind returns, biting at Alexei's ears and nose, keening with a mournful, almost-sentient cry. He flattens his ears, but the fox's words still ring clear. When the people no longer trust their leader, death follows.

It sounds suspiciously like the way his mother used to talk about the government, when she suspected that there might be something different about Alexei: they have your best interests at heart, what are you going to do, leave your mother country, go out to die on your own? Cold needles dance across his fur. How will you help me?

The fox turns dark brown, shadowed eyes on him. Will you accept my help?

When Alexei looks around again, the field is a football field. He thinks about the exhilaration of the moment in which he was in control of the game, the peak compared to the valleys that came before it, the crushing rift with Sol, the moments spent out on the sidewalk where he felt powerless, directionless. And after all, this is a dream, is it not? What harm can the fox do? The confidence he will give Alexei is Alexei's to use. He called the ghost; he can send the ghost away if he becomes troublesome.

So he nods his head and he speaks. Yes.

The word echoes, taken by the wind and then returned over and over, icy affirmation against Alexei's ears. The fox nods gravely. He stands, and now he looks down on Alexei, and his military coat sparkles with medals. From the front, the gold sash is even more stained, and torn in places; the coat, too, is rent. But that does not detract from the authority, the almost regal bearing. I will teach you to be a good soldier, *he says.*

I don't want to fight, *Alexei replies.* Only to be happy.

The fox's eyebrow, the one with the scar, rises. He gestures to the field. Do you believe that happiness comes without a struggle? I may guide you to your goal, but you must still strive for your destiny.

He reaches out and grasps Alexei by the shoulder. The touch is hard and firm; Alexei flinches but stands tall beneath it. What is your name? *the younger fox asks.*

I am Konstantin Vasilyevich, *the older fox says.*

Chapter 13

"Konstantin." Alexei woke with the name on his lips. Immediately he thought of the name he'd spoken in the ritual: Nikolai Konstantinov. If that were truly Niki's name, then his father's name would be Konstantin. Could this be the ghost of Niki's father? If so, would he be inclined to be helpful? Alexei didn't remember Sol ever saying anything about Niki's father.

But he got out of bed with energy, tail arched and step springy. Konstantin would teach him confidence and passion, and Alexei would have—*did* have—his own ghost story. He could tell Cat about it.

The thought made his tail wag, and then another brilliant idea came to him. There was something he could do for Cat after all. He had only to wait until the next dream, then ask Konstantin to go visit her, to inspire her. Surely a ghost could go back to Samorodka without any trouble at all, could visit dreams there as easily as here. Konstantin had been steeped in Siberia, and yet he had come to Alexei in Vidalia. So distance was no trouble. True, the ghost had not seemed like the suggestible type, but Alexei was sure that he must have seen Cat's letters. After all, he had been watching Alexei, knew his name, and he had mentioned "servant to the Tsar," just as Cat had written about being servants to the emperors.

On the way to work, he asked Sol what he remembered about Niki's father. The wolf looked around them and didn't answer immediately, his ears half-down. "The father of that fox you used to know," Alexei said, in case Sol was worried people might think it strange to be talking about a ghost.

"Yeah," Sol said. "I don't…I don't remember talking about him very much." He stared down at his paws. "Why?"

Alexei, ready for this, said, "I had a letter from my sister. She says our father is getting worse, drinking and sitting apart from the family."

"I'm sorry." Sol looked at him more fully than he had since Alexei had dropped the picture, his green eyes sympathetic.

"I just wondered how perhaps other foxes in Siberia…if their fathers are better or worse."

The black wolf nodded. "I don't think he was very nice to Niki. He mentioned being beaten, told he was useless."

Alexei folded his paws together. It was something he could believe of Konstantin, assuming the old ghost was much as he had been in life. "And," Sol said, "his ears were all torn up. I think his father might have done that."

"Perhaps," Alexei said, thinking again of the long notch in Konstantin's ear. "Other cubs do that as well. In these days it is easier to heal."

"I guess you're right." Sol looked past Alexei to the street they were passing. "I think he wasn't happy at home. He ran away from it."

Alexei curled his tail into his lap. He wished again that he had been more successful in calling Niki rather than his father—if Konstantin was his father. Konstantin's experience with love had been to see a pretty vixen and go after her. He had had rivals, perhaps, but in those days things were all more structured, guided by the mechanisms of society. He had not run away from home, like Alexei and Niki—or perhaps he had.

But then again, Alexei thought, Sol's story of Niki had not had very many happy turns. Perhaps Niki would not have been the best confidant for him. Niki had been gay, though, and would understand that. "Did he run away because…" he started to ask, and then changed his question, not wanting to say the word "gay" aloud on the bus. "Do you miss him?"

He hadn't asked Sol that in several weeks. For one thing, the care Sol took with the picture made his feelings plain. For another, nothing had happened with Niki since before Sol's birthday, months ago.

"Yeah," Sol said. "Even though it was really stressful having him… around, you know? Like, that stuff really freaked me out, the stuff that would come back…" He didn't have to say, *come back from the dreams*.

"Did something always come back?" Alexei had not noticed anything out of the ordinary that morning. "After every…time?"

"Yeah," Sol said. The wolf's ears flattened and he turned back to the inside of the bus. Of course, Alexei thought, cursing himself, the painting was one of the things that had come back. He sighed and leaned against the glass.

In the evening, though, Sol was friendly again, and the rest of the week passed without any further letters, arguments, or dreams. Alexei was aware of Konstantin as a presence in his memory, a shadow waiting for the right moment to bolster him. He added a small paragraph about the ghost in the letter to his sister, and then mailed it.

Saturday, Alexei received a call that the picture had been repaired, but it was in the afternoon, and he and Sol had the VLGA dinner at the Playtime restaurant and arcade. Much as he wanted to get the painting back soon, it would be better to wait until Monday.

The Playtime dinner would be the first time Alexei had seen Mike since Wednesday, and on the bus on the way there, Sol talked about whether he should have invited Mitch, whom he'd seen again Thursday night. Alexei listened with half an ear while thinking himself about Konstantin, and whether he would help Alexei this night. Get me a date with Mike, Alexei thought. That's all I want right now, that same cool confidence, the boldness to seize the moment. Even if Konstantin had not approved of Niki being gay, would not approve of Alexei chasing a boy, the worst he could do to Alexei would be to leave him alone again. As long as he provided Alexei just that one more moment of confidence, that one burst of courage, the young fox felt he could handle the rest.

But when they arrived in the restaurant, Kendall was already sitting next to Mike. Sol took the other side of the pine marten and nodded Alexei to the seat beside Mike, but Alexei did not want to compete with Kendall all through dinner, giving the fast-talking marten the chance to put him down. He would get to talk to Mike afterwards, while they were playing games.

So he sat next to Liza and gave her the fifty he'd borrowed, first thing. She took it reluctantly, with motherly questions about whether he could afford it, and he had to assure her twice that he could. Alice and Zayda, the hare and red squirrel, were on Alexei's left, so all through dinner, he mostly listened as they talked about their friends, including some of the people at the other end of the table. "Is it tonight, you will ask Mike out?" Liza asked Alexei, when they were all looking down the table at the sheep.

"Leave him," Alice said. "He's a sweet kid, Mike will figure it out."

"Mike deserves better than Kendall," Liza answered.

"Ah." The hare waved her off. "Kendall's just a bunch of hormones. Once he gets Mike to say yes, he'll lose interest quick."

Liza nudged Alexei. "She thinks this is okay."

"It's how boys are." The hare picked at her salad.

"Like you are better," Liza said, and then Alice turned and glared at her so furiously that the ermine turned to Alexei and started chattering about a movie she'd seen.

Alexei knew Alice had some sort of history, but he hadn't previously thought that it might be with Liza. Or maybe it wasn't, but Liza just knew about it. Anyway, it was clear she didn't want it discussed, not with her fiancée Zayda sitting just on her other side.

"So why aren't you sitting down there with him?" Alice asked when she'd finished her salad.

"Not the right time," Alexei said, with a glance down the long table.

"What about Sol?" Liza turned her sharp eyes on him.

Alexei looked back, confused. "What—we are not boyfriends. You know this."

"I mean, why are you not sitting with him?"

"I see him every day." Alexei smiled at her. "*And I like your company*," he said in Siberian.

"Don't be rude," Alice said. "Speak English."

Then Liza asked about his sister, and Alexei told her about the letter he'd received, and Alice and Zayda talked about their wedding on his other side, and he put Mike and Konstantin in the back of his mind. Before he knew it, the waitstaff were clearing plates, and people started getting up to go play the games. Mike, Kendall, and Sol were still talking when Alexei followed the girls down a dark staircase to the bright, chaotic basement.

Below the very ordinary-looking restaurant lay a glittering world of flashing lights and sounds and smells. Alexei had no plan in his head save to take advantage of the game-playing time to get Mike alone and ask him on a date. Sol had again offered to distract Kendall, and Alexei had gratefully accepted his assistance.

But when Sol and Kendall, with Mike in tow, came over to see him finish up his shooting game, Alexei didn't have a chance to get Mike alone before Sol said, "We were heading over to shoot some hoops. Want to play?"

The basketball shooting game had four stations, where players could compete against each other while shooting at individual baskets. Alexei prepared to decline, but when he opened his mouth, the words he said were, "Of course."

He'd been about to shy away from a challenge? That was—

A smile touched the corners of his muzzle. That was not what Konstantin would have him do. Well, even if he was not good at the shooting, he would play with them. Then he could ask Sol to challenge Kendall to something afterwards, something that would occupy them both. So he said yes, and took up his place at the fourth station, with Sol beside him and Mike at the far end.

When the basketballs dropped, he did his best to launch them at the hoop the way Sol was doing, in quick succession, and he thought he was doing well, missing only about every other one. When he found a groove, he sank five baskets in a row, and then lost the groove when the basket retreated and shots were worth three points. His ears flattened as his last four shots caromed off the sides of the small enclosure. Still, 42 was a good score, he thought.

He looked up at the board that tracked the scores. His 42 showed fourth, both in location and in rank. Mike had scored 55, and Kendall had barely edged out Sol, 64–62. "Woo!" the marten said, pumping his fist. "Just call me K-Hop. I got the shootin' touch."

"Let's go again," Sol said, and Alexei had no choice but to stand in at his station and wait for the next game to begin. This time, trying too hard, he scored a miserable 34, while Mike stayed steady at 54. Sol improved, scoring 65, but Kendall did too, and won with a score of 69.

"That's my lucky number," he bragged, and patted Alexei on the shoulder, right in front of Mike. "I know they don't really play hoops in Siberia. Keep practicing, you'll get the hang of it. Might be as good as Mikey there in a month or so."

"Kendall," Mike said, with an edge to his voice.

The marten shrugged. "I'm just trying to cheer him up."

Alexei swallowed the sharp retort that came to his lips and twisted away from the condescending paw. He opened his mouth to ask Sol if he could talk to him privately, and then over the wolf's shoulder he saw Alice and Zayda hopping back and forth on the dance machine, and with cold clarity, he realized that he did not want to get Kendall out of the way. What he wanted was...

He turned back to the marten. "Let's dance."

Kendall affected surprise. "Oh, you're cute, but the music here isn't my scene, and anyway, there's no dance floor."

Alexei walked toward the dance game, pointing forward. "There."

"I guess I'm up for it," Sol said.

"No." Alexei stared at Kendall. "Me against him. Mister K-Hop."

"Sure," Kendall said. "Anything you want. It's not real dancing, but I'll still teach you a thing or two."

Maybe you will, Alexei thought. Or maybe you'll learn something. But he kept his muzzle shut. Better to let your fighting speak for you, that was what his father had said. Or had he? No, his father had simply told him to hit back when he was being bullied by five larger cubs. Still, the words, in Siberian, rang familiarly to him.

Kendall laughed about his basketball score while they waited for the ladies to finish. "I can hit 69s in other places too," he told them, and Mike and Sol laughed. When Alexei didn't, Kendall spread his paws and looked innocent. "I mean golf," he said. "You play?"

"No." Alexei replied, when neither of the others did.

"Ah, you'll have to come out to the links sometime. Mikey and I played last week. He's pretty good."

Alice and Zayda finished and stepped aside. When Alexei and Kendall stepped up, the fox made sure to catch Mike's eye. The sheep had been pretty quiet throughout the evening, which Alexei interpreted as putting up with Kendall's obnoxious swagger. So he gave the sheep a smile and said, "This dance is for you."

"This game is screwed up"

He couldn't say whether that had been inspired by Konstantin or not, but it provoked a reply. "Oh ho," Kendall said before Mike could respond. "It's on. What's your beats?"

Mike gave Alexei a smile, and settled back with arms folded, clearly watching him. Alexei hesitated, but then breathed in, feeling confidence infuse him. He grinned broadly and said, "Loser's choice."

"Then go ahead," the marten said. "Unless I wasn't reading those hoops scores right."

"I was not talking about scores," Alexei said.

Because he was looking at Kendall, he saw Sol's startled look beyond him. Kendall's smile soured, but he didn't make any reply, just stabbed at the screen and picked a song that Alexei thought might be completely at random.

"GET READY," the screen warned. Kendall and Alexei both dropped to a crouch, and when the music started, they took off.

Here, Alexei had no problems with second-guessing, as he did shooting a basketball. He'd used these games to practice footwork and reaction times for football all the past year with his host family, and for the last month with Sol. He knew how good he was, and what he was capable of. After an early misstep, he caught the rhythm of the song and let himself go along with it. He was aware of the scroll of "PERFECT" scores down his screen, but he tuned out everything around him save for the arrows telling him where to jump. He barely even registered Kendall's lithe form beside him, though he did hear the marten mutter curses twice. He grinned, because he could do that without losing concentration, and fierce joy blazed inside him at matching the pattern, the screen telling him where to step and his feet following every instruction perfectly. He felt, for that span, in tune with the world.

When the song came to an end, Alexei stood straight while Kendall bent over with his paws on his knees, both looking at the screen. Alexei's score, nearly two hundred thousand more than Kendall's, flashed next to the word "WINNER."

"That's a crap song," Kendall said. "Again."

"That band's local," Mike said. "I've seen them a couple times."

Kendall ignored him, waving at the screen. But Alexei turned to Mike and smiled. "I like the song," he said.

"You're really good," the sheep replied, and that alone was enough to put an extra bounce in Alexei's step, a quick wag in his tail. He let Kendall choose the music again, and again he let himself go, found his place in the song, and stood proudly at the end as the winner.

"Okay, this game's timing is off." Kendall stepped off the pad. "I know I hit more combos than it gave me credit for."

Alexei was about to step down as well; his point had been made, and Kendall was quitting. Mike had paid him a compliment and the small sun was glowing in his chest. But as he gripped the rail of the game and lifted one foot to step down, a cloud hid the sun inside him. A deep, gruff voice in his head spoke.

Do not let your enemy walk away wounded. Defeat him soundly.

He paused, flicked his ears, and then turned around. Kendall was already off the platform, and had regained his smile and easy manner. In a moment he might propose they go play another game, something Alexei was not as good at, and this victory would fade. So Alexei pulled the chill from his chest and put it into his voice, projected toward Kendall. "I understand they don't have dancing in Vidalia so much. Don't worry. You might be good in a year or so, if you practice."

Sol stared at him again. Even Mike's smile faltered a little. But Kendall was the one Alexei was focused on, and the marten's jaw clenched, his ears flat and his hackles rising on the back of his neck. "All right," he said, stepping back up onto the platform. "One more time."

The third time was almost laughable. Kendall, flustered and upset even though Alexei had let him pick the song for the third time, missed many steps outright, and the song hadn't even finished before he said, "No, this game is screwed up," and jumped off the dance pad.

Alexei finished up while Kendall stalked away, his only worry that Mike might go after the marten. And the sheep did look after Kendall, but he waited to see Alexei's final score. "Nice," he said. "Maybe you could teach me some moves."

"I would love to." Alexei smiled at Sol. "The wolf here has practiced with me a lot."

"Yeah," Sol said. "I think I'm gonna go see if Kendall's okay."

"I'm sure he is fine," Alexei said, trying to tell Sol there was no need to keep the marten occupied, but Sol walked off anyway. Mike, happily, stayed.

"Kendall's just...he's really competitive," he said. "He's a nice guy."

"He cannot be the best at everything." Alexei stepped off the machine and took one more look at the two screens, the "WINNER" flashing on his.

"Yeah. Look." Mike scratched his ears. "On Saturday, I told Kendall it looked like he was picking on you with the water balloon. And I know he doesn't have issues with that—he didn't come out 'til college and he never got bullied. But a lot of us do, so I just asked him to be more considerate."

"Okay." Alexei tilted his head. "Thank you, but—"

"So I'm going to ask you the same thing. Because what you were doing with the dance could be construed as bullying. You were taunting him, you humiliated him."

A warm flush flattened Alexei's ears. "He taunted me. At the 'hoops.'"

The sheep moved out of the way of a pair of swift foxes who wanted to play the dancing game. "I know. I reminded him then, too. I'm not mad, I'm just saying, be more considerate."

"It's just—" The unfairness of it, that Mike would think he was as bad as Kendall, tore at his chest. "He is always around when I want to talk to you. He never lets me see you alone. This is the only way I could do that."

"Really." Mike folded his arms.

"Yes!"

The golden horns tilted. Mike smiled. "If you wanted to talk to me alone, why didn't you just ask me out?"

Alexei gaped. The room felt quite warm now, and the shame he'd felt just five seconds ago was gone. "I…I never had a chance. You were with Kendall…"

"I'm not dating him."

"Well." The fox recovered a little of his poise. "You did not seem interested in asking me out."

"Until a week or so ago, I thought you were dating Sol. You guys do everything together and he didn't like me. I thought he was jealous that you did, or that you wanted to have a threesome and he'd said no, or something."

The thought of a threesome—with Sol!—broke Alexei's mind for a moment. "No," he said, trying not to laugh. "No, we are not—well, I—" He gathered himself to ask a question, but for a moment his jaw seemed to go numb. Whether it was from the surprise of Mike's suggestion or the lingering image of a threesome (*where would everyone go?*), he struggled to form words.

His phone buzzed with a text message then, and he pulled it out. Sol, saying, *You okay?*

Mike grinned and straightened. "You're popular."

"It's only Sol. I'm turning the phone off so we will not be interrupted again." Alexei slid it back into his pocket.

"You don't have to do that," the sheep said.

"I want to." Alexei smiled. He gloried in the unusual feeling of being someone Mike wanted to talk to. Alone.

"So," Mike grinned. "Are you going to ask me out?"

I could have let her walk off into the night... "Maybe in a little while. I think I must first convince myself that I am not dreaming."

The sheep laughed. "You don't need a pickup line. I'm already interested. But all right. So where did you learn to dance like that?"

Alexei told him about his practices with Sol and asked Mike if he danced at all. They talked about local places they could dance, and then high school proms that allowed gay students to take dates, gay relationships, and the way the country was progressing to accept gay people. "I don't know that we will ever be accepted," Alexei said. "There is too much tradition built up against us."

"Traditions change." Mike smiled. "It's actually happening. All those football guys and basketball guys coming out, and I read there's a baseball player who's thinking about it. I'm just doing family law now, but I want to—" He hesitated.

"What?" Alexei prompted him.

"Ah, it's a silly dream." The sheep ducked his head. "I want to be a judge one day. Maybe on the Supreme Court. And rule on equality laws."

"It's all right to dream," Alexei said. "The world needs dreamers."

Mike smiled at that, and his smile made Alexei's tail wag. Talking about gay relationships excited him with the transgressive feeling of being an underground hero, a rebel in a just revolution. Having grown up in a country whose history was littered with revolutions so muddied that just and unjust became as meaningless as colors on a flag, that feeling was shiny and new. He felt kinships here that he had never had in Samorodka with anyone but Cat; with Mike, the conversation held additional promise, hope for many things in the future, some of which ran through Alexei's mind despite their distracting effect on his conversation.

They wandered through the games with no particular objective until they arrived at a colorful, exciting shooting game, paused to watch it, and grinned at each other when it became clear they both wanted to play. There was a cooperative mode, with no object other than destroying robots sent back in time to kill them, and Alexei was delighted when the game was over and Kendall still had not reappeared.

"I never played many video games," Mike confessed when they finished. "My ex was into them and I have bad associations."

Alexei's instinct was to shy away from the subject of an ex, but Mike had brought it up, and he was intensely curious about the sheep's prior relationship, if only to find out what things he should not do. At the same time, it was a struggle to ask a direct question about it, possibly because he could not figure out what to ask. He settled for, "How long ago did you stop dating?"

Mike dropped his big brown eyes and shook his head. "Two months ago—no, three now. Brad—you wouldn't have met him, he moved away right after—he just up and left one day. Said he was taking a job on a cruise ship out of South Beach and maybe he'd see me when he got back."

"Maybe," Alexei repeated.

"Yeah. So I said…well, I said I would keep in touch. But he hasn't written and I haven't written and we haven't talked. So it's pretty much over."

"I'm sorry." Near the shooting game, Alexei found a small table with one empty glass. He moved the glass and gestured to Mike to sit in the other chair. "I cannot understand why someone would leave you."

"Oh, it's not that strange." Mike sighed and dropped into the chair. "I guess I'm pretty boring. Brad was always wanting to travel, and I have a job I can't just leave at the drop of a glove."

"Brad had a job with a lot of vacation?"

"Well, he wasn't exactly working," Mike said.

Alexei began to get a picture of the relationship, and part of him felt a wash of pity for Mike, taken advantage of. But a deeper, colder part of him scorned the weakness of someone who would let himself be used.

He hid his surprise at the feeling and said, "I'm sorry," again, focusing on the sympathy.

Mike laughed. "I won't deny it hurt," he said. "But you know, people had been telling me for months that he wasn't good for me, and I dunno. I just thought he'd get his act together. He had so much potential, you know?"

"Sometimes you can wish for people to change for a long time, and it never happens." He breathed in, and for a moment the memory of the rotted wood of his bedroom wall, which was now home to a hive of bees, tickled his nose.

"Amen." Mike looked down at the table, and then up with a determined let's-change-the-subject smile. "Heard from your sister?"

Alexei nodded. "She has met a fox who might help her come to this country."

"Wow, that's great!"

"Yes." He twisted his paws together. "I wish I at least knew his name. This helpful fox."

"Did you ask her?"

He nodded again. "But for the letter to come back, for her to answer..." He sighed. "Two weeks perhaps. If she writes back quickly."

"It must be hard. Did she say why she didn't write for so long?" When Alexei didn't say anything, Mike lowered his voice. "Was it your parents?"

"I think so." The words spilled out and then Alexei shut his muzzle quickly.

His ears flattened, and Mike must have seen his alarm. "You said your parents weren't very understanding, and I know parents of gay kids sometimes take it out on their other children if they're sympathetic, that's all." He looked away and fidgeted with his hands. "Do they...hit her?" He met Alexei's eyes again. "Did they hit you?"

The fox delayed answering until the silence itself became an answer. Then he nodded, once.

Mike sucked in a breath. "Jesus. I'm sorry." His large frame hunched in as though feeling the blows himself. "For a parent to abuse—that's just about the worst—God, I'm really sorry."

Gratitude and affection warred with surprising contempt in Alexei. It was one thing to acknowledge another's pain; it was something else to let oneself be weakened by it, succumb to it in a way the bearer of the pain never had. Mike had had an easy life, and Alexei could have stood sympathy better than this suffering by proxy...

He shook his head. What kind of thinking was that? Mike was sweet; that was what had attracted Alexei to him in the first place. "I survived," he said, and when Mike looked up, he pushed aside the bad feelings and forced his ears upright. "I wanted to achieve my potential."

At that, Mike's smile returned. "I think you're doing a good job of it so far."

Alexei gathered his courage. "Would you like to perhaps have dinner with me?"

"I'd love to." The sheep's expression brightened as though they hadn't discussed it just half an hour before. "Like when?"

"Any time." Alexei's heart thudded against his chest, though he remained oddly calm. Chill, Sol would call it, and indeed there was a chill at the tips of his ears—the air conditioning, perhaps—and at the pit of his stomach.

"Well, tomorrow's not good. Is a weeknight okay? I know we have our game Wednesday, and that guy from the Peaches is going to be there with his friend. So you have to practice hard Tuesday. How about Thursday night?" He grinned. "Maybe we can celebrate you becoming a Peach."

"Yes," Alexei said. "Thursday sounds good."

"Great." Mike glanced to one side of the room and then turned back to Alexei, his expression clouding and then clearing. "Just text me sometime after six. Tell me where we should meet. We can talk about it after the game, too." He'd gotten shorter with his language, and was now very determinedly not looking at that side of the room. Alexei flicked his eyes in that direction and saw Kendall gesturing angrily, Sol with a paw on his shoulder.

"I would like to talk at the game." Alexei hoped that having Mike want to talk to him, with Kendall there, would be another way of cementing his defeat of the marten. He risked another look at Kendall, now sulky and quiet, and felt a surge of fierce joy. But no; Mike had warned him about that, about taunting and humiliating his enemy.

Pah. What did he know, anyway? He had grown up soft, with a loving family, never wanting for anything, not on the hard ground of Siberia with stern, cruel eyes watching him every moment in case he misstepped. Someone like this could afford sympathy for his enemies.

Mike turned back to look at Kendall too, perhaps following Alexei's glance, and Alexei watched the broad muzzle, the brown eyes, with increasing estrangement. How could he have thought Mike would be as attractive as a vixen? Those stubby ears, the strange pupils in the eyes, the pale white fur…none of them matched the vixen he'd seen in his vision. And his scent, distinctly male—

Uncomfortable, Alexei leaned on the table and turned to his left, away from where Kendall and Sol were. He wanted to have the dinner with Mike. It was just strange asking someone on a date, and he was nervous. That was all it was.

His eyes strayed to another shooting game he had only briefly glanced at, now empty of players. The grey battlefield that formed the background of the game, made up of jagged pixelated rocks, held his attention. He knew that landscape, but from where? He was sure he'd never played this game before. The name, WAR ZONE 5, was almost completely unfamiliar.

Mike remained quiet, perhaps still staring off away from Kendall, perhaps waiting for Alexei to answer, but the fox barely noticed, transfixed by the static field. He was certain there had been moving figures on it when they'd first stepped up beside the console, but now the field was empty, scarred rock. It was unusual enough that he wanted to reach out to Mike, to ask what he thought of it, but the words died before he could form them in his throat.

Onto the empty field, the pixelated figure of a fox in a blue military coat walked slowly, in profile. One arm hung at his side, swinging before the gold belt at his midsection. The other carried an ancient-looking sword. When he turned, Alexei could see the crimson red collar and the deep notch in the fox's ear.

Cold air rushed down around him, the air conditioning kicking in. His fur prickled, his chilled ears flattening. The fox's black pixel eyes stared out of the game at him. His throat closed as he tried to call Mike's name. Konstantin's glare bored deep into Alexei, and he heard the gruff voice. *This is what you wished for? This is how you use your soldier's passion?*

He struggled to answer, to recall his place in this situation. He had called Konstantin, and the ghost should be bound to his will. This self-assured contempt was not his; all he wanted was a date with Mike. His stomach churned as he tried to wrench his gaze away from the fox who was not a character in the video game.

No. You will not show weakness before him.

Strength flooded his muscles, braced his legs and lifted his muzzle. He turned back to Mike and tried not to think of the game or his dreams or anything except being with the sheep. "Shall we get something to drink?"

He didn't want a drink, not now, but perhaps he needed one. Mike tilted his head, said an uncertain "Sure," and got up from the table. Alexei wanted to grab his arm, to point at Konstantin and demand to know whether Mike saw him, but if the sheep didn't, then Alexei would seem crazy, and if he did, well, that would be even worse.

Upstairs at the bar, the bartender asked Alexei what he wanted, and he stared, still seeing the pixelated Konstantin in his head. "Red Devil," he blurted out, then realized that that might just be Meg's concoction and started to take it back, but the bartender, a lanky cheetah, just nodded and turned to Mike, who gave Alexei a strange look as he ordered one of the same.

"IDs please?" The cheetah looked down at both of them, his gaze lingering on Alexei.

Mike produced his wallet and handed a plastic card over. Alexei's paw lingered on the pocket containing his new yellow wallet, and frustration clipped his words. "I—lost mine."

"Sorry," the cheetah said. "Can't serve you."

"Coke," Alexei said, forgetting that here in Vidalia a "Coke" might be anything carbonated. He took the wallet out and slapped a five dollar bill down on the counter.

They took the drinks over to a high table at the edge of the bar area. Mike sat and lowered his voice. "Did you think he wasn't going to card you?"

"I do not drink often," Alexei said. "I forgot."

The sheep smiled and sipped his drink. "What is this, anyway? I've never heard of it."

"Regional flavors and Siberian vodka." Alexei looked at the reddish-orange drink. He could smell the sweetness of peach, the sharpness of vodka. "May I have a drink?"

Mike glanced toward the bar. "Uh…if he sees you…"

"Never mind." Alexei gulped down his Coke, which actually was a Coca-Cola, tart and fizzy and cold. He wanted it to warm him, relax the tension, but all it seemed to do was chill and tighten his chest. He put it down and breathed.

Mike hesitated, then slid the drink across the table. "I guess it wouldn't hurt…just a drink, I mean."

Alexei smiled. "Thank you. I promise I will not tell the police." He picked up the drink and tipped just enough into his muzzle to run across his tongue and fill the back of his mouth, then handed the drink back to Mike and swallowed.

The sheep sipped. "It's pretty good." He lifted his head and looked up at Alexei. "Are you…okay?"

Alexei nodded curtly, breathing in the peach aroma, feeling the tension inside him fight the warmth of the alcohol. This drink was weak, fruity. He picked up his Coke again in case anyone had seen him drinking, and took a sip to cover the alcohol on his breath.

Sol came up on Alexei's other side. "You're not answering your phone."

"I am talking to Mike," Alexei replied, setting his glass down on the counter with a crack.

The black wolf sniffed at Alexei's breath, nostrils wide. "I thought you didn't drink."

"Not any more. Not very much," he said, but the whirl of emotions was settling. With the vodka calming him and Konstantin's voice receding into memory, Alexei's ears came up. He turned to Mike and gave the sheep a warm, full smile, lifting the Coke to him. Mike met his glass with a clink and a return smile, and that warmed Alexei more than the drink: just what he needed. He drained the glass and put it back on the table.

"Is that what happened to you? How did you even get a drink without your ID?" Sol leaned on the table and looked at Mike. His voice sharpened. "Did you buy him a drink?"

"Just a swallow." Mike's smile vanished and his eyes widened.

Alexei's fear and anger at Konstantin bubbled up again. "I have not broken any laws," he snapped at Sol. "Your father gave you beer."

"That's different," Sol said, but he flattened his ears and stepped back. "I just want to make sure that you're not going to be drunk out here in public. Without your ID. You could get in a lot of trouble. Make some bad choices." The wolf glared again at Mike.

Alexei raised his voice. "Mike is *not* Carcy," he said, challenging Sol with his eyes.

The wolf's ears did not come back up at the mention of his ex-boyfriend's name. "Fine," he said, and turned on his heels to walk off.

Fox and sheep stared down at their glasses. Alexei watched the ice shift as it melted, and ran his finger down the condensation on the side. He wanted to go after Sol and apologize, but he didn't want to leave Mike. At least he no longer felt the dual emotions of Konstantin's presence; here at the table with Mike, warmth enveloped him and his tail hung behind him, swishing slowly. He belonged here, and Mike wanted him here.

"Are you mad at him?" Mike asked.

Alexei shook his head slowly. "He is mad at me," he said, and emotion drained out of him, leaving him tired enough that he had to grip the edge of the table. "I think perhaps I should go home."

But on the way home, the insulating cocoon created by the swallow of vodka frayed and thinned, and the shadows outside the bus window loomed sinister as they slid past. Alexei wondered what they might be concealing. Sol sat in silence beside him, and without conversation, his eyelids drifted down.

The rocky field swam into his mind's eye.

He drew his arms around himself and forced his eyes open. The field had remained bare, no fox in military coat. But the possibility hovered there, so real that he could swear he saw the flip of a coat in the play of a streetlight as the bus rounded a corner.

It was nothing, merely a trick of the light. Alexei held on to his pride, to the date with Mike and the sweet nature of the sheep, the exhilaration of the conversation they'd had. He could not put off sleep forever, and soon he would need to remember those feelings, he thought.

Chapter 14

At fifteen, I made the friendship of a reindeer who was also training to be admitted to the Semenovsky regiment. His name was Pavel, and like me, he had a military father. Unlike me, his father was his blood father, a reindeer from Finnska with a dubious military career of his own who had come into a small fortune during the disastrous war twenty years back. With it, he bought his way into the lower levels of the aristocracy, and his son a Semenovsky candidacy.

At first, I was wary of Pavel. Vasily warned me against the aristocrats, those who valued their personal fortunes over the welfare of the Empire, and I carried myself very carefully around Pavel at first. But his easy manner and devotion to his duties wore down my suspicions, and when he took my side in an argument over the proper way to conduct our training, I extended a paw to him, and he took it. His family, he told me, kept always in their minds the source of their fortune, and were determined to repay the Empire for its generosity. Using the fortune to purchase a candidacy only served to further their service.

Some of the other candidates resented him for having bought his place, but I did not; they resented me, too, for the patronage of Vasily Petrovich. These candidates were the ones whose fathers had served in the regiment, and yet they did not feel that this chance of fate was as unearned as my adoption or Pavel's father's wealth. Pavel and I trained together, fox and deer, and we agreed that by whatever means one reached the regiment, one still had to apply oneself to meet the qualifications of the regiment.

In the class ahead of us, for example, there was Rurik, a wolverine whose situation was similar to Pavel's. He had inherited a fortune from his father and had spent it freely to be able to wear the Semenovsky uniform. Rurik was universally despised in his regiment, for although he was unable to master the finer arts of obeying orders and marching in formation, he excelled at fighting his comrades over the smallest slight. He was rumored to have attempted to buy his way into the Preobrazhensky regiment, but thankfully that regiment remained true to its standards and exclusive to tigers. As much as I ached to wear the brilliant gold and dark blue, it was almost worth it to me that Rurik, too, would be excluded.

Prior to induction into the guards, the candidates underwent a week-long intensive training exercise during which they were to remain on the grounds, eating together and completing physically grueling courses. The evenings were to be spent in meditation on the duty to Siberia and the tsar, in preparing the mind as rigorously as they were preparing their bodies. I would undergo this training the following year, using that time to review not only my duty to my mother country and ruler, but also my duty to my commander and to my family, when I should start one. A soldier functions best when his loyalties are clear; one who stops on the battlefield to think of his unborn child may well be the weak spot in a line of defense, or the one whose failed attack dooms an entire advance.

And yet Rurik spent at least two evenings in a bar in Petrograd, frequently fighting, often thrown out. It was clear that the furthest thing from his mind was being a loyal, effective soldier. He preferred to drink and carouse, and of course there would be no room for him in the Semenovsky Guards. Pavel and I said that surely Rurik would see his dream of belonging to an elite regiment ended, and we would be quit of him.

Instead, he was inducted with those loyal, hardworking officers who had dedicated their lives to the pursuit of this honor and the upholding of that ideal. Pavel and I spent some time in a bar that evening ourselves, railing bitterly against the unfairness of it. It was then that Pavel said that he hoped there would come a day when a person would be judged on his merit and not on the money he could raise, or the accident of his birth.

I believe he thought I would be sympathetic, but I, just as much in my cups, said that some births were noble, and not accidents. Pavel shook his head, insisting that a noble birth was as much an accident as an ignoble one. Surely, I said, he did not mean all noble births. Most surely, I said, he did not mean the noblest birth in all of Siberia.

All noble births, Pavel said, for if we make exception for the greatest, how then do we differentiate the next greatest? As though the Tsar and his nobles were fish to be measured side by side at the market. I grew angry, and Pavel, though he knew my temper, still insisted that he thought the Tsar had proven his right to rule by his actions and not by his birth.

When I woke the next morning, I did not specifically recall how I came to be lying in my bed with one side of my face aching. Pavel, too, woke with a sore jaw. I did, with the clarity of a cold day, recall his words about the Tsar, and when he laughed about how we had let ourselves go the previous night, I did not smile. I asked if he had been serious in what he said.

He evaded the question, growing more ill-humored, and finally barked that yes, he had meant it. I asked whether he would repeat that once more, sober and in the light of day, and he said that he meant no disloyalty to our fine and capable tsar, but that he believed truly that a more just society would choose its leaders based on merit and not on their birth. Kings had a place, he said, but we had only to look to the nations to our west to see that progressive societies no longer trusted them with absolute power. People around the world were banding together, leaving their countries or forcing the governments to change when the government no longer suited the people.

There were no words I could say to convey the depths of my despair at this conversation. I had considered him a friend and believed that he, as I, trusted in the sanctity of purpose of the guards we worked so hard to be worthy of. And yet, in a single breath, he destroyed that bond. He repudiated the very land we would be called upon to defend, called into question the society that had allowed him and his father to succeed, and proved his unfitness for the post. Government suit the people? That he called upon the decadent, chaos-plagued powers of the West, suffering gruesome wars nearly every decade, as examples of his philosophy showed the rot at its core. The people suited the government; the emperors ruled by right, and what they decided, the people carried out. To doubt that foundation was to doubt Siberia herself.

I reported his conversation to the commanding officer that very noon. When confronted, Pavel did not deny the charge. He was dismissed from the regiment, and I gained the favor of some of the officers. My classmates thought that the desire to curry that favor was the force behind my actions, but the truth is that I would have acted the same even if I were sure that censure would follow. They said that I had betrayed Pavel, but Pavel was the one who betrayed us all. If you do not believe in the right of your lord to rule you, how can you be trusted to fight for him and his country, to value their welfare over your own?

Friendship can suffer many pressures and remain intact, but when the most private and personal beliefs strike across each other, then the friendship must needs crumble. That conflict will always lie between the former friends, a gulf that may never be crossed.

Years later, I would meet Pavel again, and he offered me forgiveness. I told him that he had nothing to forgive me for, as I had done him no wrong.

Chapter 15

Alexei did not dream of Konstantin that night, and he woke Sunday with his sense of accomplishment dominating the lingering unease. He had his date, and he didn't need the old fox and his "soldier's passion" now. Maybe the ghost would go away, disgusted, and leave Alexei alone. That would be just fine.

Sol came out while Alexei was eating cereal and got himself a bowl, but didn't say anything. His flat ears and curled tail would normally prompt Alexei to ask him what was wrong, but the fox had a pretty good idea, so he kept quiet as well.

Then Meg opened her door and stood there, yawning, while Sol poured his milk. "So," she said, "let's hear it. How did the night go?"

"Alexei was pretty hardcore," Sol said. "He showed up Kendall twice on the dance machine."

"Three times," Alexei said.

"He went off in a huff and Alexei got to talk to Mike."

"I asked him on a date," Alexei said, sitting up and lifting his muzzle proudly.

Meg raised her eyebrows. "And he said...?"

"Yes, of course." Alexei grinned.

Sol squinted at the fox. "You were getting kind of belligerent at the game, too. And then you had a drink."

"Just a swallow of Mike's. It calmed me down," Alexei said, and then nodded to Meg. "Your Red Devil was better. Too much sweet in theirs."

"Grenadine? The cherry flavor?" Alexei nodded. Meg yawned again, her piercings glittering in the light, and smiled smugly. "Maybe I should apply to be a bartender."

Sol crunched down a mouthful of Corn Flakes and swallowed. "Seriously, though, what got into you? You were bitchy at me, too."

Meg walked up and sat down while Alexei was chewing, composing his answer. "What'cha mean?" She looked back and forth from wolf to fox.

"It is nothing," Alexei said. "I decided I was tired of putting up with Kendall."

He avoided Meg's gaze as Sol went on. "He was being all up in Kendall's face. Like when they first picked music to dance, he called him a loser right there. I mean, you know Kendall—well, no, you don't. But he's all about…" Sol waved his paws. "Kendall's one of those guys who wants everyone to like him and think he's awesome. And he's okay if you don't like him as long as you still think he's awesome."

"He is not awesome," Alexei said.

"No, but…well, he's a pretty good goalie," Sol said. "And he knows a lot of stuff. Hey," he said, when Alexei glared at him, "I mean, I know he's obnoxious, but he was really opening up last night. We talked about going on this march to Potomac."

Meg leaned forward, her rings clinking as she set her muzzle on her paws. "So let me get this straight. Alexei was getting all confident and belligerent."

To disrupt the conversation, Alexei asked, "What is belligerent?" though he was pretty sure he knew.

Sol and Meg both explained it while he finished his cereal, and then he said, "I was not so belligerent."

"I never saw you act like that before," Sol said.

"I decided I wanted a date with Mike," Alexei said. He still didn't look at Meg.

"Uh-huh."

She let the words hang there, but still he kept his muzzle turned away from her, toward Sol. "Shall we go to the park and practice today?"

The wolf's ears remained partly down. "I guess," he said. "Weather looks good if we go early. Supposed to be nasty by the end of the day."

They walked down the street, tossing the soccer ball back and forth until they got to the park, and they did not talk much, both lost in their own thoughts. Three cubs from the block were already there, playing with their own ball, so Sol and Alexei kicked around with them for a while. Only when Alexei took out his phone to check the time did he realize he had never turned it back on after the previous night.

A few moments after he replaced it in his pocket, it chimed. He ignored it until they were done practicing and then took it out as Sol was talking to the cubs. Sol was better at that than Alexei was, because inevitably the cubs asked where they played, and Sol had to talk very delicately about the VLGA. The wolf stayed away from specifics, telling the cubs about "a group of my friends," as Alexei looked at the number that had called him.

It was an international number, from Siberia, but it wasn't his parents' number. His heart raced. He glanced at Sol, held up his phone, and called up the message.

"*Hello, Alexei,*" his sister's voice said, in Siberian.

He froze. For a moment, the brightness of the day flooded his eyes with white, and he smelled the rotting wood of the bedroom wall he'd talked to his sister through. He said, "Caterina?" before remembering it was just a voicemail.

"*I am on a public phone. I stole ten rubles from Papa. I don't know how long that will let me talk. I wrote you another letter today, but before I could give it to Kisha, the phone rang in our house. Papa answered and it was the fox from Vdansk, asking after me. Papa yelled at him and then locked me in my room.*

"*I had stolen the money to go to Vdansk later, but I had to call you, so I jumped out the window. I didn't hurt myself much. I landed on my ankle badly, but I can walk on it. It's like the time I fell out of the tree. Lexi, I will not go to Vdansk today because the next time I go, it must be to leave forever. So I will take Papa's punishment when I come back and I will go fish again, but I needed to ask you this favor first. Please, if you can reach this corsac fox and tell him not to call, but ask him to meet me in the same café in Vdansk. If he tells you when he will be there, I will make sure to go there and meet him, if I have to smash all the windows in our house to go. I know that we are meant to respect our ancestors, but also our ancestors are meant to protect us, and if Mama and Papa will not protect me, then I must leave and protect myself. I think Prababushka would want me to go.*

"*The fox's name is Bogdan Chichikov and I do not have a phone for him. But he is on leave from the civil service and he lives in Moskva. It is an unusual name and I think he should be easy to find so please, please, Lexi, find him for me and I will come join you. Love you so much.*"

The phone clicked and then a smooth mechanical voice said, "End of message."

"Hey," Sol said behind him. "Hey, you ready to go?"

Alexei stared down at his phone. Sol stood a short distance from him, arms folded. "Was that Mike?"

"No," Alexei said. "My sister."

The wolf took a step closer, his shoulder brushing Alexei's. "Oh. Is she okay?"

Alexei curled his tail around his leg and lowered his ears. "She twisted her ankle."

"That doesn't sound so bad." Sol squinted ahead at the street. "Come on, the light's green."

He tossed Alexei the soccer ball, but Alexei, when he caught it, did not toss it back. "Come on," Sol said as they hurried across the scorching asphalt through exhaust fumes to the other side of the street. "I'll buy you a Coke."

Sol ascribed to the Vidalia custom of using "Coke" to refer to any fizzy Coca-Cola product, and often not even that brand. Alexei was used to Coke being inflexibly associated with red and white, and sweet cold carbonated cola with a distinctive bite, so he had gotten used to specifying to Sol that he wanted an actual Coca-Cola. But he was distracted by his sister's call, and Sol didn't ask, so this time Alexei got a Pepsi because that's what the newsstand had in the cooler.

The over-sweet soda did at least stop him panting quite so much. Sol chatted about the pieces of Niki's story he was going to write that evening, his tail swishing more freely than it had earlier, but Alexei only half-listened, his thoughts chasing each other around his head. He panted in the muggy heat, the air full of automobile fumes and people and the cool, delicate scent of the trees as they walked beneath them. It felt crowded and alive, and Alexei liked that he could move through it undisturbed when he wanted to, sometimes jostling people talking on cell phones and to each other, and though his ears caught all those conversations, he didn't parse the words. Midland was larger than Samorodka; Vidalia was larger by at least two orders of magnitude, a city that Alexei had at first been afraid of getting lost in. But he had started from his apartment, added the parks and the VLGA and his workplace and his co-workers, and now he could tune out the noises and smells and flashes of different fur and walk confidently down a street, knowing that he had a home and a job and that he belonged here.

On this walk, he focused on plans to find this Bogdan…Chichikov? Shchichikov? The word blurred in his memory; he would have to listen to the message again. Learning the name did not make him feel more confident in the fox, but it didn't matter; Chichikov or Shchichikov would not throw bottles at Caterina, would not constantly belittle her and think of her as good for nothing but marrying, and so Alexei was determined to find him.

The beaver who'd processed his exchange program would be a good place to start. But Rozalina wouldn't be in her office until Monday morning, Moskva time, which would be…Alexei tried to work out the numbers in his head. Something like midnight here. He could stay up and call, if he did some research while Sol was writing.

So in the afternoon, he told Meg he would help her with dinner, and then spent an hour looking up Bogdan Chichikov online, with no success. He looked through forums to find various branches of the civil service in Moskva, but there were a dozen agencies that might qualify, and a thousand jobs, and though there were three Chichikovs, none of them even had the first initial B. Siberia had not yet reached a point where everything was copied online, and it was entirely possible that this Chichikov, who had to be moderately well-placed to have a son in the exchange program, was just low enough to be ignored online.

There would be nothing more he could do without calling, and nobody in Moskva would be around on what was their Sunday night. So Alexei helped Meg prepare some kind of fish she had gotten from the market. "You actually left the apartment?" he said.

She slapped him. "I go out plenty."

"You are always here. Where do you go?"

"The market." She waved at the window. "Couple shops out that way."

"Riverwalk?" He knew of no other shops in easy walking distance.

"Somewhere with fish and lemons." She pulled three bright yellow fruits from her bag and set them on the counter, their knobbly forms wobbling across the formica.

Alexei unwrapped the fish and drew a claw across the bluish-grey skin that glistened under the kitchen lights. The sight was both familiar and unfamiliar; the fish he'd caught for years in Samorodka were longer and thinner, their fins differently placed and shaped. And none of them, in the fifteen years he'd fished, had had skin this healthy. "I can clean this fish. I have practice."

"Really? I hate cleaning fish."

Alexei did, too, but not when he was offering to do it and it made him feel like part of a family. He brought the fish to the dining room table and allowed his paws to do the automatic work while he thought again about Cat and what else he could do.

He could call his parents. He could make them let Cat go—but no, they would never listen to him. He reviewed the names of his school friends, anyone he could talk into helping Cat, but the names had faded after a year, and he could only think of one, a hare, who might still remember him well enough to be willing to help.

"Wow," Meg said. "You did that fast."

Alexei had hardly realized that he'd finished. "I told you," he said. "Practice." He scooped the skin, bones, and organs into the garbage.

The fish was delicious, fresher than most Meg had brought home, but it disappeared quickly, and for Alexei, dinner passed in a blur of thoughts of Mike and Cat and Konstantin. Sol had to ask him twice what his plans for Monday night were. Tuesday, of course, was their regular practice, and Wednesday was the game, the one where the Peaches would be watching him.

"I don't know," Alexei said. "I have to look at some things for my sister."

"For her ankle?"

He shook his head impatiently. "She is trying to escape Samorodka— Siberia."

"Oh." Sol leaned forward over his empty plate. "I thought she couldn't call you any more."

"She cannot. She stole money to make a public phone—to use a public phone."

"Good Christ," Meg said. "Don't cubs in Siberia have cell phones?"

"No." Alexei wiped his paws on his napkin and set it back on the table. "No, not in Samorodka. Moskva, yes, perhaps. We heard stories from the people there. Some probably were not true. But no, my sister and I used one phone, in our parents' house."

"How did you survive? Did your parents—" Meg started.

Alexei pushed his chair back and got up. "I am sorry," he said. "Thank you for dinner. I need to look on the Internet for Cat."

Meg offered to wash up, so he left his plate and silverware in the soapy water in the sink and retreated into his room.

Though he couldn't think of anywhere else to look online, he returned to the Moskva civil service sites, sitting at the desk until Sol came back in, then ceding the desk to the wolf and sitting cross-legged on his bed with his back to the wall and his tail beneath the laptop on his knees. When he'd gone through all the civil service sites, he looked at information on the exchange program. Then, because he kept looking over at the space on the wall where Niki's picture had hung, he looked up the tsars and their guards. He couldn't remember the name the fox had spoken in his dream, but when he called up images of the Semenovsky guards, he recognized the uniforms, the navy blue coats, red collars, and gold sashes.

The image of Konstantin in the video game came back to him. He found it difficult to look away from the pictures even as he read the descriptions of the elite non-tiger regiment assigned to protect the noble families and keep order in Petrograd, and later Moskva. None of the few names mentioned in the articles Alexei found matched Konstantin, or an adopted fox, and he had no idea what Konstantin's last name might be. There was one picture of a guard, a stern-looking red fox, and every time Alexei's eyes traveled away from the picture, he expected it to move. He had to copy the page's text into another window and close the page before he could read it properly.

None of the images did move, and again Alexei had the creeping feeling that he'd been abandoned. It is a good thing, he told himself. The old soldier was hardly a benign, helpful ghost. But…what if Konstantin could help his sister?

Alexei rubbed his whiskers and thought. The spirit could easily travel to Moskva; in fact, he was familiar with it. He could find this Bogdan Chichikov, could perhaps come to him in a dream…Alexei closed the display on his laptop while he thought about this. If there were no other way to bring Cat here to the States, then he would make sure Konstantin understood how important it was. The ghost might be angry at him for Saturday night, but here was a child in danger. How could a soldier say no to that?

At midnight, he tried to call Rozalina, and she didn't answer. Perhaps she was out today, or getting in late. He set his alarm for five-thirty. He would try again when he woke up.

Chapter 16

The more I grew to know Mariya Frolova, the more I admired her inner beauty, which matched the outer. She had the ability to melt the hardest heart with a smile, to right any wrong with a word, to lift the darkest spirit with but a touch of her sleek brown paw.

I do not know how she came about that gift, for it was not present in any of her family. Those noble foxes sat on many councils and held grand dinner parties, and took great pride in the nobility of their company and their exhaustive knowledge of every rule of etiquette. My rough manner and experience shocked my neighbors at the first dinner I attended, but Mariya, without scolding, told them I had lived a difficult life and had known little but soldiers. She guided me through those social engagements with a gentle paw, pointing out which painting I should compliment and why, which bright silver utensil I should pick up, when I should let the servants bring me food and drink, when I should talk and when I should be silent. Often, she had to remind me that not every complaint about the government was a cry of treason against the Tsar.

It was difficult for me to adapt to these evenings. Vasily hated them and would have nothing to do with them, leaving me alone. Without Mariya's guiding paw, I should have given up after the first awkward silence. I felt more comfortable on the field, where I had risen to a rank of Lieutenant and was partly responsible for training new recruits, along with my assigned Colonel. There, my unyielding style earned praise from my superiors and respect from my trainees.

I was not, of course, assigned to train the Tsarevich, who would become Nicholas the Second. Then, he was only Nicholas, a young tiger well-liked by all the other soldiers. He showed none of the battle-readiness of his father; rather, he took after his mother with his charm and sociability. I envied him that. Even at the age of ten, he fit more neatly into formal dinners and dances than I, nearly ten years his senior. So I joined the crowds around him and talked with him when I could. Anxious as I was to be accepted by the Frolovs, I found myself captivated by the young prince's charm.

One day, Mariya came to see me on the practice field. She did not understand the necessities of the exercises we practiced relentlessly, and I admit that I faltered in my instruction, worried that she might see me as harsh. But Nicholas, with all the charm of a young cub, approached her when he saw her watching me, and told her that I was such an excellent soldier that I would surely have been one of the Tsar's personal guards, had I had the good fortune to be born a tiger. Mariya asked him why we needed to scold the soldiers so, and he assured her that to prepare them to defend the Tsar and country, soldiers needed to be prepared to instantly respond to any command given on the field, that they had the honor of being the force wielded by the tigers whose experience and intellect gave shape to Siberia's defense.

She repeated his words to me as I escorted her from the barracks area, and with a sparkle in her eye and the warmest love in her voice, she said that she was proud of me. I had no appropriate response except to thank her for her confidence, and to bolster again in my heart my unwavering devotion to the Tsar and his line. I believe it was that moment that made our marriage possible, for her parents had always been somewhat distant toward me, as though I were a passing fancy to tide their daughter over until a more suitable candidate presented himself. The week following Nicholas's conversation with Mariya, her father approached me and asked me what I would need to start a family with Mariya.

My officer's pay was adequate for my purposes, and though I did not feel comfortable discussing the details of it with him, he seemed to know approximately how much I made. He assured me that they would stand by me and keep our family comfortable. After that, we discussed the unrest in the country, the foreign wars and the news from abroad that Siberia's way of life was out of date. Peasants rarely toiled for landowners in other countries, but in Siberia, that was how we had always done it. I came of peasant stock, which Mariya's father had mentioned often prior to that week, but I had improved myself through diligent work and dedication to my country, which he spoke of more often in the weeks following.

We were married in a small ceremony in Petrograd with many nobles and officers in attendance. The few I counted as friends were vastly outnumbered; my adopted father's presence made it important to be seen, and the Frolov household was not without importance in the area. I heard whispers that the marriage benefited me far more than Mariya, but I paid them no more mind than she did as our eyes met and we spoke the words that would join us.

Once we were married, there were few changes in our lives, as we had already begun to attend the same functions. I moved out of the quarters I shared with two other lieutenants, and Mariya moved out of her family's home. The house we shared was modest: a brick building near the edge of Petrograd, with a small columned porch and a stable in back. Modest it might have been, but sufficient for both of us, and affordable on my pay (nonetheless, her father insisted on paying for half of it, and though it rankled me, I allowed him). Mariya brought carpets and wall hangings, curtains and chairs and couches, pictures and silverware, but above all, she brought herself. From the first, that little house became our home, completely naturally.

Tradition dictated that we should go away to spend time as newlyweds, but Mariya had little desire to travel, and I had my duties. My colonel had given me leave, but I knew that would place him under undue strain, and as Mariya preferred to remain in Petrograd, I did not take advantage of his offer. Instead, Mariya and I set immediately to the joyful task of establishing ourselves as a family.

We attended dinners together, at which I still needed her guidance; still, my confidence in social situations grew with each week. With her at my side I felt worthy of the noblest audience. Marriage into her family brought me access to other meetings, groups of male foxes and wolves and reindeer and rats who discussed the country's situation while their wives spoke of other matters in the other room (Mariya would tell me the talk was all of the faithfulness of husbands and wives, the success of husbands and children, and some sophisticated conversation that rivaled the males' on the subjects of government and aristocracy). At these meetings, I listened more than I spoke, reminding myself that these nobles wished the best for this country and that their dissatisfaction did not mean they were treasonous.

They had much to complain about. The Emperor at the time, Alexander, had far fewer social graces than his wife or son. He was known to pass gas in public, and laugh raucously after the disruptive noise. He valued loyalty over thought, and indeed one of the grievances often echoed in those rooms was that some flawed or destructive policy had been passed into law because the creator was a favorite of the Emperor. He rarely attended social events, and when he did, did so always in uniform, a giant of a tiger barely contained by his navy blue coat, his gold epaulets and medals seeming as impermanent as clouds on a mountain.

And yet, when it came to the state of the country and its prestige, in Petrograd and Moskva as well as abroad, Alexander kept a firm grasp of what needed to be done and what he wished for Siberia. Even the dissatisfied nobles could not dispute that the country under his rule appeared stronger to its enemies, both internal and external. We had lost a small amount of prestige in a foreign war near the end of his father's life, but Alexander's strength united the country. He was, in effect, Siberia. When the nobles talked of discontent with policies and practices, they rarely criticized the Emperor directly, preferring to talk of his underlings, as one criticizes parents by discussing the children. I inferred the criticism of the Emperor, but a lieutenant, even one in the Semenovsky guards, could not speak up against these nobles, for fear of exclusion from their society.

I could not risk that; I would not have minded for my own sake, and my adopted father cared as little as I did, but the company of her friends and family was Mariya's lifeblood. But she loved my passion as well, and when we had left the great marble-floored halls and velvet chairs, the rarefied conversation and the lifted muzzles, we both of us looked forward to the ride home in our carriage, where we laughed together over the people who thought themselves wiser than the Tsar. The work is easiest for he who watches it being done, my father used to say. Though Mariya did not always understand a soldier's life, she respected the effort I made, and my dedication to guards and country.

After a year of marriage, Mariya announced that we were expecting a cub, and our lives filled with delight. She left the house more rarely after that, and I stayed with her; even had I wished to attend more tedious social events, I would have missed them for her sake. A few of her friends visited her regularly, and with that and my company she seemed quite content. I have rarely felt joy as I did during those few months, watching her grow larger and more beautiful with impending motherhood, and making preparations for our cub to arrive. All my fellows took to slapping me on the shoulder or shaking my paw, even the ones who thought me too harsh, too disciplined. Family, they said, sets all of us right in the end, and with a wife and cub, my life would be complete.

On a cool spring morning, the sun shone, flowers bloomed, and little Tatya was delivered to us. She was a delicate little thing, with thin charcoal fur and paper-thin ears, a tail barely longer than one of my fingers. Her eyes, when they opened, would be blue, Mariya said, but they would change as she grew, becoming perhaps brown like mine or green like her own.

I did not care what color her eyes were, nor whether her tail would bear my thick white tip or Mariya's smaller one, nor what shape the shadow on her muzzle took. I knew she would be beautiful. I stood at my wife's bedside, looking down at my daughter, and I promised I would keep her safe and protect her for all of her life.

And within two weeks I was forsworn. She developed a cough, which wracked her weak body. The nurse could do nothing to stop it. By the time the doctor arrived, he was too late.

She never even opened her eyes.

Chapter 17

Tombstones face away from Alexei in rows that stretch too far ahead of him to count. They are of all shapes and sizes, but like kinds are grouped in families. His paws rest on cold, polished white marble. Near him, the tombstones are all like the one he stands beside: large, elaborate monuments in rose, white, and grey. Farther away, brown clusters of small, plain sandstone markers dot the field. Clouds roil overhead, but the wind that blows is not the biting cold he remembers from earlier dreams. The smell is the same: broad, Siberian, empty.

Around him, regular plots below the stones mark graves. He wonders whether this is a vision of a real cemetery or simply a spiritual resting place for ghosts, and the thought makes his fur prickle and his tail wind tightly around his leg.

He looks around at the front of the tombstone he is resting on and sees a tiger's head and the name, in Siberian characters: Princess Yekaterina Orlov 1845–1898. On each surrounding tombstone, the interred person's name and species are recorded, some in standard characters, others in individually designed images that may or may not actually represent the person buried below them.

There is no evidence of anyone else in the cemetery, but Alexei has the feeling of being watched. He walks around to another tombstone, and another, his steps leading him toward one stone in particular. There is nothing distinct about this stone; it is rose granite, polished on the front and rough on the back, but there are other rose granite stones and red sandstone. There are other square markers, others with flowery reliefs along the edges. But each time Alexei steps forward a row, or around a stone, this rose granite stone is closer.

When he stands in front of it, he reaches out to brush the letters. They read: "Tatya Galitzin, 1879," below the picture of an infant fox.

I have no more help to give you, *comes Konstantin's voice, soft steel across the wind of the boneyard.*

You have to help me, *Alexei calls. He turns, trying to see the fox, but he is still alone amidst the rows and rows of the signs of death.* I summoned you. You have to help me!

I will not be a party to your perversion of nature.

It is unsettling, talking to a disembodied voice, but Alexei pictures Cat and stands tall, though the breeze grows colder. I need you to save my sister.

The Tsar is the land, the servant of God. His servants must follow God's plan. *Konstantin's voice grows louder.* Marry a vixen, start a family. Your family joins the other families, your children grow up to have children, and the world continues on and you are part of it. This twisting of God's gift, placing you outside the world, it is an affront to the fur you bear, the parents that bore you. I am disgusted to be talking to you, ashamed to have been a party to this sickness.

The words burrow into him, curl his fingers, toes, and tail. He knows them too well, and knows the answer, that he is as God made him, but the words fail when he tries to speak them. The image of his sister gives him strength, and those words he can speak. My sister is in danger! She needs to reach someone in Moskva.

Row upon row of silent stones give him no answer. He turns, and turns again, but they stretch away from him in every direction, unbroken by a red tail or a blue coat. He falls to his knees, the ground hard and dusty and cold. Please, *Alexei cries.* Listen to me!

For agonizing moments, eternities, only the wind hisses against his ears. He reaches out a paw to the rose granite stone. Cat's image, hazy and translucent, takes shape atop it, her tail swinging back and forth through the stone. Her face is indistinct, save for her smile, which is the brightest thing as far as he can see. He whispers, They will kill her.

Konstantin's voice comes softly, very close to him. Why can your parents not protect her from any danger?

The image of Cat on the tombstone wavers and vanishes. My parents are the danger, *Alexei says.* They care nothing for their children. Cat, she is so smart, she could be a teacher, but my mother says she must marry, cannot go to university…once they beat her so badly I had to help her walk to school for a month. *He does not talk of the time his father heard the rumor that he liked boys, the time he broke a bottle over Alexei's back, his mother screaming that they would send him away to be cured, his father's shouting: I'll see him at the bottom of the river first. His fear now is like his fear then, only for Cat rather than himself.* We looked out for each other, *he said,* and she helped me escape. But now she has no-one.

He turns, and Konstantin is there, crouching beside him, the red collar flat against his shoulders and chest, blue coat defining his stiff, squared shoulders, his ears splayed so that Alexei cannot see the notch in the right one. The fox's eyes, dark and brown, bore into Alexei's, and the younger fox thinks Konstantin can see those memories he is hiding. A parent who puts their cub in danger, *he says, and then stops.* But to beat a daughter…

His paw rests on the rose granite tombstone. Alexei holds his breath, trying to peer into Konstantin the way he feels Konstantin is looking into him, but he sees only darkness there. He wishes he had Konstantin's confidence to meet the older fox. Will you help me? *he says timidly.*

The soldier holds his eyes. Finally, he speaks, his voice low and gravelly. If you wish my help, you will have to abandon this unnatural way of life.

It—it is not unnatural, *Alexei says.* Not any longer. In your time—

If you wish my help.

Silence hangs over the stone markers and stretches on and on, out into the horizon. Alexei feels unmoored, floating in the dreamworld, even though in the dream his feet are solidly on the ground. The stone beneath his fingers feels very real, the smell of earth and desolation in his nostrils just as solid.

What Konstantin is asking of him feels like returning to Samorodka, to the rot and ruin and the hiding of his nature. He sits down with his back against the granite marker and it is like being back in his bed at home, tail curled around himself, desperately spinning through the cycle of desire and denial. He'd escaped that for good, he thought. But for Cat…

He closes his eyes, which in the dreamworld has little effect; he is still acutely aware of the clouds, the granite, the earth, and Konstantin, waiting. It is my life, *he says, and his voice is small, not very confident at all.*

Konstantin comes back to him, soft and firm. Your life is not simply your own. It is the contract you make with those around you. What you feel in your heart sometimes must be denied for the good of all.

The earth is cold below him. Its grit is in the fur of his tail. He brushes at it with his paws, but it simply spreads to his fingers, to his palms, working into the creases between the pads and the fur, a maddening itch. Will you help Cat? Find the person she is looking for? Tell him to call her?

The older fox stands, arms folded over medals glinting on his chest. Konstantin's ears are flat and his eyes stare down the length of his muzzle. Will you live a proper life?

Alexei takes a breath and feels fine grey dust on his tongue. Yes.

Konstantin does not speak, but his ears rise and he smiles. And Alexei is again in his bedroom, listening to Cat tell him there is nothing wrong with him; he is at the Samorodka schoolhouse feeling again the oppressive fear digging claws into his chest, looking every day at the other boys and wondering if any of them were like him; he is in Midland writing the letter to Sol, the first time he had confessed to being gay to anyone but Cat; he is outside the school as Sol comes out to him, and he has just thrown all this away. Wait! I need—I can't do what you ask—

But Konstantin is gone.

Chapter 18

He'd taken it back, he told himself when he woke, heart racing. He hadn't thrown away everything he and Cat had sacrificed to earn his freedom here. But the itch remained in Alexei's pawpads, though he scrubbed them clean in the morning and again once he arrived at work. In between carrying boxes around, he scraped claws around the pads on his palms until they were sore and tender.

The day was overcast and drizzly, doing nothing to help dispel the pall of his dream. In the sunlight and reality of dust and heavy packing boxes, his conversation with Konstantin felt unreal, the more so because he had called Rozalina in the morning, with light just glimmering through the kitchen window. It had been strange falling back into Siberian, but easy, perhaps because of the dreams.

Rozalina had told him that the name Bogdan Chichikov wasn't familiar. She had checked the phone listings in Moskva and had not found him, but there were other places she could look. He said that his sister had met the fox in Vdansk, so Rozalina promised to check there as well and to call him back if she found anything. Her warm, motherly attitude had reassured Alexei, but it did not stop him from worrying about Cat, nor from thinking about his dream.

Even if the threat of Konstantin felt less substantial during the day, Alexei had to wonder what it said about him that he had agreed to give up his pursuit of Mike—and more, give up being gay, or at least acting gay. In the waking world, he could tell himself that he'd taken it back, that it would be only until Cat was safe, that it would be only until Konstantin went away. But all the same, it required him to accept Konstantin's belief that he *could* give it up.

The way Konstantin had phrased it: deny what is in your heart for the good of all—that stuck with Alexei. He couldn't really see where denying his attraction to Mike, or to males in general, would benefit anyone apart from perhaps Konstantin himself. Still, all of his accomplishments from Saturday night now scraped like grit in his mouth.

But as the relentless normality of Monday pushed his dream farther back into memory, Alexei's confidence rose. He would perhaps get a call from Rozalina that night, or the next, with the phone number of this Chichikov, and then he would set up the meeting with his sister, and he could tell Konstantin to leave him. Maybe he would have to get Meg to look up a ritual to dismiss him, but he would be free, he would have his date with Mike, and everything would go well from here on out.

When he got home, he walked into his bedroom, saw the blank space on the wall above Sol's bed, and realized that he'd forgotten to pick up the repaired picture again. He stood staring at the wall, tail swishing against the bed, trying to decide what he'd say to Sol. *I am sorry, I was distracted by this dream I had where a ghost told me to give up being gay so he could rescue my sister.* He shook his head. Best just to say nothing. He pulled his sister's letter from his desk, more to look at her handwriting and feel her presence than to read the words again. He had promised to help her and protect her, and even though he told himself he was doing his best, the feeling of powerlessness made him shove the letter back into its drawer and get out his Siberian metal music again.

In the morning, Sol said nothing about his painting. In fact, he did not say much at all, but Alexei did not talk much either, preoccupied with wondering why Rozalina had not called, and why he had not dreamed of Konstantin. Waiting was worse, because the longer he went without hearing anything, the longer he thought about his sister at their father's mercy. What if he'd beaten her for stealing money, for sneaking out of the house? His mother had always—usually—protected them on the rare occasions when their father had completely lost control, but what if she, too, were angry with Cat? What if they had gone too far?

While Sol was in the shower and Alexei getting dressed, he turned to the window. The morning sun caught the dust from the construction site, playing with it in swirling patterns. Alexei watched the lazy dust motes float through the air. Funny, he thought, that one looked like a "K."

It was a "K," he realized with a jolt. And other letters formed beside it, Siberian letters. The first word of a question: *What.*

He stayed frozen where he was, fur prickling, as the dust drifted lazily into more letters, the question forming slowly. He wished Sol would come back, wished Meg were awake. He tried to call, but his mouth would not move, his tongue dry. A short, soft whine forced its way out of his throat, not enough to be heard anywhere else, not through Meg's door, not over the noise of the shower.

What is answer?

The letters hung in the air, and there was no question for whom they were meant, nor to what they referred. So Konstantin *had* heard his retraction and still required him to answer. "I," Alexei squeaked, staring at the dust as though he could will their improbable message away, as though he could force them to break apart. If he turned around, he would no longer see them and he could walk out of the room. Or if he could close his eyes and open them again, the letters would be gone; it was impossible that they were there in the first place. But they remained, stubbornly hovering on the other side of his window.

"I don't know," Alexei forced out. "I need more time!"

Movement behind him broke the spell, made him whirl and see Sol, a towel wrapped around the black wolf's middle. "Okay," Sol said, "but don't take too long or we'll miss the bus."

Alexei spun back to the window. Nothing floated beyond the glass except formless dust.

If Konstantin could come into his world, as Sol said Niki had done once, then that made things more dangerous, his bargain more binding. More than once as he lifted and moved boxes at work that day, he was tempted to call his parents, demand to talk to his sister. They would hang up on him, he was sure, but at least it would be something he could do. The problem was that doing so would make things worse for Cat. If he called and let them know that he was working with her, then they might make it harder for her to get away when the time came.

Is it more important to me to go out with Mike, or to rescue my sister? When put like that, the question was ludicrous. But Cat had helped him escape, had told him he should go first and she would follow. Live life, she had told him, and I will come when I can. Still, he knew what his answer should be, and he was furious at Konstantin for making him choose, furious at his parents for creating the danger to his sister, furious at himself for taking such a long time about it.

So Tuesday evening, in the continuing drizzles, he took out his frustration on the practice field. Mike and Kendall and most of the rest of the VLGA's soccer team showed up drinking beers. Kendall wanted to tell everyone about some store chain that had just adopted benefits for same-sex partners, attributing the change, of course, to the petition he'd started on the Internet. The discussions of same-sex partners and lives together prickled the memory of Alexei's dream until, restless, he took the soccer ball and just did footwork drills by himself, the way he'd done back in Samorodka.

Sol came out to work with him, which reminded him that he still hadn't picked up the picture. At least tonight he had the excuse that they were practicing, and he wouldn't want to bring the picture to the park. Still, guilt over forgetting one more time on top of the rest of his turmoil kept Alexei quiet and focused on his exercises. When the rest of the players joined in and they moved on to game drills, Alexei dedicated himself to stopping anyone who tried to drive the ball past him, to kicking with force and precision, and to working as hard as if he were playing a game. Wet grass slipped under his feet, but he was the only one who didn't fall at least once. When it wasn't his turn to work with the ball, he left Sol and Kendall talking on the grass and ran two laps around the park.

He felt the need to prove himself, much as he had that weekend, but in the course of running alone with the wind whistling past him and the light fading, with drizzle seeping into his fur, he wondered whether he was proving himself to Mike or to Konstantin, or simply to himself. If he were to give up his gay life, as Konstantin demanded, should he simply leave them all and keep running, past the border of the park, out to the street and down the pavement and home? Should he run beyond that, out to Millenport, perhaps, a larger city where he could begin over, with people who didn't need to know that he was gay? Was this something he could run away from?

Shadows lengthened around him. He felt he could just slip into one of them and vanish, reappear somewhere else as a different fox, a fox who had fled Samorodka not because he was not allowed to love there, but because he wanted a better life. And then he came around a corner of trees and saw Sol talking to Kendall, Mike standing by himself near the beers bending over to get another bottle, and a powerful rush of belonging surged through his chest. Run away? Start over? No, he had a good life here, and he would remain here. Konstantin couldn't force him to leave.

He slowed, panting, breathing in the humid evening air across his tongue. The flood of rebellious determination reminded him of that rare confidence he'd felt Saturday night. Tonight, it had been focused on everyone rather than just Kendall; he had tried to show them up in the practice and then had drawn apart from them while he ran. Konstantin, maybe, again. He shook his head to clear it, looked up, and stopped where he stood.

Behind a large oak tree at the back of the practice field, partially hidden by the shadows of the leaves and trunk, a figure stood motionless. At first, Alexei took it for one of those people who took advantage of shady corners to drink, or to smoke not-quite-legal substances. But this figure was not smoking, nor drinking, and its large, vulpine ears pointed straight up, and a long, bushy, vulpine tail snaked out from under a long square-shouldered military coat, and the eye that glittered from above the broad, flared collar of the coat appeared to be looking directly at Alexei.

He stared back, and the figure did not move. His chest grew cold and hard as ice, his lungs compressed so that he had to labor to draw breath.

His tongue hung out, but he could barely force air over it, and his throat felt raw.

It couldn't be. This wasn't a video game or a dream. It was just some other fox behind the tree, someone dressed in an overcoat.

"Hey," Mike said, walking over with a Bolt. "We're winding down. Thought you might like a…" He stopped three feet from Alexei when the fox didn't turn. "Are you okay?"

Alexei tore his gaze from the tree, looking up into Mike's wide, honest eyes, framed by those golden curved horns. "I beg your pardon?"

"I said, are you okay? You look like you've seen a ghost."

Alexei jumped, stumbling backwards a step. "What did you say?"

"I just—" Mike frowned and set the energy drink down. "Hey, you're shaking. What's wrong?"

"Nothing!" Alexei took another step back as Mike walked toward him, arms out. He swung his head around to look at the tree where the vulpine silhouette had been standing.

It was gone. There was nothing there but the tree.

Mike followed his gaze. "Oh, shit, is that guy back? The creeper?"

"No." The ice in his chest had melted; humid warmth drenched Alexei. With an effort, he forced his ears upright. "Did you see someone? A fox in…in a long coat?"

"Sounds like a flasher. Oh, uh, a guy who, he'd be naked under the coat and then he'd…" Mike frowned, looking down at the fox. "Are you sure you're okay? What did that guy do?"

He reached out and put a hand on Alexei's shoulder. The fox jumped again and swatted at Mike's arm, knocking it away. "I'm fine," he said, loudly. "I am fine."

Mike held his wrist for a moment, his eyes hurt. "Fine," he said. "Sorry." For a moment, he just stood, the silence between them awkward, and then he turned and walked back.

Alexei's throat closed up. He wanted to run after Mike and thank him, tell him he wanted the Bolt and wanted the touch and wanted the affection. But the remembered glitter of the eye in the shadow held him transfixed, the overcast sky bore down on him, and the dirt when he finally walked forward again felt soft and moist. He scratched at his paw pad, walked past the Bolt without touching it, and sat down alone at the side of the field. He didn't even care that Mike and Kendall were talking, shooting glances his way. He sat where he was until Sol came over to take him home.

On the bus, Sol asked him twice whether he was okay, and by that point Alexei had recovered some of his composure. Even though his heart still beat quickly, he tried to talk to himself logically. His date with Mike was a whole two days away. Anything could happen in that time. He just had to keep control of himself and not act too crazy. He wished he'd thought of this before leaving the park, so he could apologize to Mike, but at least he had the sheep's phone number and could text him. *Thanks for the drink,* he wrote. *I am sorry for acting strange. Thought I saw someone I knew.*

Mike hadn't answered by the time they got home. The rain had increased, so they hurried up to the front of the building. As they slipped in the front door, Sol said, "Hey, I don't mean to press, but, uh, do you know when the picture will be ready?"

"Oh," Alexei said. "It should be soon. I know that we have practice today and the game tomorrow, but I think Thursday for sure."

"Okay," Sol said. "Just wondering."

And Mike wrote back just then saying, *Hey, no problem. Talk to you tomorrow.*

So Alexei felt better, and as Sol was sitting down at the desk, the fox sat on his bed facing the wolf. "Sol," he said. Sol's ears flicked, and then he turned to look at Alexei. "I am sorry if this is difficult, but…when you were having dreams, when things were coming back, as you said…"

Sol looked away, but his ears stayed mostly up and his shoulders mostly squared, not slumping. "Yeah?"

"I know that there were some things…" Alexei stopped. "Did…did you ever think a person might have come back?"

The wolf shook his head in a sharp motion. "I…" He breathed in deeply and then slumped forward as he exhaled. "He did, once. Just for a short time. But he couldn't stay."

"Was that when your…boyfriend…"

"He wasn't ever that," Sol snapped, his head rising to glare at Alexei. A moment later he softened. "I thought he was. Yeah. Niki saved me from him. And then from myself. But he didn't stay."

But the ghost fox had been able to strike the sheep who was going to force himself on Sol, to throw a scared wolf across a bathroom to stop him hurting himself afterwards. And if Niki could do that, what might the ghost of his father do to Alexei? He had already inspired Alexei with courage, had perhaps made him feel disgusted at Mike's—at Mike's sensitivity, the thing Alexei loved about the sheep.

He came close to telling Sol then, right there. But the longing in the wolf's voice when he described Niki coming and going pierced Alexei's heart again. How could he tell Sol that he had succeeded in contacting a ghost? Sol would be jealous, and then perhaps he would redouble his efforts to connect with Niki again, when he should be focusing on dating Mitch here in the real world. Alexei bit his lip with one canine tooth and said, "I wish I could have met him."

He had said that before, and Sol responded as he had the other times. "I do too. I wish he could have gotten another chance."

Alexei nodded, rubbing the flat of his paw along his thigh because it was itching again, and it hurt when he scratched it. "How are things going with Mitch?"

He'd intended it to perk up Sol's spirits, but the black wolf didn't respond with a smile. "Good. He's going home this weekend for a visit with his parents."

"Oh, good." Alexei rubbed his paw harder. "Have you talked to your parents recently?"

Sol turned back to his desk. "Mom, yeah. I talked to Dad a week or so ago. It's just hard to talk to him about my life here, you know? 'I play soccer with some friends…I'm seeing someone…'" He stared at his computer screen. "Just too vague."

"Does he ask questions?"

"No." Sol drummed claws on the desktop. "Still. I feel bad about it. It's just easier not to say anything."

Sol's parents were nice people. They did not drink, they worked hard, they believed their cubs would grow up to be good people like they were. Their disapproval of Sol's homosexuality felt mild to Alexei, and even though he had read that there were places in the States that were better still—Yerba, Port City, Crystal City, Freestone—he was happy to live in a place that did not fear gay people.

He thought that Sol's parents would get over their anti-gay bias. His mother already had come to visit and had asked if Alexei—not Sol—were dating a "nice boy." Sol had talked to his father on the phone a few times, and things seemed to be cordial with them. His father wanted to know if Sol was playing baseball and Sol told him he was playing soccer and softball (the VLGA fielded a softball team that played for beer and fun; Sol played when it didn't conflict with soccer). That seemed to make things all right.

But Sol wanted to share more of his life with his parents. Alexei thought he should just go ahead and do it, but the fox wasn't about to push Sol, not now when the blank space above his bed reminded them both of the tension between them. Before the end of the summer, perhaps, but he had enough to worry about, with Mike, and his sister, and how he would remain friends with Sol. Once those were resolved, he could think about helping Sol deal with his parents.

Her voice had called him back to the wall

What *was* he going to do about Mike? Again, lying in bed, he remembered the dream and Konstantin's demand. Here in the real world, the attraction to Mike was much more clear, and Konstantin's threat diffused. But the sharp feeling, like claws around his heart, at the thought of giving up a life where he could date whomever he wanted—the memory of that remained.

Cat alone of all the people in Samorodka had known his secret. He'd crouched by the rotten wall and seen her russet fur on the other side, shading to ivory at the base of her ear. She had just asked him if he'd wanted to go out with…with…he couldn't even remember the vixen's name now. And he'd said no, and she'd asked why not, that she thought the vixen pretty.

And Alexei had looked at the fur on the other side of the wood and had imagined his words released, traveling that small span, reaching his sister, a confession he could never take back. And he had realized that if he didn't tell her, if he kept it in, it was going to gnaw away his insides until he was nothing but an empty shell. So he had taken a deep breath and said, "I don't think I want to go out with any vixens."

Cat had stayed quiet. She'd asked if he liked that female wolf in his class, and Alexei, embarrassed, had said "Never mind," and tried to crawl back into bed, but her voice had called him back to the wall.

"Oh," she'd said. "I saw about that on the Internet. Are you gay?"

And she'd used the formal term for it, not the derogatory term he had heard on the schoolyard all his life. He'd choked out the single word, "Yes," and leaned against the wall, in the darkness and silence that no longer felt quite so alone.

The next morning, she'd given him an extra-big hug, and he'd forgiven her for breaking his pencils the week before. Whenever they'd fought in the past, it had only lasted as long as it took for one of their parents to heap abuse on them; from that day forward, Alexei had forgiven her nearly everything immediately. Cat, in her turn, aware of what a fragile thing she held, had talked to him gently and even spread rumors at school about what vixen he'd moaned about in his sleep, so people wouldn't suspect.

She'd covered for him when he met with the engineer, distracted his parents while he ran away to Vdansk. He never forgot the hug Cat had given him before he left, nor the words she'd whispered to him. He'd whispered to her that he loved her, and that he would see her again.

Wasn't it worth any price to make those words come true?

Would Cat approve of the price?

He sighed and closed his eyes. Once Cat was safe, he could stop having these thoughts. Her safety was the only thing that could make him give up this part of who he was. He had run out of alternatives; he had no recourse but to accept Konstantin's help. He would keep trying to convince the old soldier that his homophobic attitudes were out of date, and if that did not work, then he hoped Mike would wait for him. As much as the principle of giving up his right to love bothered him, the ordeal shouldn't last more than a month or two.

Unless, a voice whispered in the back of his head, *you cannot make Konstantin go away.*

Chapter 19

When Nicholas had been born to Sasha, as Alexander III was known before he became Tsar, there were celebrations throughout the country, but the celebrations were muted. We were of course grateful to the mercy of God for a male heir to the throne, but in those days, even with the best doctors available, it was always in the back of our minds that a sickness or an accident could carry off the young, vulnerable cub at any time. With each day that passed, our hearts grew easier, and I recall that on the night when young Nicholas celebrated his eighth month, one of my comrades in the Guards turned to me and said that our Emperors would continue on.

Nearly eleven years later, I mourned Tatya's death in the company of two of my peers who had also lost cubs. We commiserated with vodka, talked of how excellent our wives were and how little they deserved our ill fortune. The other soldiers spoke meaningless comforts, but in their words we could all see their true feelings: "Why are these people cursed by God?" As though it were our fault, as though our thoughts and actions were transmittable to our newborns.

My comrades in misfortune had their families gathered around them, with support and reassurance and love. Vasily attended Tatya's funeral, but shed no tears, and when it was over, he slapped me between the shoulders with that great tiger paw and said that I must leave off dreaming of what might have been and immediately go to work on producing another cub. Mariya's family clove to her, but clearly shared the view of the soldiers, that Tatya's death had its root in the fault of one of the parents. Only one, mind you.

I grieved in my heart, but remained outwardly stoic. To lose a cub is a terrible thing, but I had lost two parents, and I knew that in life, losses and gifts come at the whim of the Almighty, and to grieve overmuch is to question His plan. Though Vasily's sentiment was not tactfully phrased, I understood the message: go on, live life; that is what a good soldier must do. I endeavored to follow those sentiments and to convey them also to my lovely wife.

And yet, in the wake of Tatya's death, Mariya fell away from me into a deep depression. Her lovely tail grew filthy unless I washed it, her fur matted and coarse, and her ears sagged as though bereft of any life. She had rarely known loss, so although I spoke of God's plan and the life we were creating together, she did no more than nod and stare out of the window. Our servant was little help, slinking around the house telling Mariya that the constant snow that followed Tatya's death was "frozen tears." Nonsense. God does not weep for the deaths of the innocent any more than the Emperor weeps for the death of his soldiers. We mourn because they have passed from this world and we have lost the joy of their presence. But they are not beyond His sight. God sees them every day He looks out upon his kingdom, and the Emperor sees the spirits of his fallen soldiers in the grandeur and glory that is Siberia. He feels it every day in the breath of the land, in the reports from his ministers of the harvest and the planting, the plowing and the sowing. We who have lost them, we may weep, but God and the Emperor are above such things. And in the end, we shall be reunited with the ones we love in God's kingdom, where there are no more tears.

Mariya did not share these views. She received her sisters and her mother, but none of them, even with their prettier, softer words, could move her any better than I could. They left with barely a word to me, speaking among themselves of how she had changed, how she had been so joyful before her marriage. They spoke in low tones, but being foxes themselves, they knew well how their words would carry, and knew full well that I heard each one.

So I ceased to call upon them. They had accepted me as their family in our wedding ceremony and then turned their backs on me. Mariya, in her state, would not call upon them either, and so they faded from our lives.

But I continued my work with the Guards, where the young Tsarevich expressed his sympathy at my loss with an eloquence far beyond his eleven years. I thought him so charming then, thought that his way with people was a strength and not a sign of his weakness. He had no need to be strong at that age. The other cubs deferred to him; he had no challenges in which to prove himself, no father striking him to temper his steel. I did not see this at the time. I saw only the grandson of our Emperor, bestowing his favor upon me.

I said to Mariya, look, the Tsarevich wishes us well. He knows that this tragedy is but a small one in our lives. We could yet have a cub worthy of him. I professed my love for her, told her that God would not let two people such as us, full of devotion, remain barren. I promised to do all in my power to keep her safe, that the doctor would attend our next cub from the moment of birth.

My passion stirred her, and six months after Tatya's death, in the bright dawn of summer, she smiled for the first time and took my paw in hers. I felt again the happiness I had when I married her, now made stronger by the misfortunes we had suffered and borne together. I saw that happiness reflected in her eyes, and I knew that all was right with the world. Watched by God and the Emperor, Mariya and I would rebuild our life from the debris of our tragedy. Her depression was but a passing weakness, and the strength I had seen in her now rose again to the surface.

I had given myself wholly to the Guard, but when the leaves turned in autumn and Mariya declared that she would be ready to accept another cub, I took a leave from the Guard to go abroad with her, the first time we had done so. The doctor recommended a change in climate for her health, but my dear would not go unless I accompanied her. So we traveled to the south, to a hot spring known for its healthful effects, and we spent two lovely weeks there.

And yet we were not blessed with a cub. She sank into depression again once a month, and all my efforts to cheer her spirit were in vain for some three to four days. She cried that she was not meant to be a mother, that she would never know the joy of holding her cub to her and watching her son or daughter grow. I told her she was foolish, that one as lovely and caring as her could never be without someone to look after. Days went by, the sun rose and set, and she accepted my words, and kissed me, and for another month her smile returned.

It was nearly a year later that this cycle was broken, in the heat of the following summer, when she rushed into my arms one morning and told me that we would have our family after all. I held her close and laughed with her, our noses and whiskers brushing, our tails curled around each other. And the first thing I thought was, I must tell the Tsarevich Nicholas. He will be so happy for us.

Chapter 20

Crumbling buildings surround them, gaping windows rimmed with shards of glass and tatters of curtains. The wind keens and cries through cracks in the stone, chilling Alexei's nose and ears in gusts. He curls his tail around his legs and shifts his feet on loose gravel and dry, musty-smelling earth. Above him, clouds gather thick and black, but the stones glow with a soft, eerie light, as though at sunset. No matter where he turns, though, there is no sun to be found.

Konstantin stands in the ruined street next to him, a head taller. His coat snaps in the wind and his sash streams out behind him like a tail, though his own tail remains properly tucked beneath the coat. Now his scent is strong in the air; now it is not only Alexei's whiskers and eyes that acknowledge his reality. He looks down his long muzzle at Alexei, the scar over his eye wrinkling. He does not have to ask the question.

Yes, *Alexei says.* I will…I will give up…only save Cat.

The soldier nods once, curtly. I will do what I can.

Why? *bursts out of Alexei.*

The unscarred eyebrow rises, the ears come up to stand straight. Because I promise to do so.

No, I mean. *He struggles for words, and it is as though he is speaking English again for the first time, though the conversation is in Siberian.* Why do you care? About Cat, about me. What is it to you if I date Mi—males or vixens?

The older fox glowers, and his muscles tighten in a way that sets off warnings Alexei has not felt in a year. He steps back, tail curling tighter, and half-raises an arm. But Konstantin does not move any further, simply gathers himself and speaks, his voice chill and precise. Because once a soldier took me from a path that led to damnation and raised me up. He gave me a chance to be more than my parents could.

Alexei swallows, encouraged somewhat by this opening. I have that chance too, *he says.* In this time, you know, it is not…as it was. I know, in your time, boys who like boys are—

There were places where it was tolerated, *Konstantin says.* Not spoken of, not encouraged, but tolerated.

The curl of his lip shows what he thinks of those places. Alexei has encountered this argument, and on the Internet and in the VLGA he had heard counterpoints. It is simply love, *he says.* Affection. You might not be familiar with the way it is expressed, but—

Love! *Konstantin glares, then turns away.* What matters love in all this? Love is for—love is for— *He hesitates.* Dreamers.

Behind the older fox, a section of building slides to the ground as silently as in an old film. Dust rises from it, but does not approach the foxes. Alexei watches it spin into clouds and tendrils, half-expecting it will form letters. But no; that was Konstantin's doing, and the soldier stands before him now, staring into the distance, his ears flat though the wind has died to a flutter. Alexei says, tentatively, What about your vixen? Maria?

Once I was a dreamer. *The fox's voice, hollow, drops the words like glass.*

Alexei, afraid of the edges that further questions might bring, changes the subject. You can help my sister?

Konstantin's attention snaps back to him and the breeze rises again, gains strength. Yes, *he says.* If you live a virtuous life. I will not help someone who is unwilling to help himself.

But, *Alexei begins, and then flattens his ears and squints up as wind buffets his muzzle, as the dark eyes of Konstantin fix his. He takes a step back. Gravel crunches under his feet, and he clasps his paws together in front of him.*

You have given your word, *Konstantin says.* Do not be forsworn.

But it is not so simple…

The clouds thicken; the light on the stones dies. Konstantin raises an arm and points it at Alexei, the coat flapping about his legs like a great beast reaching out to pull Alexei in. You have given your word!

Alexei's heart pounds and he takes another step back. Gravel slides and slithers under his paws and he falls backward, hitting the ground with a snap—

Chapter 21

—that woke him with a jolt. He clutched the sheets to himself in the darkness, panting hard. The noises of construction rumbled in the background, but in the other bed, Sol slept peacefully. Alexei lay back in his bed, closed his eyes, and tried not to think about what he had promised.

All day Wednesday, he was jumpy. He thought he saw a fox in a long coat behind the newsstand when they passed; he thought he saw the glint of medals on the homeless coyote who was only a shadow until they approached. It didn't help that the day was overcast and drizzly, grey and hazy, so that even Sol, walking at his side to the bus, sometimes blurred and seemed to be someone else.

The only thing Sol said on the way to the bus was, "If this rain keeps up, it'll be slippery tonight," and the only thing he said on the bus was, "Have a good day," when he left. Alexei, eyes skittering to shadows and sniffing the air for scents of earth or military coats or any trace of Konstantin's severe scent, only said, "Yes," to the first, and waved to the second.

On the bus, and later, at work, he felt more secure, but even at the warehouse, he thought he caught a whiff of earth. He froze for a solid ten seconds, tail bristled, until the reassuring scent of one of his co-workers overwhelmed it with a cheery, "Working hard or hardly working?" Alexei shook his head and gave a short laugh, and delivered the box.

He didn't talk to his co-workers about his private life. As far as they were concerned, he was just a nice, single fox. So would there really be a big difference in his life at work, if he followed Konstantin's orders? Here, his sexuality meant little or nothing. That thought, which he'd begun to reassure himself, only made him wonder what part of him was real, if he could pretend that nothing inside existed and live as a shell of a fox, smiling to the world over an empty, deserted soul.

That dark mood persisted as he changed for the game, arrived at the park, and refused pre-game beers. Sol left him alone, but Mike came to talk to him. Alexei breathed in the warm, comfortable smell of the sheep, accentuated in the rain, and for a short time, that calmed him. *Tell him you can't make it for the date*, he kept telling himself. But even when the conversation paused, Alexei felt so grateful for Mike's presence, so happy that the sheep was talking to him after his behavior the day before, that he could not bring himself to cancel the dinner. So they talked about how their days had gone, and that the team they were playing, an informal team from

Vidalia College, looked pretty fit, but also had an impressive pile of empty beer cans stacked over on their sideline already.

It was a good sign that Kendall didn't come over to bother them. He was over by the cooler in a white t-shirt he'd gotten from a 10K benefit run, talking to Sol. Alexei didn't know whether Sol was intentionally occupying the marten, but he was grateful, because in his current state, he didn't know how well he would be able to handle Kendall's indirect insults. In addition, the t-shirt was far tighter than it needed to be.

"Oh, hey," Mike said. "That muskrat from the Peaches showed up with some other guy."

"Vic," Alexei said. He looked up and wiped rain from his eyes. Colin had walked up in a windbreaker and baseball cap, and beside him was another figure, probably a weasel of some sort, but it was hard to tell in the hat and jacket. Could be a rat; Alexei couldn't see his tail. They looked around and then the muskrat pointed at Alexei. He raised a paw, but didn't move toward them.

"You want to go talk to them?" Mike started to move in that direction.

Alexei shook his head. "I want to focus on the game."

"Okay. I'll tell 'em." Mike paused, and then wrapped his arm around Alexei's shoulder. "Good luck," he said, his muzzle next to Alexei's ear. "Play great. I know you can."

When he left, the absence of his warmth almost made Alexei run after him. Why did Mike have to be that way, why? Why was he making this so hard? Why couldn't Alexei just tell him, I can't go out with you because I'm trying to save my sister?

He squeezed his paws together and rocked back and forth, tail curling and uncurling. Because that sounded crazy was why. He didn't even know if Konstantin would be able to help Cat. Wasn't Alexei doing all he could? He would call Rozalina again tonight, and she would be able to help him, and then he wouldn't have to keep his promise. Konstantin could yell and give him nightmares but Alexei wouldn't care, not if Mike would stand next to him and whisper warm words into his ear with the soft touch that made him feel able to do anything.

Running out onto the field soothed him, even with the grass wet and the drizzle making it harder to see. All he had to worry about out here was the white and black ball, and the tiger and the white rat and the raccoon in bright green shorts who wanted to get it past him. Kendall chattered away in goal again, but Alexei ignored the marten as he usually did, focusing on the play ahead of him. For the first time this summer, running onto the football field felt familiarly like an escape, a haven from a world he preferred not to think about.

The college kids were good. They had probably been better before they'd emptied the case of beer, but they still provided enough of a challenge that Alexei was able to lose himself in the flow of the game. When he felt the urge to run up and attack the play, he hesitated half a second, deciding whether it was really the right thing to do or if it was just his borrowed confidence pushing him. And sometimes he moved up, and sometimes he didn't.

Whatever he was doing produced good results. Twice he intercepted passes, and once ran up to break up an attack that got around Sol. He and Sol worked pretty well together, and at the half-hour mark, even Kendall had little to say. When Alexei glanced at the sidelines, Colin and his weasel friend looked absorbed in the game. Even when he didn't look, he felt their scrutiny.

During the five-minute break, Alexei talked to Liza, not about the game, but about Mike. She asked when they were going out, and he smiled and told her, forgetting that he had promised to break the date. She clapped him on the shoulder and said, "*Good,*" in Siberian, and he stared at her, his train of thought broken even as she went on talking in English.

Her fur was wet with the rain, the narrow summer brown of her muzzle dark and striated with dripping water. He caught himself staring at her small ears, at the curve of her smile, and then down to her tight-fitting shirt, her arms, her hips, her legs. He had never before thought of her this way and it disturbed him, to the point that he interrupted her in the middle of a sentence and said, "Sorry, I have to go," even though they hadn't ended the short break yet. He jogged back alone to the field, head spinning.

Was this Konstantin's doing? Was he able to change the way Alexei looked at his friends as well as changing how he played on the field? Or was Alexei making himself see females as sexy? If he took the credit for playing more aggressively, if he felt he had simply taken cues from Konstantin and had made himself play better, then did he not also have to take the blame for now looking at Liza as though he wanted to date her instead of Mike?

No, it wasn't him. He stood on the wet grass and wiped water from his eyes, pressing his wet fur down. The other players filtered back onto the field, and Kendall and Sol jogged together toward Alexei's end. He ignored them both, making up his mind that he was going to play more aggressively, and that that was going to come from him, not from Konstantin. He would prove that he could play hard, and then he would go to the sidelines and he would talk to Mike, not Liza, and everything would be all right.

His wet tail slapped from side to side as they started play, and for a little while, he fulfilled his promise to himself. He charged plays, and though sometimes that left Kendall alone behind him, Alexei played well enough to break up the attacks of the college students each time. Kendall chirped at him about taking risks, and Alexei ignored him.

It was about ten minutes from the end of the game that Alexei and Sol both ran out to counter an attack. It went to Alexei's side, and he was on course to intercept it when a cold breeze struck his chest, through the damp fur, and chilled him inside as though it had penetrated his skin. He staggered, stopped, and then saw, limned in unearthly light on the patch of grass just behind the opposing goal, a fox in a navy blue military coat with a gold sash, medals sparkling through the rain.

Alexei saw him clearly, but for only a moment, and then one of the college kids, a raccoon, plowed into him, shoulder to Alexei's chest. The fox saw grey sky and smelled the raccoon, strongly, as the sound around him seemed to die out, leaving him in suspended silence for a count that seemed much longer than two seconds.

He slammed into the ground on his side, his ribs twinging. His nose drove into the grass, and almost immediately, he sprang to his feet, now unable to smell anything but the thick, herbal odor of grass. He ran after the players in time to see a perfect pass and kick from the corner of the goal that soared past Kendall and into the net.

When Alexei turned, there was nothing behind the opposing goal save for a celebration.

The game ended in a tie, and only Kendall seemed to mind, stalking off the field while the rest of the VLGA were shaking paws and hands with the college kids. The marten stood by himself while Mike, Liza, Sol, and the others made their way back to the beer cooler. The drizzle continued, but the air was warm and muggy, so they didn't mind standing around getting damp. "Hell, we're already soaked," Alice said as Alexei approached them, slowly, still looking back at the opposing goal, and then all around when there was nothing there.

The rain and fading light placed a shadow behind every stand of trees, making it impossible for him to see anything properly, and the closer he got to his team, the more the scents of wet fur masked anything else that might be around. He kept his ears up, flicking them to clear the water out every few seconds, listening for anything over the soft background noise of rain.

The muskrat and weasel walked toward him, both smiling. Colin raised a paw, and Alexei shook off the confusion of Konstantin to change course to meet them. Liza, who'd been waiting for him, nudged Mike, and the two of them beamed through the drizzle.

"Hi, Alexei," Colin said, and indicated the weasel. "This is Vic. He's the team captain and also our head scout."

"Pleasure to meet you," Alexei said, and extended a paw.

The weasel shook with a firm, wet grip. "Looked good out there. Got distracted once or twice, didn't ya?"

"Er—" He was trying to figure out how to explain that he didn't expect an ancient Siberian ghost to appear at most of his games when a sharp voice interrupted him. Alexei flicked his ears backwards.

"Hey!" Kendall, mud spatters decorating his white t-shirt, strode toward the fox. Alexei lay his ears back and shifted his feet to stand defensively.

Liza hurried quickly to intercept the marten. "Leave him alone," she said.

Vic and Colin glanced at each other. Alexei felt a chill in his chest, and he clenched his fists, then relaxed them. "I am fine," he told Liza, and stepped up to face Kendall. "What?"

"I told you to stay back." The pine marten stopped a couple steps in front of Alexei. Sol came up on Kendall's right, and Mike was plodding slowly over, two or three of the others behind him. "I told you, and you still ran out there—"

"He did great," Liza said.

"It was not my fault." Alexei edged forward to stay in front of Liza. It annoyed him that she was trying to fight his fight. He was aware that the annoyance was not completely rational, and yet it gnawed at him like a flea bite.

"You let through the attack that tied the game!"

"So what?" Liza said. "It's a game! We are not in some Premier League. We play for fun. You remember fun, yes, Kendall?"

"I told him to stay back!" The pine marten yelled now, pointing at Alexei. "If he'd just played a little more conservatively—"

"Or if you could block a shot," Alexei said, deliberately taunting, because Kendall had blocked about six shots during the game. "I take this game seriously." After all, Alexei's ability to stay in this country might be riding on how well he played, and the marten was trying to dress him down in front of the people who could make that decision. What did Kendall have at stake except puffed-up pride? Behind their group, the muskrat and weasel stood the way strangers would watch a family quarrel, unwilling to intervene, unwilling to look away.

"Hey, look," Sol said, placing a paw on Kendall's arm.

The pine marten shook him off, glaring up at Alexei. "What did you say?"

"I slipped," Alexei said. "I fell. But still they had to kick past you to score. Did you slip? Or did you just miss?"

"I had no help!" Kendall shouted.

Sol grabbed Kendall's arm again. "Calm down," he said. "Alexei made a mistake, it's not a big deal."

"I made a mistake?" Alexei lifted his muzzle to stare at Sol. "I made a *mistake*?"

"You slipped." Sol let go of Kendall, who was trying to twist his arm away anyway, and shrugged. "That's all I meant."

The accusation stung. He'd thought Sol would always support him, as he had always wanted to support the black wolf. He felt the familiar urge to curl up, step away, and nurse his grievances, but it was overwhelmed now by a fire in his chest, indignation that none of these people appreciated him, with the possible exception of Liza. "Well," he said coldly, "you ran out there too."

"I told him to go attack," Kendall said, stepping forward and gesturing back at Sol. Alexei could smell his breath, hot and sour with the aftertaste of beer. "If you'd stayed back where you should have been, even if you'd slipped, you would've slowed them down enough for him to get back, or for me to get into position."

"Not my fault you were not in position." Alexei's chest was tight, but his head was cold and clear. "Not my fault you know nothing of basic football strategy."

"You think you're so clever because you're a fox, because you grew up playing soccer. Soccer." He jabbed a finger through the air toward Alexei. "We call it *soccer* here, not football. And it's about being part of a *team*."

"Hey." Mike came to stand near Liza and Alexei, facing Sol and Kendall.

Alexei ignored the big sheep, letting his frustration out at Kendall. "What would you know about team? Is all about you, always."

The pine marten wiped rain out of his eyes, raised a paw, and waved it around. "Says the guy who just runs off and does his own thing."

"Always showing off," Alexei said. "Always puffing out your fur. Always putting down others."

"At least I have something to show off about," Kendall snapped back.

Liza stepped between them. "Hey," she said, lifting her paws to both shoulders. "We are all friends. Have a beer and we will talk about the picnic in two weeks—"

Kendall slapped her paw away. "This isn't about being friends. It's about winning games."

He said a few more words, but Alexei didn't hear them, because his ears were rushing with more than wind now, the cold clarity wavering dangerously. He put himself between Kendall and Liza, chest bumping the marten's. "Don't strike her," he said in a low, iron voice that he barely recognized as his own.

"Strike her?" Kendall leaned his weight into Alexei, smirking. "Is that some Siberian thing? She touched me first."

Sol reached around to try to pull Alexei away, and in pulling out of his grip, Alexei bumped into Kendall, pushing him back. Later, he would admit to himself that it was not entirely accidental, but he had not planned to do it when he pulled back from Sol.

The pine marten reacted immediately, shoving Alexei in the chest with both paws, knocking him back into Liza. She clutched at his shirt, missed, and fell.

The rushing sound in Alexei's ears got louder, as though the rain were heavier, and the edges of his vision frayed and blurred. The world took on a reddish tinge, so that the mud spatters on Kendall's shirt became the dark rust color of bloodstains. Sol was speaking, but Alexei only saw his muzzle moving; he heard none of the words. He panted, tension coiling in his chest like a spring, and before he knew it, he'd cocked a fist and punched Kendall in the stomach.

It felt good. His blood sang, and the impact, the whoof of breath leaving the pine marten, the flesh against his fist, all rang with triumph. He watched Kendall stagger and fall on his butt on the ground, and smiled. A large hand came to rest on his shoulder and he left it there for the half-second that the pine marten actually stayed down.

And then Kendall bounced back up, fists coming right for Alexei, and the fox had only a moment to adopt a defensive posture before meeting those fists. But Kendall was weak and didn't really know how to fight, and Alexei blocked most of the blows aimed at his face, sending a couple more into the marten's gut. The joy of the fight blazed up in him even as hands tried to pull him away from Kendall. "Weak," he spat at the marten, easily knocking aside another punch, and then both his arms were held from behind just as Sol was holding Kendall.

At Alexei's insult, Kendall twisted and writhed and squirmed free. He leaped on the fox, his weight tearing Alexei out of Mike's arms, bearing them both to the ground with a hard thud that crushed Alexei's ribs, drove the breath from him.

"I'll show you weak," Kendall snarled, and Alexei felt sharp teeth close in his ear.

Never bite in a fight. Unless in close quarters, and then tear away quickly. If someone bites you, they have made their head a target. Hold it. Strike it.

The words came to him in a flash, in images and barked orders—

—and memories, soldiers grappling in close combat under a grey sky, flakes of snow drifting between them—

—that he processed in the length of time it took him to shift his weight to roll to the side of the ear Kendall was biting, and then drive his head down sharply into soft flesh and the bone beneath it with an impact that hurt his skull. He brought a fist up to the trapped jaws and got in one good blow with a satisfying snap before the hold loosened, and then people were dragging him away again, across the slick ground. Grass and blood filled his nose along with the smell of wet pine marten, and he turned his head to one side and spat as he struggled to his feet.

The first thing he did was look sharply about him, ears perked for any further threat. But Sol was helping the pine marten to his feet, and Kendall had one paw to his mouth, looking dazed.

Mike's comforting bass, anxious, asking how he was. Liza, higher and sharper: "Your ear."

"I am fine," Alexei said, though his head was ringing.

"Oo oke aye oof!" Kendall said, trying to focus on Alexei.

"It's over." Sol looked between the pine marten and fox, and then past them, at someone Alexei couldn't see.

"He broke," Kendall said, still holding his jaw, "my tooth!"

"You bit my ear." All the ice of a Samorodka winter was in Alexei's voice.

"Did not," Kendall muttered.

Liza's fingers brushed the soft, wet fur around Alexei's ear. "It's bleeding right here. Definitely a bite."

He had had his ears bitten before, on the playground; they healed well with iodine and bandages, but walking around with bandaged ears was not a badge of honor, as bandages on the battlefield might be. Still, Liza's touch felt good, and then he turned and realized that it was Mike holding his ear, Liza simply looking on.

The urge to pull back, jerk his head away, spread through his muscles like fire, but equally strong was his urge to lean into Mike, to let the sheep take care of him. He shuddered with the conflicting pulls of those violent impulses, and Mike let go of his ear. "Does it hurt?" he asked.

"A little." The cold in his voice would not thaw. He forced out warmer words. "Thank you."

Kendall had his mouth open for several of the others to examine his teeth. "Yeah," Alice said. "That left canine is loose, probably gonna fall out. Shouldn't have bit him."

"Didn't," Kendall muttered again, as best he could with his mouth open, and then, when he snapped it shut, "He just slammed his head into my jaw."

"Look," Mike said, "it's not worth getting this worked up over a game."

Kendall leaned on Sol, and the black wolf supported him. "I feel kind of woozy," he said. "Your friend has a thick head."

"You should get some rest," Sol said.

"Maybe something to eat," Kendall replied. "If I keep it down, then I probably don't have a concussion."

"Is your head so soft you get a concussion from grass?" Alexei said.

"Hey." Mike grabbed him, turned him away. The sheep's hands felt good, and again, Alexei felt the warring impulses in him. Liza was there, too. He should go with her, shouldn't he?

No, that was ridiculous. He shook his head, slowly. Liza didn't like boys.
Better than a perversion.

She wasn't even a vixen. They couldn't have a family.

You fight like a soldier and then renege on your promise. What about Caterina?

The promise felt unfair, a pledge made with his sister's life held over his head. Mike was here, Mike was real. He set his teeth, staring at the ram's white fur and golden horns until he felt again the draw to stay with him, to follow through on their date. Behind him, Sol and Kendall were talking, and Liza was saying something to Alice, but Mike was focused just on him, with a soft, "I'm not mad at you. I didn't hear who started it, but I saw Kendall charging at you, so...talk to me, Alexei."

Do not think you can abandon your promise so easily.

His resolve faltered. The implied threat prickled his fur, chilled his ears, but he said, silently, *I am only keeping a friendship, not breaking my promise—and you have not kept yours, either.*

In that moment, when a gust of wind blew rain into his face and he had to wipe his eyes clear, the urge for him to court Liza vanished as though blown away. He almost fell against Mike then, almost shook and collapsed into his soft strength, but he saw a shape among the trees of the park, a fox in a military coat, walking away. Leaving him—no, not leaving him. Not conceding, not surrendering; preparing for their next battle.

He straightened, called on his own inner strength, and focused his attention on Mike again. "Thank you," he said, stretching his mouth into a smile. "I think I should go home."

"Don't go home just 'cause of him."

Alexei shook his head. "I have caused trouble here, and I think it is best to let everyone cool down." Though he knew they were gone, he turned anyway, to look for the muskrat and weasel. There was no sign of them.

Mike followed his look. "The Peaches guys? They must've taken off. Well, I'm sure they'll get in touch with…"

Of course they would not. What team needed a somewhat-talented player who got into fights? Alexei had always felt that their consideration of him had been at least partly motivated by charity, and here he had shown himself to be belligerent and violent; he had punched Kendall, unmistakably escalating what had been just a shoving match. As clearly as if he had seen it, he knew that Colin and Vic had looked at each other and come to agreement without speaking. And he knew what Mike had only realized on the cusp of finishing his sentence: that the muskrat's connection to the team had been Kendall.

It took a great effort to keep his shoulders square as he turned back. He put a paw out to the rain, and wiped the fur around his ears. The place where Kendall had bitten him still ached, but it wasn't bad. His fingers came back smelling of blood, but only a little now.

Mike searched his eyes and reached for his paw. Holding it, not shaking it. "I'll see you tomorrow night?"

Alexei swallowed. "I will call you," he said. "I may not feel up to it."

Mike's eyes creased in disappointment, and Alexei's heart sank. "Well," the sheep said, "I guess I understand. But I'd still like to have that date. I can maybe help you figure out how to stay in the country."

"I will try," Alexei whispered. But if Caterina's well-being hung in the balance, there was no question.

"You've got my number."

"Hey," Sol called over, interrupting them. "I'm going to take Kendall over to Starbucks on the corner there." He pointed through the trees and the drizzle, where a green-and-white sign glowed. "You coming?"

Alexei shook his head slowly, again. "I will not."

"All right. I'll see you at home." Sol turned his back and slipped an arm around the marten's chest. Kendall draped a paw over Sol's shoulder and leaned on him, and then, as they left, the marten looked over his shoulder with a malicious smile that set Alexei's wet fur to prickling.

Mike stood at his side, and Liza came closer as well. "It seems Kendall has given up on you," she said to Mike.

"Yeah." Mike, too, looked through the rain at the black wolf and pine marten. "I suppose when I talked to Alexei at the Gameplay the other night, he didn't like that."

"Good riddance," Liza said.

"Oh, he's not so bad," Mike said. "I like him."

Alexei stayed silent. He watched Kendall lean on Sol, watched the pine marten's paw slide lower on Sol's side as they crossed behind a tree, toward the Starbucks and out of sight. He did not feel as though he had won anything.

Chapter 22

Meg poked her head out of her room with a clink of earrings. "If you guys didn't have dinner, there's leftovers...What happened to wolfy-boy?"

Alexei closed the front door behind him and moved over to drip on the kitchen floor. "He is looking after Kendall."

So Meg asked what happened, and he told her, and she clapped her paws together when he told her he punched Kendall. "That's the guy who was mackin' on your sheep, right?"

"I...suppose so." He grimaced and rubbed his ear, where the pain had steadily increased. He had stopped at a pharmacy on the way home and couldn't find iodine, so he asked one of the cashiers for something to put on an ear bite, and she'd given him a tube that he hadn't looked at. He pulled the tube out of the bag and squeezed a greyish paste onto a finger, then rubbed it on his ear. "But that was not all that happened."

So he told her the rest as well, including the departure of the people who might have hired him to play soccer. She gaped at him open-mouthed as he washed the excess salve off his fingers. "You want a hoop to go in that hole in your ear?" she said when he was done.

"There is no hole," he said. "I think. The skin is broken, but..." he scraped at the bite with a claw and winced, "the ear is not pierced."

"You should," she said. "You'd look good with a pierced ear. So what pushed you to fight? I never heard of you getting in a fight."

He crossed to the bathroom and stripped his wet shirt off, keeping the wounded ear folded down. "I fought in Samorodka," he said, although the way he'd fought Kendall had been very different, and he was trying hard not to think about where that had come from. Thinking about Samorodka also reminded him that now he might have to return there.

"And this after you got 'in his face' at the game place the other night."

He folded both ears back. "I have to take off my pants," he said stiffly. "Perhaps you should go back into your room."

She turned her back. "I won't look. But I think maybe you're tryin' not to answer the question. You didn't the other day, either."

"What question?" He didn't want to just take his pants off while she was there, but he had already said he was going to, so he had really no choice. He unfastened them and slid them down his legs.

"The question of what's gotten into you. You used to be easygoing, more cheerful. You smiled a lot more and joked with me." He didn't answer.

"Look, nothing happened when we did that ritual the other night, you know. I don't know if you've talked yourself into thinking Niki is speaking to you, or," her paws made air quotes, "'empowering' you somehow. But nothing happened. It's all coming from you."

"You don't know," he said, and then stopped. He kicked free of his pants and threw them into the hamper.

"Ha." She half-turned, enough that he could see her grin spreading her whiskers. "So you do think something happened."

To put off answering, he walked quickly past her into his bedroom and grabbed an old pair of sweatpants Sol had given him. He jammed his legs into them and stood there, wondering whether he could just stand here and wait her out, or if he should try running to the shower. What he really wanted was just to towel his tail dry—it was dragging water all over the carpet—and then go to bed and not answer any questions about Konstantin or Mike or the muskrat or the ritual.

Meg said from the bedroom door, "I'm sticking my head in in a minute, so you better get on whatever you want to be wearing."

"Don't come in," he said automatically, annoyed that she had forestalled him.

"You've got fifteen seconds."

"I need to dry my tail."

She didn't say anything, but he heard her walk away. He barely had time to feel relieved before she returned, her black-furred face grinning from behind one of their green towels. She stood in the doorway and threw it at him. "So tell me. What do you think has been happening?"

He scowled, gathered up his tail, and wrapped it in the towel, losing himself in the pleasant feeling of rubbing the moisture from the fur. "It is probably nothing," he said, staring down at the green cloth slowly darkening with the moisture it was absorbing.

"What is probably nothing?"

"Dreams," he said, slowly, pushing the towel down toward the tip of his tail, which dripped onto the carpet. He curled it up so it would drip into the towel.

"Like Sol had?" She leaned against the door frame, her eyes fixed on him.

He shook his head. "I do not think so." When he looked up, she had her eyebrows raised and was making a "go on" gesture. He sighed. "Sol told us he was dreaming, what, that he *was* Niki?" She nodded. "In my dreams I am talking *to* someone."

"And this someone is…?"

Alexei shook his head again. "Do you think it is possible," he said, "that I might be imagining conversations?"

"If they're all dreams," Meg said, "of course. If you're seeing him in real life…" She waved a paw back and forth. "You might be having hallucinations."

"That is bad." Alexei had gotten to the tip of his tail and held it wrapped in the towel. He squeezed his paws around it. In one respect it would be reassuring if Konstantin were only a product of his own mind. In another, though…he would rather the old soldier were a ghost than imagine that his own mind were going to so much trouble to torment him. "It is also bad to listen to the dreams?"

Meg tapped the door frame. "Are they telling you to kill the district attorney?"

"What?"

She waved a paw. "Old States history."

"No." He shook his head. "They are telling me not to do things."

"Dreams are created by the subconscious. And you know, you're under a lot of stress. You and Sol are fighting, and if you don't get this soccer gig, you might be deported, and then there's the thing with your sister, which is probably a lot more stressful than you're letting on."

The towel had absorbed so much water that when he released his tail and ran his paws through the fur, the tip was still damp. But it wasn't dripping, so Alexei let it go, hanging down to the carpet. "Sol and I are not fighting," he said.

"Come off it." Meg's tail swished. "You guys used to talk all the time coming back from games, going off to work. He's upset about his picture and you're stressed about it. How's the thing with your sister going?"

Alexei had the wild urge to say, *It depends on a dream.* Instead he told her about Cat's voice mail, and Meg sighed when he was done.

"Yeah," she said. "That'll give you a whole steaming pile of stress. You want some weed?"

In his month living with Meg, even though she was considerate enough to smoke when the canids were out, or else outside on their stoop, he had smelled the distinct herbal odor of marijuana, and had deduced what Meg meant by "weed." Back in Samorodka, they had thought of marijuana as something that rich people did in Moskva, and he had not yet gotten used to the idea that high school and college students routinely smoked it here. "No, thank you."

"Better than alcohol," Meg said.

Alexei shook his head. "I do not want a drink, either," he said softly.

"Well, look." She unfolded her arms and rested her paws on her hips. "If you want to talk about shit, and Sol's not around or still pissed at you, you know you can bother me." His expression must have shown his skepticism, because she said, "I promise I won't make fun of you all that much."

That got him to smile. "If only I could believe that."

"Hey," she said, "I can be nice. Ask Sol."

"Sol says that if your tongue were any sharper your cheek would be pierced too."

She laughed. "Yeah, well. Not gonna say he's completely wrong. But I can keep it in."

He dropped the towel to the floor, and she made a 'tch' noise as she walked over to pick it up. "I'll toss this in the hamper."

She lifted her tail for balance as she bent over, moving fluidly, and he watched the lines of her body, barely concealed by her baggy clothing. The thought stirred in him that he could mollify Konstantin with her rather than Liza. If he asked her, would she pretend to date him? Would pretending be enough for Konstantin? Or could the fox hear his thoughts even now, would he know that Alexei was trying to trick him?

The older fox, if he were present or watching, remained quiet. Alexei felt a flare of anger that Konstantin had so invaded his life that he couldn't even look at a friend without seeing a potential mate. He'd lived with Sol for nearly two months and they were only friends. Sexuality wasn't about sleeping with the first available person of the correct gender; it was about finding the right person. And Meg was definitely a friend, no more than that.

No, this scheme of Konstantin's to get him to be straight in exchange for Cat's safety, even if he had agreed on it, was not right. He could not change his nature and the old ghost was wrong to ask.

Anyway, Meg had a boyfriend, or a sort-of boyfriend, and remembering him gave Alexei an idea about how to get rid of Konstantin. He was careful not to think overtly about it. "Athos is visiting this weekend?" he asked.

At the door, she paused and nodded. "That's the plan."

"I look forward to meeting him," Alexei said. "I would like to ask him where he learned of the ritual."

"Oh," Meg said with a paw on the door frame. "I wouldn't ask him about that. He's real touchy about it."

Alexei frowned. "He is..." He flexed his paws in front of him. In his preoccupied state, it took him a moment to properly translate "touchy."

"It's just that he does a lot of research into historical things," Meg said. "He's always paranoid that someone's going to steal it. I know, like there are people out there just dying to publish his formula for getting rid of vampires. Come to think of it," she rubbed her chin, "I guess some high schools might want that. But no, he's ridiculous about it."

"It can do no harm to ask." He scratched at the fur between his pads. It felt like some of the mud from the game was still in there. Maybe he should shower after all.

Meg looked on the verge of saying something more, and then she just said, "You know, he's…he's touchy. It took me months to get him to tell me anything. I mean…" She gestured with both paws, slapping the towel into the door. "Just to get him to tell me that ritual, I had to promise that I would delete the e-mail right away, that I wouldn't let you read it, that you wouldn't tell anyone else about it…"

Alexei flicked his ears and nodded. "Well," he said. "All right. If he is so concerned about it." He let Meg walk off to drop the towel in the bathroom, and sat down on his bed, damp tail and all.

The night of the ritual remained crystal-clear in his memory, and he was certain that Meg had not asked him not to tell anyone else about it. She had said that she was not allowed to tell anyone else, and when Alexei had said he'd hear it, she dismissed that because, she said, he wouldn't have memorized it.

He hadn't, but he remembered some of it, especially that he had rung the bell once to summon the spirit, and had not rung it the second time to release it. It hadn't seemed that complicated, certainly no more so than many he'd found on the Internet, and anyway, if Athos was as paranoid as Meg claimed, would she not have made more certain to tell him not to tell anyone else? Alexei ran paws through his tail's fur, which definitely was dirty from the game. The only problem with asking Athos questions was that the grey fox was not here now.

There was not very much he could do right now, except go to the kitchen to eat leftovers. He had several hours before he could call Rozalina again. And later, he would have to sleep, and most likely deal with Konstantin. If Alexei could hold onto the memory of his sacrifice, of Cat's sacrifice, and the anger at the old ghost—or hallucination—interfering, then he might be all right. Anger and pride: Konstantin understood those. Alexei was beginning to as well.

Chapter 23

Clouds loom overhead, not the Siberian grey of previous dreams, but thick and black, thunderclouds straining downward. The air is tense with the pressure of rain, still like a held breath. Alexei's fur stands on end as he looks around. He tries to remember his anger, but there is nothing here to be angry with.

He stands on flat paving stones, with grass struggling up between the cracks. Near him, just out of arm's reach, a wall rises, rough stone and mortar beneath a top row of heavy ash-colored granite, broken away at the top. The wall stretches away to two corners, and around to define a square. Opposite Alexei there is a gate, closed, of thick iron bars with a crest in the center. He cannot make out the crest from where he stands, even in the dream world: he squints, but it shifts and blurs.

And in the center of the square is a statue of a tiger, tall and wide in the shoulders, fangs bared toward an invisible enemy. He wears no shirt, only pants with stripes carved into the sides. In his foremost paw he holds a sword as long as Alexei is tall. In the paw held down at his side, he holds a flag, a banner with the emblem of Siberia emblazoned on it.

Alexei walks forward. The statue is dark bronze, polished, and the tiger's muscles seem to ripple with the reflected churning of the clouds. The base, a wide block of marble that would easily have fit Alexei's bed atop it, has no plaque, nor inscription, on the sides facing him.

He expects to hear Konstantin's disembodied voice at any moment, but the only sound is the hiss of wind. It buffets his ears, swirls around his stomach and tail, and then he feels the touch of the first raindrop. He hugs his arms around his bare chest, burying his fingers in his fur, and hurries around the other side of the statue.

Here, facing the gates, is a plaque, dark against the marble. The words, carved in relief on the bronze, are difficult to make out. Alexei leans forward as raindrops spatter between his ears.

Alexander III, Emperor of Siberia.

Movement catches his eye. He looks up. Did the bronze sculpted flag just shiver in the wind? When he lowers his head, the plaque has changed.

There has been no statue erected of Nicholas II, *the words now say.* He was weak. He placed himself above his duty.

What does that mean? He looks again up at the tiger, and jumps in shock. The fierce jaws that had been facing away to his right now face him directly, and above them, the empty metal eyes flicker.

Alexei backs away, his heart pounding louder than the wind. The gate, he thinks, but if he turns his back on the tiger, it will certainly leap after him and destroy him. So he backs up, and the statue watches him go. He takes two steps, three, and then lands awkwardly and looks down to be sure of his footing.

When he looks up again, the tiger is standing in front of the pedestal. Alexei backs up another step, keeping his eyes on the statue, fixing it with his gaze. But even as he backs toward the gate, getting lightheaded with fear, the statue advances on him, another step, and another, the muscles rippling for real now.

Raindrops smack his fur and ears. Alexei stumbles backwards, slips on rain-slick stone, and falls. The tiger continues to advance, inexorable, and Alexei has time to get up and run to the gate. He knows the tiger is behind him, but he can run faster. He is a fox; he can get away, he can outsmart his foes.

The gate is locked. Not with a visible chain or padlock, simply closed and refusing to open to Alexei's increasingly desperate pulls. Behind him, metal footfalls come with the regularity of a clock. If I die in my dream—

A scrape, so close behind him it might nip his tail. He turns, back to the gate, and the tiger is there in front of him, the sword barely a foot from his nose—but it is not a sword, not up close. It is a long, clear, unlabeled glass bottle.

The bottle draws back, swings forward. Alexei, as he did so often on the playgrounds against much less deadly opponents, ducks and slides to the side, running along the wall. He is faster than the statue, he thinks as he reaches the corner, even if he can do nothing but run from corner to corner, before a pursuer who moves slowly, but never tires. The clank-clank of feet behind him punctuates the static hiss of the rain.

There is a crack in front of him: a bottle shatters against the stone, fragments of glass bursting like stars. He jumps, runs the length of the wall, and another crack sounds behind him, another in front of him, fireworks exploding in glittering points, and he avoids them all, gets to the next corner, and turns—

—and the tiger is there, impossibly, and this time he thrusts the flag at Alexei like a spear. Alexei flattens himself against the wall and the long metal pole and metal cloth pass inches from his fur. Cold radiates from them onto his wet stomach.

The fangs, the eyes lock on his. The flagpole draws back again. He hears the words in his head: If you will not be strong, then this will be your fate.

The voice is Konstantin's. He bends his knees, dropping below the flag and trying to roll forward, hitting the flag and then rolling around it, and he is away again, and this time he calls, Konstantin! Konstantin! Wait!

A crack of lightning answers, nearly blinding Alexei, followed almost immediately by a peal of thunder. The fox keeps running, his feet wet and cold, the wind lashing his face with rain. He is close to the gates—

He slips again on the stone, and stumbles. Lightning flashes again, and with the roll of thunder he sees the tiger in front of him, cutting off his escape. The right paw now holds a sword again, drawing it back as the teeth flash, and in that moment as Alexei tries to catch his balance, he hears a deep, guttural voice, and this one is not the old fox's voice. It is not a familiar voice, and yet Alexei knows it is his father's voice, the deep growl of the formidable tiger. I should never have believed in you.

The sword descends quickly. Stone against his back holds him in place. He squeezes his eyes shut, senses light and pain against his side where the sword's arc ends, and the stone gives way beneath him.

Chapter 24

He hit the floor with a yell, the rasp in his throat momentarily disconnected from the sound in his ears until he realized that he was the one who was yelling. He closed his muzzle with a snap.

The dark room was full of the smell of wet wolf and wet fox. His back and tail still felt damp, but that could have been from the rain last night. His side hurt, but it seemed not so much from the blow of a dream sword as from landing on his elbow. Alexei closed his eyes and perked his ears, inhaled to catch all the scents of the room, until he was satisfied that the only smells were himself and Sol, the only sound the thumping of his heart. He felt slightly dizzy, so he lay on the floor another moment until his heart slowed.

His head, however, spun faster than ever. Why had Konstantin only spoken, not appeared? Was he furious, or simply away doing what Alexei had asked? Or was Meg right, and this whole set of dreams was simply in his head?

No. He'd seen Konstantin on the football field, he knew he had. And if it was simply "stress," as Meg said, then what had changed to remove Konstantin from his hallucinations and dreams? The soldier had been intimidating, never threatening, never physically pursuing him. But perhaps Konstantin had enlisted a more primal, vengeful spirit to frighten him... one that knew Alexei's past.

He sat up, now worried that a tiger statue would come through the window, a fierce, shirtless statue of Vasily—

The name came to him as easily as the name Konstantinov had come during the ritual to summon the ghost. Alexei chewed his lip with one canine tooth. The tiger had been Alexander, not Vasily. Alexander III had been the Emperor before Nicholas, but the pictures Alexei had seen in his history books melded together, a parade of tigers in different uniforms, in black and white or color oil portraits. The tiger statue from his dream might have been any of them. He was sure none of them had been named Vasily, though.

The other line on the statue's base, about Nicholas II, referred to Alexander's son. Alexei knew little of them beyond the basics: Alexander had fought to keep Siberia together in the face of Western society and technology that threatened to change the fabric of their lives. Nicholas had seemingly been cursed from the start, too weak to impose his will on the nobles or the would-be revolutionaries who had been active since the time of Alexander II.

Alexei huddled on the floor. Sol had not woken, his breathing slow and regular, but Alexei still did not stir from the carpet, drawing his knees up and his tail around them and rocking forward. The bottles from the dream were all too familiar, and those had likely come out of his own memories, whether dredged up by him or by Konstantin. They had served another purpose, though: to remind him of the danger his sister faced. A broken paw, a twisted ankle, and who knew what else she was concealing from him?

When he stood up, he saw glimmers of dawn out of the window. It was four-thirty, almost not worth going back to sleep. So he took his phone out into the kitchen and called Rozalina's office.

She answered, and although she had not yet been able to locate Chichikov, just talking to her calmed him. She asked how he was doing and whether the exchange program had been successful, and he told her that it had, although he was still exploring ways to remain in the country permanently. He asked if she knew of any options, and doubtfully she suggested he call the local State Department office to ask.

Liza had told him that alerting the government that you were attempting to remain before you had a specific plan was a quick way to get yourself sent back to where you'd come from. But his only plan at the moment was to march into the Millenport office and seek asylum based on his sexuality, which at the moment felt to him like basing his hopes on drawing a playing card from a deck. So he thanked Rozalina and said he would look into that, with more cheer than he felt.

"*You know,*" she said, "*of course we would love for you to remain in Siberia, but I cannot fault you for leaving your town. Moskva will be best place for you if you return.*"

"*I hope it will not come to that,*" Alexei said. "*I am happy here.*"

"*There was a news article about desperate cubs in many small towns,*" she said. "*We knew about terrible conditions in some places, yes, but there have now been,*" she lowered her voice, "*suicides.*"

Alexei's ears perked. "What?"

"*Suicides,*" she said. "*I recall Samorodka was mentioned. One moment.*" He heard a rustling of papers, and then she came back. "*I cannot find it, my apologies. But I believe it was written that there were...two suicides? A teenaged wolf jumped from a high building, and a younger hare one week later. Very sad.*"

"In Samorodka?" The room felt colder.

"*Yes. Did you have friends, wolf or hare? I am so sorry.*"

"*No,*" Alexei said. "*I have not kept close to anyone except my sister.*"

"*Oh, well.*" Rozalina sounded relieved. "*They have blocked off the rooftops there, so I believe no more will jump. It is a sad thing, but not all cubs are smart and driven as you are.*"

"*Driven, perhaps.*" Alexei wanted badly to call his sister. *Since Slava left,* she had said. Had Slava been the wolf who jumped to his death? Why would he have done that? If he hadn't killed himself, then where had he gone that Cat was reluctant to talk about? Had he simply broken up with her? "*Rozalina? Could you do something else for me?*"

He read off his parents' phone number and asked if she could call and ask after his sister, make sure she was doing all right, and then he would call her back.

"*I would be happy to,*" Rozalina said. "*But if your parents do not want to talk to me…*"

"*I know.*" Alexei felt relief. "*Do whatever you can.*"

He sat at the kitchen table after hanging up and stared at the glow of his phone in the slowly brightening room. Could he call his parents himself, force them to put his sister on? What would he say if he called them? He was powerless, here in the States, but now that he had turned eighteen, his parents were equally powerless. They could try to contest his student visa—had done so—but even if it expired or were revoked, now, he would just return to Moskva. He would never go back to Samorodka.

They knew that. So there was no threat sufficient to make them put his sister on the phone. Rozalina, a neutral party, would have the best chance.

The phone blinked off because he hadn't touched it in two minutes. He set it on the table and sat, thinking about his sister, until the day brightened and he decided he should shower before Sol woke.

They walked out in silence down to the bus. The rain had cleared but the humidity remained, making Alexei's fur sticky and rough. He rubbed his paws down his arms even though he knew it would not help. Sol rubbed the back of his paw, his tail tight against his body.

When they reached the bus stop, Sol cleared his throat. "Kendall isn't sure his insurance is going to cover the repair on his tooth."

Alexei made a noncommittal noise, as if he cared. Sol looked at him, but Alexei kept staring forward at the cars passing in the street. "I told him I'd talk to you about paying for it if it doesn't."

"I will not pay for it," Alexei said.

"I mean, you did break the tooth," Sol said.

"He bit my ear." The ear with the healing wound was on the other side from Sol. Alexei flicked it anyway.

Sol sighed, his tail uncurling and relaxing. "I know. I told him that too. I said you own up to mistakes. He was saying you wouldn't even care if he needed dental surgery."

Alexei could hear Kendall saying those words, too. The thought made him grit his teeth. He ran his tongue over his own unbroken canine teeth and smiled. "I hope he does not need dental surgery," he said, at least partly sincerely.

"That's what I told him," Sol said, but he didn't sound so sure, and his tail was flicking like it did when he was thinking about one thing and talking about another.

Alexei rubbed his paws together, wondering if he should say something, but after the dream and the conversation with Rozalina, he was worried about Cat all over again. Slava had killed himself—the more he thought about it, the more he was sure of it. And Cat, if she didn't get out of Samorodka, who knew what desperate lengths she might go to? He wanted the day to be over, the moon to rise so he could call Rozalina and hear her confident Siberian voice saying, *Your sister is fine. She sends her love.*

"I know you don't like him," Sol said, "but he's not that bad a guy. He said he didn't realize you were interested in Mike, and so he's stepping back to give you a chance with him."

"I see," Alexei said. "By the way, I will get your picture back tomorrow."

He said it hoping that Sol would lapse into one of those silences that might be uncomfortable, but would at least spare him having to hear about Kendall. But when they got on the bus, Sol didn't even mention the picture. He talked more about Kendall while Alexei tried in vain to stop his mind from picturing Slava leaping from a rooftop. He didn't remember exactly what Slava looked like, so he could only see the face of one of his wolf friends from year six, and the resulting picture was even more disturbing.

It wasn't until lunch in the small sandwich shop down the street from his warehouse, when his phone beeped with a text message, that he remembered about the date with Mike that evening.

He could beg off. He could say that he was still stressed from the fight, from losing his visa chance, and that he would not be good company. He could say that his sister was having a hard time and he was worried about that. Those stories had the advantages of being true. Of course, Mike had a younger brother and therefore maybe Mike would offer to talk to Alexei about his sister, and Alexei would rebuff him and Mike would feel bad. Or Alexei would talk to him about Cat and would have to tell him more about their childhood, the terrible conditions in Samorodka, and maybe Mike would be horrified that he'd left Cat there, or he would pity the two of them, ask how he could help. And he couldn't help, no more than Alexei could, and probably significantly less.

Anyway, even if Alexei politely rescheduled, it would only postpone the date a couple days. He would still have to figure out if he were going to give up on Mike for good, as Konstantin wanted, or if he could just walk a careful line until the older fox had helped—or failed to help—his sister. The thing was that the same stubborn confidence that Konstantin had helped him build with his play in the games, with the dance-off and later the fight against Kendall, now pushed at him when he thought about giving up Mike. *Do not give in*, he heard in Konstantin's voice, even though he was thinking about the old fox himself.

Where *was* Konstantin? The vision of the soldier at the game was fading in his memory to a trick of the light, a shadow, and he had heard nothing but a few sentences that might have been in his head, a voice in a scary dream. The threats from the nightmare felt like bullying he'd endured back in Samorodka, his father yelling, *I'll see him at the bottom of the river*, his friends pushing him in the mud until he cried out whatever they wanted to hear. Konstantin had promised to help his sister, but so far he had produced no results. Had he simply used that as a lever to twist Alexei's arm? Or had Alexei himself changed worry over his sister into guilt at his own freedom, as Meg would have him believe?

He closed his eyes and inhaled the smell of fresh-baked bread, the sweet smell of sliced meats, the musk of patrons coming and going, and pressed his paws over his face. The sandwich shop felt warm, cozy, and altogether too blandly normal for any ghost or hallucination to invade. If only he could stay here forever, and bring Cat, huddle with her in the alcove and look out over the flowing crowds together.

His phone chirped again, because he hadn't opened it to answer the text, though he could see the words on the alert. *Still on for tonight, Playtime at 7:30?* Alexei felt a small wash of irritation, that special irritation reserved for people asking questions that were relevant but shouldn't have been, as far as they knew, like someone asking for the exact card you'd just picked up at Old Maid. In the normal course of things, if he'd made plans and then told Mike he wouldn't feel up to it, he wouldn't mind Mike checking to confirm them—would expect it, even.

Alexei turned his phone over. Sometimes he wished he could just stop thinking so much about things. Of course Mike couldn't know that Alexei had been ordered not to go out with him, could not know that his simple question was what the fox had been agonizing over for hours and days, whenever he wasn't worried about his sister or his visa or, now, that Sol was going to start dating Kendall.

Okay. He took a breath. Sol was not going to date Kendall. He had that guy, Mitch, the one he liked. And there was nothing Alexei could do about his sister that he wasn't already doing. Same for the visa. He turned the phone back over and stared at the message. He hated feeling bullied; he hated worrying about Cat. He worried that he would lose the rapport he was building with Mike; he worried that he would lose his already-tenuous connection with his sister. So what he had to decide, what he had to figure out right now, was whether he was going to reply to Mike with a yes or a no.

Chapter 25

Of course, the young Tsarevich had many better things to do than to occupy himself with the family of one of the Guards. He had his training, his royal relatives to visit, his political connections to cultivate. And yet, when he saw me on the grounds, he would ask, "How comes the family, Kostya?"

That he remembered at all was a great blessing and I thanked him every time. I told Mariya his words and she agreed that he would be the greatest tsar we had seen, though we hoped we would see many more years before his accession. How could one who so easily remembers and keeps the dreams of his people in his head and heart do wrong?

When Mariya told me it was time, I summoned the doctor, and he attended at her bedside while the child was delivered. I waited outside to be presented with little Nikolai or Aleksandra, readying to make the same promise I had made almost two years before. It was in the heat of summer this time, so we had high hopes that our cub would survive to six months without an illness.

Mariya's cries tore at me as she again suffered the pain of bringing a life into the world, but there was nothing I could do but stand and wait. I paced, my tail curled nervously behind me, and then I heard the wailing of a strong, healthy cub, and I clapped my paws together. But the doctor did not emerge.

After Tatya's birth, I had held her in my arms in a matter of minutes, cleaning her fur, pressing my nose to her stomach to hold her scent in my memory. But fifteen minutes passed, and then thirty. "Is all well?" I called in to the doctor. Our cub had not stopped crying the whole time. I wondered if perhaps he or she had broken an arm or a leg; I knew such things happened.

The doctor did not respond then, but five minutes later he called, "Boil more water! Get me clean rags!" and I sent the servants off to follow his instructions. I called in again to ask what was wrong, but again he would not answer, save to snap at me to remain outside.

When the servants returned, the doctor met them at the door holding a small form bundled in blankets. He thrust the blankets into my arms without a word. I barely looked down at the face of my newborn son, barely heard his cries. Words choked my throat and remained unspoken, so I had to beseech the doctor with my eyes, but his small cat's ears remained down, and he looked at the floor and would not meet my gaze. "Take them away," he said to the servants, who had moved closer with the pot of steaming water and the rags. "They are no use now."

"They are no use now"

Chapter 26

As soon as he sent the text message, *Yes*, Alexei felt queasy. But it was too late to take it back, or at least, take it back in a way that didn't make him seem weak or indecisive. Besides, thinking about retracting his words didn't make him feel any better. After all, confirming the dinner didn't mean he was going back on his promise to Konstantin. It was just dinner. He wasn't going to do anything beyond that.

After four hours of the solid, dusty reality of cardboard weight in his arms, he felt better, almost looking forward to his date. He smiled and joked with co-workers as they loaded up trucks. Vlad noticed his ear and asked if he were planning to get a piercing. "Not to be modeling on Pierre, yes?" the big tiger said, gesturing to the hutia, whose ears fairly dripped silver, and everyone laughed.

And then Alexei went back into the warehouse by himself, searching through the shelves, and heard a hiss of a soft voice. He perked his ears, at first thinking it was one of his co-workers, but then the whisper came again, and the words reached his ears clearly.

"*I am watching you.*"

He whirled, looking for the fox in the military coat, and the box he was holding thumped to the floor. The aisle before him was deserted, lined with shelves and boxes that remained immobile. The lights in the warehouse and the windows that let in the cloud-filtered sunlight banished most shadows, but Alexei hurried down the aisle, around a corner. He poked his muzzle between rows of boxes, ears and whiskers alert for any movement.

"Where are you?" he hissed.

"Am here," Vlad said from around a corner. He emerged into the aisle, black stripes flexing over his arms, long tail lashing. "Where did you go? Did box fall?"

"I—" Alexei shook his head. "I thought I heard voice." It was easy to slip into Siberian cadences when he was talking to Vlad. "Thought one of you was talking to me."

"We are all at dock." The tiger reminded Alexei uncomfortably of the statue from his nightmare, so close, looming over him like this, though Vlad's smile was friendly and he held a clipboard rather than a sword.

Still, Alexei took a step back. "I am just getting package—getting the package. I will be there in a moment."

"All right." Vlad waited a moment, then turned and walked back to the dock.

Alexei breathed with one paw set against the nearest shelf until his heart had returned to normal, and then he looked around at the dust motes drifting through the beams of light. "I do not care if you are watching me," he said. "You have done nothing." He picked up his box and walked back to join Vlad.

◆

Though the rain had passed, its weight lingered in the air as he left. He picked up an energy bar from the break room before he left to help calm his stomach, hoping he was just hungry. That was one thing he loved about life here: the infinite variety. In Siberia, they had sometimes had dry, tasteless bar-shaped snacks that filtered down unwanted from the stores in Moskva where the good ones were snapped up. Here, he could choose from a dozen brands and a million flavors, and though he had only been here a month, the casual acceptance of the other employees—some of them even griped that the warehouse only stocked one brand—told him they were a common thing. Alexei found it delightful to have something like this at all, much less provided for free by an employer.

The snack did settle his stomach by the time he got to Playtime. The restaurant, loud and bright, looked much the same as it had on his last visit: dotted with plants in strategic corners, a black-and-white tiled floor, and red-coated waiters and waitresses dodging about the open area. Behind the dining room, the long stair led down to the games room, a loud, clanging backdrop to the buzz of conversation.

Restaurants all had a unique smell to Alexei, which Sol had told him was a blend of the most popular dishes and the most common cooking oils and seasonings used in that restaurant. Playtime smelled like peppers and cheese, burgers and fried potatoes, and very little of any particular spices—a smell which now evoked in Alexei an echo of the feeling of satisfaction he'd gotten from watching Kendall lose his composure the previous week. Tail relaxed, he took a breath and walked in.

Mike was waiting for him by the host stand. "They wouldn't seat me until everyone was here," he said. If it had been Sol, he would have put air-quotes around "everyone" and rolled his eyes while saying it, but Mike just smiled as the hostess took two menus and brought them to a small two-person table near the back of the restaurant.

"How are you feeling?" Mike asked as she left them, before he even picked up the menu.

"Oh, a little nervous." Alexei wagged his tail. "But I am glad to have some time with you."

"I meant…" Mike touched his ear. "From the fight."

"Oh." Alexei's ears lowered and his tail stilled. "I am fine."

The silence lasted only a short time. "I'm sorry," Mike said. "I wanted to ask. For what it's worth, Liza told me how it started. I think Kendall was being a dick."

Alexei nodded. "I did not want to fight, but he pushed Liza."

"That's very noble. Although I don't think Liza needs people standing up for her."

"No, I think she was mad at me for it." Alexei smiled. "No matter. I stand up for friends when they are in trouble."

"You have a lot of friends in trouble?"

The fox shook his head, though he was thinking of Sol, of Cat, of Meg and her mysterious friend, of Konstantin. "Not a lot. More than I would like."

"My brother helps people a lot. Older brother—well, Kenny does, too, though he's more into his music right now. He used to write a column for his college paper about social issues."

"Sol's a writer," Alexei said, grateful that he wasn't going to have to talk about Cat, which would remind him of Konstantin and the bargain he was maybe not keeping very well right now.

Mike, to Alexei's surprise, glowered down at the table and picked up his menu. "I had the Swiss mushroom burger last time," he said. Veggie burger, of course, where Alexei'd had meat, but the toppings were the same across the different varieties. "What did you have?"

They discussed the sandwiches available while Alexei tried to figure out what Mike had against Sol. He knew why Sol hadn't liked Mike initially, and felt he had started to change the black wolf's view. But Mike had always seemed pleasant and friendly to everyone. In the back of his mind, Alexei felt a small pulse of anger, the need to defend Sol to Mike, because even if Sol was being a bit dense sometimes—stone-headed, they used to say in Samorodka—he was a good person, and still Alexei's closest friend.

Mike didn't mention Sol again throughout dinner, and Alexei forcibly kept the anger from growing any stronger, focusing on their conversation. They were picking at the remains of the immense pile of fries they'd each gotten when the subject of Sol came up again. Mike had mentioned a book he'd enjoyed, and how he'd tried to write while he was in high school. "Terrible emo poems," he said, laughing.

"Sol is writing a story," Alexei said.

Mike set his jaw. "Oh? What about?"

And Alexei now could not tell Mike what the story was about, because that would mean telling him about Niki and Sol's dreams, and he couldn't do that. It was also edging too close to telling Mike about Konstantin, and he certainly couldn't do that. So he just said, "I don't really know. He has only mentioned one or two details. I think it is about a fox."

"Maybe he'll change it to be about a pine marten," Mike said in a low voice.

"What?" Alexei flicked his ears forward. He wasn't sure Mike had meant for him to hear that. A lot of people who weren't used to being around canids—foxes in particular—said things in what they thought were inaudible whispers.

Mike's golden horns shook from side to side. "Nothing," he said. "Only it seems like he's not interested in foxes anymore so much as pine martens."

"We were never together, me and Sol." Alexei frowned, the pulse of anger returning. "We are just friends."

"I know," Mike said. "Just seems like he switches sides pretty quickly."

Alexei curled his paw tightly around the napkin in his lap. "He has been a good friend. We had a fight recently, but that was my fault."

"No, I'm sure he's a great person." Mike softened. "Sorry, I don't want to spend tonight talking about him."

But the anger was brighter now, and joined to it, Alexei felt again the tinge of disgust, as though he were looking at Mike through a tinted glass that made the sheep less desirable, an opponent rather than a partner. "He's my roommate," Alexei said, "and my best friend."

Mike held up two rough hands, palms out so the thick black fingernails were barely visible. "I shouldn't have said anything."

"No, you shouldn't," Alexei snapped, and then pushed his chair back from the table and stared down at the paws in his lap. That tinted-glass disgust, the shift in perspective—this was familiar, like his vision going red the previous night before he'd seen Konstantin walk away. He fought against it, reminding himself that he wanted to date Mike, that this vision was being forced on him from the outside. "I'm sorry," he said through gritted teeth, flattening his ears. *Don't apologize*, said a rough voice in his head, and he told it to be quiet.

"No, look," Mike said. "I know he's a good friend of yours. He's just been rubbing me the wrong way for a little while now, and I shouldn't have said—"

"Don't apologize!" Alexei wrestled with the words that wanted to come out, choking back the contempt the older fox's ghost had for weakness, for boys who liked other boys and flouted the rules of nature and God, for boys who'd run away from their families. *Traitor*, the voice said. *Dishonest. Disloyal.*

Now the sheep's head and curled horns tilted to one side. "Are you okay?"

"I'm…" When the subject was himself, it was easier to vent the turmoil. "Disloyal. A traitor."

"Oh, God," Mike said. "No! You're the most loyal person I know. You—you don't look good."

Alexei kept his muzzle clamped shut, breathing through his nose and twisting the napkin this way and that. Inside his mouth, his tongue worked to form words, terrible words like *you abandoned your family, just like me*, and *I am destined for better things*, words he did not believe but was being forced to see the truth of through another's eyes. "I'm—I am fine," he said with harsh breaths and a snarl that he was aware conveyed exactly the opposite impression.

"Should I get our waitress?" Mike craned his neck, looking around, then back at Alexei with his wide brown eyes. "Are you having a seizure or something?"

"No!" He could do this. Konstantin had taught him enough strength, and besides, he had strength the older fox knew nothing of, strength forged from his father's belt and the rotting wood of their house, the broken houses and choked river he walked by every day.

A 'strength' of avoidance, of running.

Survival!

To survive in such a way is barely better than death.

Mike said, "I'll get the check. You need to lie down."

What I need, Alexei wanted to say, is an exorcism. But he had no sooner thought that when Konstantin's dry, harsh laugh echoed in his ears. *You have called me, and I will not be soon dismissed. You will not run away from me this time.*

It was impossible that he could never be rid of the ghost. Not possible. What he'd done could be undone, couldn't it? He could repair the glass over a broken picture; he could also remove the ghost from his life. Or the hallucinations. There were drugs, therapy.

The waitress brought the check and looked down at Alexei with concern. "Is he okay?"

"He'll be fine. We're just getting him somewhere to lie down." Mike fished his wallet out and gave the waitress a credit card.

Alexei shoved a paw in his pocket and came out with cash. He threw it on the table blindly, without looking. "I don't need to lie down," he growled, and then clamped his jaw shut. Even letting out those few words had felt dangerous, as though more might escape.

"You do need to lie down," Mike said, his eyes soft. He picked up the cash and held it out to Alexei. "I'll take care of dinner."

"Keep it." Alexei shoved back his chair and stood up, tail curled tightly around his leg. His polo shirt and jeans were unbearably warm, even though fans spun lazily above him.

Mike stood, too, and walked around the table, putting a hand on Alexei's shoulder before the fox could stop him. "I'll walk you out," he said.

Konstantin hated the gentle touch with a surge of disgust that overwhelmed Alexei long enough for him to shrug Mike off and back up. "Leave me alone," he snapped, and then fought back the words. "I mean— it is not a good time. I'm s-sorry." The last word he had to force out with an effort that left him panting for breath.

"No, I'm sorry," Mike said. "I didn't realize—"

"Don't be weak!" Alexei yelled, loudly enough that the whole restaurant turned to stare at them. The waitress, returning with Mike's credit card and slip, halted as well. The moment remained frozen, the hurt in Mike's eyes, the burning curiosity in everyone else's.

This is a dream, Alexei thought, nothing but a dream. The harsh lights on the white tile, the smell of cheese, the sour taste of oil on his tongue, the throbbing ache in his ear as it lay back flat, the faint queasiness in his stomach, all of these were too fine, too detailed to be real. The shock on Mike's face was too comical and horrible, and the silence in the restaurant too dramatic.

Alexei did not act this way. He stood up for the weak; he did not chastise them. He was quiet, because to make noise was to draw attention to oneself. He had their attention now, all of it, and his fur prickled all over. He felt the need to apologize to Mike, to the whole restaurant, at the same time as the gruff, foreign presence in his mind told him that they were all weak, that none of them deserved to be in this room with him, that he should tell them so and make sure they heard the message.

"Is everything okay, boys?" the waitress said, and that broke the spell. Diners returned to their meals, the low hum of conversations louder now. Even with his ears folded down, Alexei could hear snatches of conversation around him.

"—foxes're all high-strung—" "—on drugs, Ah bet yew—" "—couple faggots—" "—business out in public—"

"I don't know," Mike said in a low voice. His muzzle, inches from Alexei's, exhaled warm breath, filled with the scents of the meal they'd shared.

Alexei tucked his lower lip under both canine fangs and bit, the habitual action and familiar small pain sending him spinning back down into his past. He looked into Mike's eyes and saw confusion, hurt, emotions for which he had no answer in this place, in this time. He couldn't tell him it would be all right, he couldn't tell him that one day they would get away from this place, from the people causing the hurt, because this time the one causing the hurt was him.

Konstantin held his throat in check, but he was able to force out the word, "Sorry," in two choked syllables before turning and running toward the nearest exit, down the stairs to the room full of games.

Blessed cacophony enfolded him, lights and noise and the scents of fifty or so people in the heat of competition. Even though his head had begun to pound, Alexei lost himself in it, stumbling between rows of video games and islands of multi-player competitions until he came to rest against a shooting machine. With one trembling paw, he clutched the console, looked over, and saw—

—a public square, the statue of a tiger in the middle of it, filled with zombie soldiers in military coats lurching toward him—

—and he yelled and ran until he hit a uniformed goat, barely older than he himself was, who grabbed his shoulders and said, "Hey, hey, no running."

"Got to get out," Alexei sobbed.

"Jesus Sheep," the goat swore. "Okay, okay, there's a bathroom out this way. Don't puke on the floor."

He led Alexei to a back hall and held the door of the bathroom for him. But Alexei caught the red glow of the exit sign up a narrow, dark staircase, and said, "Outside."

"Suit y'self." The goat let go and retreated a couple steps, making sure Alexei wasn't going to head back to throw up on his carpet.

Alexei stumbled up the stairs and threw himself against the door. The hot, muggy air did nothing to relieve the pressure in his throat and chest, nor did the silence of the alley help clear or distract his thoughts. Rotting food and smoke fought with car exhaust from the nearby road to offend his nose. Alexei ran to a dumpster and leaned back into the corner it made with the stone wall behind it. The smell of garbage, terrible, nearly overwhelming, was what he deserved.

Weak.

"It is all right to be weak," he said. "It's all right. I don't have to beat up everyone. Mike is a nice guy."

Out here in the alley, the words flowed more easily, the constriction in his chest loosening. But the other voice was still there in his head. *If you show weakness, people will exploit it.*

"Who? I am no soldier!"

Military, government, family, society. It is all the same. And you are forsworn.

Alexei shuddered. "I haven't done anything," he said. "I was just having dinner with a guy."

Yes, and what were your intentions regarding this sheep?

The word "sheep" echoed with disgust. Alexei clutched his head below his ears. "Did you help my sister?"

The tension in his chest vanished, though the pounding in his head remained, a thick pulsing that pushed against the space between his eyes from the inside with every heartbeat. He closed his eyes, and as he did, another smell intruded on the thick smell of refuse, a smell of cold and stone and ice, a smell of fox and earth and thick wool. His stomach fluttered, and he pressed himself back into the wall as Siberian words echoed off the concrete wall, the metal dumpster.

"If you care so little for your promises, then how shall I regard those I made to you?"

The voice sounded strange in his ears here in the real world, without the filter of dreams. *"You are not real,"* Alexei rasped through gritted teeth, the tightness in his chest all his own now. *"You are stress and worry and…"*

"And sadness." The voice moved closer to his ears. *"Yes. All of that."*

Alexei felt the wave of it, and then felt movement with his whiskers. He shrank back, but nothing touched him. The weight of his sister's plight came down on him again. He had been a fool to trust a ghost, a hallucination, to produce any effect in the real world. *"You've done nothing to help Cat. I was a fool. You only wanted—"*

"I promised." The fox's growl echoed in the alley. Alexei's whiskers registered motion in time for him to flinch, not quickly enough for him to escape the cuff to the side of his head that sent it into the metal wall of the dumpster.

Pain shot through his skull and sparks flared behind his closed eyes. A moment later, his ear rang and the side of it where it had been crushed into the dumpster throbbed with pain as well. He squeezed his eyes shut as his legs nearly gave way; he would have landed on the ground had he not thrown out an arm to steady himself.

Konstantin's words penetrated the red haze and the ringing in his ears. *"…dreams are difficult to navigate. I will continue to search, as long as you hold to your promise."*

Alexei wanted to keep his eyes closed. He could imagine that the voice was in his head, that his nose was addled with the horrible smells, that he had slipped and banged his head into the dumpster. He did not want to open his eyes and see the military coat against the backdrop of the alley, the gold sash bright against the navy. He wanted his ghosts to remain in his dreams, insubstantial, where they belonged.

"*Think of your sister,*" Konstantin said. "*If you value her future…*"

"*You'll help her get away from my parents.*"

Fingers gripped the end of his muzzle and lifted it. Alexei could not keep his eyes closed; they flew open and he stared into the cold dark eyes of the older fox.

Here in the darkness, details about him were not as clear as they were in the dream, where Alexei could focus on the grey patches on his muzzle and around the edges of his ears, or the short cropped fur along his cheeks. The notch in his ear seemed to glow with the light behind it, but otherwise Alexei's gaze jumped about, taking in the dry black nose, the tips of the canine teeth visible over the fox's lip, the black smudge down his muzzle. He could not smell Konstantin's breath as anything other than moist, wet earth, like the smell from his dream.

"*I will find this Chichikov,*" Konstantin said. "*Your parents I will judge when the time comes.*"

Alexei's heart hammered against his chest. He did not feel Konstantin's false confidence inside him, but when the issue was his sister… "*My father drinks,*" he said roughly. "*My mother does too. They don't love their children.*"

Konstantin narrowed his eyes, searching Alexei's. "*I know this.*"

"*They abandoned us. The life they chose—it was killing us.*"

"*They would have made you marry, and have cubs.*"

The old soldier was about to go on about the laws of nature, Alexei knew, and he barely had the strength to meet that argument. His head still rang and his headache had gotten much worse. So he interrupted. "*They did not care for their family,*" he said. "*They struck us, harmed us.*"

Konstantin's rough voice bored into Alexei's ears. "*To correct you. To discipline. To make you a better person. Where they failed, I will—*"

"*For no reason but their own weakness! Being parents doesn't make your actions right!*" He and Cat had said these words to each other many times, but he had never said them to another.

They rang against the metal of the dumpster, echoed, and vanished. Konstantin's ears flattened and his eyes flickered; light struck them, showing Alexei the wide slits of the older fox's pupils. He felt as though he were looking into a carnival mirror that showed what you would look like in forty years.

For a moment, he thought Konstantin might strike him again. The fox's breathing quickened, harsh and loud, and he glared at Alexei for a full ten seconds before his eyes and whiskers relaxed and his ears came back up. "*I will see you again*," he said, and then the fingers released Alexei's chin.

He sagged back against the wall as Konstantin straightened, brushing a paw down his dark blue coat. The sash he wore bore stains, but not as many as Alexei remembered from his dream. It shone in the darkness, and then swept out of view behind the dumpster.

The alley went still to his ears, eyes, and whiskers. He lay against warm brick and cooler metal, inhaling refuse and urine and trying not to think about what had just happened. A hallucination was anything imagined, so he supposed that he could have imagined the feelings, the conversation, and the smack on his muzzle. The pain all down one side of his head, whatever the source, was very real. He closed his eyes and tried to relax.

"Hello?" A voice came to him from the other side of the alley, and footsteps sounded. "Hello? Someone here?"

If he didn't respond, perhaps she would leave. But the footsteps grew louder, near enough him that Alexei opened his eyes. A moment later, a white-tailed deer stepped into his field of vision. "Hey," she said in a soft voice. "You doing okay? Had a little too much?"

He shook his head slowly. "I am fine," he said, pushing himself to his feet.

"You aren't from around here, are you?" Her drawl indicated that she definitely was.

"No." He put one paw to his head, pressing in on the spot that had hit the dumpster, and he winced. "From Siberia."

"Oh, that's what you were speaking."

He lifted his eyes to focus on her soft blue ones, above a warm smile. "I suppose so." He wanted to ask if she had heard only him or if there had been another voice, but he was afraid that she would say yes, and he was afraid that she would say no. So he kept the question stifled in his head and said, "I am sorry for causing a disturbance."

"It's no problem. I work with the homeless shelter, and so when I hear someone in an alley...do you have somewhere to go?"

"I do." He nodded, which made his head throb again, so he stopped.

"Oh, all right." She sounded almost disappointed. "Is your head hurt?"

"I hit it…when I fell. It will be all right." He gritted his teeth.

"You sure you don't need to visit the hospital or something? Let me see if I have some aspirin in here…"

"No." He lowered his paw and breathed in, trying to settle the ache in his head. His ear hurt, and it was the same one Kendall had bitten; a trickle of blood made its way down his fur. He hoped she would leave before she smelled it.

Thankfully, she did, gathering her yellow dress around her and walking back out the alley the way she'd come. Alexei watched her go and then looked the other way, the way Konstantin had left. Slowly, he walked in that direction until he reached the street, and then he turned mechanically toward the bus stop. People passed him in either direction, but he barely noticed, wandering through a haze of light on warm concrete, smells brushing his nose like feathers and then vanishing.

At the bus shelter, he leaned against a giant glowing poster for the upcoming WonderWolf movie. The wolf looked determined, his fist poised to strike whatever evil the filmmakers had lined up for him. And he was smiling, he was confident, he knew that whatever happened, he would come out the winner.

Alexei stared at the eyes of the wolf in the poster, wishing for that same confidence. He didn't know what would happen to his sister. He had wanted very badly for Konstantin to be real, and now he wanted nothing more than to never see him again. At the same time, that confidence in the wolf's eyes felt very much like what Alexei had felt when Konstantin was possessing him. He wished he had that confidence when it came to approaching Mike, talking to Sol, or, most of all, when it came to reassuring his sister that he would do everything in his power to help her get out of Siberia. He closed his eyes and waited.

The bus took him to the transit center downtown, which he almost missed because the bouncing along the pothole-filled streets made the pounding in his head worse. He had his eyes closed and his paw to his ear again, and only because a lot of people got out at the transit center did he notice that he had to follow them. By the time he struggled up from his seat, people were already boarding, and he had to push past an annoyed red wolf and Dall sheep to get out. He whirled after the Dall sheep, convinced that it had been Mike, that Alexei hadn't recognized him, but the sheep wore a denim vest and his larger, awkward horns did not shine like Mike's.

Then the bus he needed to get home was just leaving, and he ran after it in vain, only to watch its red lights vanish through the hazy night around a corner. He could walk home from here, and to hell with it, he thought. The next bus might be twenty minutes away, so the half hour walk was worth it not to have his head bounced around like a football.

Not that the walk was much better. Drained from the date with Mike and the conversation with Konstantin, his feet dragged along the sidewalk. To avoid the lively gay neighborhood of Riverwalk with its rainbow flags and cheerful same-sex couples, he trudged two blocks over, past closed office buildings, vacant apartment homes, and overgrown parks. He passed from starkly lit concrete, pale and featureless, to hazy, disquiet darkness, and every time he saw a shadow flicker or heard the tap of a footstep, he jumped and looked around. There was no reason for Konstantin to come back, but that was what he feared more than being attacked in the street. A live assailant he could manage, or at least understand.

When he finally dragged himself up the front step of his building, he leaned against the door for a moment. The sensation of being home was such a relief, and yet he knew that before long he would be needing to sleep, and after meeting Konstantin and having the nightmare of the statue the previous night, he was not looking forward to what his dreams might bring. Perhaps he could ask Meg to mix him another drink, something that would help him sleep. With that thought in mind, he turned his key in the lock and opened the door.

The babble of conversation came to his ears almost immediately, and then paused. Facing him from the kitchen table when he looked in were Meg, Sol, and an unfamiliar grey fox, his fur a salt-and-pepper mix except for russet patches around the sides of his face up to the base of his ears. Alexei had met grey foxes in the States before—never in Siberia—but he had never met one who wore a white starched collared shirt and a black cape fastened around his neck with a golden brooch, nor one who had apparently darkened the fur around his eyes to give himself a hollow, spectral appearance.

It was not really the thing Alexei wanted to see, and he might have turned around and run back out of the apartment if the fox hadn't immediately stood up and extended a very real black and white paw with orange highlights in the fur, and said, "You must be the other roommate. I'm Athos."

"Of course," Alexei said, willing his tail to uncurl from around his leg. He grasped the other fox's paw; he had a soft grip and Alexei immediately thought, "Weak," and hated himself for that. "I am Alexei."

"From Siberia, right?" Athos had a soft, understated manner, and though his precise East Coast voice was not hard to hear, it was a notch lower than Sol's or Meg's, which was disconcerting in the apartment. Nobody other than the three of them and Sol's parents had ever been inside. A window was open, so the noises of cars and the construction crew starting up outside intruded more than they normally did.

Alexei nodded. "One year ago," he said, to indicate the amount of time since he'd left. Again he felt the flicker of disbelief that one short year could encompass so much change.

"You know," Athos said, sitting down, "I've always wanted to go to Siberia. There's such a rich tradition there, and all kinds of unexplained phenomena. I mean, starting with Rasputin and Tunguska, but so many things less famous than that."

Alexei knew something of the Tunguska explosion, variously rumored to be an alien attack, a natural fission bomb, a black hole, and an asteroid, which had struck a remote part of Siberia over a hundred years ago. It was now widely presumed to be either a small asteroid or part of a comet. "Yes," he said, dazed, wondering how he could be having a conversation like this when his head was throbbing and his ear was bleeding. Could none of them see what was happening? "It is a large country."

"I'm mostly intrigued by the ghost of the revolutionary who is said to wander the streets of Moskva at night. Did you ever see him?"

"No." Alexei shook his head. "I spent very little time in Moskva. If you will excuse me…"

"There was a ghost in his town, though," Sol said. "Some great-grandmother or something."

Everyone turned to look expectantly at Alexei. He weighed his response. "It was not a real ghost," he said. "It was wind and old house and rumors and fear."

He walked to the bathroom and took an analgesic from the medicine cabinet, and then after some thought he took a second one. A glass of water washed them down. He wondered how long it would take for his head to stop hurting.

"You okay?" Sol called from outside the bathroom.

"Fine," Alexei said irritably. He wished people would stop asking him that when he clearly wasn't. He examined the wound in his ear, which had opened again, and put another bandage on it.

"How was your date?"

Mike's words about Sol and Kendall came to his mind. "Not so good," he said, and then, before Sol could ask any questions, "When are you going to see Mitch again?"

"Oh, um." Sol leaned against the wall outside the door. "I don't know. We were going to get together this weekend, but Kendall wants to take me to this foreign movie that's playing downtown that he thinks I'll really like. Hey, maybe you and Mike can come along too."

"I didn't think you liked Mike." Alexei applied a small metal clip around his ear to hold the bandage in place.

"If you're going to date him, I guess I should give it a try." Sol shifted his weight. "I guess not all sheep are like Carcy. I just see him whenever I look at Mike. I know, that's not fair."

"I would rather go with you and Mitch," Alexei said. "Mitch likes movies, yes?"

"Yeah, but…" Sol sighed. "I'm going away at the end of the summer, y'know. Anyway, Kendall doesn't hold the fight against you. He'd be okay with it."

"I think you are wrong about that," Alexei said, staring at himself in the mirror. He tried to keep his ears up, but they kept sliding downward, his whiskers drooping. When he tried to summon the conviction and power Konstantin had shown him, he merely looked desperate. "I think he dislikes me very much."

"He said he didn't."

"Of course," Alexei said. "But why do you think he now wants to date you instead of Mike?"

"I told you," Sol said. "He didn't realize you were interested in Mike, and—hang on. You think he's only interested in me to get back at you?"

Alexei didn't say anything, but he didn't have to. Sol's muzzle appeared at the door, ears flat. He lowered his voice. "You're wrong about that," the wolf said. "He likes me. He just thought we were a couple."

"I am sure that is what he told you," Alexei said. "He attacked me and bit my ear."

"You shoved him." Sol frowned. "What'd you do, make it worse? Did Mike hit you?"

"No!" The fox glared. "For God's sake."

"Then what—"

Alexei closed his eyes and shook his head. "It is not important," he said, and turned, pushing past Sol to walk through the living room.

"Hey," Meg said, but he ignored her. In the bedroom, the window had been propped open by the fan sitting in it, though the fan was off. Alexei turned it on and stood in front of its breeze, eyes closed, and then retreated to the bed. He sat cross-legged, drew his tail around himself and folded his paws in his lap.

A moment later, Sol came in, ears still flat, tail wrapped tightly around his hip. "Hey," he said. "First of all, you don't know Kendall. You just don't like him because—well, I don't really know why."

"He puts me down," Alexei said in a low voice. "He is sneaky and does not want people to know he does it, but I notice."

"Well, that's easy, isn't it? Like a ghost only you can see."

Alexei jerked upright. "What?"

The wolf pointed a black finger at him. "I'm just asking you to give him a chance."

"Sol," Alexei said, almost in a whisper, "when your ghost struck Carcy...did you see him?"

"What?" Sol's bright green eyes blinked, and his ears came back up halfway.

"Did you smell him? Was it real?"

"I—I think—" Sol frowned. "Don't change the subject."

"I am sorry," Alexei said. "I—I wanted to know..."

And something in his expression must have tipped off Sol, because the wolf stared at him, and Alexei could not look away from those eyes. "Are you seeing a ghost? Are you seeing Niki? Is that why you haven't brought my picture back? Are you talking to him?"

"No," Alexei said, weakly. His head pounded.

"Christ," Sol said, green eyes burning. "I can't believe you wouldn't tell me. What are you talking about? Did he talk about me?"

"No!" Alexei got up. "I am not talking to him! I would tell you. But I knew you would be like this." He stood, rising on the balls of his feet, but his nose still was not quite level with Sol's.

"He was my friend—I was him for a while. Are you having those dreams? Are you dreaming you're him?"

"I am not dreaming about Niki." Alexei tried to keep his voice under control, but it was getting away from him, wavering, rising in volume.

"Then what is going on?" Sol, eyes narrowed, clearly didn't believe him.

Alexei wasn't sure he could blame Sol. He must look a mess right now. He wondered if Sol could see his headache pulsing in his eyes, maybe as a twitching of the fur on his muzzle whenever he winced. If he told Sol about Konstantin, then Sol might be able to help him—but no, another part of him said, Sol only cared about Niki. He wasn't even asking why Alexei looked so bad, hadn't said, *Are you okay?* Well, okay, he had said that, but then he'd immediately started asking about a double date with Kendall. He was angry at Alexei for dating Mike, for not liking Kendall, for maybe talking to Niki.

The room felt even more stuffy than usual. Sol's scent was thick in the humid warmth as the wolf leaned closer and said, "Well? What's going on?"

It reminded Alexei of his father, without the smell of alcohol on his breath. "I am dreaming about Niki's father," he said, fast, to get it over with. "That is all."

He turned to sit back on his bed, but Sol grabbed his shoulder. "His *father?*"

Alexei twisted out of the grip and pushed Sol away from him. "Yes!" he yelled. "His father, Konstantin."

Trembling, he waited for Sol's response, waited for the wolf to ask how it was going, to express sympathy, to ask whether Konstantin was coming into the real world and if that was why Alexei had asked about it, and he would say, *Yes, yes, yes,* and Sol would put arms around him and say that they would figure this out. Athos would come in and help them exorcise the ghost—once he'd helped Cat, of course—and Alexei would get Sol's picture back and everything would work out.

He watched Sol's eyes flicker and narrow as his forehead creased. The wolf's ears lay back. "But you were *trying* to talk to Niki, weren't you?"

The growl in his voice, the accusation—more hurtful because it was true—and the collapse of Alexei's fantasy all squeezed the fox's chest tightly. He fought to draw in a breath, clenched his paws into fists, and willed himself not to let the pressure behind his eyes escape.

"Weren't you?" Sol demanded again.

There was no way for Alexei to escape the conversation, save one. He turned quickly and half-walked, half-ran to the bedroom door.

"Hey!" Sol said behind him, but Alexei didn't stop. He strode past Meg and Athos, who turned to look at him in surprise, and flipped the lock on the front door, then yanked it open and slammed it behind him. Indistinct words filtered through the door of the apartment, and Alexei fled.

Chapter 27

Nobody came after him, all the way to the front of the building and out, down the front stoop and under the streetlights. This time he did not pause at the sidewalk, but turned left and walked down along the road, under the hazy orange glow.

A block away, he turned back to look at his apartment building. It sat silent and still. Nobody had appeared at the front door, nobody hurried down the walk after him. He'd been a fool. Sol didn't care about him, not if Mitch or Kendall were around for him to date, not as long as Niki remained his. Meg had her vampire fox. Mike…who knew what Mike would think about him after this night. Even Konstantin, who had promised to watch him, had abandoned him.

He turned, tail swinging loosely behind him, and stalked on down the road. Between the game the previous night and all the walking tonight, he was starting to tire, but he pushed himself on through the night.

Again, he avoided Riverwalk. He could have asked Liza for a place to stay, but he feared what Konstantin—or Alexei himself—might do now if he were in her house, surrounded by her scent. So he followed the same path back that he'd taken from the transit center, through the decrepit buildings and closed office parks. Not many people were out walking this street, and they observed the same unspoken contract that Alexei did: they looked up, acknowledged each other, and went back to their solitary walks. One group of young otters in denim jackets, laughing and pushing each other, came close enough to him that he could smell the whiskey on their breath. He ran through scenarios in his head, how they would pick on him, start by following him and escalate to shoving, and to stop it, he would punch the nearest one and then threaten the others until they ran off.

It scared him to think of that, and when he thought further, he doubted his ability to go through with it, notwithstanding the fight with Kendall (which he had won, he reminded himself). So he just shoved his paws into the pockets of his pants and moved to the side, and the otters barely noticed him.

With his ears back and his head down, he walked all the way back to the transit center, and there he stopped. Memory stirred, lifting his ears to what passed for a night breeze in this humid city. Only one bus idled out back; otherwise the hum of the electric lights remained unbroken. But in the shelter of the overhang out in front of the transit center, four people lay huddled in blankets.

Here was a place he could spend the night so he didn't have to go back to the apartment, didn't have to face accusations and questions. Not tonight. Alexei walked up and then, through the glass doors, saw three more people lying across seats inside the station. He glanced again at the people outside and was about to go in when a sound stopped him.

The closest person to him, a big cat who was either a lioness or a puma—wrapped in her blanket, it was hard to tell, and the smells of the busses and the rank odors from the blanket drowned out any identifying scent—lay with her eyes open, looking at him. But Alexei got the feeling that she wasn't actually seeing him. The sound she'd made had been a word, but he didn't understand it. It might have been a name, or it might have been a foreign language.

As he watched, she lifted a paw and reached out to a point a foot to his left, and moaned the word again. "Jio," she said in a low voice that made his fur prickle. "Don't, Jio. Not now."

His paw closed around the door handle, but he couldn't make himself pull it open. He stared in fascination at the lioness. She spoke again. "I'm sorry, Jio. You don't have to. I can fix it."

Was this what the deer would have seen in the alley if she'd arrived five minutes earlier? Alexei wanted to help the lioness, but he could not escape the vision of himself lying on the ground, pleading with empty air. He pulled the door open and fled into the transit center.

Bright fluorescent light dazzled him from the ceiling and reflected off the chilly tile. The air, cool and chemical from processing, was enough of a relief from the outside air that he just stood and panted, letting it flow over his tongue.

Whenever Alexei had been here previously, the lobby had been a hum of activity, busses belching exhaust out back, people of all species milling about, queuing at the ticket window, sitting patiently on the chairs. But fewer than half a dozen people occupied the chairs, a large red "CLOSED" sign blocked the ticket window, and only one uniformed person, a coyote in a bus driver's uniform with a gold hoop in his ear, stood in the lobby. He yawned, waiting for the coffee machine to fill his cup, and when he pulled it free and sipped from it, he closed his eyes and sighed. Then he squared up his shoulders, turned, and noticed Alexei.

"You waiting for the Millenport bus?"

Alexei shook his head. The coyote glanced toward the people on the seats and then back. "Ah, heading out in the morning, huh?"

"Yes." Alexei swallowed against the dryness in his throat.

"All right." The coyote raised his cup and walked to the door leading out to the bay where his bus sat idling. "Last call for Millenport!"

Nobody moved. He looked around one last time and then walked out.

Alexei could go to Millenport. He could get on the bus and just go. It was a bigger city, where he'd never been, and perhaps the ghost couldn't follow him there.

No, that was ridiculous. He shook his head. The ghost might be the only part of his current life that *could* follow him there. And as he had that thought, he looked up at the list of departures and saw...

The board that had a moment ago read, perfectly plainly, "Neely – Penderton – Jack's Crossing – Whiteside – Millenport," now bore Siberian letters, spelling out a short message: *You are safe here.*

Alexei stared. His eyes watered, the letters blurred...and when he'd rubbed his eyes clear again, the stolid list of bus stops had returned. His fur prickled, but only lightly. He was too tired to go anywhere else, and the message had been reassuring, if in a creepy kind of way. Well, he would stay here tonight, he could catch the bus to work in the morning, and then...and then he would figure out what to do from there.

He found an unoccupied seat two rows back from a snoring fennec fox, feeling better closer to another fox, and lay back against the plastic rest, his tail hanging down to the floor. He closed his eyes, which did a little to shield him from the brightness, and let the hum of the lights and the soft snores of the fennec lull him.

Sleep came fitfully. He woke once to see through blurry eyes the clock reading nearly 3 am, impenetrable darkness outside the glass doors. He yawned and closed his eyes again. The next time, the clock read just after five, and a small group of a possum, a skunk, and a mouse waited patiently at the ticket window, one standing, the other two sitting on the floor.

Noise woke him again less than an hour later. The line outside the ticket window had added a wolf and another possum, and though the sign at the window still read "CLOSED," there was a doe behind it arranging some stacks of paper.

Alexei calculated how long it would take him to arrive at work, and when the bus that Sol usually traveled on would arrive here, and decided he had another forty-five minutes. He stumbled to the coffee machine and got a coffee with milk and sugar which proved to be the worst hot drink he had tasted in his life, including the time he and his sister had played tea party with mud when he was five.

He choked it down anyway, and by the time he was ready to walk outside and catch his bus, it had woken him up some. Sol was not on the bus that pulled up first, so Alexei paid his fare and sat staring out the window. When the bus pulled away, it was almost like getting back into his normal routine. If he tried, he could pretend that he was just going to work early.

But even as he pretended, the stiffness in his back and soreness in his leg from sleeping in a plastic chair reminded him of the things that did not submit to pretense. He had not dreamed, but he knew that meant nothing, really. Konstantin might be off exploring other people's dreams, but he had not given up watching Alexei. Or Alexei hadn't given up imagining that Konstantin was watching him.

Unlike Sol nor Meg, who hadn't come after him or even called. Mike hadn't followed him out of the restaurant. Only Konstantin had pursued him even though he'd gone back on his word. The ghost was his, bound to him, and Alexei found something familiar in those ties. Going out with Mike again would make Konstantin angry; trying to spend time with Liza would make him happy. Konstantin had become more real than most of the other people in Alexei's life.

He got off the bus and dragged his feet into work, where Vlad looked up from the supervisor's station and greeted him with a hearty, "Ha! Same clothes as yesterday…you have a good evening or just slept in clothes?"

Alexei smiled automatically and said, "Slept in clothes."

Vlad had not expected that answer, and Alexei saw his confusion, so he forced a laugh. "Kidding," he said. "I had a date last night."

"Oh-ho," Vlad said. "Hey, Pierre, our fox has love life after all."

The hutia had just come in. He squinted at Alexei. "Good for him," he said. "Plenty of vixens up here. Not so many hutia for Pierre." He gestured to himself.

"So you have fun with the vixens." Vlad's laugh boomed throughout the small office, and Pierre's slight wince told Alexei that the hutia had been having some kind of fun the previous night.

"Sometimes. So, pretty vixen?" This was to Alexei.

"Sheep." Alexei searched for a gender-neutral species, then thought of the deer in the alley. "Blue eyes."

The lies came more easily than he would have thought. Pierre gave him a comradely punch in the shoulder, and when their other co-workers came in, he made a point to ask them, "Hey, what you notice about the fox?" Alexei squirmed under these observations, but confessed to a fictitious romantic night with a blue-eyed sheep again and again, until he actually felt bad for not being able to make up more details. But he was tired, and his mood vacillated between enjoying the deception and feeling deeply ashamed of it.

At lunch, his co-workers pressed him for more details about his date, and he said vaguely that he'd met her at Playtime and he didn't want to "kiss and tell," a phrase he'd heard them use in the past. This provoked laughter, a "he's got manners, not like you" remark, and a long story about a rabbit from Pierre.

Alexei brooded toward the end of that lunch. Sol and Meg still hadn't called to ask if he was okay. For all they knew, he could have walked out and been hit by a car. He could be lying in a hospital bleeding to death, or he could already be dead, and they wouldn't care. Maybe he should look for another place to live.

In fact, if he had to give up his gay lifestyle, living with Sol would get more difficult and that might be a good idea. Liza. His fatigue-blurred mind pulled her image from Wednesday and presented her as a solution—a temporary one, yes; she was gay, but she didn't have a partner, and maybe she would be sympathetic to his problem. He couldn't tell her about the ghost, because whether the ghost was real or not (he was real, Alexei was sure, or at least, pretty sure; at least, *right now* he was pretty sure), the story made him sound crazy. But he could tell her that he was having doubts, that he wanted to talk about life. No; he could tell her that he and Sol had had a fight and he was looking for somewhere else to live. That would be better. That was an immediate problem she could help him solve.

So he took out his phone to send her a message, and found it dead. He sat staring at it as though unable to understand how it could be. And then more thoughts filtered in: When might the phone have died? The battery usually lasted a day, but he didn't know how much longer. Maybe Sol and Meg had called him as early as last night; maybe his phone had been dead when he'd walked out. He put it back in his pocket and sighed. He would have to go back to the apartment where his charger was.

He put that out of his mind for the afternoon and only thought of it when Vlad came over around four and said, "You get here early. You can leave now if you like."

It might be good to leave early—he could get home before Sol did, and plug his phone in. But all he wanted to do right now was lie down, and he only had one bed in which to do that, and Meg would be home anyway. If he stayed, he would put off the confrontation a little longer. "I will stay," he said. "One more hour. It is not much."

"Look at this work ethic!" Vlad bellowed to the rest of the team, who looked up. "He has been laid and still works full day and more!"

"He *got* laid," Pierre corrected, but the team laughed, and a couple of them told Alexei he could go home, while others said he didn't get to go home just 'cause he got laid. All in all, it was very friendly, and Alexei would have felt better if he were not starting to feel the effects of the lack of sleep that much more. By the time five o'clock finally rolled around, he could barely keep his tail off the ground as he dragged his feet out the front door. At least he had a bus ride home in which to organize his thoughts.

Or so he'd hoped. As he walked toward the bus stop, he saw an otter waiting there, and at first he took no notice, thinking it was just another person waiting for a bus. Then he saw silver glinting from jewelry in her ears and face, and thought, how odd that another otter would have piercings. And even when she leaned forward and he saw that the black on her face was not just shadow, it wasn't until she said, "Good, you didn't get hit by a bus," that he recognized Meg.

"My phone died," he said.

She shrugged. "We thought maybe you turned it off."

He shook his head, leaning against the plastic at the back of the bus shelter. Meg didn't get up from her seat. She wore a button-down white shirt that he thought probably belonged to Athos, untucked over a pair of black jeans. "Nice shirt," he said.

"Where did you spend the night? I said homeless shelter. Sol said you probably went to Mike's place."

"Bus terminal," he said, and stifled a yawn. Just the memory of the sterile glow and relentless hum of the fluorescent lights made him sleepy.

"I'll be damned," she said. "Athos won the bet."

"I have to go home and charge my phone," he said. "Then I will look for another place to live."

"For what it's worth," Meg said, "Sol feels bad about yelling at you." Alexei didn't know how to respond to that without telling her that he didn't care, so he kept quiet. "Well," Meg went on, "he feels bad now. After I yelled at him about it. He needs to get over his goddamn crush on that painting."

"The painting," Alexei said, and squeezed his eyes shut. "I should go pick it up."

"Yeah," Meg said. "Sol wanted to come and make sure you did, but I told him I would do it so you guys didn't end up yelling at each other in the middle of the framing store." She pushed herself up off the seat. "Also it's good to see you standing, if barely."

He gave a short laugh and shook his head. "I managed to work today. How is Athos?"

"He's off at a shop that sells arcana or something. I had no idea there was anything like that here." She waved a paw. "Which way is this framing store?"

They walked toward it together. When Alexei didn't say anything, even to ask what "arcana" meant, Meg talked about Athos and how he was much more normal than she'd been expecting. She told Alexei that he'd slept on the floor in her room, emphasizing that detail, he thought, so it was clear they hadn't slept together. He liked fish, like she did, but not garlic, though she thought that it was a real dislike of garlic and not just an affectation. "I won't know for sure for a couple days though," she said, which made Alexei wonder if she was planning to sneak garlic into his food, and he thought about that while she told him about Athos's polite manner and earnestness about his occult fascination.

"He knows it's not real, but he's really interested in why people think it is," she said, and laughed. "I said I wasn't, but I mean, look at who I'm rooming with: two guys who dream about dead people. So maybe he has a point. I guess I never asked you guys why you wanted to believe so much, but if you talk to Athos, he might."

Alexei could think of few conversations he would less like to have with anyone right at this moment. He held the door for Meg as they entered the store. "Is that his shirt?" he said, mostly to change the subject.

"Yeah. He said he wanted to see it on me, so I tried it on. Kind of like the look, except the color, you know? I like basic black."

"It looks good on you," Alexei said honestly.

They unwrapped the picture at the counter and showed him the unbroken glass. He and Meg inspected it for cracks or marks, which in Alexei's case meant staring at the fox in the picture and wondering how he'd handled his father, if he'd run away at fourteen or eighteen, if he could possibly come to Alexei and help him.

"There's a fingerprint on the glass," Meg said, pointing. "It's on the inside."

"We could re-do it," the skunk behind the counter said, leaning over to take a look. "It would take another four days."

"Let's bring it back to Sol." Alexei shook himself free of his imaginings. "If he has to wait four more days…he won't believe me."

"I'll be a witness," Meg said, but she didn't argue with him.

"He can decide if he wants it re-done," Alexei said. "But I think he needs to see it."

"What about you?" Meg said as they left the store. "I think you need to see a couple things yourself."

Holding the large picture, Alexei shuddered. There were things he did not need to see again. As if she'd heard him thinking that, Meg said, "Have any dreams at the bus terminal?"

Slowly, he shook his head. The letters did not count, because he'd been awake. "Okay, then," she said, "What the hell was going on with you last night? Sol said you just blew up."

"He blew up at me," Alexei said, gripping the picture more tightly.

Meg walked along with him for a few steps without saying anything. "It sounded like you were asking him about something, but he wouldn't tell me what." Alexei didn't respond. "I'm guessing it has something to do with the dreams, and then he yelled at you because he wants his goddamn precious dreams back."

"Sort of," Alexei said cautiously.

"If I'd known those dreams were contagious, I never would have agreed to live with you two," Meg said. "What is going on with you?"

"Nothing," Alexei said, more strongly.

"Are you all right?"

Her tone eased the words he wanted to say. "I am having these dreams and Sol wants to have them too, but they are not what he thinks they are and I cannot tell him that."

He expected Meg to ask him how they were different or ask him more about them, but she only nodded and said, "Preachin' to the choir. You can't tell that woofer anything sometimes. He needs to get over that dream fox. In fact, I'm not at all sure we should be taking this picture back to him."

Alexei paused. For a moment, he envisioned going back to Sol, telling him the store had lost the picture. Sol would be furious, yes, and…and he could not do that. He knew how much Niki meant to Sol, and it wouldn't be right to take that away.

"I'm kidding," Meg said before he could answer. "That'd be like…like taking weed away from my folks. Well, maybe not that bad. I'm pretty sure Sol could function without the picture. He'd just be sad."

"He is writing a story," Alexei said.

"Yeah, I'm not sure that's healthy either." Meg shrugged. "But a lot of writers are a little bit nuts, so who knows? Maybe that's his calling."

"I am worried that he is seeing Kendall," Alexei blurted out.

"Kendall," Meg said as they reached the bus stop. "That's the guy from your team? The goalie?" He nodded. "I thought Sol was going out with some bear or something."

"Mitch," Alexei said. "He sounds like a very nice guy."

"There's Athos," Meg said, lifting her paw.

Across the street, the grey fox nodded toward them. He wore a grey t-shirt, dark slacks, and the black cape around his shoulders. He carried a small brown bag.

"Anyway," Meg said. "You boys get all too worked up about dating. Isn't it supposed to be easier for you? You all want the same thing, right?"

"I thought so," Alexei said in a low voice as Athos came within listening distance.

"The stores here," the grey fox said, "are curious. I would have thought there would be more *voudon* material there, but there was more of the standard things you find in these kinds of stores. Mostly fakeries and old things without any interest."

Alexei wasn't sure what "voo-don" was, and then he realized it was probably the word for what in Siberian was "vudu." Black magic practiced in some states to the south and west, not so much around here. "What did you buy?" he asked, to be polite.

The fox laid his ears back and slumped down into the plastic seat. Meg, next to Alexei, kicked him in the leg. "Don't drop that picture," she said, when he stumbled.

He looked again at the brown paper bag and remembered Meg's warning about Athos being "touchy" about his interests. He remembered, too, his plan to ask Athos how to dispel Konstantin. That desire felt dull now, remote. The ghost had been through last night with him, and he now placed more hope in hearing about Cat from Konstantin than from Rozalina.

He sat by himself on the bus on the way home, while Meg and Athos sat together two rows back. Since Athos was drawing strange looks in his black cape, Alexei was not terribly upset by this. He didn't know where the grey fox was from, but wherever it was, it was a place where wearing black capes in public did not make one a target. Or else it was, and the fox just thought that since he was visiting here, he would wear his cape around and nobody would care. It annoyed Alexei slightly to think that, but then again, Meg did walk out with her fur dyed black, and once someone had yelled at her to wash her fur, and she'd flipped them off (that was what Sol called it), and there had nearly been a fight.

That had been back in Midland, though, not here in Vidalia. If Alexei looked out the window, he knew he would see lots of dyed fur. No capes, but at least dyed fur and piercings. He didn't look, though. He held the wrapped picture in his lap, inhaling the woody smell of it and the wax of the crayon with which they'd written his name on the paper. The streets passed by outside, and as he drew closer to home, he tried to think about what he would say to Sol, but his mind refused to play the conversation beyond him giving the repaired picture to Sol. He had no idea whether Sol would apologize, whether he would be distracted by the painting and not even talk about the previous night, whether he would still be mad at Alexei for walking out.

Trying to imagine all the possibilities threatened to return the headache from the previous night. His head and ear were still a little sore, but not too bad, not at all. The physical pain was nothing to the worry about Cat, and Konstantin, and Sol, and Mike.

It had been nice of Meg to come get him, even if it had also been partly for Athos to explore his shops. He'd caught a snatch of conversation between them, Athos grumbling about the distance he'd had to walk, and Meg saying, "I showed you the bus routes." Alexei inferred that they had stopped at his stop even though there was a closer bus stop to where Athos had wanted to go, and he felt warmly toward Meg for that. He would miss her when he moved out.

His fingers hurt from holding on to the frame. Behind him, the wolf slouched in the seat had his music turned up so loud that Alexei could hear it even over the bus noise. He smelled like dirt and other wolves. Two rows back, Meg and Athos talked in low tones that Alexei could hear, even if he couldn't pick out words. But other people on the bus sat alone, absorbed in their own thoughts, their books, their music, far more than sat in couples. Perhaps all of them had ghosts as well, spirits that helped dictate the course of their lives. Yes, he thought. He would be all right on his own.

Sol was not home when they arrived. Alexei placed the painting carefully on the wolf's bed and then stretched and sat on his own. The sensation of rest was so different from sitting down on the bus, or in the break room at work, or in the plastic seats at the bus terminal that he closed his eyes, curled his tail around his hips, and let his whole body sag back. Before he knew it, he was falling backwards, and then he was lying down on the bed, eyes closed, relaxing for the first time in over a day. Konstantin was not bothering him, he was not worried about Sol or Mike or anything right now, just letting go and drifting.

"Hey," Meg said, "we're going to make tuna casserole for dinner. You in?"

"Sure," Alexei said without getting up.

He wasn't aware of falling asleep, only of waking to the smell of cooking cheese and tuna oil. He rubbed his eyes and sat up. Konstantin had not appeared in his dreams; maybe he was still searching for Chichikov. Even the faint hope and fear that he was gone barely registered now.

Alexei rolled over and felt something hard in his pocket: his phone. He plugged it in, watched the light come on, and then walked out to the kitchen, but the oven timer showed that there were ten minutes left to go, and Meg and Athos were in her room with the door closed. Sol was still nowhere to be seen. He sighed, and just then, his phone beeped, so he hurried back into his room.

The voicemail listing showed Sol's number yesterday evening, Mike's late this morning, and in between, two Siberian numbers. Heart pounding, he sat on his bed and brought the phone to his ear.

"Hey," Sol's voice said, strained. "Sorry about tonight. Look, come back—don't run off like an—like that. Come—"

He skipped the rest of it. The second message started with crackles and pops, so that for a moment he thought he'd skipped it by accident, and then he heard his sister's voice.

"Alexei! Where are you? Oh, it is so exciting, Bogdan has called again and said he will be coming to Samorodka tomorrow morning to pick me up. I need only meet him where the road comes into town, by the sign that says 'Leaving Samorodka.' He wanted me to come to Vdansk, but I said I did not know when I could go there. So he said he will come down to fetch me. Oh, Lexi, tomorrow I will be in Moskva! I asked Bogdan how long it would take to fill out the paperwork to send me to the States. He said it would depend on getting my records from the school, but that he has already entered my name into the program, so it should happen rather quickly. There are several programs for social work, and he says that with my grades and ideas, I should certainly gain admission to one of them. He is not sure it will be close to you, but he says that once I am in the States, it will be easy for us to travel to see each other.

"The way he called was very clever. He told Papa he was from the National Siberian Achievements Board and that they had been sent my examination scores and wished to interview me for a possible award. Papa had been drinking a little, but he still asked many questions, and Bogdan answered them all well. He must be acquainted with the National Board. Perhaps he does work for them as well as being in the civil service. When he talked to me, he told me I must be very brave and also that the exchange program might cost fifty rubles in fees.

"This is what I wanted to ask you. I did not know that your program cost so much! Did you get it from the engineer? Or did someone else help you? I think Mama has that much in her room, and I should be able to get it, but I do not want to steal it if someone else is supposed to give it to me.

"I will try to call you again once I am in Moskva. Dear brother, I hope to see you soon again once more and feel your arms around me. I must hurry back now and pack the things I wish to bring with me. It will be sad to say good-bye to this town, but I know I will return one day."

In his haste to hear the next message, his fingers fumbled, pausing it and then stabbing down to get it to play. Rozalina's voice spoke in his ear::
"Alexei, I called your parents, but they shouted at me and I was forced to hang up. I hope that no complaint will be filed. I am afraid all I learned was that your sister may already be gone."

There were two more clicks, and then silence.

Chapter 28

We buried Mariya on one of the hottest days of the year, under the beating sun. Her family gathered on the far side of the grave, while I stood with my comrades from the Guards, my adopted father Vasily, and the nurse I had hired to tend to my son.

Mariya's family panted, even sheltered under their white parasols, their russet fur darkened almost to brown in the shade they created. We Guards, more disciplined, kept our muzzles shut and suffered the heat, knowing the limit of our tolerance. There was much weeping on their side of the grave; on ours, only the nurse wept, her large black ears flat against her head, tears staining her fur. Not even my one-week-old son cried. Not once, the whole day he rested in her arms.

I looked over to make sure he had not passed out from the heat, but even though his ears were perked and his eyes precociously open, he could not possibly have known what was transpiring. For all he knew, the nurse using the corner of his blanket to wipe her eyes was his mother, and we were at the funeral of a distant relative. His eyes, the clear blue of the sky, took everything in without reaction.

After the service, only Mariya's sister came to talk to me and tell me how sorry she was. Mariya's mother, her aunts, her uncles and cousins, all stayed clustered in a tight group, anger the only emotion they showed me when they looked at me at all. As if there were more I could have done, as if I had not had a doctor standing by her side throughout. Mariya's sister said they were merely grieved, that they did not understand. I said that I did not care whether they understood. They had already grown accustomed to living without her, while that long and unwelcome task stretched ahead of me still.

Barely were the funeral clothes pressed and folded before I had to don them once again. Where Mariya's funeral had been a small, personal affair, the passing of Tsar Alexander II brought most of Moskva and a good portion of the populace of Petrograd, who made the journey to stand in the ceremony. The Semenovsky Guards presented arms second, after the Preobrazhensky regiment. There were speeches and wailing—again, not from the guards. Alexander III, who would be inaugurated later that year, spoke in his loud, forceful voice about continuing his father's work and keeping Siberia whole. The Tsarevich Nicholas stood at his side, like a reed beside an oak tree.

Nicholas came to express his condolences to me as well. I told him I had named my son Nikolai for him, and he beamed and said that he hoped my son would prosper in his service. He said he would like nothing better than to see my son in the Guards uniform, joining me in protecting our native land.

At the time, that seemed the only brightness in my future.

◆

The time of Alexander III began with promise. The Tsarevich returned to the palace of Petrograd, his time in the Guards over. Now that he was next in line for the throne, he would have to learn affairs of state, visit foreign nations, and so on. I devoted my life to the Guard, knowing that someday I would be called upon to protect him.

For the first two years of his life, I left my son in the care of his nurse. He grew strong and healthy, worthy of his father. I would say that those were good years, but they seemed to pass by in a blur. I watched Nikolai crawl, saw him notice his tail for the first time, watched him stand and then talk, and his first word was "milyenkiy" (darling), something his nurse said of him all the time, though he could not say more than "mili." It was clear what he meant, though, because he pointed to himself.

I rose to third in command of the Guards. Vasily showed some pride, though always with the expectation that I would rise higher. Prior to Nikolai's birth, he expressed this through moderation of his compliments: that is not bad, he would say. It is what I would expect. After Nikolai's birth, he greeted news of my promotion with mild congratulations and a wish that Nikolai would someday rise to the heights that I could not. As though my career were already on its decline, as though I had nowhere left to go but to live through my son. He insinuated that Mariya's death had changed me, that I was lost in grieving and dreaming of what might have been. I brooded over these remarks when we parted company, and perhaps I should have been more careful around my son, or left him at home—but I wanted him to know his grandfather, and I wanted Vasily to be proud of Nikolai.

He never got to see my son's life, nor even his third birthday. My father had always imagined his death would come in battle, but we do not control the manner of our passing. He complained of chest pains one night in fall, retired early to his bed, and never rose from it again.

Nikolai, ever precocious, understood that the funeral service had something to do with Vasily, but he did not yet understand death. The nurse had to take him aside several times to answer his questions, spoken so loudly that all of us standing at attention in the Guard could hear him. Where is he? he wanted to know. Why is he not here?

Eventually, at the conclusion of the service, the nurse made him understand that Vasily was in the ground, in the box, and Nikolai ran to the edge of the grave and stared at the box, his eyes wide with wonder. Why does he not come out? he asked, turning to me. Is he playing?

The nurse pulled him back, strewing apologies before her. I had thought my son would miss Vasily, and it was pleasant to see it so, not because Vasily's death was causing him sadness, but because he might be of an age where he would remember his adopted grandfather.

So I thought, until the conclusion of a speech by the Grand-Duke Demenok, the commander of the Preobrazhensky regiment, praising Vasily and his service. I had not been called upon to speak, but the Grand-Duke knew my story and signaled down for the commander of the Semenovsky regiment to ask me if I would like to speak. I was not prepared, but I felt I owed Vasily this acknowledgment. So I told my story briefly, how I had been rescued from a terrible life by Vasily and given the chance to serve the Tsar, which I had striven my whole life to repay him for.

And at the end of my speech, Nikolai burst free from the nurse and ran to the coffin again, pointing at it and calling out, He was a bad tiger!

The nurse leapt and nearly fell in her haste to recall him. The other guards stood at perfect attention, showing no sign of the embarrassment I am sure they felt on my behalf. I allowed the unpardonable sin of faltering in my speech, and then mumbled an apology on behalf of my son—cubs, I said, did not understand the totality of a life lived. In looking back on it, I see that this apology only worsened the moment. It allowed the mourners to believe that Nikolai was justified in what he said.

My comrades, perfect gentlemen, said nothing more of the incident, and Vasily was interred with all honor, guns fired off a in salute that made Nikolai press his little paws over his ears. I exchanged solemn words with Gregor, Vasily's natural son, now a captain of the Preobrazhensky regiment, and I was somewhat surprised to hear that he, too, thought he had disappointed our father, and hoped that his cub, now five years old, would have redeemed him in the old tiger's eyes. I said that now it's his son who must please him, but the prospect did not seem pleasant to Gregor. We promised to meet again, but both knew that with our separate lives, this would never come to be.

I had previously left Nikolai's discipline to the nurse, but that night I struck him on the arm five times, once for each misspoken word. He cried then, as he had not cried at the funeral, and afterwards I asked him, Why did you say that? What evil spirit possessed you to dishonor your grandfather?

His eyes, now sea-green, looked guilelessly into mine. Because, Papa, he said, he made you sad.

Chapter 29

Alexei sat staring at his phone. Still muzzy-headed from sleep and fatigue, he felt a creeping wrongness around Cat's message. Fifty rubles? No, the program he'd gotten into had been paid for by the state. There was a program for disadvantaged cubs from small towns, a fund that covered their expenses and gave them some living money. Perhaps this Bogdan did not know about the fund, but that did not make sense if he were as clever as he claimed. It could be that the fifty rubles was simply his way of extracting a bribe from a young cub who might not understand that she was meant to offer one, but…

No, it did not feel right, but none of this felt right. Konstantin must have reached Bogdan, gotten him to call. There was his proof that Konstantin had kept his promise, and therefore Alexei would have to fulfill his end of the bargain. He could not give up being gay while living here with Sol and Meg; he would need a fresh start.

Numb, but with a small sense of relief at having the decision made for him, he dialed Liza's number and listened to the ring-ring, ring-ring, until her voicemail picked up. Her friendly, accented voice said, "This is Liza. Say what you have to say, I'll call you back."

"Hi," Alexei said into the phone. He pictured Liza's brown and white muzzle, small nose, kind eyes. "I might need your help. I mean, I do need your help. I need to find another place to live. I will talk to you later."

He hung up and sat there with his phone in his paws. He had done it now, had spoken the words to make it official. Curling his legs below him to sit on the bed, he pulled his tail around into his lap. Now that he wanted to talk to Konstantin, of course, the ghost was nowhere to be found. He'd fallen asleep twice since seeing Konstantin in the alley, and had talked to him neither time.

"Hey," Meg said, poking her head in the door, "dinner's about ready."

When Alexei sat down at the table, she asked, "Do you know where Sol is?" He shook his head, scooping a big hunk of casserole onto his plate, cheese dripping and pooling around the pieces of tuna. His stomach growled; it smelled wonderful. The slightly burned cheese concealed soft noodles and cream sauce as well as tuna. He returned the spoon to the casserole dish and looked up to see Meg and Athos both looking at him.

"What?" He looked at his plate, but they both had scoops of the casserole on theirs as well. He flicked his ears toward Athos. "Did you want to say Grace?"

The grey fox smirked. "Only to Count Dracul, or perhaps Baron Samedi in these parts."

"Dracula?" Alexei had always heard it with the trailing 'a.'

Athos rolled his eyes, and Meg cut in. "So what's with you moving out? You said something earlier, but I didn't think you meant now."

Alexei folded his ears back. "That was a private conversation," he muttered.

"Then you shouldn't be having it in a room next to someone with fox ears." Meg pointed to Athos, who did not even look abashed.

He'd forgotten about the fox. Meg usually couldn't hear what was going on, but they must have stopped the music or come out to the kitchen at just the right time. "Well," Alexei said, "I have to move out. That is what is with my moving out."

"Is it something to do with Sol?" Meg said. "Come on, I mean, you guys have had fights before."

"It is not—not entirely about that." Alexei hesitated.

"So what is it? Is it me? Because fuck you if it is. I mean, I know I'm not your best friend like wolfy-boy there—"

"He is not my best friend," Alexei said, "and it is not about you."

"Then what?" He stayed silent in the face of her demand, scooping a forkful of the casserole into his muzzle and chewing stoically. The food was hot but he did not taste any of it. Meg shrugged and took a bite herself. "Okay," she said, "you don't have to tell me. But Sol's gonna be upset, so I'm giving you a chance to rehearse what you're gonna say to him. And I'll tell you the parts that are stupid."

"You cannot change my mind," Alexei said.

"I'm past trying to figure out boys." Meg grinned when Athos, next to her, snorted. "I don't know why you would leave a place where your best friend—sorry, I guess a good friend—lives, and another friend who helps you perform nonsense rituals—"

"They are not nonsense," Alexei snapped, feeling his ears flush. The paw holding the fork itched; he scratched around the pads with claws.

"So is it about these hallucinations?" Meg laid her fork down. "You know, if the voices are telling you to move out..."

"They are not hallucinations."

Though he was staring down at his plate, he saw Meg and Athos exchange glances. Athos spoke. "I understand the need to believe that there is more than just what we see with our eyes, smell with our noses. But you have to keep it all in perspective."

"Your absinthe started this," Alexei said.

"My—" Athos faltered, ears askew, bewildered. "How?"

"Jesus," Meg said. "All right, you remember that absinthe you sent me for the school project? Sol got buzzed on it and had some weird dreams and that's what turned his eyes bright green."

"The absinthe?"

"Probably. I dunno, the doctors just said it happens sometimes and that it wasn't going to hurt him. He thinks it happened from talking to some ghost in his dream."

"It did," Alexei said.

"And now," Meg said, "foxy here is convinced that *he* is having dreams where he's talking to ghosts too. Only instead of turning his eyes green, they're telling him that he has to move out. Is that about right?"

"They are not just in dreams," Alexei said. He lifted a paw to his muzzle, rubbed where it was still sore.

"Right, hallucinations too." Meg sighed. "Does that under-the-table job you got have benefits that cover mental health programs, by chance?"

"I have been under a great deal of stress." He focused on the food in front of him, but the rich, hot smells seemed faded now. He didn't want to talk about Konstantin's reality, but if he had to, these were the second and third people in the world he would want to tell. "And anyway," he said, "he has gone into the dreams of a fox and made him call my sister. To help her." I hope, he added silently.

"Did you talk to this guy?" Athos's voice had a soft edge, the way you talk to someone who might go crazy and hit you if you said the wrong thing. "This fox? Did he tell you he had a dream?"

"No," Alexei said. "But he called my sister."

"Obviously it's a ghost, then," Meg said. "Because there's no other way someone would call your sister. I mean, people in Siberia don't just use phones to call each other."

"My friend at the exchange program could not find him." Alexei glared at Meg. "She has not called me back to tell me any news."

"Look." Meg glanced at Athos.

"Don't tell him," Athos said.

Alexei swung his muzzle back and forth, between the two of them. "What? Tell me what? Have you seen him?"

Meg sighed and looked at Athos. "I have to. Otherwise he's gonna end up like Sol, freaked out over nothing."

"It is not nothing," Alexei said. He leaned forward. "What? What is it?"

Meg put her fork down again and leaned forward across the table. "You know that e-mail Athos sent me with the ritual?"

Alexei nodded quickly. Athos had leaned back in his seat as though he wasn't feeling well from the meal, staring down into his lap. "I did not look at it," he said.

"Well, what it said was…" Meg took a breath. "It said, 'Burn some wormwood, get something related to the spirit, and say something about summoning the ghost from beyond. Oh, and use a bell.' That's all it said."

Alexei blinked. "You made up the words?"

Meg nodded slowly. He leaned forward. "But…but it worked." He turned to Athos. "It worked, I promise you."

She sighed. "It can't have worked. It wasn't a real ritual."

"Well," Athos said. "Let us hold on for one moment here." Alexei's ears perked up and he turned to the grey fox. "A ritual doesn't have to be something that's been used over and over again. I mean, technically that is the root of the word, from *rite*, which was a word used to describe religious customs, things which had been repeated."

"I'm not a priestess," Meg said. "And you're not helping."

"Rituals exist outside the supernatural, too," Athos said.

"But…" Alexei leaned across the table. "Perhaps the words did not matter. Perhaps it was the intent."

"Yeah." Meg tapped her claws on the table. "Listen, Athos, I'm trying to help out foxy here. I'm trying to narrow down what's happening to him to 'things in the real world.' You told me it didn't matter what I said."

Alexei looked between the two of them. "Perhaps it did not matter because the incense and the item were most important."

"What I'm saying is," and here Athos leaned forward and uncrossed his arms, "that people who claim that these things do work use the rituals as a sort of crutch. If a ritual fails, they will decide that it was something minor they forgot, or that the phase of the moon was wrong, or that the subject of the ritual was flawed—you know, like, if your ritual had failed, you might have explained it by saying you couldn't summon a ghost outside his native land. If rituals succeed, though, people attribute the success to the ritual even if many of the elements weren't quite right. The most important element is the belief of the people involved. They can trick themselves—"

"It is not a trick!" Alexei tried to stop his voice from climbing, but he was trembling now. "It is not in my head, it is not! He helped my sister— that fox called her, when he had no reason to, and she is going to Moskva to be safe now."

"Okay," Athos said, again in that soft voice that people in movies used when they were telling their friends that of course they were not crazy, "what I'm saying is that because you didn't know it wasn't a ritual that had been used before, for you, it held power."

"So it might have worked."

"No." Meg clutched her head in her paws. "Jesus, have you not been listening?"

"You will have to see him," Alexei said.

"Sure." Meg looked up at him through webbed fingers. "I'll just hook up our 'Inception' machine. It lets Athos and I come into your dreams and find secrets." She turned to Athos. "Got your token?"

"I told you," the fox said evenly, "that it was not just in dreams." He had to clasp his paws together to keep them from shaking.

Both otter and grey fox stared at him. Athos reached down to rub fingers along the side of his cape. "So," he said, slowly, "you can just call him up?"

Alexei took a deep breath. He pulled his tail up into his lap and rubbed the tip, combing through the fur. The motion soothed him. "Not… exactly."

Haltingly, he told them of his encounters, starting with the dreams. As he was describing the cemetery, and Athos was leaning forward with wide eyes, Sol came in the door. Alexei stopped, and all three of them at the table turned to the black wolf.

"What's going on?" Sol let the door swing closed behind him and took a step toward Alexei. "Jesus, where the hell were you? You scared the hell out of us."

"I know," Alexei said. "I am sorry."

"Sorry." Sol shook his head. "You just fucking disappeared, didn't answer your phone—"

"It was dead."

"—we didn't know where the hell you were, if you were dead—"

Alexei stood up, quelling the urge to meet Sol's belligerence with his own so easily that he knew Konstantin was nowhere near. He met the wolf's aggressive stance with swept-back ears, but he didn't turn his muzzle aside. "I had to get away," he said. "I am sorry."

"If you remember," Meg said, "you were kind of crazy last night. I probably woulda run away from you too."

Sol's tail flicked to the side. He didn't look at Meg, but to Alexei he said, "I didn't mean to scare you. But…"

It was a half-apology, and in the past, it would have been enough for Alexei. Now he stared levelly back at Sol and said, "Are you trying to say you are sorry?"

The wolf shifted on his feet and his eyes flicked down. "I guess so."

"Then you should say it."

Sol's eyes widened, and Alexei felt the stiffening of Meg and Athos. "I…" Sol started to reply angrily, but he hesitated, and Alexei jumped in.

"I have said I am sorry," he said. "But you also behaved badly."

Now Meg looked at Sol, a grin twitching at the corners of her mouth. "He's right, woofer. Come on, own up."

Sol spared her a brief glare, and then, ears lowered, looked back at Alexei. "I shouldn't have yelled," he said. "I'm—I'm sorry. But it was Niki."

"It is not Niki," Alexei said.

"It's his father," Meg put in. "And he's kind of a jerk."

That got Sol's attention. He turned to Meg and said, "Hang on, so you believe in this now?"

"Fox-boy believes in him, and thinks he can prove it, so I'm going along as official skeptic." She looked sideways at Athos as she said that.

Sol rolled his eyes and looked back at Alexei. The fox managed to pull his lips into a weak smile and said, "At least she is willing to try to help look for a ghost."

The black wolf surveyed them all and then grinned, his green eyes flashing. "That's something, I guess," he said. There were no more chairs, so he leaned against the sink. "So how are you going to look for him?"

With Sol's acceptance, words came more easily. Alexei told about seeing Konstantin on the fields, about the encounter in the alley, all the while with an eye on Sol. The black wolf listened keenly, green eyes flickering with interest, especially when Alexei talked about the fox entering their world. He sucked in a breath when Alexei told them about being slammed into the dumpster, and his eyes flicked to the bandage still on the fox's ear. Sol's ears stayed as low as his voice. "Were you going to do something—something bad?"

"No. He did not—he does not want me to be gay."

"That's ridiculous," Sol said. "What else could you be? That's why you came all the way from Siberia."

"He is helping my sister," Alexei said. "I love her. I need to bring her safely out of Samorodka."

"But this is who you are," Sol said.

Alexei breathed in. "Yes." He ran his fingers over the plastic wood grain of the table. "But it is not who I can be right now. And so I must leave."

He had planned to say more about leaving the apartment, but Sol and Meg both jumped in at the same time with an emphatic "No!"

"I have to!" Alexei said.

"You belong here." Sol stabbed a finger down at the table. "I mean, if you wanna go because I yelled at you…well, I said I'm sorry."

"It is not that." He breathed in and let the breath out slowly. "Sometimes we must give up something precious for those we love."

"That's—it makes sense, but—" Sol shook his head. "You can't just stop being gay."

"I can stop behaving gay."

The room fell so silent that Alexei could hear workers talking on the construction site, where no trucks or cranes were running. "You know," Sol said, his ears back, "that's exactly the sort of shit that the VLGA tells cubs not to fall for. The whole 'deny what you are and act straight.' That's probably what he wanted Niki to do. That's why Niki ran away from him."

"I am…bound to him," Alexei said softly. There was a twisted kind of caring in Konstantin's determination to change Alexei's life. Alexei's natural father had wanted his son to be straight so that the town would not ridicule them; Konstantin wanted Alexei to be straight so that his life would have meaning—as Konstantin saw it. "He wants my life to be…"

"What, normal? Screw him," Sol snapped. "What does it matter to him? He's just trying to fuck you up the same way he fucked up his own son. We'll help you fight him."

"Listen, fox." Meg leaned toward him. "What Sol's saying here is that we'd rather have you living with us and trying not to be gay than have you out there on your own. We care about you."

"But you shouldn't try to not be gay." Sol's voice had a deep growl at the back of it.

Alexei had rarely heard that from him. It reminded him of Sol's father, but he thought this was not the moment to bring up the comparison. He lay his ears back. "He watches me," he said.

Silence fell over the table. Athos perked his ears and lifted his nose, while Meg and Sol glanced back and forth to either side. "Like…right now?" Sol said.

"I don't think so."

"Does he watch you in the bathroom?" Meg asked. "Because then he's a pervert."

"He doesn't watch me all the time," Alexei said. "But he knows about Cat's letter. And he knew when I was on the date with Mike."

"Jesus," Sol said under his breath.

"It was the same for you." Alexei looked up at him.

The black wolf shifted. "That was different," he said, and looked over at Athos. "It was only once."

Athos smiled. "All these years of finding nobody who had really seen a ghost, and now two of you."

"They haven't really seen a ghost," Meg snapped.

"I thought you believed." Sol folded his arms, his tail smacking the cupboard under the sink.

"I believe," she said, pointing at Alexei, "that foxy here is in a bad way over something he thinks is happening. And I'm happy to help him deal with whatever he thinks is going on. But if there's one thing I've learned from a lifetime of having the mystical goddamn universe shoved in my face, it's that there is always a logical explanation for everything."

Athos leaned toward her. "But doesn't the possibility of something supernatural excite you? Just a bit?"

"No," Meg said. "It makes me fucking worried is what it does. So can we just agree that we'll stay with Alexei, and if he has an episode of whatever the hell is bothering him, we'll be there to help him deal with it and objectively tell him that there are no such things as ghosts?"

Sol met Alexei's eyes, and in the bright green, Alexei saw brotherhood, belief, and trust. For the first time that evening, he managed a small smile. "I would be glad to have your company," he said, and to himself he added, *until the moment I must leave.*

"Right, then," Meg said, and got up. "I've got a ritual we can do. Let's play Uno and see if this Siberian ghost cares about card games."

Chapter 30

As Nikolai grew, I watched him, eager to see signs of Mariya in him. His nurse remained with us, luckily, as Mariya's family did not grow closer to us after the funeral. On one occasion when I sacrificed my dignity and pleaded with Mariya's mother to come see her grandson, she turned up her nose and hurried away, and her maidservant reprimanded me for bringing up the name of her dearest departed daughter.

I understood that they hated this coarse soldier with no proper family, that they blamed me for Mariya's death and that dear Nikolai was but a reminder to them of the daughter they had lost. Nikolai liked to play at hiding under couches with his tail peeking out, a game in which his nurse or I would catch his tail and he would squeal with delight. On the rare occasions when Mariya's family could not escape their obligation to visit, Nikolai tried to play with them. But even when he would switch his tail below their seats, begging them to catch it, they remained unmoved. He was a painful reminder, because he was not theirs, but belonged to that same coarse soldier.

And yet Nikolai showed little of his father. He took after his mother, gregarious and happy, always smiling. If I could have changed one thing about him, then, it would have been to share with him my love for the army and the service to Siberia. He attended practices under sufferance when young, with polite restraint when a little older, because he was not allowed to talk to the soldiers during drills. Many of them broke rules to speak to him anyway, he was so difficult to resist, and yet my son far preferred mealtimes, when the soldiers were free to converse. He showed no interest in joining their occupation, but professed to love dancing, and I allowed him to study it, because it had a noble Siberian history, and because his teacher told me he excelled.

He worked hard to make friends with the noble cubs he attended school with, although his relationship to me hurt him in that regard. Only one cub, a bear, became a regular visitor to our house, and he often pulled Nikolai out to the town, to the coffee shops and markets. I could not deny him that pleasure, even as he grew older and began to visit those places by himself.

The friends he brought home were less frequently his age and more often in their later teens, young intellectuals who scorned me with their eyes when Nikolai cautioned them against speaking their true feelings. They were dancers and students and writers, not one of them an honest worker. A builder, a carpenter, those I would have respected. Even a groomer does work with his—or her—paws, where these friends of Nikolai's sat and drank coffee and vodka and pretended that their dreams were meaningful. They were bad sorts, unreliable and flighty, and I knew they would put him in danger.

What sort of danger, Papa? he asked, and only when he was thirteen did I tell him the story of his blood-related grandparents, of how they too had fallen in with the wrong sorts of people and had dreamed of revolution rather than working to appreciate the land and the Tsar they had. I told him that I had been granted a miraculous chance by Vasily's benevolent nature, a chance that I was sharing with him, and I pleaded with him not to waste it.

He said that the chance was his to do with as he pleased, and he was trying to improve both our lives. He asked whether my life would not be better if I were allowed to rise to the ranks held only by tigers, or if I were permitted to hold land which now was reserved for the nobles. Many of my peers had purchased a small farm and negotiated with the peasants on it for their income, but I felt that would provide too much distraction, what with worrying over the harvest and traveling to the land. I told Nikolai that the Semenovsky Guards had already improved my life immeasurably. How many people had the chance that Vasily had given me, he asked. How could a just society allow some of its people to know nothing but suffering while others enjoyed the fruits of their labors?

Because, I told him, people are born to their lives, and when people are allowed to choose their destinies, a nation falls into chaos. The Tsar, I told him, is as bound to his life as we are. He shook his head at the mention of the Tsar, and said he was an aristocrat who knew nothing of the real Siberia. At those words, which I knew were not his own but parroted from his friends, I cuffed him as Vasily would have done. Only rather than straightening and accepting his punishment, as I would have, he cowered, and hurt shone out of his bright green eyes.

There was one friend in particular, a bear who recited poetry, and Nikolai was very affectionate with him. He sat close to him in our parlor, often put a paw upon him in laughter or concern, and smiled at the mildest witticism. The poetry rankled me, amateurish and sloppy, and yet Nikolai hung on every word. For my son's sake, I tolerated this pretentious fool, until one particular evening.

It was summer, and I had returned home from a difficult but honorable week, sent to attend to Nicholas II at the summer palace in relief of the Preobrazhensky Guards, who were being given the time off. I had performed well, but had become disturbed at what I had seen of the Tsarevich. He had gained nothing of the strength or determination of his father and grandfather; rather, he continued to favor his wife's family, preferring conversation to decision, etiquette to action. The guards I spoke to and the ministers I overheard all said that it was a good thing the Tsar remained in fine health, for Nicholas was coming into his birthright more slowly than anyone had expected. Blame lay with Alexander, for allowing him the space to chart his own course and for not insisting that he become part of the government with his father.

When I returned home, wishing only to see my son and embrace him, I found him on a chaise with his head on the thigh of the bear, who was writing in a notebook. At my appearance, Nikolai did not look up, but the bear did, and regarded me with a smirk. He proceeded to recite a poem that mocked the guard, mocked the Tsar, and held them up as outdated puppets in a show with no audience.

I did not let him finish, but told Nikolai to escort him from our house. When my son sat up, looking mutinous, I promised to evict this bear by force if necessary. Niki pleaded his case, saying it would do me good to hear what he said, but I told him I had heard enough.

That night, I told him he was no longer to visit the coffee houses, but that he would attend me at the Guards and train to be a soldier himself. He had enough strength not to cry; if he had, I might have relented, or I might have cuffed him harder for his weakness. But had I thought then what I suspected later, that he went to hide his sorrows in the self-styled poet's arms...I might have locked him in his room and never let him out, not even to become a soldier.

Chapter 31

He stands in front of a decrepit, empty house on a street down which ragged grey leaves blow in the cold wind. The houses to either side are smaller, the ruin more complete in them, as though decay had whetted its appetite on smaller meals and was only now beginning to tackle the main course.

A central arch rises three stories in the center of the house facing him, white stone against the ochre of the walls. It is merely decorative, as the wall continues both inside the arch and out, but it is imposing nonetheless. White trim defines the large windows inside the arch as well as the smaller ones outside it. To the right of the arch, the house rises two more stories to a pointed roof, and on the right corner a circular tower room ends in a sharp green point. To the left of the arch rise two more stories in a large block beneath two chimneys, one of which has mostly crumbled.

Only half the windows are intact. The roof on the left hand side of the house is missing so many of its pure black shingles that the few remaining ones appear to be a blight on the underlying wood. And in front of Alexei, the door hangs from its top hinge, askew in the frame. Beyond it, the darkness smells of rot and mold.

But it is the decoration on the door that freezes him, holds him in place in the chill wind as leaves rattle around his ankles. Carved into the dark wood is a relief of a tiger, and though the pose is different, Alexei knows that it is the tiger whose statue chased him around the courtyard in his last dream.

This time, it does not move. He is afraid to run lest it chase him; he is afraid to approach lest it come to life and pounce. His tail wraps around his legs and he tightens his arms around his chest, rocking back and forth.

The relief becomes the focus of his attention, so much so that he does not see at first the shape behind the door. Then Konstantin steps in front of the relief, appearing to materialize out of it, and Alexei is badly startled, enough that he jumps and his dream-tail bristles out behind him.

I have found your Chichikov, the older fox says, advancing on Alexei.

Alexei's heart pounds from the initial surprise, but it does not calm down. He has the sense that the tiger is waiting behind Konstantin or inside him. I know, he says. He called Cat. He will be rescuing her.

The skies overhead thicken with clouds, darkening as Konstantin's expression does. I did not tell him to call her, he says. He is not a good person.

Not good? A gust of leaves blow against Alexei's muzzle. He flinches. How, not good? You promised to help her.

Not this way. He has... The fox pauses. Bad thoughts. Harmful thoughts.

Is he going to hurt her? *Alexei finds his footing, takes a step forward. His body thrums with the rage he felt at Kendall, a thousand times fiercer.* You have to protect her.

This Chichikov takes laudanum, or some such. He does not dream. I cannot reach him. I can see the thoughts in his head like scum on the water, but it is frozen; I cannot step inside.

You promised!

Alexei runs forward two steps and raises a fist before the fox, intending to strike the bright gold sash that hangs loose, the spotless red collar. Konstantin glowers down and the world darkens further. You will not strike me, *he says.* It is not your place.

My place is with my sister. You betrayed us!

I did not! *The dream-voice echoes in Alexei's head so hard he thinks it will burst open. He clutches his temples and staggers back.*

Konstantin follows him, shadow growing. The wind howls, the clouds descend. The top of the house is no longer visible. A low growl comes from the wood as the wind batters it, pushing at the heavy door. I am trying to help *you.* You have no understanding of family, of what it means to be loyal to someone. You will do your sister more good by learning to respect your family than by infecting her with your scorn.

My father was a drunk! *Alexei shouts back at Konstantin.* My mother vicious and cruel!

And you never thought to ask why. You never thought you could help them.

He repeats what Rozalina told him once, so long ago. It is not my job to help them!

Shadow-fingers reach down to his shoulders, grasping them with cold ice. They do not feel like real fingers, but more like the ghost-sword of the tiger statue. Konstantin's broad muzzle looms inches from his. When Nicholas was growing, he disappointed his father on many occasions. He was not strong, forceful; he was weak and would sooner sit at court with his mother's relatives than learn to rule the country. Alexander allowed this because he loved his son, because he did not see it as betrayal. I did not see it. None of Siberia saw it until Nicholas became the Tsar.

Alexei raises his arms to try to break the shadow-fox's hold, but he has only enough strength to twist his shoulders back and forth. And what did you do? Did you follow him anyway? Your beloved Tsar? *He intends the words to be a taunt, but they falter in the face of the stormclouds.*

Yes! *Konstantin's eyes, dark and haunted, bore into Alexei's until the young fox feels their chill in his heart.* Because the tsars had taken me in, and they were my family. I owed them my loyalty and I gave them all of it. It did not matter that they were not what I wanted them to be, what Siberia needed them to be. I stood by them. I did not flee to Lutèce, as many of the aristocracy did later.

You should have, Alexei says *because he is thinking it, and in this dream the line between thought and speech is blurred.* You should have saved yourself.

What good is it to save myself if my world is gone? What is my life worth if I have abandoned those who needed me?

I needed you! You betrayed me, *Alexei says*, and I will have no more to do with you. My friend will banish you and then I will live the way I want to.

The old fox thrusts his muzzle forward, teeth bared. You will not leave me, *he says, and his eyes, now the color of dried blood, fix Alexei and he cannot look away. The fingers holding his shoulders seem to be boring into them; ice crystallizes in his muscles, growing a lattice around his heart. Behind Konstantin, clouds have enveloped the house, and not just hidden it from view; it is the clouds that eat away at the buildings. As their tendrils snake around the turret, it crumbles, sending bricks to the ground in a muffled clatter. Grey mist steals over the roof, dissolving the last remaining shingles.*

Alexei is dragged forward, toward shadow-Konstantin, and the gold sash falls aside, and the coat hangs open, and inside it there is nothing—no, wait, there is the same grey mist as the clouds. He tries to dig in his heels, but there is no purchase.

You cannot make me come with you! *he yells.* My sister needs me!

The icy fingers pull. Alexei's resistance falters. Konstantin says, She is beyond your help. Come, *lisenok.*

That is more chilling than the ice in his chest, the cold breath on his whiskers. But Alexei feels the ghost's insistence, and he knows he cannot resist for much longer. I am not your son! I am not Niki!

He shouts it desperately, because his paws are beginning to go numb, and the flaps of the coat hang around his nose, and the scent he breathes is old earth, old blood, old sorrow. What will happen if he is drawn into the coat he does not know, and does not wish to discover.

But it is Konstantin's turn to falter. He breathes a word across Alexei's ears: Nikolai… *His breath is warmer, or perhaps Alexei's ears are colder. But the pull stops, and Alexei wrenches his shoulders to one side, losing his balance, but Konstantin's arm is there to catch him, and it is warm and solid and real—*

"You will not leave me"

Chapter 32

"Hey, Alexei!"

Warm arms around him, a voice in his ear that is not a hundred years old, warm breath, warm blankets. He shudders, the ice around his heart slow to melt, and clutches at the arms, presses his head to the chest. Still he feels the decrepit landscape around him.

It is Sol's voice that reaches him. "Hey, you were having a nightmare."

He lifts his muzzle from the black-furred chest into the gleam of green eyes in a dark room. "Yes," he says. Automatically, he adds, "I am sorry I woke you," even as his mind races with the terror of the dream. He sees Konstantin behind Sol, for a moment as clearly as if a lightning flash had illuminated him.

"Ahh!"

He yelled and scrambled to the nightstand, grabbing for the light. The lamp toppled over and fell with a crash, and Alexei came completely out of the dream. In the darkness, he could see very little in the room. Even Sol's green eyes had disappeared. The wolf was still grabbing at him, but the image of Konstantin burned into Alexei's eyes made him hypersensitive to touch, and he shoved Sol away.

"He's here, he's here!" Alexei yelled over the wolf's curse.

Even with his ears flat against his head, he could hear Sol's harsh breathing in the silence that followed. "Where?" the wolf whispered. "In the room?"

Alexei breathed in through his nose. The only smells in the room were fox and wolf, dinner and the dust of the silent construction site outside the window. No smell of old earth, no smell of decay. "I thought," he said, and scanned the room. The darkness yielded to his eyes, which stretched as wide as he could open them.

Sol waited for several beats and then spoke. His dark fur blended into shadow so that his light blue boxer shorts seemed to float in the air, and when the dim light caught his green eyes, they flashed toward Alexei like beacons. "When I saw Niki," he whispered, "it was just for a second. But it was really important. Were you dreaming?"

"It isn't Niki." Alexei knew Sol was just likening their experiences, but he felt he had to convey that Konstantin was not the same kind of benevolent spirit as Niki, who had reached out across a century and an ocean to protect Sol. Konstantin was reaching across the same century, the same ocean, but he wanted to draw Alexei back with him. And he had been unable to help Cat. *She is beyond your help.*

"I know," Sol said, but the rest of his words were cut off when the door opened and light flooded the room, making both canids squeeze their eyes shut.

"What's going on?" Meg's voice sounded unnaturally high.

Behind her, Athos said, "Is it him?"

"I have to call my home." Alexei pushed Sol away and swept his paw across his night table, looking for his phone.

"It's two in the morning," Sol said.

"Not in Siberia," Meg said. "Why? What happened?"

The phone was on the floor next to the broken lamp. Alexei grabbed it, stabbed at the buttons until his call history came up, the number Cat had called from last. He pressed "Call" and flipped the mike out, breathing heavily against it. Ethereal whirrs and clicks filled his ear.

"I don't know," Sol said to Meg.

"Konstantin isn't here?" Athos pronounced the name wrong, without the proper depth to the "o," but Alexei didn't correct him, nor respond. On the other side of the world, the phone was ringing.

"He had a dream, I think?" Sol got up.

Alexei curled his tail around his legs, knees drawn tightly up to his chest, and worked his way back against the wall, the bed and desk on either side of him bracing him, holding him up. The phone rang again and then the ring cut off. A clatter, and then a harsh, familiar voice said, "*Yes?*"

He spoke quickly, in Siberian. "*Cat,*" he said. "*Caterina.*"

Before he could say anything else, his mother snarled, "*Aleksandr. How dare you call? Did you know about this? It is your fault. If not for you, my Caterina would be here at home! Did you know? Did you help her run away?*"

"*It is not my fault.*" Sol stared at him. Meg turned over her shoulder to say something to Athos. Alexei barely noticed them. Surely, surely if something terrible had happened to Cat, she would have told him. "*She was never happy there.*"

"*We could have been happy if you had been a better son!*" His mother sounded close to wailing, her words distorted and stretched.

He wanted to hang up, to cut them off again, but he had not spoken to them in over a year. "*Let me talk to Cat!*"

"*We gave you a home.*" His mother's voice held no more love, and Alexei wondered now if it ever had. "*We gave you food, gave you shelter, promised you everything.*"

"*Not what we needed,*" Alexei said. "*You thought only of yourselves. Never of us.*"

"*We thought of nothing but you!*" his mother shrieked. In the background, he heard his father cursing at him. "*You abandoned us and lured your sister away and now look at what has happened!*"

"*Caterina only wants to come live with me, with her real family who loves her,*" he said in spite. "*We will start—*"

"*No!*" His mother's cry drowned out his words. "*She will be buried here!*"

She shouted more curses, but Alexei didn't hear them. His fingers on the phone went numb, as though the phone were a block of ice, and his breath caught in his throat. "*Buried?*" he choked out.

His mother didn't hear him. "*You ungrateful cub. I wish I had drowned you in the river. I wish you had never lived! I would rather mourn a dead newborn than this, than to see how you corrupted and destroyed my Cat, my darling.*"

"*You never loved her,*" Alexei said, trying to suppress his reaction to the words. He'd known his parents despised him for leaving, but wishing him dead? His tail curled tightly on itself; he drew his knees up, hunched on the floor. "*What happened to her?*"

In the background, he heard his father say, "*Hang up. Hang up! Do not waste breath on him.*"

"*She's dead!*" his mother screamed into the phone. "*Dead, and you killed her!*" And then there was a click, and silence.

Alexei sat without moving. He kept the phone pressed to his ear, though nothing but silence came through. Dead to us, that's what his mother must have meant. Cat would be buried there in Samorodka—eventually. But his blood remained cold, and his muscles refused to unlock.

Sol and Meg stared at him; Athos had gone. "One more call," he whispered, and dialed Rozalina's number—the home number she had given him, since it would be Saturday morning in Siberia.

"What's happening?" Sol said. "You were angry and then went quiet."

"And not a good kind of quiet," Meg added.

He held up a finger for them to wait, and they did. The phone rang and rang, and on the third ring, Rozalina picked up. Alexei identified himself quickly. "*I am worried about Caterina,*" he said. "*I called my parents too—*"

"*Why did you call your home? You should not have done that.*"

"*—and they were very upset.*"

"*I told you they were upset.*"

"*I think something may have happened to her. Please, can you see if any young vixens were reported...*" He couldn't bring himself to say the word. "*In Moskva? She said she was going to Moskva.*"

"*Why do you not ask them?*"

He could have, he supposed, but he did not trust them to give him an honest answer. They could easily say she was dead just to spite him even if she were just upstairs. "*They were very upset,*" was all he could think to say.

She tapped on a keyboard. "*Your father called this office eleven times when you left.*"

Meg and Sol were talking softly to each other and watching him. "*I know. I am sorry.*"

"*It is not your fault. But you should not call and antagonize them. Now he is going to call here again and they always send the calls to me, and there is nothing I can say to him. He will yell at me and call me terrible names and hang up, and then call back to do it all over again.*"

What else did she want him to say? "*Don't talk to him.*"

"*Then he reports me and I have to suffer through a review and explain your family again.*" They're not my family, he wanted to say. Not anymore. "*I am not seeing any reports in the news. There is...wait.*"

Her voice softened, and Alexei's heart filled with dread. His ears flattened back. In the room, Sol and Meg quieted, watching him. For three, five, ten seconds there was no sound but keys being tapped, then clicks, and then not even that. "*There is a report,*" she said slowly, "*that a young vixen fell from a building and died. They think the roof, perhaps a high window.*"

"*Like the wolf from Samorodka,*" he said before he could help himself.

Sol and Meg glanced at each other at the mention of Alexei's hometown. Rozalina sucked in a breath. "*And the other one,*" she said, but Alexei cut her off.

"*She was dating the wolf, the one who jumped.*"

"*You don't know it was her, Alexei,*" Rozalina said, but he did know, could feel it like a lump of ice lodged in his chest. He could see her looking at the window and remembering Slava, how if all other avenues of escape were closed to her, at least she had his lead to follow. He thought of the times he had talked to her about ghosts, about living beyond death, and how she must have thought she would see Slava again. In trying to protect her, he had led her to Bogdan, encouraged her, and it had been a trap.

"*The corsac fox,*" he said, with as much clarity as he could. "*The one I asked you to look up. Bogdan Chichikov. He did this to her.*"

"*Alexei—*"

"*Promise you will tell the police about him. Promise.*"

She paused. "*Bogdan...Chichikov.*" She spoke slowly, as though writing down the name. "*I will tell them. But—*"

"*Thank you*," he whispered. Before she could answer, he hung up the phone.

"Well?" Meg said. "You going to translate for us?"

In his head, the words were in Siberian: *Caterina is dead.* He understood Meg's words but could not for a moment cross the barrier to form words to say back to her. "My sister," he said, reverting to some of his first English lessons, struggling to pull words together. "I hear my sister has…" Jumped, died, suicide: the words clattered around in his head, refusing translation, refusing to pass his throat. He squeezed his eyes shut and dropped his phone to the floor, barely noticing the thump as he pressed a paw over the bridge of his muzzle.

His whiskers twitched as Sol knelt next to him. Crammed into the space between the bed and the desk as Alexei was, it was difficult for Sol to get an arm around him, but the wolf crawled halfway under the desk and got one paw on the fox's shoulder. "Hey," Sol said. "Come on out. Let's get you something warm to drink."

"He doesn't need coffee," Meg said. "Maybe he just needs to be alone."

"No." Alexei and Sol said it at the same time.

"We promised we'd stay in case Konstantin came back," Sol said.

"I just meant that maybe he doesn't want to talk about his sister," Meg snapped back. "Maybe we can just talk about, I dunno, movies or some shit."

Sol and Alexei shared a look, and in that Alexei saw Sol's sympathy, the experience they shared. Sol had never lost a sibling, but he had been lost in a different way, his world falling apart around him. "Do you need someone to listen?" the wolf said softly.

Alexei's ears came partway back up, and his whiskers rose and fell. He exhaled and crawled out from the corner he was in. At least listening to Sol and Meg seemed to have restored his ability to speak properly. "I do not know what will do any good," he said. "I fear I have done a terrible thing to my sister."

"In your—" Sol's ears flicked toward Meg and then back. "Dreams?"

"No. In…" Alexei circled his finger around in the air. "In this world. She wanted to escape. I am afraid…"

Sol reached out for him then, and Alexei let the wolf hug him. After a moment, he hugged back and rested his head against Sol's shoulder.

At the table, a little later, he was able to tell them more. They were silent, and then Meg said, "Well, that sucks."

"Nice." Sol glared at her. "Any other obvious unhelpful remarks to make?"

"I'm being sympathetic, smart-mouth," she retorted. "If you have an idea for a more practical response, I'm all ears."

Sol turned back to Alexei. "I know you said Konstantin wants to make you stop being gay, but...does he want to help you? Can you ask him...?"

"I already did." Alexei shook his head violently. "This is why—" He stopped himself. It was not why this had happened; Konstantin had in fact tried to warn him about Bogdan, but had done it too late. Alexei himself was the one who was at fault for encouraging his sister to leave, for filling her with false hope and a desperation strong enough to make her easy prey for a cunning predator who recognized her spark shining out amidst the desolate small town.

He slumped back in his chair and covered his muzzle in his paws. "Hey," Sol said. "Hey, come on, keep it together." Another of those expressions that Alexei had to focus to understand. Together? He was coming apart, alone, powerless to control even his fate, let alone his sister's or anyone else's. It would be best to do nothing, to sit here in this room where he could not hurt anyone, most of all himself.

Chapter 33

Alexei spent Saturday sitting on his bed staring at his phone. Around him, Sol and Meg hovered, with Athos throwing in statements on occasion. Meg made him chicken soup for lunch, after he'd refused to eat breakfast.

"I know it's for like, when you're sick with a cold, but in case you get some psychosomatic shit happening, this isn't going to fuck with your system any."

He shook his head. "I am not hungry," he said.

"Well, you're not going to starve." She stood with paws on her hips and stared down at him. "And I can stand here all day until you finish it, so you will eat it."

When he still didn't move, she added, "And I'm not gonna reheat it. So you're better off eating it while it's hot."

He sighed and turned toward the bowl. The soup did smell good, and best of all, it smelled nothing like anything his parents had made for him, brought back no memories of home. He brought the spoon to his muzzle and sipped. "It's good," he said.

"It's Campbell's," Meg snorted. "I dumped it out of a can. Keep going."

The taste did, for a short time, drive off the memories. He watched the noodles float in the golden broth, watched the patterns the chicken fat made on the surface, and emptied his mind until his spoon scraped the bottom of the bowl.

"Right." Meg took the bowl to the kitchen and returned a moment later with a plate and two slices of bread. "Here. In case you get hungry. Athos and Sol and I will be out in the kitchen." She looked down at her feet. "If you wanna talk. Or something."

"Thank you," Alexei said softly. He barely noticed when she left. Sol spent the morning and early afternoon with him, then left to run some errands, after making sure Meg would be home if Alexei needed anything.

All day, he was thinking of Cat, of the time that beaver had stepped on her tail and Alexei had knocked him down; of the time their father had whipped her with his belt and she'd hidden in Alexei's room sobbing; of the time the two of them snuck out and just sat in the moonlight in the overgrown weeds; of the time with the loaf of bread, the time with the pencils, the time with the half-eaten fish. And he thought of Konstantin telling him that Chichikov was a "bad sort," of how overjoyed Cat had been in her letter to him, of how desperate she must have felt standing on that roof.

Slava's death must have weighed on her. She had probably stayed up nights just as Alexei was now, thinking of the wolf's body diving into free-fall, arms outstretched, just as he could see her standing on the edge.

The skies are grey behind her. She stands perfectly still. The stone is sunlit-warm beneath her toes, and up here, the wind pushes against her as though desperately trying to hold her up. Her tail flows out behind her, catches the sun, but does not shine as it once did. Inside her there is something black, something gnawing, sapping the brightness from her fur and her smile. She extends her arms as perhaps Slava did—

Or:

There is nobody on the roof; he checks before coming through the door. The slight weight of the faded vixen is no trouble for the stocky corsac fox. She lies limp in his arms, drugged (already dead?). He crouches, scuttles to the edge of the roof, and lifts her body—

Or:

He is not her savior. She runs from him, escapes the apartment somehow and finds the stairs. She goes up, hoping he will think she went down, but he hears her or smells her or he has done this before and he knows. She runs to the roof and then there is no more escape. He is not worried; they always come down. But not this one. She is new, her spirit still flickering, and she has nothing to go back to. She climbs onto the roof, and when he advances one more step—

Alexei buried his muzzle in his paws. He heard Cat's laughter, smelled her as though she were standing beside him, felt her hug him good-bye and kiss him on the cheek, heard her whisper, "Good luck." He saw her writing the letter, determined that she would come and join him, tongue tip sticking out of her mouth like it did when she was concentrating on something (one of the many unladylike habits she had). He saw her falling from the tree they had climbed, the time she scraped her ear, the time she twisted her ankle.

He saw himself promising they would make it out together. He felt the rough wood of the wall against his nose again, felt the splinters catch in his fur as Cat asked him, "Are you gay?"

She had understood, and whom else would he have told there? How else would he have had the courage to escape? Anger at his parents surged in him, but at the same time he felt that was no more than a diversion to escape his own guilt.

Later in the afternoon, he became convinced that Caterina was not really dead, that it had been some other vixen, that his mother had been drunk or hysterical. His phone had rung three times, twice from Liza and once from Mike, but he hadn't answered it, and only Liza had left voicemail, which he hadn't listened to. Still, he kept his phone near him, and when in the evening it rang with a Siberian number, he jumped to press it to his ear. In his excitement, he heard a female voice and said, "*Cat?*"

"*Yes,*" the caller said, and then, "*I am so sorry, Alexei.*"

"*What? Where are you?*"

"*In Moskva. Alexei, this is Rozalina. I have just talked to the police on your behalf. They confirmed that the vixen who died was Caterina Tsarev. I am so sorry.*"

"*No. No.*" He shook his head. "*Cat is going to call me.*"

"*Did you receive a message from her?*"

He bit his lip. Rozalina kept talking, but he didn't understand all the words, until she said, "*Chichikov,*" and then he snapped back to attention.

"*What? What about Chichikov?*"

"*They arrested him, Alexei. He lived in the building she jumped from. They found pictures of young girls of many species in his apartment and items of clothing. He is a criminal.*"

"*And he killed Cat?*"

"*They cannot be sure. But they will tell me. I had to prove I was your legal representative. I hope you do not mind.*"

"*No,*" he said. "*Please tell me what they find.*"

"*She had a letter in her pocket,*" Rozalina said. "*It is addressed to you. Would you like me to read it, or send it on to you?*"

"*Send it,*" he said without thinking. He could not bear to hear it now, Cat's words coming to him in Rozalina's voice through the phone. He could not give himself that false hope.

"*How did you know of him? They wanted to know.*"

"*Cat told me,*" he said, and squeezed his eyes shut.

Sol came back later, when Alexei was finishing a second bowl of soup Meg had forced on him. "Any news?" he said, and then at Alexei's expression, "Shit. Sorry. I got back as soon as I could."

"She is dead," Alexei said in a voice as flat as his ears. He had not told Meg yet, and now she hovered in the doorway, staring.

Sol turned to her. "You didn't tell me."

She pointed. "*He* didn't tell *me.*"

"What happened?" Sol asked, softly, sitting on the desk chair so his knees were inches from the edge of the bed where Alexei sat cross-legged.

"She wanted to do what I did. She trusted a bad fox and then…" He spread his paws. "Perhaps he threw her out of a window. Perhaps she jumped, like her boyfriend did."

"Jesus," Sol breathed.

"Fuck," Meg said. "Look, no way is that your fault."

"I asked Konstantin to help her escape," Alexei said. "I drove her into his arms."

"You can't blame yourself for some other sick fucko." Meg spat the last word.

"And you're definitely not moving out," Sol chimed in. "Not now. Anyway, he didn't help your sister. You don't have to do what he says, now."

Alexei had not heard from Konstantin in a very long time, it felt like, and yet he knew that the older fox was not gone. Konstantin knew grief and loss; Alexei had seen that in his eyes in the dream. He was bound to the old soldier now, with shared history and experience, an intimacy as close as family. Konstantin's current absence was respectful, but Alexei knew that very soon he would have to face the soldier again, and this time, offered the chance to escape the guilt and tragedy of the world, he might not have the strength to resist. "I do not believe it is that simple," he said softly.

"You can't be alone."

Alexei curled his tail around his ankles and stared down at it. "I am not," he said, and Sol and Meg made approving noises, while grit itched between his paw pads and the dirt from the construction site smelled like a grave.

Chapter 34

Later in Nikolai's thirteenth year, the tiger he was named for ascended the throne of Siberia. Nicholas II became Tsar when his father died quite unexpectedly, and the twenty-six-year old was entrusted with the most noble empire in the world. He still had not displayed the fortitude expected of him given his parentage, but he had a noble wife to whom he seemed devoted, and we had hopes that with her family's alliances among the houses of Petrograd and Moskva, we might see him surround himself with capable ministers who could help him grow into his birthright.

Alas, his rule began under ill omens. A gathering to celebrate his coronation became a stampede, and many were killed. The soldiers who failed to maintain order were punished—fortunately, I was not among them—but the whispers began. Even among my own regiment, there was scorn for the emperor's weakness. He had attended a ball that very night! Did a thousand deaths mean nothing to him? I argued on his behalf in vain, for my arguments felt as weak as his character. Still, for the sake of my son and my post, I clung to my loyalty.

When my son Nikolai began his military training after his fifteenth birthday—somewhat late, to be sure—I explained that he had aspired to the ballet, and his commanders accepted this as properly rigorous physical exercise, though he was not allowed to continue once he joined the guard. He did not sulk over this, but showed such hurt when reminded of it that several times I nearly allowed him to take it up again, before remembering the focus necessary to succeed in the guards.

I had always thought that Niki would make an admirable soldier. He was smart, so smart, and he got along well with the other boys. For the first six months he was trained with the twelve-year-olds to make up for the years he'd missed, and he quickly became their favorite. Even though he complained of boredom to me, he said he liked the marching, and my heart filled with hope.

Wastrel poets and intellectuals no longer followed him home, and as far as I knew, he did not visit them any longer. He and I continued to converse on any number of subjects, and I learned much about music and literature from him. Good Siberian literature, respectful of the people and the Emperor, seemed to do wonders for his attitude. I felt at this time that Nikolai and I had mastered the challenges that life had thrown at us: the death of his mother, the death of my father, the instability of the empire. We would grow and prosper, my boy and I, and he, so much smarter than I, would outshine my achievements.

After six months, he was placed with boys his own age, and here he found the regiment harder to master. When he was living with the other soldiers, not simply visiting them, he could not resist talking of the ideas his coffee-shop intelligentsia had expounded upon or reading some of their execrable poetry, things I had thought gone from his life because he no longer spoke of them to me. The other soldiers, who preferred to talk about racing and young ladies, viewed him as an outsider, even after more than a year of training.

This I heard from his commanding officer, two months after his seventeenth birthday, but that was only the background to the chief complaint against him. Nikolai, this tiger said, barely keeping his claws restrained, had tempted other soldiers into vice, and at least one had succumbed. He did not describe the specific act, but my imagination supplied the details.

I told the tiger I would correct it, ensure that such a thing never happened again. When he left, I brought in Nikolai from the other room.

He knew what he had done, but was unrepentant. The other soldier had asked him about it, he said, and there had been no coercion nor seduction. I cuffed him and reminded him that the point was to behave like a soldier, to be strong and fierce. I told him how disappointed I was in him and that I expected him to do much better. He protested that it was not weakness, that he could be a strong soldier and still have affection for his fellow soldiers, but I saw this ridiculous notion for the coffee-shop nonsense that it was, and forbad him speak of it.

Dancing was all that he valued, it seemed, so I told him that if he received satisfactory marks from his commander after another six months, I would allow him to resume his dancing lessons. After all, it did seem to help with the marching; one area where Nikolai had never been faulted was in the precision of his steps.

It was too late for that, he said, though I could see the longing in his eyes. He would never be in the Imperial Ballet; he was far too old.

But, I pressed, he still wished to practice, and learn, and improve, yes? I saw the answer though he did not speak it. He had only to prove he was strong and he could do as he pleased. If he wanted something, the path to taking it was clear.

He told me that not everyone was meant to be strong. I retorted that strength could be taught and learned, and if one chose not to learn it, that spoke to a deficiency of one's inner character. He turned his bright green eyes on me and said, what, then, of Nicholas, the tsar you love so? Do you not love him even though he has not yet learned to be strong as you think of it?

Stop, I cautioned him, but he and I were too close, too familiar, and he saw his chance.

Do you know what they say about him, in the guards? He stepped up closer to me, daring me to shut out his words even though my ears were flat. I could not look away from his eyes. I felt the warmth of his breath on my whiskers. They say he would like me, he said. They say he would appreciate my personal attentions. They say I should enter his service.

I cuffed him harder, raked his ears with my claws, and knocked him to the floor. He bled; I could smell it, and yet I only wanted him to stop. And why, he said, do you love him and not me?

He lay on the floor without even attempting to stand against me. I told him that I loved Nicholas for his family. Truthfully, though I barely knew it then, I had begun to feel disgust for my Emperor, for the country he disappointed with his uncertain, passive leadership. And you, I told my son, I love because you bear my blood and Mariya's.

Ah, he said, so that is why. And he appeared sad, which infuriated me. Did he want me to love him as I did my Tsar? Did he want me to forswear my post, my country? I loved him; what more did he want?

He remained silent, and then softly asked if he might leave. I asked if he would dedicate himself to the guards. Slowly, he rose to his feet, though his eyes remained downcast, and he said he would do nothing that would give me cause to be ashamed of him.

Alas, the following year, another incident came to my attention, and though Nikolai said the other soldier had initiated it, I was forced to punish him again. His commander suggested I should remove him from the guards, because he had gained a reputation and the others would not leave him be. I had no choice but to comply, furious. He sat on the chaise in our parlor with his head and ears down, those scarred ears that reminded me of my temper every time I looked at them, and he did not stir nor speak for an hour, while I talked to him of my disappointment, of our duty and the noble tsars to which we owed our very lives, of his inability to show even the merest gratitude to them, let alone a whit of respect for me. I told him that his mother would have been saddened by his descent into feckless wastrel behavior.

When my fury had run its course, I stood and stared, and realized that I could not see any future for us. I would not be one of those parents who insisted on pushing his son into the military despite his unfitness for the duty, who made the other soldiers suffer for his pride. But neither could I let Niki return to the filthy poets who talked insolently of the duty of the people, who preached godless philosophy and hinted darkly at revolution. I would not allow my son to be taken in the night and buried in an unmarked grave.

Perhaps, I thought, the joke about entering the Tsar's service was not so bad a thought—stripped of its scandalous origin. Much as I despaired for

Nicholas himself, his court might well be the best place for Nikolai, and I still held some small favor with Nicholas, though I had not called upon it in years. I told Niki that in the morning I would see to a new appointment, and I told him that if he would make nothing of himself, I would make something of him. But it was a desperate hope, and he may have heard that in my voice. He replied dully, in monosyllables, when he replied at all.

When I ran dry of words and anger, he sat on the chaise still, head bowed and tail curled around his knees. I could not see his bright green eyes, only the ragged edges of his ears, and I felt a sting in my heart. But I quelled the emotions and walked up to my bed.

And when I woke in the morning, Nikolai was gone.

Chapter 35

Sol was sitting with Alexei when his phone rang. He took it out, glanced at the number, and started to put it back into his pocket. "Take it," Alexei told him. "It is okay."

"It's only—uh, I'll take it out there." Sol tapped the screen and hurried out to the kitchen. "Hey, I can't come out tonight, sorry," he said into the phone as he brushed past Meg.

She took two steps in. "You get another day to grieve, and then you get out of bed." She pointed a finger at Alexei.

"Have you ever lost someone dear?" he shot back.

"I was—" She started sarcastically, then reconsidered and shook her head. "No."

"Then you do not know how long it will take to grieve."

"No." She sat down on the desk chair, draping her thick tail over the back. "But I almost lost Sol. You know, he almost killed himself. And I thought about that some." She scowled back out toward the main room. "Don't tell him I told you. Also, I almost killed myself a couple times." At the perk of his ears, she waved a paw. "Years ago. But you can't—you can't let it take over your life. Your sister sounds like she was pretty sweet, right?" He nodded. "She wouldn't want you to screw up your life over her death."

"I know," he whispered. The thought of Cat brought pressure to his chest again. "But I cannot...I cannot do anything else."

"Not now," Meg said. "But in a day or so I'll kick you in the ass. Just giving you fair warning so you don't think I'm some kind of cold-hearted bitch."

He nodded. Then he looked up. "I thought you were proud of being cold-hearted bitch."

She got up. "Most of the time," she said. "Don't tell Sol."

Out in the kitchen, Sol raised his voice. "He is not a drama queen. If anything, you are!" Then he seemed to realize he'd been shouting and lowered his voice again.

"Speaking of bitches," Meg murmured.

"Where is Athos?" Alexei said, because he thought he knew who was on the phone and didn't want to talk about him.

"Went out to get drinks. He thought we might need more alcohol. I told him no vodka."

Alexei shook his head. "I do not want a drink," he said, although the prospect of dulling his mind and drinking himself to sleep was frighteningly appealing. "But perhaps I need one."

"Attaboy," Meg said. "I know you canids don't smoke, but I have weed, too. It'll take the edge off, you know."

Again, he shook his head. "Thank you. I will try to sleep."

"Okay. Let us know if you see your ghost, 'kay?"

"Yes." He nodded, but as she left, he wished she hadn't said that. Now he was worried about sleep, too.

But his sleep that night was dreamless, as though Konstantin knew to stay away from him. Alexei woke with a strange sense of regret. The panic of his last dream had been worn down by the relentless pounding of grief and guilt, and as he'd lain down, he'd almost been looking forward to seeing Konstantin. He wanted to ask the old fox how one could be strong enough to endure something like this. But even that small chance at comfort was denied him.

He didn't tell Sol or Meg about this, and Sunday passed much as Saturday had, the day as bleak and the night as dreamless. Monday morning, though they both insisted he stay home another day, he pushed himself out of bed and got dressed. "I will go to work," he said, because at the warehouse, there was nothing to make him think of Cat, nothing to remind him of his old life at all, and he could move boxes onto and off of shelves and conveyor belts all day and imagine himself simply a part in a vast machine that cared nothing for him. If it did not care for him, he did not have to care for it; he could simply exist.

The day was everything he had hoped for, monotonous, dusty, and brown, stiflingly warm in the warehouse so that he spent the day panting and drinking water, devoid of conversation, both from real people and from ghosts. Mike called again around lunch, and this time left a message that Alexei again did not listen to. After the way he'd treated Mike, he was afraid of what the sheep would have to say to him.

But at the end of the day, Vlad came to him as he was checking out. "Ho," the big tiger said. "Liza says you are not calling her back?"

"I've been sick," Alexei said.

Vlad extended a claw. "You will call her right now," he said, and stood with arms folded while Alexei, ears burning, took out his phone and called Liza. When she picked up and he said hello, Vlad nodded and pushed Alexei out the door.

"*Where have you been?*" Liza said in Siberian. "*What is this with you moving out? Is that wolf making you leave? Of course you may come here if you need to, but he seems nice, and I think you should stay.*"

"*I cannot,*" he said, but that too had been driven from his mind and he did not know now whether he still needed to go. To be gay, to not be gay; none of it mattered to him. He could not grow close to anyone, could not be part of this world, not now. Konstantin had no more hold over him, but Alexei now felt more drawn to the ghost than to anyone else. He had seen what Bogdan was, he had tried to help, and he had a vast loneliness inside him that Alexei now understood.

"Well," Liza said, in English, "there is a meeting tonight, and Kendall wants to have you removed from the soccer team. If you want to tell your story, you should come. If they kick you off, I'm going to quit, whether you're there or not, and Alice might quit too."

"Don't do that."

"We can always play basketball. And listen, if you need anything else, call me, please."

"I will." Alexei spoke the words without meaning them.

When he'd hung up, he listened to Mike's message from two days ago, a warily concerned message, and then the one from lunch. "Hey, Alexei," the sheep said, hesitant, uncertain. "Look, you're a sweet guy and I really like you. But you're going through some shit, it seems like, and, well, uh. I got enough shit of my own to deal with right now. Sorry. I hope I'll still see you on the soccer team, and we can still hang out, but…no more dates for a while, okay? Sorry. Really, I like you. Okay. Sorry. Good-bye."

Alexei lowered his paw, looked at his phone, and then deleted all of his messages.

Chapter 36

Alexei is wandering through his apartment, only his apartment is many stories, more even than his house in Samorodka. In his bedroom, the wooden wall adorned with posters of Siberian footballers smells familiar. A low buzzing hum comes from the walls all around, and a bee flies past him, into a rotted hole two feet off the floor. He kneels to peer through, but there is only blackness there. Cat, *he calls softly.*

When he perks his ears to listen, he hears a soft keening, but it is not coming from the hole in the wall. He straightens, brushes his bed and desk, and looks for a moment to the corner of his room, but Sol is not here. Outside the window, he feels the movement of machinery even though he cannot hear or see the big yellow bulldozers and shovels.

Cat may be in trouble, may be crying out. Maybe their father has finished a batch of his vodka again. Alexei was not there to take the blows for Cat, and as the certainty of this sets in his mind, he staggers in the doorway, guilt paralyzing him. He must hurry. He might still have time.

On the back of the door is a long poster, a picture of a ten-year-old fox cub in a smart soldier's uniform. Alexei stares, and then flicks an ear and the cub in the poster flicks the same ear. He looks into his own grey eyes and then the eyes are dark brown, but he knows the expression: it is bravery laced with fear, and Alexei has the sense that just outside the frame of the poster is a large bronze statue with a sword waiting for the cub to falter. But the cub is silent, not the source of the keening whine. With an effort, Alexei wrenches himself away and leaves the room.

The stairs outside the bedroom are not the cramped, wooden stairs he remembers, and the smell of rot and fermenting potatoes does not permeate them. They are marble, the banister polished brass, and on the wall are portraits, stern tigers glaring at him with accusatory eyes. He hurries down the stairs, glancing over his shoulder. Though none of the tigers leaps from a picture to follow him, he feels their gathering presence behind him, a weight at his back that pushes his feet faster, now skipping steps, the marble cold and hard under his pads.

He emerges from the staircase into a large living room, with marble flooring and a pair of long backless couches, between which a low credenza stretches with a mirror atop it. To one side stands an old cabinet—Alexei knows he can find the liquor there, his father's labelless clear bottles of dreams and rage—and candelabras top both the cabinet and the adjacent desk. He has sat on the couches, letting his tail hang down between the cushions and the wall unless he has company, when it is fashionable to curl one's tail along one's hips. The vision of sitting in the room with other foxes and tigers comes clearly to him, and he knows them to be relatives and friends, other cubs from school and from Petrograd, and his father the tiger. And Cat, he has looked after Cat in this room and played with her when she was little and liked to hide under the couches with just her tail peeking out.

But Cat is not here, and the keening is no louder, so she is not in this room, not hiding under the couches nor in the cabinet with the bottles. He feels a fresh wave of guilt at her departure. She is in trouble somewhere and he has to find her.

He goes to the window, but instead of seeing the dirt road of Samorodka—
—or the fine gardens and the Petrograd streets beyond it—
—or, yet, the construction machines, dull yellow amid a chaotic jumble of dirt—
—he sees weathered old sandstone buildings, rows of blank and featureless windows a street's width beyond. Here the keening is louder; perhaps the wind screeching through the canyon between the buildings and into Alexei's eyes and perked ears. He blinks away tears and turns his head this way and that. And then he looks down.

Many stories stretch down to the street below, and it is a modern street such as he might see in Vidalia, only without color, all sepia-toned and blurry. It seems to be twenty stories down, then ten, then fifty, and he cannot make out what is in the street. The wind brings the keening to him, and Alexei squints against the wind. Through his tears, he sees a figure below, and his heart leaps—Cat?

He retreats into the living room and runs to every door, but none conceals a staircase, and even the large marble stair leading up to his bedroom is nowhere to be found. He stops and stares into the mirror and sees a fox in a dark blue coat, standing on a field of ice. This fox could help Cat; this fox would be brave; this fox would not run away.

Desperate, he runs back to the window and calls: Cat! Cat!

The wind shrieks up at him. The figure below is dark, but he knows she is looking up. I'm coming! he yells, and runs back into the room, but nothing has changed: the couches, the wood cabinets, the doors that lead to closets and kitchens and no stairs. He stares at the window, and bites his lip. Then he runs at it and leaps through.

The air is cold, and grows colder as he falls. His eyesight blurs, his body chills, but the figure below waits for him, growing larger. And he sees the dark coat, the old muzzle turned upward. It is not Cat; it is Konstantin who spreads his arms and his coat, which turns blue as his form judders and snaps in the sepia street.

Keening becomes screaming in his ears, wind shrieking past him and through him, and he is falling and falling past blank windows, and below him the fox's coat spreads wide, the grey haze of nothingness sending tendrils up to meet Alexei. He squeezes his eyes shut and thinks, I am dreaming, I am dreaming, wake up wake up WAKE UP

Chapter 37

Alexei woke with a jerk, sat bolt upright, and clutched the covers to his chest. His tail wound tightly around his stomach and he panted, gulping in the warm air of the bedroom and the comforting scent of Sol nearby. He flicked his ears upright against the panic in his head, forcing himself to listen. No keening reached him from outside, only the whirr of the fan, the low rumble of machinery, and Sol's even breathing.

Just a nightmare. And yet he could not relax. His eyes searched the shadows of the room, accustomed enough to the darkness to pierce even to the shadowy corners. There was the desk, the dresser, the picture of Niki back in its place on the wall, piles of clothes on the floor. No Konstantin. No beam of light touched the room from outside.

The fox drew in a breath. He uncurled his fingers with an effort and released the covers, but he did not lie back down in bed. The night sounded and smelled like any other, but though the air was warm, the tips of Alexei's fingers and ears ached with cold. Konstantin was here, again, waiting for him.

He turned to Sol. The wolf lay on his back, his chest rising and falling, and as Alexei watched, he let out a little snort and rubbed his head back into the pillow, as though scratching an itch behind one ear. Sol would want to be woken, to help defend Alexei, and the thought brought a smile to Alexei's muzzle. But he did not want to put Sol in danger, and he did not want defending, not now.

Because Cat was gone. The sorrow of the dream remained with him, the desperate need to help her, the echo of her keening, and the guilt that circled his chest like a vise. As her older brother, he should have protected her. He should have waited until they could both leave together. He never should have left her behind.

Konstantin had visited Alexei from the grave, and that was undoubtedly where he wanted to take Alexei back to. Perhaps, perhaps, he might see Cat there, and apologize to her. Or if Konstantin was offering him nothing but oblivion, well. The alternative was an empty apartment filled with guilt and memories and a keening he could never stop hearing.

So he slid out of bed. *Don't come in*, he said in his head. *I'm coming out.*

He had no idea if Konstantin could hear him, but the ghost did not appear. Alexei pulled a t-shirt over his head and walked out into the kitchen.

The smells of dinner persisted, fish and toasted bread and rice, but the kitchen lay eerily silent and dark. He touched the back of one of the chairs as he circled the kitchen table, remembering the dinners Meg had made and the drinks she'd mixed for him, the peach and cherry and orange faint memories along his nose and tongue. For a moment, he felt guilty, thought he should leave a note, but there was nothing to write with out here. The guilt subsided. They would assume correctly that Konstantin had taken him, and it would be kinder to let them imagine it had been against his will.

A flicker of resistance burned still, deep in his chest, the spark that had kept him hopeful on those icy nights in Samorodka, his back or arms or chest aching from beatings administered by his father, his spirit bleeding from his mother's blows. Now, it felt smothered beneath a damp woodpile. In Samorodka, he had believed in a better life for himself and for Cat. Here, there was nowhere to escape to. This hell was inside him.

As quietly as he could, he threw the bolts on the front door and slid out. In the hallway, even the noises of the street outside were subdued, far away, as if he were on an upper floor and the street far below. Indeed, when he opened the front door of the building, he almost expected to look down onto the scene from his dream. But the front stoop lay empty and ochre in the light of the sodium lamps as it always was, the street outside quiet and dead save for the engine of a car fading into the distance, the buzz of insects.

And on the sidewalk below the stoop, Konstantin waited.

He looked normal here, solid and real, just an old fox in a worn blue military coat fastened with a clean gold sash. His soldier's bearing, straight-shouldered, paws clasped in front of him, did not relax as his eyes met Alexei's, but his tail swished slowly from side to side, the white tip shining in the dim light.

Alexei let the front door close behind him and stood in silence. Running away again, a voice said in the back of his head, and he pushed it aside. Running toward something now, he told it. Toward peace and structure, toward a place where I know what is expected and I need not make decisions that kill those I care about.

"*You have chosen to come with me.*" Konstantin's words sounded flat through the humid air.

"*I think so,*" he said softly. "*Where are we going?*"

"*Back,*" Konstantin said. "*Can you hear the train? The souls traveling to the land between?*"

Alexei turned his ears this way and that, and what he heard first was the keening sound from his dream. When he focused on it, it turned into a long, low whistle, a steam engine releasing pressure in a mournful cry. He turned back to Konstantin. "*So I will be dead.*"

"*In this world, yes.*"

Alexei nodded. The spark in his chest flared. "*Why?*"

Konstantin inclined his head. "*You created a bond when you summoned me, but it is not that alone. You have been treated badly by the world. I have grown fond of you. I would…welcome the company.*"

"*Can I see my sister?*"

The older fox shook his head slowly from side to side. "*We may encounter others in that land, but those we love…that comfort is denied to us.*"

"*Oh.*" Alexei's shoulders sagged. He curled his tail back and forth and breathed in the warm, humid night air. "*Can I get a message to her? Can I tell her I'm sorry?*"

"*In my experience,*" and here the older fox, too, hunched over, as though carrying some weight, "*that is not possible. But the land between is a strange place that I would not have believed possible when I lived. Who can say?*"

"*How do you know I will stay with you, then?*" A new fear had occurred to Alexei. "*I would hate to die and still be alone there.*"

"*You do not know. Nor do I. But I feel it; do you not?*" Konstantin reached out his paw. "*You have but to grasp my paw and come with me.*"

Alexei did not move, not yet. "*Why can't you just suck me into your coat?*"

The older fox smiled wryly. "*We are not in a dream, here. There are… limitations.*"

"*Is that why you're not as scary?*"

"*Perhaps I am less frightening because you are less frightened of me, now.*"

Or it could be another trick, Alexei thought wearily, for the spirit to appear old and vulnerable, to lure him in closer. But Konstantin's explanation was the simplest: Alexei had come to him willingly, and there was no need for anything more than an outstretched paw.

In his chest, the rebellious fire refused to be quenched. What about Sol, what about Meg? But balanced against them was Cat's absence, the vitriol of his parents, the weight of his guilt. To think he could have peace with just a touch of Konstantin's paw… He lifted his arm.

Noise sounded behind him, and the front door clattered open. Alexei half-turned, saw Sol in his boxers, Meg in a robe, Athos in a t-shirt and shorts, all wide-eyed. Sol cried, "Alexei!" but all three of them stared past him, at the old Siberian fox in the military garb.

"My God," Athos breathed.

"God dammit, Alexei," Meg said. "You scared the hell out of us. Who is this bum?"

Words caught in Alexei's throat. The warm, real presence of his friends overwhelmed him, but he couldn't keep from thinking, *what if I betray them as I did Cat? What if they fall as well?* And then the startling flash of realization. *"You can see him?"*

He spoke in Siberian, and then had to force his mind to translate the words into English. But even as he said them again, Konstantin was speaking in Siberian, aloud. *"Of course they can see me. You brought me here into the world."*

"I see someone," Sol said slowly. "I can't understand what he's saying."

"Oh, he's from some Siberian homeless shelter downtown." Meg grabbed Alexei's wrist. "Get back inside."

At that, Konstantin strode forward, his ears flattening and eyes narrowing. "Do not touch him," he said in English, and he stopped short of Meg, his movements clockwork-precise. He could not grow to a great height here, but he looked down on all of them from his natural stature, and he had a soldier's assurance.

"Back off," Meg said warningly, and Sol took a step forward.

Alexei shook his wrist free. He stepped to one side, away from his friends and yet not toward Konstantin. "None of you know what this is like," he said, pressing a paw to his chest. "It *hurts*. Every minute, every thought I have. Before, there was hope, and now…nothing. There is *nothing*."

"It gets better." Sol reached out to him, and kept his paw out even when Alexei shied from the touch. "You stop thinking about it quite so much. It just takes time."

"What," Alexei said, "you're talking about losing Niki?" He set his jaw. "You knew him for a month, and never even in real life! This is my sister, my little sister. I held her when she was tiny, I walked to school with her, I protected her…" His throat closed up again and the rush of his loss roared in his ears.

At the mention of Niki's name, Konstantin had stepped forward, ears up, eyes widening. "You…you know my Nikolai?" The older fox took another step forward and stared at Sol. *"Your eyes,"* he said in Siberian, his gaze fixed on the wolf's face.

"Niki changed his eyes," Alexei said, in English.

Sol's bright green eyes almost glowed in the strange light. "They're a gift," he said, standing with his shoulders and muzzle forward, a belligerent posture. "He gave me strength, and he's always with me now."

"With *you?*" Konstantin took another step forward, his paw dropping to the scabbard at his side.

"Hey," Meg said, stepping forward to grip Sol's arm. "Look, old timer, what's your name? Where do you live?"

The old fox raised his paws and his voice, still fixing Sol with his gaze. "I am Konstantin Vasilyevich Galitzin, born in eighteen fifty-nine and again in eighteen sixty-five. I do not 'live.' I have been dead for nearly one hundred years."

"Or you're a crazy person who escaped Siberia," Meg said, and then released Sol as Athos stepped back. "Don't be—hey! Where are you going?"

Athos fled back into the building as she watched. Meg took two steps after him while Alexei watched Sol and Konstantin. Both canids had their ears back, and though Sol looked afraid, Konstantin trembled as though barely restraining himself. Alexei's ears stayed fully up, all his senses on alert.

"How did you meet Nikolai?" Konstantin whispered, his voice low and dangerous.

"Sol," Alexei said urgently. "Go inside. Leave me. This is—"

The black wolf ignored him, his ears flat, eyes narrow, focused only on Konstantin. "I met him. I saw his story, after he ran away."

"After?" The fox's lips drew back. "What became of him?"

Sol frowned, glaring more furiously than Alexei had ever seen. "He died," he said. "Drowned."

For a moment, like the flickering in his dream, grief blazed over Konstantin's muzzle. Then his eyes set and his lips drew back farther, his fangs yellow in the light. "You lie."

"He slept with a rich French noble." Sol threw the words out, fists clenched. "Who hit him in the head with a candlestick and dumped him in the river."

"Jesus, Sol," Meg said.

Before Alexei could speak or react, Konstantin had lunged forward. With a growl, he drove his fist into Sol's stomach. The black wolf doubled over, staggered, and Konstantin pushed him to the ground. The soldier dropped to his knees and raised an arm to strike again—

—Alexei seized the raised arm, pulled with all his strength, dragged Konstantin back off the stoop as Sol struggled to his feet, wheezing.

"Stop! Leave him alone!" Alexei held his paws up, tried to keep himself between Sol and the ghost.

Konstantin drew himself up, seeming to grow several inches. His fangs gleamed in a snarl as he pointed at Sol. "*He tells lies about Nikolai,*" he said in Siberian.

Alexei drove forward

"*They are not lies,*" Alexei said, and switched to English. "He saw Niki. Niki helped him."

"Niki told me it was all right to be gay." Sol glared up from his knees, his breathing still labored. "He was gay, too."

Konstantin's muzzle twisted, and he lifted the pointing finger until it aimed directly at Sol's nose. "Nikolai did not understand the world. He belonged with *me*. He would not have died had he remained a loyal son."

"He hated you," Sol got to his feet, lips pulled back from his teeth, as fierce as Konstantin. "You drove him away."

"You will be silent."

"I will not," Sol said. "Niki wouldn't want me to."

Konstantin leaned forward, his muzzle less than a foot from Alexei's, his eyes fixed on Sol. "I was not asking," he said, and extended his arm fully toward the black wolf.

Alexei saw clearly the grey fur on his muzzle, the dark eyes, the notch in one ear. Konstantin's breath smelled of old earth and mold, and it was cold on his nose. Shadows crept out from behind the old soldier and pooled around his feet; blackness wreathed his arms and grew like a halo behind his ears and head, crept along his arm and out toward Sol.

The black wolf recoiled, nostrils flaring, and Alexei drove forward, life and desire flaring brightly now. "No!" he cried, and lowered his shoulder into Konstantin's chest. The military coat gave under his charge, and Konstantin grabbed at Alexei's shirt as the younger fox pushed him back off the stoop and out of the circle of light.

"Hey!" Meg and Sol ran forward, but Alexei did not stop, the burning need to keep Konstantin away from his friends driving his feet forward.

The older fox staggered backwards several steps with him and then recovered his balance. He threw Alexei aside and strode back toward Sol, determined. Alexei ran at him and tackled him from behind, shouting, "Leave him alone!" and so distraught he did not know whether he was speaking Siberian or English.

Cold earthy air enveloped him and strong arms pinned him down. "He must not be allowed to speak that way," Konstantin said.

Out of the corner of his eye, Alexei saw motion: Meg and Sol. He tried to wave them back, tried to call, "He's dangerous!" through the thicker and thicker fog surrounding him. His lungs burned with the cold, his nose wrinkled at the overwhelming smell of mold and age, rot and decay. But he did not feel fear. He would save Sol, and then his departure would have meaning.

And then, high and clear, he heard the ringing of a bell. Konstantin stopped, though his grip did not relax enough for Alexei to escape. Athos's voice, a little shaky, called out, "Avaunt, shade!"

For a moment, Alexei could only think about how ridiculous it was. He had tried so many things to banish Konstantin, and this grey fox thought he could just ring a bell? But the fog around him warmed, the odor of the grave weakened, and Konstantin's grip on him faltered.

The bell rang again, and this time Konstantin flinched as though he'd been struck. His head turned down to Alexei, and in them Alexei saw a vast and endless darkness, pain and loneliness, and his own eyes reflected in them. Points of light appeared in the darkness, and Alexei realized that what he was seeing was the night sky through the fading outlines of Konstantin. The physical grip on his arms weakened, but he could not look away from those eyes.

Meg and Sol called his name from a long way away. The fire in him hissed and wailed, but it could not burn away the blackness. Grey fog crept in at the edge of his vision and the ground slipped out from below him and he fell.

Chapter 38

Alexei stands on a flat concrete platform with a wooden building behind him, his paw in the icy grip of Konstantin. His paw, like his ears, like his tail, tingles with cold, and so the touch of the older fox's paw is not uncomfortable. His tail swishes slowly behind him. He looks around curiously.

A pair of rails runs past the station, and to his left, there is a train approaching. He perks his ears and catches the hiss of the engine. Clouds of steam escape the train's boiler and rise to join the cloudy sky, persisting for a long time against the featureless grey before finally dissipating. The landscape around the train, flat plains that rise in the distance to brown hills and a jagged, toothy horizon, is familiar. Somewhere not too far, Alexei thinks, there is a river, and sometimes fish.

Above him, a sign creaks gently. There are Siberian characters on it, but the sign is nearly directly overhead and Alexei cannot read them.

"The train will be here soon."

Konstantin speaks Siberian. Alexei's ears flick in acknowledgment. He turns to his right and follows the empty track away from the station. It stretches out across the same flat landscape, but there are no hills, no mountainous peaks on the horizon. Instead, the tracks disappear into a grey-brown fog.

Behind them, the windows of the wooden station-house are dark and empty. There is a doorway, but Alexei smells only dust and age from it, no other people. The pressure on his paw crushes his fingers, but only a little, and even if he did pull free, where could he go? He scratches behind his ears, and then down his side. His fur feels gritty, as though he has fallen into a patch of dust.

"Nicholas had a son," Konstantin says off-handedly. Alexei listens but does not reply. "His name was Aleksei."

Alexei knows this; one does not grow up named "Alexei Tsarev" without someone bringing up the son of the last Tsar in history classes. Aleksei Romanov, the hemophiliac tiger who died at the age of fourteen with the rest of his family, bore little resemblance to Alexei Tsarev the fox, as far as the fox could tell, but he listens as Konstantin talks and the train draws nearer. He thinks about Sol and Meg and wonders what they are seeing. Is he lying dead? Is he gone, disappeared?

"I attended his birth. The empire was already in turmoil, but the birth was a blessed occasion, an island of peace in the midst of uncertainty and fear. It was the last time I saw Nicholas in person, the only time I saw him happy after the turn of the century.

"When our children are born, we have such hope for them. Was Aleksei's weakness inherent in him? The spiritual weakness of the father was made manifest in the son,

perhaps—our biologists would have it so. But then whence came Nicholas's weakness? He must have had inner strength and let it languish and die. His father—his father was strong. It is impossible that the fault lies in the father, or in the mother." Konstantin's voice grew stern. "You, now, you are strong. You resisted your nature, you defended your friend. Away from the temptations of the world, with a strong guide, you will be a good fox. I will be pleased to have your company."

Alexei nods dully. This is his destiny. He wonders if he will see Cat here somewhere, which would be nice. He will not see Sol or Meg for a long time—unless Sol summons him via a ritual. Perhaps Alexei might return to the world as a spirit, the way Konstantin did. The black wolf's face hovers in his imagination as the fox last saw him, ears back, eyes blazing. Fighting for Alexei, fighting to protect him.

Failing to protect him. Just as Alexei failed to protect Cat. Alexei feels a wash of love for Sol, sympathy and friendship. We both tried our best.

Konstantin squeezes his paw. "Come," the older fox says, "it is not so bad. I have tales of battle, tales of the mounted troops, tales of society. I will teach you chess."

Chess: a complicated game for old people. Is there room to kick a football on the train? Alexei watches it approach and regret consumes him, a clear, single note that encompasses in a wash all the things he will miss, is already missing. Sol's laugh and Meg's sharpness, the sweet and heady taste of her drinks, Sol's scent and the construction outside his window, the hot, humid air and the cool, dry air conditioning, Vlad and Liza and Rozalina and his host family and Mike and the feel of the football coming off his foot and soft, flaky fish and greasy fast food chicken...

The train's whistle drowns out his thoughts. He watches its approach through blurred vision. But even as tears render the train indistinct, his thoughts sharpen, as though the sparse landscape and imminent train have focused his mind.

Konstantin pulls him forward. He resists, and the soldier turns with surprise and annoyance.

"There is more to strength than fighting," Alexei says.

The old fox flicks ears down. "Eh?"

"You say I am strong because I fought you to protect Sol, and because I fought Kendall, I suppose. But I left Samorodka and that was strong as well."

"Abandoning your family?"

"Yes. To stay, to bear my parents' abuse: you might think that strong, but it is giving in to them, admitting they are right about me." He sees it now with the clarity of distance. "Cat saw it too. She was not in danger as I was. She chose to remain behind because she loved me. And I would have sent for her because I loved her, too." Alexei stares off at the train. Bright lights precede it, but he does not need to shield his eyes.

Konstantin is silent for a moment. "I am sorry for your loss," he says. "I also lost my wife. And..."

"And you drove your son away."

The older fox glares down at him. "He left."

Alexei is silent for a moment. "When your wife died, did you feel there was a hole in you that would never be filled?"

"Yes."

"And yet?"

Konstantin shifts from one foot to the other. "I hoped to encounter her here in..." *He gestures about him. "Heaven? But I have not seen her." The arm not holding Alexei's paw drops to his side. "I have not seen...any of my family."*

"But you did not think to kill yourself then, even though you suffered a great loss."

"I had a cub to care for!" The older fox's ears shoot up, and his paw tightens. He opens his jaw to say more, and then closes it quickly.

Alexei lets the silence hang. The train will be at the station soon. "How did you die?"

"Defending Nicholas and his family. The guards kept order as long as we could, but were overwhelmed by the revolutionaries rushing the palace, the people who cared only for their immediate gratification, who sought to place themselves above the emperor and Siberia. I believe it was a length of pipe that struck my head from behind." He speaks dryly, steadily.

"I'm sorry." Alexei cranes his neck to see the back of the soldier's head: smooth, russet fur. No wound, no mark. "You never had a chance to escape."

"Escape?" Konstantin barks. "Flee, you mean. As everyone else did. I had chances to flee, of course I did. I chose to stay, every time, every day. That is what loyalty means. That is what I hoped to teach you, after you deserted your family."

"Still?" Alexei's anger builds. "Look, and I will show you family."

He does not know how to summon images as Konstantin did. But he draws on his memories, his father's cries, his mother's words, the bottles and boards and bruises, a kaleidoscope of childhood horror, and the soldier's eyes widen. He winces, and his paw squeezes Alexei's again. "Still," he says, "you could..."

Everything else fades before the bright image of Cat crying against Alexei at the shed, the realization he felt in that moment, the understanding that his parents would not protect him. Konstantin falls silent.

And then, the warmth and understanding from Sol, the moment of connection when Alexei confessed his sexuality—yes, even this he shares with Konstantin without flinching. The joy he felt in being asked to live with Sol and Meg, the sense of belonging, the freedom that came with the openness to discuss his life with others in the VLGA, all of these fill him and, he hopes, Konstantin.

Still the soldier does not speak. Alexei takes a breath. "Why are you making me flee those who mean the most to me?"

Konstantin stirs and looks down. "Did they pursue you when you ran, or search for you when you did not return? Do they care more than I? Do they need you more than

I?" It is all there in the soldier's voice, in the emptiness of the vast plain that stretches out before them, in the long low howl of the steam engine as the train slows.

"They need me, too. And I love them." Alexei speaks so softly that were this a normal train, even Konstantin with his fox's ears would not be able to hear it over the screech of brakes, the huffing of the steam engine. But here in this desolate station between life and death, Alexei's words echo from the boards of the old station platform.

Now Konstantin looks down at him, his pupils narrowed to slits from the train's bright light. "Love is for dreamers," the old fox recites. "That is what Vasily—my father taught me."

The boards creak as his weight shifts. Grey dust rises at the train's approach, narrowing the world around them to the platform, the train, each other. Alexei looks back. "And what are we doing now but dreaming?"

Again, Konstantin's stony expression flickers. His ears curl uncertainly behind him. "It is too late for that," he says.

Flat black train cars with no name roll past, no decoration adorning them. Faces stare out, deer and ermine, coyotes and wolves, rabbits and otters. Their eyes sweep over Alexei and Konstantin as though the foxes are no more than fixtures of the station. Behind them, all is darkness. The carriages go on and on and on, and slowly come to a halt.

"It is not too late," Alexei says.

Before them, a door opens, sliding noiselessly to one side. Inky blackness spills down the stairs like a viscous fluid. Alexei shrinks back, but Konstantin holds him firmly and pulls forward. "Do not be frightened," he says.

"Do I have to go?" Alexei whispers.

"Yes." Konstantin pulls again, then stops. This is not a station where passengers disembark, and yet there is movement from the door nearest them. From the blackness emerges a cornflower-blue dress, wrapped around a young vixen with a sad smile. She holds up one coal-dark paw, palm out.

Alexei's muzzle drops open. He cannot push the word past his throat, is afraid to say it lest he be wrong, lest her name banish her, but he cannot take his eyes from her. And then she meets his eyes, and she says his name, and the word bursts forth from him. "Cat!"

"You don't have to come," she says gently.

The words do not sink in. He can only hear the sadness, cannot help but remember her last message to him and the bright hope in her voice that is gone now. "I am so sorry, Cat," he says.

"He is coming with me," Konstantin says. "He has decided."

"Wait!" Alexei pulls back against the older fox's grip.

"Look." Konstantin points to the carriage. "Your sister is here, just as you wanted. Who can say whether this chance will come again?"

"Kostya," Cat says gently, familiarly as if she has known him for years, "it is not yet his time, if he does not wish it."

"He is the reason you are here! He—"

"No," Cat says. "I am the reason I am here. The mistakes I made, they are mine."

"Do you not wish his company? Do you wish to be alone?"

"Kostya. I have come to see my brother. Who has come to see you?"

Konstantin whips around, glaring, but Alexei does not stop pulling, prying at the other fox's fingers with his free paw. The soldier draws himself up, growing a foot taller, two feet taller, staring down with eyes growing dark and cold. "Will you leave me as well?" he cries, and behind his voice is the sharp keening of the wind, of the train whistle, the sound calling out across miles and years. "What of your guilt, what of your loss? Are you so eager to return to them, alone?"

"They are mine," Alexei says. His eyes do not leave the older fox's, but he is aware of Cat near him, and he draws strength from her. "And I will not have to bear them alone. There is also love, there is also hope. I serve no tsar, but I serve those who have given their hearts to me, and who have kept mine safe in return. That is as sacred a duty as your commission to the Emperor. You must not deny what is in your heart. You must cherish it."

It is as if Sol is behind him, and Meg, and Mike and Liza and Vlad. Even as Konstantin's shadow engulfs him, he stands tall. "Love!" the older fox says again.

"Yes," Alexei says, and then he reaches up and he touches the very tip of the older fox's chin, the only part he can reach. "And you are among those I love, but you are not the only one. Do you love me, dyedushka? Will you let me go?"

At the Siberian word 'grandfather,' Konstantin's eyes widen. He exhales, his shadow retreating, returning to his regular size. And then the old fox is no more than an old soldier in a worn, bloodstained coat, and his paw holds Alexei's a moment longer before releasing it. It remains out before him and then drops to his side. "You will not come?"

"Not now," Alexei says. He risks a look at Cat and sees her smiling, her eyes moist. "Someday, I promise. I will not forget you."

Cat speaks again, gentle and firm and sad. "Come, Kostya. For you, it is time."

The train whistle keens again. Darkness withdraws into the body of the train, and Cat takes a step up. Now her tail is not visible at all, and the back of her dress vanishes into the black.

The older fox bows his head and reaches out a paw. Alexei looks warily at it, but the soldier only ruffles the fur between Alexei's ears. The pads are cold, covered with a thin layer of dust, but Alexei does not mind. Konstantin's expression is serious, sternly paternal. "I know you will not follow the path I set forth for you. Show me, then, in your own way, how you are strong." He pauses and then his paw stills. "And because you have shared yourself with me..."

Memories, golden-bright and clear as a crisp Siberian day, flood Alexei's mind. He sees a cart in the dead of winter, a giant tiger, betrayal and salvation in one night, the unworthiness he will spend his life overcoming. There is a sword flash and a pain in his ear, a recurring nightmare of a tiger statue with a sword. Warmth in his heart at the memory of Mariya, the betrayal of her untimely death, the pain again of being left behind. And the years watching his son grow, with pride and hope, at first. Niki's bright spirit, their joy together, the distance growing between them, the shine in those bright green eyes diminishing. The harsh mantle wrapped around himself after the final betrayal, the final abandonment.

"He left me," Konstantin says. "He left. I did not drive him away. I was, at the end, the only one worthy of my father, the only one loyal." But the confidence he bequeathed to Alexei is nowhere in his voice, nowhere in his eyes. He speaks quickly, as though using the sentences like sandbags against a rising flood of uncertainty.

Alexei remains silent. Konstantin leans closer. "Tell me what you know of my Niki," he says urgently.

The soldier's eyes stay fixed on his, as Alexei tries to remember everything Sol has told him about Niki. "Your son was good," he says. "Strong. He helped my friend, and he inspired others." He pictures the painting, hoping Konstantin can see it, and indeed, the soldier's eyes widen. "Sol—the wolf you saw—he was so lost, and Niki saved him. Your son led a sad life, but you should not think you failed in raising him."

His own memories run through his head, shorter: that first time talking to Sol on the bleachers, Sol coming back after Carcy's visit, the beautiful painting and the artist Niki inspired to create it, Sol telling him Niki's story, all of it, the sadness and beauty, and he thinks too late that he does not want Konstantin to see the sadness, but it is a part of the story and he cannot help it.

Lines crease around the older fox's eyes. He withdraws his paw, gently, and now Alexei sees the train through the outlines of the blue military coat. The golden sash is a faded, translucent yellow, but clean of stains. "I wish he had not gone. I wish I had not..." He stops. "Thank you for sharing his story with me. And thank you for sharing yourself."

The whistle sounds again, but this time it is apologetic, if no less firm. Konstantin rubs a paw across one eye and looks down at Alexei. "I must go. You will not see me again, save perhaps in dreams."

"Don't be scary." Alexei perks his ears up and focuses on Konstantin's eyes, which remain solid and brown though the fur around them shimmers and the train gleams through it. "In my dreams, I mean."

That brings a brief smile to the fox's disappearing lips. "I make no promises, lisenok," he says, and bows. He takes a step back, then turns and boards the train.

Cat makes way for him, and he pauses for a moment to look down as he passes her. The last thing Alexei sees of him is the tail of the sash, trailing over the fox's tail, as both fade and vanish.

"Thank you." Alexei smiles at Cat, tears gathering in his eyes as well. "I'm so sorry."

"We were granted our wish," she says. "You are living for both of us now. I will see you when the winter is over."

The ebony car begins to move, silently. He jogs to keep pace. "What wish?" he calls.

"Good-bye, Lexi." Her eyes sparkle, with love or tears or both. "I will be watching you, too."

He tries to keep up, but the black train pulls away too quickly. The last he sees of Cat, she is raising a paw and waving. He stands and waves back, and then tears fill his eyes and the grey dust rises over him. He strains to see through it, but it grows thicker and thicker, colder and colder, and with each blink, he finds his eyes harder and harder to open. Then they stay shut, and he panics, pulling himself out of the dream—

Chapter 39

—his eyelids felt stuck. He forced them open with a cry and then shut them immediately against a bright light. A growling moan made its way out of his throat; his ears tried to flatten against a pillow and could not. He lifted a paw to his eyes and smacked his tongue against the sour taste in his mouth. His body ached, but it was warming, as though he'd just come out of a winter day and his mother had lit a fire.

"Hey!" A voice pierced his ears. It took him a moment to recognize Athos. "He's awake!"

The intrusion of another person on his struggle out of darkness irritated him at first, and then a weight landed on him and strong arms lifted his shoulders from the bed, crushing him in a hug, and Sol's black fur pressed into his nose, the lupine scent warm and welcome. The wolf's voice and breath ruffled his cheek fur. "Oh God, Alexei, I was so scared."

"Wh...what happened?" His dream was fading, but details shone clear in his memory: Konstantin's paw, the old soldier's breath and the intense cold, the pieces of his life, and...and Cat.

"You fainted," Sol said, "and you were cold... *really* cold." The wolf's words faded out of Alexei's awareness as he struggled to hold on to the memory of Cat, but reality's assault left his dream even more fragmented. He remembered her looking at him through darkness, being frightened for him—but not for herself. He thought she was at peace.

But that was only a dream.

Meg's sharp voice pierced the warm shell of Sol's halting monologue. "I told you he'd wake up." Alexei shifted and saw her, smiling uncharacteristically as she walked toward Sol's bed to sit beside Athos.

Sol released Alexei but remained sitting on his bed, and Alexei sat up. "We didn't know what happened to you," he said, the stubbornness in his voice telling Alexei that this had been a topic of argument between the wolf and otter. "After Athos banished the ghost—"

"Scared the Russian bum away," Meg corrected. Athos, next to her, scowled.

"You just collapsed. You were barely breathing."

"You were in shock." Meg folded her arms. "He was cutting off your oxygen. You just needed some rest."

Sol's head was down, but he was looking at Alexei and his ears were perked. Athos leaned forward, eyes wide and curious. Alexei looked around at all three of them and said, "I—I don't really remember. I had a dream…"

"What was in the dream?" Athos's voice sounded high. "Take your time. Try to remember details."

"There was a train." Alexei closed his eyes. "And Konstantin was there, and my sister. And I think she saved me from him."

"That bastard." Sol's growl rumbled through the bed.

Alexei curled his tail into himself. "He was very lonely."

"He drove his own son away!"

"He wanted…" Alexei was not sure what Konstantin wanted. "He had a very hard life."

"Look, you two." Meg got up from the bed. "Write your story another time. I'm gonna get something for him to drink. You hungry?"

This was to Alexei, who began to shake his head and then felt a gaping void where his stomach should be. "Yes, thank you."

Meg left, and Sol reached over to hug Alexei again. The fox returned the embrace, then sat up and followed Athos's gaze to the doorway. "She does not believe in ghosts," Alexei said softly, looking up at the painting of Niki and then down at Athos.

The grey fox met Alexei's eyes and then dropped his head, his tail swatting the bed. "No. I thought she'd keep an open mind, but…"

Sol's green eyes flashed. "She's just stubborn. I don't know what she's afraid of."

Alexei shook his head again. It was hard enough sorting out his own life without worrying about Meg's. "I am glad the two of you believe me," he said.

"I wish you'd had a better experience." Sol squeezed his shoulder. "I miss Niki, but I'm really glad I met him. Sounds like his dad wasn't all that much fun."

"Well." Alexei looked up at the picture again. "I would like to have met Niki. But I think I know a little about him, now."

"We all have the experiences we are meant to have," Athos pronounced.

"Jesus, give it a rest." Meg came back in with a small tumbler and handed it to Alexei.

He caught a whiff of the fumes before he reached out, and held up a paw. "No alcohol. Just water."

"It'll do you good," she insisted.

He shook his head, and she retreated. "Fine, fine."

The three boys sat quietly, and then Alexei said, "May I tell you about the dream?"

They listened with perked ears, respectfully, as he tried to reconstruct the dream from the blurry watercolor details. There was the train, Konstantin leading him onto it, and a moment between them that Alexei didn't quite remember. And Cat, forbidding Konstantin, saving him. "But he was not evil. Not completely. Perhaps a little bit. He was desperate and lonely."

"Ghosts are like that," Athos said. "When they die, they're trapped at the point of death, and they can't ever get past it."

"You have seen a ghost?" Alexei tilted his head as Meg re-entered the room with a glass of water and a stack of buttered toast.

The grey fox scratched behind an ear. "Well, no. But I've read a lot about them."

"Fiction," Meg said. She put the glass of water on the desk and handed Alexei the plate. "That's what you told me. You laughed at how gullible people were."

"Some of those stories...but you were there! You saw it!" He gesticulated in the direction of the front door.

Meg curled fists against her hips and glared at him. "It was dark, it was late, we were all freaked out by that homeless guy, and Alexei's talk about ghosts just made all of you suggestible."

Athos stood, and at the severity of his expression, Alexei leaned against Sol. He'd never seen anyone take on Meg like this. "I always kept an open mind, and I thought you would too. We saw the ghost Alexei described disappear, and wound his spirit as it left."

"He was in shock—"

"It was more than shock!" Athos raised his voice. "Did you feel how cold he was? It was a spiritual death."

Meg twisted her muzzle up and then looked back at Alexei. "Let's not have this conversation here, genius," she said, and then, softer, "Sorry, fox-boy."

"It is all right." He lifted a paw. He would have told them to stay, but he wanted to talk to Sol.

They left quickly, both scowling, and they'd barely closed the door to Meg's room before their raised voices came through the wall.

"Wow." Sol stared out the doorway. "I wonder how much Meg can hear of us in here."

Alexei laid a paw on Sol's arm. "Thank you," he said. "For believing me, and trying to save me."

"Oh." Sol flattened his ears. "I mean, yeah. It was just, you know, I wasn't going to let him just take you. And thank you for saving me from him, too."

"And…" Alexei swallowed. "I am sorry. For yelling at you, and for doing all of this in the first place. And for taking your picture without your permission." He held up a paw as Sol started to talk. "I do not think I understood what Niki meant to you, though you told me. When you compared your loss to losing Cat…"

"It's not the same." Sol cut in quickly. "I know. I'm sorry. It was all I could think of. I didn't even really know my cousin that well."

"You should not be sorry for the life you lived," Alexei said, and he found a smile coming easily to his muzzle. "I can't understand it, as you can't understand mine. But we can try. I want to try harder."

"Me too."

"People, even the people close to you…" Alexei thought of his anger at Sol, thought about Konstantin's anger toward Niki, thought of his family. "They can only be what they are, not what you want them to be."

"I guess Konstantin wanted you—and Niki—to be straight." Sol frowned, and his eyes flashed green.

"Yes. But also, he wanted us to be his sons. And for a short time, I wanted him to be my father. When we are afraid, uncertain, we want someone to tell us everything will be fine. And a good father knows when to rule, and when to let go. It is a hard thing to know." Alexei met the wolf's green eyes. "I told you about my father, I think."

"A little. I didn't want to press."

"Konstantin would be an improvement."

Sol was quiet, and then he took the fox's paw in his. "I'm really sorry about your sister. I can't even imagine."

"Thank you." The aching sadness of the previous days—had it been only three days?—had not dulled, but he had found that remembering love and life made it hurt just a little less. "I think she would want me to live my life and be happy."

"So, uh." Sol flicked his ears. "You're not moving out?"

Alexei tilted his muzzle and then remembered his decisions, the phone call to Liza, the arguments with Meg and Sol. "No," he said. "I do not think that would be good for me."

"Good." Sol squeezed his paw and then let it go. "I know I gotta go off to college in September, but I want us to stay friends. I think if you and Meg stay together when I go, it'll be easier. I'll come back and see you guys."

September seemed so far off as to be nearly irrelevant. "I am sure we will stay friends." Alexei smiled. "How many other people have seen ghosts of old Siberian foxes?"

Sol grinned, and his tail thwapped the bed. "I want to hear more about what you remember. Sometime."

"Some of it was scary." Alexei still remembered the terrifying parts, Konstantin's coat and the tiger and the decaying building. "But not all of it."

Sol leaned forward and brushed his nose past Alexei. "Get some rest. You wanna maybe go to a movie? My treat."

"Maybe this evening." The fox curled his tail back and forth. "I have to think about some things. What to do about soccer, and the visa."

"Oh, shit, right," Sol said. "Look, I can talk to Kendall if you want, get him to call his friend—"

"No." Alexei cut him off. "Perhaps…next year." The future was barely a glimmer to him, but it was a glimmer nonetheless. He did not know where he would be in two months, when Sol went to college, much less next summer. But at least he felt he would be somewhere, a place where he belonged.

"You know, Kendall *can* be kind of a jerk." Sol said it without prompting.

"Really." Alexei wasn't sure how to respond to that.

"Yeah, I know, I know." Sol laid his ears back. "But he can be really nice, too. He was concerned about me and making the transition to college and all."

"Did he offer to come with you?"

Alexei'd meant it jokingly, but when Sol ducked his head, the fox's fur prickled. "He sorta hinted he could move around maybe…"

"What a…" He could only think of words in Siberian.

"He's a guy." Sol leaned against Alexei. "He's got issues, yeah, but he's just a guy. He's not my best friend."

Alexei started to reply and then couldn't form words. He wrapped an arm around Sol and hugged him, and breathed in the comforting scent. The room felt quiet; Meg and Athos's argument had died down and so, for the moment, had the traffic noises outside. Alexei closed his eyes, enjoying the peaceful stillness that enfolded him and Sol.

They remained like that until Sol broke the silence. "So what are you going to do about the visa?"

"I have not even been thinking about it."

"When do you have to do something by?"

Alexei tried to remember. "I don't know. End of the summer, I suppose."

"Liza will help."

"I don't want to think about it, not right now."

Sol hugged him again. "I understand," he said, and Alexei knew that he really did, and Alexei loved him for it.

Chapter 40

Athos left early the next morning. After the argument he had with Meg, the grey fox slept on the floor of the living room that night. Alexei found him there when he went to take his shower, blinking sleepily in the light Alexei'd turned on. Not knowing what to say, discomfited by the unexpected shape in his living room, Alexei said only, "You could sleep on the couch," and when Athos mumbled a reply he couldn't hear, the red fox hurried to his shower.

Later, when Sol was showering, Athos had folded up the mess of blankets he'd slept on and stood when Alexei emerged from the bedroom dressed. "Sorry if I startled you," he said.

Alexei looked at Meg's bedroom door, still closed, and flattened his ears. "It is not a problem. I am sorry as well."

The grey fox extended a paw. "Thank you for allowing me to share in this experience. It has been...indescribable."

"I do not believe I had much choice in the matter." Alexei took the proffered paw. He was still burdened with thoughts of Cat and Konstantin, but he had slept an entire night without dreams, and the implacable reality of the world had begun its work of reassuring him with its solidity and constancy. There was heat that made him pant, dust that washed off with a shower, smells of earth but also of frying fish and automobiles and best friends. And there were the letters from Cat.

"Regardless," Athos insisted. "It changed my life. I have so much to think about now. I want to go back and reread all of my books, and talk to people. Not about your story," he added hurriedly. "Unless you would want..."

Alexei shook his head. "Not now, no," he said.

"But can I stay in touch with you?"

"Yes, certainly. You can get my e-mail from...well, here, let me give it to you." He wrote it out on a slip of paper while Athos did the same, and they exchanged the papers.

Sol came out of the bathroom. "Ready in a minute," he told Alexei, and held out a paw to Athos. "Taking off?"

"I think I'd better." The grey fox shook Sol's paw and looked down, pointedly not at the closed bedroom door. "Tell her...well, just take care of her, okay? I think someday she'll want to believe."

"Don't know about that," Sol said. "Hey, why aren't you wearing your cape?"

Athos looked down and flicked his ears back. "Seems silly now, doesn't it? I mean, I don't think they're real, but..."

"Vampires," Alexei said, "are completely make-believe."

The other two stared at him, and only when he smiled did they get that he was joking and laugh. He could not quite laugh with them, but he was glad to hear the sound. It was another brick of reality, a reassurance that the world was not cold, grey stone, but also joy and friendship and love. He was beginning to wake to this world again; he could move through it, and it could touch him.

They walked out with Athos. Sol wanted to bang on Meg's door, but Alexei told him it wouldn't do any good, and Athos said it didn't matter. Even though Sol and Alexei could both tell it was a lie, they left the apartment and closed the door without another word.

"She could probably hear everything we were saying," Sol said on the bus after they'd seen Athos off. "She could've come out anytime."

"She chose not to," Alexei said. "It was her choice to make."

"Selfish." Sol folded his arms.

Alexei stared past him. "Sometimes when people are not who we want..."

Sol turned toward him, ears perked, when he didn't finish. "What? We just turn our backs on them and leave them?"

"No, of course not." The fox looked into the wolf's bright eyes. "But it is difficult. I think they will still be friends. Meg is not...old and set in her ways."

Sol searched his eyes. "What did Konstantin say to you?" he asked in a low voice.

Alexei braced himself as the bus lurched to a halt. "This is your stop," he said.

Sol got up. "You don't have to talk to me about it if you don't want to."

"I do." Alexei forced a smile. "But not now."

He walked slowly to the warehouse, but before he could punch in, Vlad called to him from his office down the hall. Alexei padded down and stood before the large tiger's desk. "We did not expect you in today." Vlad handed Alexei his shift assignment. "Have already called temporary worker."

Alexei held the paper and met Vlad's eyes. "Sorry," he said. "I didn't call..."

"Liza called. She said you are having difficult times. I think, poor boy, new town. I remember how it is when I come from Siberia. You are going to keep up with the football?"

Alexei shook his head slowly. "I don't think I can. I got in a fight."

"Ha." Vlad leaned across the table. "Did you win?"

"Yes," and here Alexei switched to Siberian, which they did not usually use in the office, "*he bit me and then complained to the team about it.*" He pointed to his ear.

"*You complain as well. In States, they listen to both sides. Unless he is the son of a judge.*" The tiger tapped his claws on the table. "*Is he a son of a judge?*"

"*He is a son of a something.*" He cut off Vlad's protests. "*But if I want to get a visa, the scout for the team would have to see me and recommend me, and he saw the fight. He thinks I am a troublemaker...*"

"*You are no troublemaker. I know troublemakers. Back in Siberia I knock heads together.*" He demonstrated on two imaginary heads. "*But yes, they see this... so what do you do?*"

He hadn't before thought to wonder whether Vlad knew about Liza. Of course they knew each other, but that didn't mean she told him everything. Still, she had spoken to him about soccer, and therefore maybe about the league they were in... Vlad's golden eyes gleamed in the light of the office, and Alexei took a breath. "*For some people... like me... there is political asylum.*"

The tiger nodded. "*It is difficult in Vidalia, I understand.*"

"*Perhaps.*" He forced a smile, because Vlad seemed to understand right away. "*I have hope.*"

"*If you need a character reference...*" The tiger pounded his chest with a fist.

Alexei's chest tightened. He had to swallow twice before he could form the words, "*Thank you.*"

"*Da.*" Vlad looked away, and then waved abruptly with a paw and switched back to English. "Go work. I will deal with temporary worker."

On the way to his station, Alexei thought impulsively that he would like Cat to have met Vlad, and his eyes blurred with tears. Liza, Vlad, neither of them knew about Cat. Weakness buckled his knees, sent him clutching at the wall to brace himself. He could go back, he could tell Vlad that his sister had died, he could go home.

But home held more memories of Cat than his workplace did; it was no escape. He fought away the image of his sister receding from him like the shadow of a train, squeezed his eyes shut, and took a breath. He stood upright. Grief no longer weighed down on him, but the ache centered in his chest spread through him.

The monotonous work did its job. He checked zip codes, moved parcels, checked zip codes, lifted boxes. After some time, one of his co-workers punched him on the shoulder and told him it was time for lunch.

Alexei followed, though he could have sworn that only an hour had passed since he'd come in. He ate in silence, except to say, "Yes, I feel better," when asked, and returned to his work.

On the bus ride home, he stared out the window without seeing the houses as they passed. To avoid thinking about Cat, he wondered if Meg would be out of her room, how she would talk about the things that had happened. He would have thought that Sol's eyes would be incontrovertible proof of supernatural events, but Meg had discounted that, and had even manufactured a story to explain the appearance and disappearance of Konstantin.

He would be able to talk to Sol, though. His ears did perk up at the end of the bus ride, as he walked down the street toward his apartment building. If nothing else, he would be able to talk to Sol.

When he entered the apartment, there was no smell of cooking, no fried fish or boiling pasta water or tomato sauce. No noise came from behind Meg's closed door. He sighed and walked to the bathroom.

Washing his paws, he looked up into the mirror. Sol had his green eyes, but what did Alexei have to remind him of his time? Not that he would have wanted Konstantin's scarred ear, or grey muzzle, but it would have been nice to have a reassurance that the experience he'd had was real. He searched the mirror for any trace of Konstantin, but his eyes were the same, his ears were the same, his whiskers were the same. Everything about him was the same as it had been before…

He turned his head and the light caught it a certain way, and Alexei froze, staring at his reflection. With his ears tilted that way, the left side of his muzzle showing, and his lips curled… He stretched them into more of a smile.

That completed the image. He stared into the mirror, and Caterina smiled back at him.

When he let his smile fade, the likeness disappeared. He smiled, and it returned. The thought that she might be there in the other side of the mirror looking at him brought warmth and joy, and as his smile stretched wider, her likeness shone out of his reflection like the sun.

Chapter 41

Meg came out of her room later that night, when Sol and Alexei were sitting at the table in the kitchen talking quietly. She looked around and then sat down at the table with them.

"You doing okay?" she asked Alexei. "Holding up?"

He nodded. "Work was good." He and Sol exchanged glances, and then he said, "How are you?"

"I'm fine," she said. "Just been working all day. Didn't stop for dinner. You guys eaten yet?"

And that was that. She asked Alexei about his sister, but didn't want to talk about Athos or Konstantin, other than to say that maybe she should start carrying around pepper spray if there were going to be homeless Siberian foxes lurking around their building. Alexei told her she wouldn't have to worry about that, and that closed the subject.

With Sol, though, he talked that night, and the next, and the next. Sol was only too happy to relive his dreams with Niki, if in somewhat more of a rosy wash than Alexei remembered the wolf feeling about them. He could understand that; the memory of his dreams with Konstantin still terrified him, but in the manner of a scary movie he'd seen rather than an imminent threat.

Still, there were moments during which he'd jump at shadows; or when a scent would float to him on the breeze and he'd whip his head around to find nothing there; or he would hear a word whispered in Siberian and his ears would perk straight up. But nobody lurked behind him, no shadows visited his dreams, and after a surprisingly short time, he even lost the little shiver of trepidation when he lay down at night.

He talked with Liza, too, the night of the VLGA soccer game (she and Alice had both quit when Alexei was removed, despite his plea). She told him frankly that being granted asylum would not be easy. "If you go to Port City, yes, better chance. There is community of Siberian refugees, and I can give you names for places to stay. Six months average, maybe more, maybe less. Here, it depends on the person. But you know who knows laws, who knows people in Millenport office?" Her eyes sparkled. "Mike."

"Oh." Alexei nodded. "I should ask him."

Alexei did not know if Mike would talk to him. But he did not want to go to Port City, where he would not know anyone. He had already moved to a strange new town one year ago, and now that he had friends, he did not want to give them up.

So he sent Mike a text asking if he could call him, because he didn't want to call out of the blue, and Mike replied when he was done with the soccer game saying sure, and so Alexei sat in the bus shelter while busses pulled up and left, and he thought about Mike's warmth, the comforting pressure of the sheep's hand on his shoulder, and he closed his eyes.

"Liza said I should talk to you about getting asylum in Millenport," he said when Mike picked up.

"Oh. Sure, I can help with that." Mike paused. "I'm sorry about Kendall and the team. I tried to talk him out of it, but…"

"I appreciate the sympathy." Alexei's tail twitched, the beginning of a wag, at Mike's friendly tone. "It is my fault. I should not have fought him."

"Well, no, but…" The sheep sighed. "You guys just won't ever get along."

"I do not think so." Alexei paused, and then said, "Thank you for talking to me."

"Hey, I told you I still like you." Mike's voice softened. "Are you doing better? I mean, are you okay?"

He considered that. "I am not better," he said, "but I am okay."

"Well, you don't have to talk about it. I mean, I don't have any right to ask, I know, but if you need someone to listen…"

Alexei took a breath. "I found out that my sister died."

"Oh my God. Oh God, Alexei, I'm sorry. I didn't know—I'm so sorry. How—I mean, what happened?"

Another bus pulled up. Deer, ermine, coyotes, and wolves looked out the windows through the reflections of the shops, the bustling crowds, and the lively neon signs. The bus's doors hissed and folded back, but only a portly vixen in a broad floppy hat came out. No darkness, no Cat.

Alexei closed his eyes and uncurled his tail into the warmth of a sunbeam. "Do you have a little longer?"

◆

He talked to Mike for almost an hour, and at the end of it Mike had asked him to coffee, ostensibly to discuss his asylum, but Alexei knew that it was more than that. The fox felt confident that he could navigate this almost-date without yelling at Mike now that Konstantin was gone. Telling him about Cat had been easy, comfortable, and almost as though he were introducing the two of them. If Cat were watching him, he hoped she would approve of Mike. He hoped that perhaps even Konstantin would, in time.

At home that evening, he found an envelope from Samorodka and a package from Moskva. The envelope was addressed in the handwriting of Cat's friend Kisha, and held the letter Cat had mentioned on the phone, a one-page note in which she said that if Bogdan did not contact her, she would simply take a bus to Moskva and save up money until she could take a train to one of the western countries. Kisha had attached a note saying she was sending it along even though Cat was gone because she did not know what else to do.

Alexei folded the letter and carefully replaced it. He did not want to think about what might have been, but as painful as the letter was, he could not bring himself to part with it. He turned to the package, reluctant to touch it. But he would have to sooner or later, so with the shadow of the letter still on him, he ripped the paper open and pulled out the contents.

Inside, there was a short letter, an envelope, and a burst of familiar scent: no particular person, but a uniquely Siberian mix of paper and dust and air.

The letter read:

Dear Mister Tsarev,

Accept our condolences on the death of your sister Caterina. Her effects have been returned to your mother and father, except for the enclosed letter, which was addressed to you. If you have any questions, you may contact us for assistance.

Yours sincerely,

Captain Vasily Petrovich Lukashenko

The envelope, unfamiliar paper and glue, bore his name in his sister's script. He teased a claw under the flap as he turned it over, and only then noticed the brownish stain in one corner.

His paws jerked back, and the letter fluttered to the floor; fortunately it landed face-up, so he didn't have to look at the stain or think any more about what it might be. Quickly, holding it gingerly by the opposite corner, he pushed it back into the larger envelope with the policeman's letter. He left the whole thing lying on the kitchen table and then walked into his room.

He couldn't sit down or lie down, though. His tail swung from side to side as he paced, and he came to rest staring at the portrait of Niki. "I can't read it!" he said. "I don't want to remember her like that!"

The green eye of the fox watched him steadily. Niki, the last time Sol had seen him, had been drowned at the bottom of a river, and yet Sol kept this picture. Alexei's tail stilled, and he knelt on Sol's bed, careful to keep his paws away from the actual painting. He could know his sister and yet remember the essence of who she was. He had her other letters, and he had her smile.

"*Thank you*," he said to the painted fox, smiling, and then leaned closer. In Niki's features, for the first time, he saw the traces of Konstantin's. Not the eyes, but the shape of the muzzle, the ears, and even the proud posture. He was his father's son and yet something different, something he himself had fashioned from the life he'd been given. He had taken Konstantin's inflexible devotion to an ideal and turned it to another end; so, perhaps, could Alexei take his sister's love and Konstantin's strength and build his own life. Someday he would read her last letter, but he would need more of Konstantin's strength for that, would need the shock and the tragedy to recede.

Sol walked in, and Alexei hurried backwards off the bed, ears down. "I was only looking," he said. He hadn't even heard the front door.

The wolf smiled. "It's okay. You can look. If you want a copy, I can send you the scan."

"Yes, I think so," Alexei said.

Sol pulled off his red polo shirt and searched for a t-shirt in his dresser. "Meg wants to go to dinner, just the three of us, to celebrate you staying here. You are staying, right?"

Alexei sat back on his bed. "Yes. I have made the decision to stay." An old, harsh voice in his head added, *for today*, and he said, yes, tomorrow is another decision, and the day after yet another, and every day after that another one, but those days are not here yet.

"How are you going to work the legal stuff?"

"I talked to Mike."

The wolf turned, a t-shirt in his paw. "And?"

"He is going to help me." Alexei could not restrain a smile. "We are having coffee together."

Sol grinned widely. "Good luck," he said, and pulled the shirt over his head. "If it goes well, y'know…" He kept his ears up, though his tail was curled down and he tapped his paws on the dresser drawer. Alexei waited patiently. "Maybe you could invite him over sometime."

"Yes," Alexei said. "I would like that very much."

◆

The next morning, Alexei woke disoriented, sitting quickly up in bed with the vanishing feeling of having been sitting with his sister in some strange place—a church, perhaps, but one with people shuffling regularly through it. She had been talking about the letter she'd written him, but he could not remember what she'd said. The scent of old stone and his sister faded into the smells of construction haze seeping through the cracked-open window, and his own vulpine scent strong on his sheets.

Cat's last letter, he thought, and with foreboding, he walked out to the living room to pick it up. But when he lifted the envelope from the couch, only the letter from the police was inside. Cat's envelope had vanished.

Sol came out of the bathroom then, with a towel wrapped around him. Alexei held up the envelope. "Do you know where the envelope that was in this envelope is?"

Sol blinked and shook his head. "I just put it on the couch. I didn't take anything out of it. Maybe Meg did."

Alexei set the envelope down slowly. He did not think Meg had taken Cat's letter. So when he walked into the bathroom, the first thing he did was look into the mirror and turn his face to the left. When he pulled his lips into a smile, there was Cat, smiling at him.

"Did you not want me to read it?" he asked softly.

The more he stared at his reflection, the more he felt it was a silly question. Cat had wanted him to be happy, he knew that, and reading her last letter would only have made him sad. He would grieve for her, but she would always be with him, and he had many other reasons to be thankful. Happiness, too, seemed not so far away.

He turned to face the mirror. Cat disappeared, but his smile remained.

And always then I think of you

Chapter 42

Dearest Alexei,

I do not know if you will ever be able to read this. I have to trust in God that you will, although I do not know if God exists in this place. I have not seen Him.

It is strange. Ever since arriving here, I have barely thought of Mama and Papa at all, or of Kisha or even Slava. I thought Slava might be here, but I have walked up and down the train and he is not. Most of the other people on the train will not talk to me, but the old fox who was trying to pull you on board, Kostya, he does. Sometimes I sit with him. He tells me that he does not understand the workings of this train, when we shall arrive at our destination, and who we may meet there. We think, both of us, that loving bonds make a difference, and he thinks that perhaps we continue to feel them for as long as we ride. And then he lapses into silence and stares out the window, and I do not want to bother him and I leave.

So it does not surprise me that I think mostly of you. I promised you that I would see you again, and although I did not imagine that it would be in this land of spirits, I had faith that I would keep my promise.

I wish now that it had happened another way. You told me that ghosts are real, and I imagined that I would be a freed spirit, allowed to roam our world without the hindrance of walls or borders. But you did not tell me how sad it would be, how the air on the train radiates longing and desperation. I feel it myself, often; I find an empty compartment and I draw my knees up onto the seat and I watch the grey landscape pass by, always the same. And always then I think of you, and I am so sorry that I left you alone in the world.

For that reason, I do not want you to read my last letter, the one I wrote so hastily that I misspelled words and smeared the ink, the one I tucked into my pocket the day Bogdan chased me to the window and I leapt. It is a desperate, angry letter written by a trapped girl, and I fear you might take from it some guilt over what happened to me. You should not. I accused you of misleading me, but the truth is that I was anxious, I was hasty. I wanted to escape our home, and you would have warned me about Bogdan if I had given you the chance. I ran away from a monster, and that was my mistake;

I was no longer running toward life, and so I lost it. Kostya has told me you tried to protect me. I love you for that, and so I ask you to remember me in love.

Do not despair, my dear brother. I wish I had been brave like you were on the platform, like you have been all my life for me, but I have only been that brave for you, never for myself. I am glad that at the end, I was able to help you with Kostya, and I hope that I may provide good company for him as we ride together. Now that I am here, I will do my best to help all the poor people on this train. Just as you tried to help me escape, I will try to help them appreciate this world. After all, it is something, and that is more than nothing. Perhaps some of them can write letters, and if the world is kind, their loved ones can read them.

In whatever way is possible or permitted, I will be with you.

Your loving sister,

Caterina

Epilogue

The first tsars swept down from the cold northlands, and they laid waste to the world with their fierce claws and rending fangs. They filled the streets with blood and cared not what they ripped open, if it stood in their way. They saw in the land a vision of the future—their future—and they twisted the people until they realized that vision.

And the land they conquered was harsh, yes, with icy winds that screamed through noses and ears, with furious rivers that swallowed bridges and travelers, with arid wasteland and barren mountains. But it was beautiful, too: shimmering lakes and fertile farmland, warm summer days and endless verdant forests. Beauty and softness are not weakness, but merely a different kind of strength: acceptance rather than resistance, confidence rather than armor.

My ancestors lived in tune with the land, not above it as the tsars did. They knew it to be gentle and harsh, giving and demanding. They knew that the winter would pass, that new life would come each spring, that the harvest would feed them each autumn, and then the world would pass again into death, each season in balance.

Nicholas II understood this, I now believe. He saw the changes in the world and envisioned a future in which Siberia could change with it. Few of us then understood him: not we Guards attuned to the old ways, not the revolutionaries impatient for change. We fought over how to survive the winter, while Nicholas looked ahead to the spring.

I have lost a daughter and a son, and gained, perhaps, a granddaughter and grandson; each season in balance. It is a comfort not to be alone, but a small one. For I know they too will leave me, and I cannot prevent it. My spirit is shaped to ice and barren mountains; their cold wind hisses through my ears and nose, their strength and determination hold me fast. But I have not the soil, the summers, the forests. I exiled those long ago, and now I sit at a window that rolls past a timeless desert and I search for them. Surely, surely, if I pass them, I will be able to leap out and reclaim them, to take them in my arms and make myself whole again.

Oh, my boy! Oh, my Nikolai!

About the Author

Kyell Gold is best known for his gay fiction using animal people to represent human archetypes. He has won the Annual Anthropomorphic Literature & Arts (Ursa Major) Award twelve times for his novels and short stories, and the Rainbow Award twice (2009, Best Gay Novel and Best Fantasy Novel, for *Out of Position*). He has also been nominated for a WSFA Small Press Award ("Race to the Moon," 2009).

His various online presences are linked from *www.kyellgold.com*, and you can follow him on Twitter at @KyellGold. He lives in California with his husband, but can often be found at conventions around the country and internationally.

About the Artist

Rukis is a fantasy artist and comic creator who achieved commercial success with her comic *Cruelty* and went on to create the ambitious *Red Lantern*. She has since authored *Unconditional*, a comic sequel to *Cruelty*, and *Heretic*, a novel in the Red Lantern universe. Her cover for *Green Fairy* was awarded the Ursa Major for Best Published Illustration of 2012. Her work can be found at *www.furaffinity.net/user/rukis*.

About Sofawolf Press

Sofawolf Press was founded in 1999 to provide a venue to showcase great writers of anthropomorphic fiction and to promote the genre to a wider audience.

Since the debut of its flagship publication, *Anthrolations*, a literary anthology of short stories, the Press has added to its lineup other magazine-length anthologies, novels, shared-world anthologies, and other novel-length collections, comics and graphic novels, artists' sketchbooks, and calendars. The Press continues to seek out new and creative ways of expanding its offerings of printed creations.

Please visit our website at *www.sofawolf.com/catalog/* for a full list of titles available. Thanks for reading!